PAGAN MAGIC
of the
NORTHERN
TRADITION

"Nigel Pennick's *Pagan Magic of the Northern Tradition* is a treasure trove of ancient folklore of magical rituals and charms for the protection of people and homes, of barns and livestock, of temples and churches, for good luck and healing as well as causing harm when the rituals are not followed. It describes daily ritual activities of the people of these Pagan times and how they experienced the dangers and evil spirits of the world they lived in. Some of the magical rituals were quite bizarre while others may be of value for living in today's world. Pennick compares the customs and rituals of a wide range of cultures across Europe and beyond, as well as across time, tracing their origins, similarities, and differences. The book is well researched, well organized, and a valuable and impressive resource for understanding the spiritual journeying of our ancestors."

NICHOLAS E. BRINK, PH.D., AUTHOR OF *BALDR'S MAGIC: THE POWER OF NORSE SHAMANISM AND ECSTATIC TRANCE* AND *BEOWULF'S ECSTATIC TRANCE MAGIC*

"Whether we call it magic or folklore (or even superstition), the traditional, often pre-Christian knowledge described in *Pagan Magic of the Northern Tradition* is fascinating. I've been referring to Pennick's books for years when I need a fact or an example of some interesting early magic to cite in my books and blogs. I learned something new on every page!"

BARBARA ARDINGER, PH.D., AUTHOR OF *PAGAN EVERY DAY* AND *SECRET LIVES*

"Magic was a part of everyday life for our Pagan ancestors, a spiritual approach to the environment used by everyone and embedded in all the practical skills of living, from farming and building to music and healing. Nigel Pennick shows us that it is a tradition that still flourishes and rewards us in the modern world."

ANNA FRANKLIN, AUTHOR OF
THE SACRED CIRCLE TAROT,
PAGAN RITUAL, AND HEARTH WITCH

"Nigel Pennick's book offers a well-documented overview of everyday magic, the last recourse against all evils. It introduces us to a strange Pagan world haunted by spirits and supernatural owners of nature and rehabilitates the studies of magic as an important part of our common cultural heritage. Pennick's book is well worth a read!"

CLAUDE LECOUTEUX, PROFESSOR EMERITUS
AT THE SORBONNE AND AUTHOR OF
THE TRADITION OF HOUSEHOLD SPIRITS
AND DEMONS AND SPIRITS OF THE LAND

PAGAN MAGIC
of the
NORTHERN
TRADITION

Customs, Rites, and Ceremonies

NIGEL PENNICK

Destiny Books

Rochester, Vermont • Toronto, Canada

Destiny Books
One Park Street
Rochester, Vermont 05767
www.DestinyBooks.com

Text stock is SFI certified

Destiny Books is a division of Inner Traditions International

Library of Congress Cataloging-in-Publication Data
Pennick, Nigel.
  Pagan magic of the northern tradition : customs, rites, and ceremonies / Nigel
Pennick.
     pages cm
  Includes bibliographical references and index.
  ISBN 978-1-62055-389-3 (pbk.) — ISBN 978-1-62055-390-9 (e-book)
  1. Magic—Europe, Northern. 2. Occultism—Europe, Northern. 3. Paganism—
Europe, Northern. I. Title.
  BF1591.P46 2015
  299'.94—dc23
                                                              2014037912

Printed and bound in the United States by Lake Book Manufacturing, Inc.
The text stock is SFI certified. The Sustainable Forestry Initiative® program
promotes sustainable forest management.

10 9 8 7 6 5 4 3 2 1

Text design by Priscilla Baker and layout by Debbie Glogover
This book was typeset in Garamond Premier Pro and Gill Sans with Galliard and
Neue Hammer Unziale used as display typefaces

All photographs and illustrations are by the author except where otherwise noted.

To send correspondence to the author of this book, mail a first-class letter to the
author c/o Inner Traditions • Bear & Company, One Park Street, Rochester, VT
05767, and we will forward the communication.

Contents

Preamble

Magic is an integral part of culture. It has often been ignored by historians, who, not believing in its efficacy or even recognizing that in the past many people did believe, thereby have dismissed any belief in it as beneath mention. Alternatively, when they have mentioned magic and the occult sciences, they have been portrayed as worthless superstition, or irredeemably diabolical and evil, unspeakable rites to be shunned because they might taint the reader. But to present magic as a dangerous subject that ought to be censored lest it seduce the reader into criminality is unhelpful, for it pushes students of magical history into a ghetto when students of human depravity and violence, such as crime and war, are welcome in the mainstream. Magic played a significant part in shaping people's lives. Magic is an integral part of our cultural heritage, ancient skills, and wisdom that are a perennial response to universal situations and problems. Unraveling the history of an undocumented tradition in a definitive way is impossible. The only way to understand the themes embedded in the fragments is to take notice of historic parallels and examples, and draw conclusions from them.

Introduction

Northern Magic

MAGIC AND RELIGION

The traditional worldview is practical, consisting of what works or what is perceived to work. Ancient Pagan religions in Europe were concerned with rites and ceremonies; there was neither creed nor essential doctrines. All members of the family, clan, tribe, or nation participated in ritual activities, but belief was not demanded of the participants. There was no orthodoxy, and no heresy; participation was all that was required. In premodern times, life was unimaginably hard by the twenty-first-century standards of developed countries. People were reliant on agriculture, herds and flocks, hunting and fishing. There were no effective remedies for disorders, diseases, or epidemics of humans or livestock. Crop failures brought frequent famine; peasants often lived in grinding poverty at the edge of starvation. If a hurricane or flood occurred, there was no back-up to rescue survivors, who had to get by as well as they could, having lost everything. Traveling was difficult, and wayfarers and voyagers ran the risk of attack by wild animals, robber barons, bandits, outlaws, or pirates, or dying crossing rivers and or in storms at sea. At home, there was always the risk of attack by marauding bands of fighting men, bringing rape, torture, death, or enslavement to those who could not resist or flee. Numberless diseases, disorders, and ailments beset the people, and their only recourse for a remedy was to practitioners of traditional medicine. Magic was an indivisible part of the craft of wise men and women as well as professional doctors. In such a fragile environment, people needed wisdom and skill to survive and flourish.

Magic practiced by the common people in pre-Christian times was part of everyday culture. It was embedded in the practical skills of everyday living. As in all parts of traditional society, there were specialists. Those in the handicrafts included smiths, wrights, carpenters, shoemakers, and other skilled workers who made things necessary for living, and there were also practitioners of herbalism, medicine, and divination whose arts were heavily on the magical side. But all of these arts and crafts had no theory; functionality was the operative criterion. They may have had origin-stories and mythical founders, but theory is something different, the arcane pursuit of philosophers and theologians. The Christian church, unlike traditional Pagan observance, insisted on belief in stories and doctrines that it asserted were essential to the afterlife. Belief in doctrines became confused with the practice of ethics. It

Fig. I.I. Celtic stone image, Echterdingen, Germany.

was asserted that one could not be an ethical person unless one believed everything the church demanded. The northern Pagan point of view, however, is expressed in the Old Norse poem *Hávamál* (The Words of the High One), attributed to Odin. *Hávamál* describes desirable and undesirable behavior in terms of *mannvit* (common sense) and *óvítr* (foolishness). Behavior is defined as either skilled or unskilled behavior, and the outcome of unskilled activities is social: loss of face, ridicule, and outlawry. The concept of eternal damnation is not part of this way of understanding. One's personal belief or disbelief does not matter, so long as one is a good citizen.

A SHORT HISTORY
OF NORTHERN PAGANISM

The history of indigenous religion in northern Europe provides some explanation of the context of traditional magic over the last sixteen hundred years. From what we can determine of ancient northern European religion, there was no distinct barrier between gods and lesser spiritual beings. The early religion of the northern peoples appears to have been centered not on an abstract universal deity, but upon the veneration of a divine ancestor and the natural forces of the world. The king's ancestor was also the tribal god, and this principle was maintained among the Angles and Saxons in England. Seven out of the eight Anglo-Saxon royal genealogies descended from Woden, as did the royal line of Sweden. Ancestral holy places including homesteads, grave mounds, and battlefields were venerated as places where the ancestral spirits remained. Folk-Moots, the forerunner of parliaments, were held on moot-hills, some of which were the burial mounds of ancestors, whose spirits were invoked in collective decision making. The ancestors also played an important role in the everyday worship of the common people. There were goddesses similar to the Norse *dísir,* a collective of female ancestral spirits honored as guardians of a particular tribe, clan, family, or individual. Local cults venerated local gods and goddesses, and Roman influence led to the construction of temples to house their images and cult paraphernalia. In parts of northern Europe taken into the Empire, the gods and goddesses of

Fig. I.2. Roman altar to Jupiter, Juno, and the genius loci. Bad Cannstatt, Germany.

local religious cults were taken over by the priesthoods of similar Roman deities under the *intepretatio Romana*. The Romans honored the spirit of each place with altars to the genius loci.

Egyptian and Persian deities like Isis and Mithras were also worshipped in Roman cities in the north, such as London and York. Astrology and various forms of magic were embedded in everyday culture.

The Roman Empire was made officially Christian in 313 CE, and soon afterward Pagans were persecuted, their temples were appropriated or destroyed, and their treasuries were looted. But in northern Europe, in Britain on the fringes of the Empire, and outside the Empire, ancestral observances continued. For example, a Jupiter column was erected in Cirencester by the Roman governor Lucius Septimius in the late fourth century, a major Pagan sacred structure set up fifty years after the supposed destruction of the temples. In 410 CE the Roman army was withdrawn, and that part of Britain was taken over by the Anglo-Saxons in the following decades. Germanic Paganism arrived with them. Pagan worship was not static; new cults arose and were refined, and new temples were erected at the same time that the minutiae of Christian doctrines were being decided upon in church councils in the remains of the Roman Empire, which by then had ceased to have control over western Europe. For example, in Old Prussia, the temple at Nadruva (Romuva) enshrining the trinity of Patrimpas, Perkūnas, and Patolas was set up in the fifth or sixth century (Trinkūnas 1999, 148–49).

The Christian religion became dominant in Celtic parts of Great Britain while the Anglo-Saxons were still Pagan. Ireland was Christianized by St. Patrick (ca. 389–ca. 461 CE), and remnants of Christianity from the late Roman Empire may have been the spur for Celtic Christian missionaries from Ireland and Wales to the Anglo-Saxons and the Picts in Caledonia (later called Scotland) and later on into Germanic parts of mainland Europe. Missionaries sent by Rome from 597 CE onward came to England and converted some of the kings, who then imposed the religion on their subjects. The wars of this period in England were not fought on religious lines between Christian and Pagan as simplified histories claim. The most stalwart Pagan king of the period, Penda of Mercia (died 655), fought against the Christian kings of Northumbria, but Penda's allies were not Pagans but forces of the Christian king of Wales, Caedwal II. The last part of England to remain worshipping the old gods officially was Sussex, whose king Arwald (died 686) was the last Pagan king in Britain.

Ireland and Britain became a center of Christian expansionism. The Northumbrian Christian monk Willibrord was sent to Frisia in the 690s to suppress local worship. This was part of the eastward expansion of the Christian Frankish Empire, a process that continued for centuries. In Saxony at the present Obermarsberg was a shrine with a very tall sacred pole called Irminsul, "the universal pillar." It was destroyed by the forces of the Emperor Charlemagne in the year 772 during a crusade against the Saxons. The shrines of the god Fosite, on the holy island of Heligoland, were destroyed in the year 785. Bishoprics were set up in fortified towns in Pagan territory as centers for colonization and religious expansion. In 831–834, Hamburg became a bishop's residence, and further outposts in the east were established. Poland was set up as a Catholic state between 962 and 992 by Prince Mieszco I. Between this state and Christianized Saxony was Pagan territory, where the Slav inhabitants strongly resisted missionaries and colonists. Now divided between Poland and Germany, Pomerania possessed several large and finely constructed timber Pagan temples, many located on defended islands in navigable rivers. A Christian state was established there in Pomerania in 1047 under Gottschalk, but he and the Bishop of Mecklenburg were killed in a rebellion in 1066.

In the Viking Age, major temples of the Nordic gods stood at Jelling in Denmark; Sigtuna and Gamla Uppsala in Sweden; Mæri, Lade, Skiringssal, Trondenes, and Vatnsdal in Norway; Kialarnes in Iceland; and at Dublin in Ireland. The temple at Retra was destroyed in 1068, and the one in Uppsala around 1080–1100. The Slavonic shrines and temples were destroyed by German and Danish expansion during the eleventh and twelfth centuries and the Nordic temples through the conversion to Christianity of the indigenous ruling elites. A proclamation of 1108 by the bishops and overlords of Saxony called for Christian volunteers to destroy the "abominable people" and take for themselves the best land in which to live (Fisher 1936, 203–5). The Pomeranian temples were destroyed by Bishop Otto of Bamberg between 1124 and 1128, and the country was officially Christianized in the latter year. The temples at Brandenburg were demolished in 1136, but the god Triglav was still being worshipped by Slavs and Saxons there in 1153. In the Baltic was the holy island of Rügen with a number of Pagan temples, the largest of which was dedicated to the god Svantovit. The temples, which had been defended by three hundred dedicated men at arms, fell to a Danish-German crusade in 1168–69, after the death of their patron, Duke Nyklot.

On the Baltic shore, Old Prussia was another late stronghold of Paganism, where in 997 Bishop Adalbert of Prague died in a failed attempt to evangelize the inhabitants. Christianity was extirpated from Old Prussia in 1009, when the leading cleric Bruno of Magdeburg was killed. In 1200 a crusade led by Bishop Albert of Bremen led to the foundation of the city of Riga, and in 1202 a military order, the *Fratres Militiae Christi* (fraternity of the soldiers of Christ), better known as the

Schwertbrüderorden (Sword Brothers Order, or Knights of the Sword), was established to impose Christianity by force. In 1225 they were reinforced by knights of the Teutonic Order, which had been founded at Acre in Palestine in 1190. Having been expelled from Transylvania by the Pagan Kumans, the Teutonic knights were sent by the pope to Prussia to colonize the Baltic lands for themselves as a religious-military state called the *Ordenstaat*.

The Knights of the Sword were defeated in battle by Pagan Lithuanian forces at the Battle of Schaule (Saule) in 1236, but in 1260 all inhabitants of the *Ordenstaat* were compelled by the Teutonic knights to swear allegiance to the Christian religion. This led to a war of genocide against the Sambian nation of Old Prussians, who refused

Fig. 1.3. Christianized megalith at Trébeurden, Brittany, France. Commercial postcard ca. 1890. The Library of the European Tradition

to give up their religion. By 1283 the Teutonic crusade had devastated Old Prussia. Its inhabitants had been massacred or forced to flee as refugees. The *Ordenstaat* continued in existence until 1525. As a response to Christian pressure from the west and Islamic pressure from the south, the Lithuanian king Mindaugas set up state Paganism in 1251 as a means to unify the nation and resist colonization. In 1259 the Knights of the Sword attempted to take over Samogitia (lowland Lithuania) but were defeated again. In 1343, Estonian resistance against Danish colonists was manifested in the Pagan rebellion of Jüriöö Mäss (St. George's Night, April 22/23) when all the churches and manors were destroyed and the Christian priests slain. Afterward, the Teutonic knights were sent in to kill the rebels. The Grand Duchy of Lithuania remained Pagan until 1387, while Samogitia came under the control of the Catholic Church only in 1414. In Lapland (Finland), church persecution of Sámi Pagan practices went on sporadically between 1389 and 1603, and a *noid* (shaman) was burnt alive with his drum at Arjeplog as late as 1693 (Jones and Pennick 1995, 167–73; 178–79). At the far eastern edge of Europe, in Russia, indigenous Pagan practices were never fully extirpated, and continue today in unbroken tradition. Although numerous indigenous religions of Europe were persecuted to destruction, beliefs, concepts, themes, and practices that were present could not all be utterly obliterated. They continued as forbidden practices, and in the customs and traditions of farmers, craftspeople, and in folk medicine.

MAGIC AND THE CHURCH

Once it had suppressed Pagan worship, the church claimed a monopoly on spiritual activities. It asserted that only ordained clergymen were permitted to deal with spiritual matters, and that meant that anyone else who made use of spiritual technologies was a criminal. Extending this, it was claimed that anyone who was not a priest who used magic, whether for good or ill, was being empowered by the devil. Dualistic belief in an evil god as an equal opponent of a good one had not existed in Pagan times. Those who practiced traditional magic that had originated before Christianization were accused of witchcraft, as the church clerics imagined their powers came from the old gods, who in the eyes of the church could only be seen as agents of the devil. Witches, imaginary or real, were labeled as deviants and transgressors, people whose way of life lay outside acceptable norms. They were viewed as part of an evil conspiracy determined to destroy society. In an era when a particular worldview was the only permitted reality, pluralistic realism—the possibility that numerous equally authentic truths can coexist—was not an option. Religious orthodoxy was enforced with draconian rigor and horrendous punishments. But because elements of pre-Christian lore and magic are present in recorded witchcraft practices and spells, certain writers have claimed wrongly that the whole body of historic witchcraft practice is Pagan. Many, if not most, recorded spells of healing and cursing especially drew strongly from Christian sources, sometimes from the mainstream Bible and occasionally from apocryphal sources (Davies 1996, 29).

In a feudal society that was based on well-defined classes and ranks, there were basically two kinds of magical practitioner: those who had an education in a monastery or university and those of a lower class who were part of a folk tradition. Clearly, the distinctions were blurred, and similar magical knowledge and theory was used in both traditions. It is recorded that some Christian monks and priests collected magical texts, and certain monasteries became well known for them. For example, the Icelandic "black books" called *Rauðskinni* (Redskin) and *Gráskinni* (Grayskin) were kept in the monastery library at Hólar. The former title was connected with Bishop Gottskálk Niklásson in the early sixteenth century. It appears to have contained magical lore from both the classical and runic traditions. In Germany a famous grimoire was attributed to the thirteenth-century cleric Albertus Magnus, and Abbot Johannes Trithemius (1462–1516), a contemporary of Niklásson, wrote around 70 works, many on magic, including *Veterum sophorum sigilla et imagines magicae,* an influential text on talismanic and image magic. The German renaissance magi Heinrich Cornelius Agrippa (1486–1535) and Paracelsus (Philippus Aureolus Theophrastus Bombastus von Hohenheim, 1493–1541) were students of the master magician Abbot Trithemius, and their works remain in print today. In addition to incantations, medical recipes, and magical formulae, these published works contained sigils and signs that were part of the repertoire of craftspeople. They are still in use.

In his 1621 work *The Anatomy of Melancholy,* Robert Burton expressed all the fears that people of his time had of magicians and witches, and the awesome powers they were alleged to possess. In the chapter titled "Of Witches and Magicians, How They Cause Melancholy," he wrote:

> Many subdivisions there are, & many several species of Sorcerers, Witches, Enchanters, Charmers, and so forth. They have been tolerated heretofore some of them; and Magick hath been publickly professed in former times, in Salamanca, Cracovia, and other places, though after censured by several Universities, and now generally contradicted, though practiced by some still . . . that which they can do, is as much almost as the Devil himself, who is still ready to satisfy their desires. . . . They can cause tempests, storms, which is familiarly practiced by Witches in Norway, Ireland, as I have proved. They can make friends enemies, and enemies friends, by philtres . . . enforce love, tell any man where his friends are, about what employed, though in the most remote places; and, if they will, bring their sweethearts to them by night, upon a goat's back flying in the air . . . hurt and infect men and beasts, vines, corn, cattle, plants, make women abortive, not to conceive, barren, men and woman unapt and unable, married and unmarried, fifty several ways . . . make men victorious, fortunate, eloquent . . . they can make stick-frees, such as shall endure a rapier's point, musket shot, and never be wounded . . . they can walk in fiery furnaces, make men feel no pain on the rack or feel any other tortures; they can staunch blood, represent dead men's shapes, alter and turn themselves and others into several forms at their pleasures. (Burton 1621, I, ii, I, sub. III)

Although written in the early seventeenth century, Burton's account reasserts earlier writings about the fearful power ascribed to magic. These beliefs are not yet dead.

1

The Web of Wyrd and the Eldritch World

It is a human trait to see patterns in all things. According to the spiritual worldview, these patterns are manifestations of a cosmic order. We can discern patterns everywhere we care to look, and our being in the world is determined by these patterns, symbolically described in our ancient myths that tell of the coming-into-being of the world. Two of the most ancient human handicrafts are weaving and pottery, and in ancient scriptures, both of them are used as metaphors for the human condition. The ancient bards perceived the multiple interwoven strands of experience symbolically to be a textile woven by the powers they called fate. The crafts of spinning and weaving are the heart of our linguistically embedded understanding of our being, for our existence is envisaged as a part of a universal interwoven pattern, known in the northern tradition as the Web of Wyrd.

THE WEB OF WYRD

The Web of Wyrd interconnects everything there ever was, is, or will be; all people, things, and events are conceived as being patterns woven in the web. Wyrd is an Old English word derived from *weorðan*, which means "to become," "to come into being," or "to come to pass." A related Old High German word, *wurt*, similarly has its basis in a verb, *werdan*, meaning "to become" or "to come to pass." It related to the Latin verb *vertere*, "to turn," and in the context of Wyrd, this means how events turn out. Another related Old High German word is *wirtel*, "a spindle," the tool used in spinning thread from raw fibers. Fortune and destiny are part of weaving in the Old English word *gewæf*, as in the text *"me that wyrd gewæf,"* "Wyrd wove me that"—that is my lot, or fate, in life. For the individual, Wyrd is his or her "lot in life," position in the world, with all its limitations and possibilities, a state of being often referred to as one's destiny or fate. But Wyrd is not the concept of fate as something that predestines us to undergo unavoidable happenings that somehow have been written in advance. The contemporary usage of the words "fate" and "destiny" contains ideas of unavoidable predestination, but our Wyrd does not necessarily doom us to a particular fate. Yet we are where we are. The Scots expression, "Let us dree our weird" exhorts us to accept where we are and use it for the best. The worst position in life is to be a "weirdless person." Someone who is weirdless has no purpose in life and never prospers, and weirdlessness denotes doing things in the wrong way and thereby failing at every chance.

The Web of Wyrd is an ever-changing process, likened to a woven fabric, constantly being added to and constantly disintegrating. In the European Tradition, the processes that shape events are personified as the Fates, who are three sisters. In ancient Greece, they were the Moirae in White Raiment; in Roman Paganism, the Three Fates; in the northern tradition they are the Norns; and in the English and Scottish tradition, the Weird Sisters. In ancient Greece, the three Moirae were viewed by the Orphics symbolically as the visible phases of the moon: the first, Clotho, is the waxing First Quarter; the middle one, Lachesis, the Full Moon; and the last, Atropos, the waning Last Quarter. Clotho spins the thread; Lachesis measures it out, deciding in which way it will be used; and Atropos, "the Fury with abhorred shears," cuts it. Whatever they are called in the different traditions, they are personified as three women involved in the processes of spinning and handling yarn. The first signifies the beginning that is the past; the second the forma-

Fig. 1.1. The Three Fates, architectural feature at Castell Coch, Tongwynlais, Wales (William Burges ca. 1880).

tive, creative process of existence, which is the present; and the third, destruction, which is the future.

The actual physical craft of spinning is significant in this mythos, as it clearly relates to the visible apparent rotation of the starry sky at night. The image of the rotating spindle and the turning millstone is a reflection of the passing of time and the outcome of events. Many northern European words to do with the development of events and the creation of materials are related to the act of turning round. The Scots word for a wheel or a whirlwind (tornado) is *trendle,* and the English word *trend,* which describes how things are developing, is related to this. A physical phenomenon called the "windings of the stars" is mentioned by H. C. Agrippa in the early sixteenth century in his *Three Books of Occult Philosophy:* the obliquity of the Earth's axis as it progresses on its orbit around the sun gives the path of the stars and planets an apparent winding motion likened to the winding of a ball of yarn (Agrippa 1993 [1531], II, XXXIV).

The names of the Norns are redolent of meanings embedded deep within our language. In the Northern Tradition the Norns' names are Urða (That Which Was); Verðandi (That Which Is); and Skuld (That Which Is To Become). Here, the thread is not just spun, measured and cut, but woven into a fabric (the web) before being destroyed. The warp or throw of the woven fabric of the Web of Wyrd is viewed as time and events, whilst the weft is composed of individual human acts within time. As the process of weaving the web continues, the pattern of interactions of the threads, which are lives and events, irreversibly comes together to exist for a while before again being torn apart. Skuld personifies the forces of dissolution. She cuts the individual thread or shears apart the intricate weavings. She represents the inevitable end of all things, the annihilation of present existence. The Norns sit at a well; it is necessary to wet the fiber of flax with water in order to spin them into a thread.

In the English and Scottish tradition, the Weird Sisters appear under that collective name, but their individual names are lost. William Shakespeare borrowed them from Raphael Holinshed's tale of Macbeth and transformed them into the fateful Three Witches.

Their names have been reconstructed from Old English literary

Fig. I.2. The Weird Sisters, from the history of Macbeth, from Raphael Holinshed's *Chronicles*. The Library of the European Tradition

evidence as Wyrd, Weorthend (or Metod), and Sculd (Branston 1957, 71). They are the Old High German *sceffarin* (female shapers who determine the shape of things to come). The shapers mete out our fate, the Old Saxon *metod*, "destiny, doom, death," and so we are subject to *metodogiscapu*, "the decree of fate" or "the shaping of destiny." Another term in Old Norse for one's fate is *sköp*, which literally means "what is shaped." The web is not a reality, but a metaphor that gives us some limited understanding of the way things happen.

The seamless textile is the prime emblem of the Web of Wyrd, symbolized in traditional dress, whole fabric uncut and unfitted, but gathered or smocked to fit the wearer. For existence is not composed of an assemblage of separate moments, but it is a seamless flow of process, the threads of which are as but currents in a river, tides in a sea, or the blowing of the winds. The Web of Wyrd is a symbolic description of the reality in which we live. Wyrd embodies the fundamental structures and processes that manifest themselves continually as recognizable elements of the physical world. These principles can reveal themselves spontaneously or may be identified by human intelligence. Traditional spirituality recognizes them as divine principles that operate throughout the cosmos, embodying everything that exists and has ever existed. In this sense, the visible world is an emanation of the invisible. The true principles of Wyrd are often viewed as the signature of divinity.

Like a piece of fabric already woven, Wyrd is something that cannot be altered or undone. But either we can be passive and allow the vagaries of life to defeat us or we can deal creatively with the situation in which we find ourselves. Wyrd weaves our place in life, and an old saying from the Borders of Scotland and England expresses creative acceptance of our situation: "Let us dree our weird"; that is, let us endure whatever becomes of us and make the best of it. It tells us that once we stop complaining and accept our Wyrd, we can turn its disadvantages into our advantages. We are within our given circumstances, living in our own time, and must endure their accompanying difficulties, but how we endure them and how we deal with our circumstances is up to us.

Wyrd works like natural magic and science: all things that come to individuals are neither rewards nor punishments sent by the gods, but they are the inevitable consequences of events, affected by the actions of individuals and the collective. But whatever happens to us spiritually is the result of how we react to the conditions in which we find ourselves, for we have free will and choice of how to act within our circumstances. Even the gods are not outside Wyrd, but subject to it, like we are. This is clear from original texts from both Northern Paganism and traditional Anglo-Saxon Christianity. As an Old English gnomic verse in one of the Cotton Manuscripts tells us: "The glories of Christ are great: Wyrd is strongest of all." Medieval Christian images of the Annunciation—for example, a fifth-century mosaic at Ravenna, Italy, and a ninth-century stone panel at Hoveningham, Yorkshire, England—show Our Lady spinning with spindle in hand, with a (woven) wickerwork basket containing wool beside her. This is the motif of the first Weird Sister, signifying beginning; in this case, the conception of Jesus. Our Lady is also depicted handling thread as Maria Knotenlöserin, "Mary the Unraveller of Knots," in a baroque painting in the church of St. Peter-am-Perlach in Augsburg, Germany. The church stands on the site of the temple of the Swabian goddess Zisa (Pennick 2002a, 107–10). Whether the concept of the *Knotenlöserin* was ascribed to the goddess is not recorded. Knotted threads and cords are certainly a major element in magical practice in northern Europe, used in warding off harm, stopping bleeding, binding illnesses, and bringing winds to sailors.

ØRLÖG: CHANCE AND FATE

Our existence is not fixed, but part of a process. Nothing exists without coming from somewhere. Every aspect of material existence now is the result of what preceded it in time. The sum of all of the events that led to the present existence of anything is called its *ørlög,* an Old Norse concept meaning both "primal laws" and "primal layers." That which has already been woven by the Norns, even if it has been torn apart in the past, is that which came before the present pattern of existence, so it has influenced it profoundly. *Ørlög* is more than just the processes of nature, or the record of history, for it includes all of the factors that go to make up the present time. Each human person has his or her own *ørlög*. Personal *ørlög* includes genetic, individual, family, and collective history and every other factor that has made the individual what he or she is. There is no escape from *ørlög*, for we cannot alter what has already happened or the circumstances that come from it. Everyone's *ørlög* also accumulates as we get older; it is the sum of everything that we do, where we are, and the circumstantial events affecting our lives. The individual's *ørlög* gives us both our possibilities in life, and also determines their limits. Because of this, *ørlög* is sometimes confused with destiny or fate, a force that is seen to favor some individuals and to destroy others.

In the Roman worldview, the goddess Fortuna presided over what would now be called random events. She is still invoked now by gamblers, who call upon Lady Luck in the hope of winning games of chance. Her emblem is the Wheel of Fortune. The concept of mathematically calculable randomness did not exist in ancient religious systems. Every event was ascribed to supernatural agency—either to a particular deity like Fortuna, or to an omnipotent creator. Religions that believed in an omnipotent and omniscient god claimed that everything that happened was under the god's direct control. The Anglo-Saxon king Alfred the Great stated that there was no such thing as chance, everything being due to the actions of God. In this worldview, nothing can happen without the god's involvement. God's will is in control of everything from the course of the planets to the weather on Earth. This concept has the consequence that everything that happens must be preordained, fated to happen. Every event and happening has been decided in advance by divine edict and cannot be changed. Randomness is not part of this deterministic belief system, as King Alfred stated. However, the mathematical principles of randomness, discovered after the Renaissance, still apply to divination even when the divinatory system is from a belief system that has no concept of randomness.

Of all forms of divination, dice have a strange position between the sacred and profane uses. The tumbling dice, though random and only predictable in the long run through the laws of statistics, produce a real and immediate outcome. When given human significance, the points facing the thrower can bring fortune or ruin. The random becomes determinate immediately the dice roll to a halt. When the dice are at rest, the success or failure of the prediction is apparent at once. Fate and doom can be decided on the roll of a die, and the saying "dicing with death" emphasizes this reality. Ancient Roman dice terminology was related to the twelvefold division of the world, as expressed in weights and measures. The German word for a die, *Wurfel,* has the connotation "to throw" (the verb *werfen*), linking their workings with the "throw" of the weave of Wyrd's web. Willard Fiske, in his *Chess in Iceland* (1905), remarks:

> Among the adherents to old Germanic mythology Wotan (Odin) was regarded as the inventor of dice. But on the introduction of Christianity several old attributes and spheres of activity were transferred to the spirits of evil, and thus the devil, at a later day, came to be regarded as the originator of dice. He was supposed to have created them for the purpose of gaining souls for his infernal kingdom. (Fiske 1905, 248–49)

The English word "fate" is derived from *fatum,* the past participle of the Latin *fari,* "to speak." The Fates are those who speak about what shall become of us. The Old Icelandic poem *Völuspá* (The Sybil's Vision) recounts of the Norns that they "staves did cut, laws did they make, lives did they choose: for the children of men they marked their fates." The Norns' name is also interpreted as those who speak, being related to the Middle English verb *nurnen,* which means "to say." The Norns' utterances or decrees are described in Old English as *wyrdstafas* "wyrd-staves" and can appear in the form of writing, the staves. Staves can mean both runic characters and the wooden staves upon which they are cut, the runestaves being cut upon a runestaff. There is an oblique reference to weaving and knowledge in the poem *Vafþrúðnismál* (The Lay of Vafþrúðnir) where Odin has a riddling contest against the giant Vafþrúðnir, whose name means "the mighty weaver." The poem contains prophetic riddles that deal with the nature of the gods, giants, and humans and their relations: the nature of the Web of Wyrd.

The runes are fundamental to understanding something of the weavings of the Web of Wyrd and our place within it. When we use the runes, we can penetrate the surface of outward appearances, and enter the realm of consciousness that perceives the basic unity of life that is the Web of Wyrd. Even in the everyday prosaic use of characters to represent sounds and numbers, we penetrate some of the mysteries that lie at the foundations of existence. At the basic level, the individual runes are various patterns that occur within the Web of Wyrd and serve as gateways for the consciousness to grasp the nature of these patterns. The alphabetic glyphs or signs that we call runes are what appear in the mind when the word "rune" is heard. But a rune is much more than just a letter in an alphabet. In addition to possessing symbolic meaning—whether as an alphabetic letter, an ideogram, or a symbol representing something—it can also mean a song, a poem, an incantation, or an invocation having talismanic power.

The meaning of the word rune itself is a "mystery" or "deliberation," as in the Old English word *rún,* the Old Norse *rún,* and the Middle Welsh word *rhin.* Similarly, the word *rún* in modern Irish (Gaeilge) means "secret" and "intention." But it is a secret in written or spoken form that is not understood by everyone, as in the Scots verb *roon* and modern German *raunen,* both meaning "to whisper," and in a common English idiom, a "rounder" is a whisperer, a person who uses barely audible, secretive speech. Within the simple letter, composed of a few lines, lies a great deal more than its surface appearance. At its basic level, a rune denotes a mystery; that is, something secret and otherworldly, something that is more than just an unknown meaning for a person who is illiterate or uninterested. Each rune stave is a unit of embedded lore, a storehouse of knowledge and meaning within human consciousness. According to the northern worldview, the interconnections of the nerve pathways in the human brain are an obvious aspect of the Web of Wyrd. As a symbol, a rune denotes a formless and eternal reality that is rooted in the world as we experience it.

THE DIVINE HARMONY

Traditional cosmology is a symbolic way of describing the earth and the heavens we perceive to be above us. Above the earth are nine spheres defined by the apparent courses of the planets, the moon, the sun, and the stars. The different planetary spheres correspond to various aspects of existence: they are ruled by the nine Muses; they correspond to metals and the colors used in Anglo-Norman heraldry, and likewise to the notes of the musical octave. The relationship between different spheres is that of numerical proportions discovered originally by Pythagoras (ca. 500 BCE), which are the basis of the Western diatonic musical scale. In 1650 Athanasius Kircher wrote in *Musurgia universalis,* "The ancient philosophers asserted that the world consisted of a perfect harmony, that is, from the earth to the starry heavens is a perfect Octave." Hence the single-stringed musical instrument devised by Pythagoras, the Monochord, is an image of the Cosmos, as Robert Fludd wrote in 1617: "The Monochord is the internal principle, which, from the center of the whole, brings about the harmony of all life in the Cosmos."

Whatever means of division we use, there is the recognition that all are present simultaneously. In his 1642 essay *Religio Medici,* the English philosopher Sir Thomas Browne (1605–1682) used the example of the seasons and the earth to explain this principle: "whatsoever sign the sun possesseth, those four seasons are actually present. It is the nature of this luminary to distinguish the several seasons of the year; all which it makes at one time in the whole earth, and successive in any part thereof" (Browne 1862, 47). Thus the parts are inextricable components of the whole. Only in modern thought do the parts become separated in a reductionist and fragmental way, and used in isolation from one another without consideration for their place in the totality.

The Greek alchemical text the *Anonymus,* expressing ideas current in the third and fourth centuries CE, places the origin of the four elements in the Mystical Egg of the alchemists, which is the Seed of Pythagoras. The author was following the traditional Greek coming-into-being symbolism of the Orphic religion, expressed by Aristophanes in his play *The Birds.* The unknown author of the *Anonymus* notes that the four

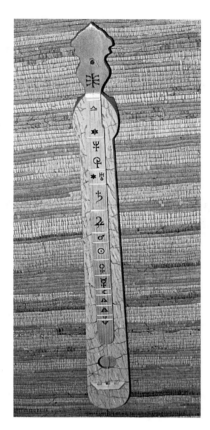

Fig. 1.3. Celestial monochord
made by Russell Paddon,
designed and painted by Nigel
Pennick, 2013.

elements are also present in music, because there are four main harmonies, and the basic row, the *tetrachord,* is composed of four elemental tones. These concepts gradually entered the north and became embedded in magical understanding. In the second century CE, Theon of Smyrna pointed out how the four main harmonies of the diatonic scale, the preserve of the Muses, combine the numbers 1, 2, 3, and 4 as the Musical Tetraktys. The four harmonic ratios are the fourth (4:3), the fifth (3:2), the octave (2:1), and the double octave (4:1). There are six possible tetrachords: Aëchos, Isos, Katharos, Kentros, Paraëchos, and Plagios. Three are ascending scales, three (Aëchos, Isos, and Plagios) descending. Combined, these make twenty-four musical elements (that can be related to the twenty-four characters of the Greek alphabet and the northern runes). By combining these in proper ways, all forms of music—the benedictions, hymns, revelations, and other parts of

Orthodox Church music—were made. There are limitless possibilities of combination. In all its complexity of endless realignments, changing relationships, and new harmonies, the "music of the spheres" reflects the limitless combinations of the elements that allow the multiplicities of the existent world to have their being.

THE TRADITIONAL VIEW OF THE COSMOS
Symbolism of the Mill

A link between the weird sisters and mills appears in medieval laws that banned women with spindles or distaffs from coming near mills. The stones that grind flour in a mill can be understood as an image of the cosmos where the sky rotates above a fixed earth as the upper millstone turns on the lower one. The original mills were querns, handmills where an upper stone driven by hand rotated upon a lower, stationary stone. The first powered mills in northern Europe were watermills built directly over watercourses. An axletree fitted with paddles dipped into the running water below the mill, and fixed to it was the upper stone. The lower stone has a hole in the middle to allow the axletree to rotate. So the upper stone turned against the lower stone to grind the grain into flour. There were no separate waterwheels or transmission gears to drive the stones, as in later, more sophisticated water mills.

Symbolically, the oldest form of water mill structure reflected the tripartite cosmos in the Northern Tradition interpretation: underworldly water (world serpent flowing, Utgard); fixed earth (lower millstone, Midgard); upper stone turning (starry heavens, Asgard). The turning but fixed axletree (the world-tree Yggdrassil) rotates around a fixed point, the Pole Star. The poetic fragment by Snæbjorn in Snorri Sturluson's *Skaldskaparmál* tells of nine skerry maidens turning a mill that is a kenning for the churning waves of the sea being cut through by the prow of a ship. Amloði's mill has been interpreted as an earthly counterpart of the celestial mill that grinds the meal of the strewn stars (Jones 1991b, 4). Amloði is identified with William Shakespeare's Hamlet (ca. 1602), and the Bard gives the First Player of the play-within-a-play the following lines, which connect it with the Wheel of Fortune:

Out, out, thou strumpet, Fortune! All you gods, In general synod, take away her power; Break all the spokes and fellies from her wheel, And bowl the round nave down the hill of heaven, As low as to the fiends! (Shakespeare, *Hamlet,* II: 2).

The millstones themselves were ascribed magical powers. Old millstones were used to block places where evil might enter, being laid in the gateways of churchyards and the entrances to places of the dead. Broken into four, they were used as foundations of the four corners of the house (Garrad 1989, 110).

THE MODES, THE PLANETARY SPHERES, AND THEIR HARMONY

The seven modes of ancient European music reflect an ancient recognition of this cosmic harmony. It appears to have originated in the speculations of the Greek philosopher Anaximander, who suggested that the heavenly bodies are carried around the earth on a series of concentric spheres. It is this system to which Plato refers. Although two thousand years later, European scientists, most notably Copernicus, determined that the earth is a planet in orbit around the sun, and not the center of the cosmos, the model created by Anaximander is still a valid spiritual metaphor that had a profound influence all over Europe. Credited to Pythagoras, who elaborated the ideas of Anaximander, the system of the octave was worked upon by later Gnostic researchers who used the concept known as the *Ogdoas.* In this eightfold system, the cosmos is ruled by seven deities who in turn were under the rulership of the Supreme One. In the ancient treatise *On Style,* conventionally ascribed to Demetrius Phalereus, we find, "In Egypt also the priests venerate the gods through the seven vowels, letting them sound one after the other, and instead of the *aulos* and the lyre, it is the sound of the letters that is heard harmoniously." Through the sound of the vowels, properly invoked under the correct liturgical conditions, material existence could be transformed to spirit. These sounds are the pure notes that Plato puts in the mouths of the Sirens.

The Neopythagorean philosopher Nichomachus of Gerasa reinforced this concept when he commented that the planetary spheres each produce their own particular tones, each of which is reflected in a corresponding vowel in the Greek language. According to Nichomachus, the vowel α reflects the sphere of the moon and the mode called *Nete*. The sphere of Mercury is expressed by the vowel ε and the tone *Paranete*. The vowel η sounds the sphere of Venus, the tone *Trite synemmenon*. The vowel ι reflects the sphere of the sun, with the tone of *Mese*. The vowel o relates to the planetary sphere of Mars and the tone of *Lichanos*. Vowel υ recalls Jupiter and *Parhypate,* whilst ω signifies Saturn and *Hypate* (Nichomachus 1994).

In Greek culture there were no separate characters for numbers, and the letters of the alphabet thus had numerical equivalents. Anyone who learned to read absorbed these numbers along with the meaning of the letters. As a result Greek culture—unlike ours, in which Roman letters and Arabic numerals have no connection—had an integral symbolic understanding of the relationship of name and number. Concepts such as that the Creator had brought matter into being by the utterance of a word, and that number is the underlying structure of existence, which to modern culture seem separate and irreconcilable, were integrated in this worldview. Belief in the power of the word is fundamental to religion and magic alike. Gnostic papyri contain numerous incantations that begin or end with the seven Greek vowels in differing combinations. One text gives an invocation that encapsulates a magical theory: "Thy name, made up of seven letters, according to the harmony of the seven tones, whose sound is made according to the twenty-eight lights of the Moon, Saraphara, Araphara, Braarmarapha, Abraach, Pertaomech, Akmech, Iao – ouee – iao – oue – eiou – aeo – eeou – eeou – Iao." The numbers seven and eight are an integral part of this spiritual current. The Greek alphabet, having twenty-four characters, is divided into three *ogdoads*, or groups of eight, each of which has a ruling letter and is thus structured 1 + 7. In common with Greek practice, the twenty-four runes of the Common Germanic *fuþark* are also divided into three *ogdoads,* called by their Norse name, *ættir*. Identically with the Greek alphabet, each *ætt* is ruled by the first rune of the group, the *ogdoad* of α (alpha) being the first group of eight in Greek and the *ætt* of *fehu* being the first in the runes.

The Gnostic magical text known as *Moses' Book of the Great Name* (in the *Papyrus Magicus Leyden W*) tells of the godly power contained in the name of the Ogdoas: "Present in it is the supreme name, that is Ogdoas, who commands and controls the whole: the angels are obedient to Him, the archangels, the demons and demonesses and all that is within creation." The use of the musical modes in initiation is recorded in this papyrus. Apotropaic and invocational music based upon the octaval system operates by recreating the vibrations of the divine name; that is, the Music of the Spheres. The modes of the Pagan philosophers are reckoned from the highest note downward, signifying, as it were, the descent of spirit into matter with the heavenly spheres. The Orthodox Christianity of the Eastern Roman Empire, the inheritor of this Greek Pagan philosophy, reckoned the same modes from the lowest note upward, seemingly signifying the ascent of hymns from the earth to heaven. The Byzantine system used the same notes, calling them the *echoi* (singular, *echos*).

Around the beginning of the sixth century CE, a monophysite monk named Severus of Antioch wrote a series of hymns for the Common of the Seasons (a cycle of rituals pertaining to the particular liturgical seasons of the Orthodox Church), using the Oktoëchos system. These hymns are sung on a series of eight Sundays in a different *echos*, beginning with the lowest mode. The first Sunday's hymn is in the first mode, the second in the second, the third in the third, and so on, through the octave. The whole Oktoëchos is based upon the Pentecontade Calendar that uses a series of seven weeks and a day as the basic unit. The year is built up from seven of these Pentecontades plus fourteen intercalary days. Thus the hymns of a particular day reflect their place in time. Each one is a proper part of a greater sequence that reflects its corresponding place in the greater divine harmony of the cosmos. With the correct enactment of a ritual that reflects the cosmic order, the participants themselves become part of that order, thereby transcending their own finite individuality. It is a means of becoming one with the cosmos, thereby taking communion with the infinite.

2

Traditional Operative Magic, Philosophy, and Theory

The traditional way of viewing the world describes the principles that rule it in simple terms. Processes are usually described as having a three-fold nature, most simply apparent in the sequence: beginning—continuance—end. Existent realities, such as matter and planar space, are understood in a fourfold way. The four directions divide the plane of the Earth's surface, while the four seasons divide the year. The fourfold division of the world into the cardinal directions and their subdivisions is discussed further in the next chapter.

The Greek philosopher Pythagoras (ca. 500 BCE) taught the significance of the divine numerical series 1, 2, 3, 4 as the creative power of the cosmos. Pythagoreans described existence by means of the Tetraktys, put in visible form as a triangle composed of ten points, arranged from the top down, 1, 2, 3, 4. Of the various forms of Tetraktys, the fourth composes the four elements, and the eighth, the Intelligible Tetraktys, the four faculties of the human being: (1) intelligence and mind; (2) knowledge; (3) opinion; and (4) sensation.

The oldest surviving description of the tetrad of principles known as the four elements comes from Empedocles in his text *On Nature* (ca. 445 BCE). The division of the matter of the world into four symbolic elements is the basis for the traditional Western understanding of the subtle nature of the human body. Within the Cosmos, the individual natures of things, both nonliving and living, can be described by means of these four principles: Earth, Water, Air, and Fire.

The four elements are thus a description of the nature of the material world. They exist within the matrix of the physical structure of the world, the dimensions, which Pythagoras classified into four parts: (1) the seed or starting point; (2) height; (3) depth; and (4) thickness or solidity. This tetrad is the archetype of all growing things and things that are made by means of the human arts and crafts.

In the European tradition, the subtle component of the human body is composed of four humors. These are blood, phlegm, black bile, and yellow bile. As symbolic (rather than physical) bodily fluids, they correspond with the four elements. Thus, blood corresponds with air; phlegm signifies water; black bile relates to earth; and yellow bile to fire. This tetrad of humors is a metaphorical way to describe the active qualities present in the bodies of all living beings. They are not the same as the Intelligible Tetraktys of Pythagoras, which is concerned with the function of consciousness, being bodily. But they have a profound effect upon the consciousness, nevertheless. According to the ancient Greek concept known as *Perisomata,* the relative proportions of each of the four humors in any one being produce or describe that individual's personal temperament. The word "temperament" literally describes the outcome of the combination of humors tempering one another. The principle of Temperance, as one of the Four Virtues, refers to this kind of tempering. According to this symbolic viewpoint, an individual's bodily strength, along with that almost undefinable quality of health, is determined by a particular combination of humors. Imbalances of the humors lead not only to bodily disorders, but to psychological ones as well.

In his *The Nature of Man,* Polybius defines health as being the state in which the four humors are in the correct proportion to one another, both in strength and quantity. They must also be mixed together well enough. Whenever there is a deficiency or an excess of one or more of the humors, or the mixing is insufficient, then a certain disorder results. When the humors are in harmony with one another, according to the basic nature of the individual's constitution, then there is balance, and she or he is therefore healthy. The Muses play their part in the creation of good humor, for traditionally music has been seen as a means of restoring balance of the humors. Temperance, the art of balancing the humors, is a health-bringing technique. The commonplace expression "being in a good humor" refers to this ancient concept.

The northern tradition views bodily powers as consisting of two separate but linked qualities: might and main. Might (Old English *meaht;* Old Norse *máttr*) is the physical strength of the body, the energy within it that enables it to live, powering its movements and actions. Main (Old English *mægen;* Old Norse *megin*) is the inner psychological strength that empowers the personality; it is transferable to other people and to objects. In Old Norse tradition, *megin* (main) is described in terms of who or what possesses it. The earth has *jarðar megin;* the gods possess *ásmegin.* When a magician empowers something with *megin,* it becomes *aukinn,* "augmented." A god or person with his or her own *megin* can also be *aukinn* with *megin* from elsewhere. The god Heimdall, for example, possessed *ásmegin* but was also *aukinn* with *jarðar megin.* Anything to be made *aukinn* must have an empowerment that aligns with the object or person's innate qualities. If something is empowered contrary to its nature, it still works magically, but there is an inner conflict, as the empowerment is *álag,* an "on-lay."

Without main, might is useless, for main includes the will to live. It is main that enables a person to exert his or her will in all realms of life. It empowers the magical arts of the human being. We must have both might and main in order to live effectively. Without one or the other, we are close to death. Inner power corresponds with outer powers, by means of being in the right place at the right time to achieve what is needful. This is shown, for instance, in the English martial arts, whose Four Grounds of effective action are defined as judgment, distance, time, and place (Brown 1997, 94). To be successful in combat requires a perfect combination of these factors. Equally, the performance of magic requires recognition of the Four Grounds. The inner human power of might and main must be balanced properly with external powers. When both are in alignment, then the human is at one with the cosmos. To maintain this equilibrium is a constant task.

Old Norse concepts from pre-Christian times do not have overt references to the theory of the four humors, but traces of the Intelligible Tetraktys theory are present. *Önd,* the breath of life, equivalent to the Greek *pneuma,* is synonymous with human existence. Every person begins life by drawing a first breath. It is the cry of the newborn baby. Regular breathing measures out our lifespan, and at death we literally expire by breathing out our last breath. Birth is thus the moment of the first breathing-in, and death, the last breathing-out. Between, we are alive, breathing. The traditional worldview envisages the human breath of life as a reflection of a greater whole, the universal Cosmic Breath that is present everywhere. Every individual possesses a mind; that is, a rational faculty dependent on consciousness and personality. The mind operates on physical, psychological, and mystical levels. According to these traditional concepts, our powers of perception, reflection, thought, memory, and inspiration are all aspects of the cosmic breath, and magic is worked through the individual's portion of these powers.

As in the Pythagorean system, there are a number of specific named qualities that make up the human being. *Litr* is health, and *læti* is the power of movement. *Hugr* is consciousness, intelligence, and willpower (intelligence and mind). *Hamr* is personal ability to control and shape images and events. *Hamramr* is the ability to shape-shift; for example, into animal form as Odin and the berserk warriors were said to do. A person changed into another form is a *hamhleypa,* and traveling in another form (out-of-the-body travel or soul-flight) is *hamfarir. Hamingja* is luck and the ability to take advantage of appropriate circumstances. The northern tradition worldview tells that luck is a personal possession; there are instances from former times that interpret luck in this way. Magnates and heroes were able to bestow their *hamingja* upon other persons as favors in order to accomplish tasks that would be impossible without magical assistance. Because it is a personal possession, *hamingja* must be nurtured, for it can also be lost or stolen. The old Irish adage, "There is no money that cannot be stolen" applies also to luck.

Soul-flight is the shamanic practice noted two thousand years ago by Roman authors and in the north as *hamfarir* in the thirteenth-century

Ynglingasaga where Odin "changed his form; the body lay there as if heavy with sleep or dead, but he himself was in the form of a bird or beast, fish or worm, and went in an instant on his own or another's errand to distant countries." This account is almost identical to the Roman accounts of Hermontinus of Clazomenae by Plutarch in *On the Sign of Socrates* and in works by Pliny and Tertullian. Hermontinus left his body and wandered into distant countries, from where he brought back accounts of things that could not be known unless he had been there. Like Odin, Hermontinus lay apparently lifeless while his soul was out of the body. His wife betrayed him to the Cantharidae, his enemies, who burned his body while he was in soul-flight. H. C. Agrippa noted in 1531 that even in his day in Norway and Lappland were very many people who could "abstract themselves three days from their bodies." When they returned, they could tell people of things they had seen far away. No other living creature or person should touch the body while in soul-flight; otherwise the person could not return to the body (Agrippa 1993 [1531], III, I).

According to Norse belief, every individual has a *fylgja* (attendant or fetch; plural: *fylgjur*). The *fylgja* is present throughout the person's life, but it can also leave the body and put on a new shape. Powerful warriors and kings had "strong" *fylgjur,* which preceded them everywhere. *Fylgjur* of magnates and heroes could actually be seen by people with second sight. To see one's own *fylgja* was an omen of impending death. *Fylgjur* could also appear in animal form, the beast being related to the individual's character. When Christian beliefs became the norm, the *fylgja* became the guardian angel. This is overtly recorded in the tale of Hall, who allowed the Christian missionary Thangbrand to baptize him on condition that the archangel Michael should be his *fylgja*. The later concept of the *fylgja* in English outside the guardian angel is the wraith, from the Old Norse *vörðr,* "ward, guardian."

Celtic tradition is recorded in medieval Breton, Welsh, Irish, and some Scots Gaelic texts. Christianity arrived much earlier in Celtic Britain and Ireland than in Scandinavia, so what may be older concepts are expressed differently from the Germanic and Norse personal powers and spirits. The physical and spiritual *Eight Parts of Man* and *Twelve Parts of the Body* appear in Welsh tradition in the medieval *Book of Llanrwst,* ascribed to the sixth-century CE bard Taliesin. The eight parts are: (1) earth, inert and heavy, the flesh; (2) stones, hardness, the bones; (3) water, moist and cold, the blood; (4) salt, briny and sharp, the nerves; (5) air, the breath; (6) the sun, clear and bright, the heat of the body; (7) spirit, soul and life; and (8) divinity, the intellect. There are also twelve parts of the body that relate to abilities, emotions, and powers: (1) the forehead, sense and intellect; (2) the nape of the neck, memory; (3) the top of the head (pate), discretion and reason; (4) the breast, lust; (5) the heart, love; (6) bile, anger and wrath; (7) the lungs, breath; (8) the spleen, joyousness; (9) the blood, the body; (10) the liver, heat; (11) spirit, the mind; and (12) the soul, faith.

THE SYMBOLISM OF THE PARTS OF THE BODY

A symbol denotes being in the world, unlike a sign that represents *the* being or *the* world. The symbol must include the observer, whereas a sign does not. Symbols permit us to progress from the externally perceived form of a given phenomenon toward its essence. Symbols do not exist to be interpreted or decoded: they draw the observer inward to participate in the world of spirit. At an as-yet-undetermined time, bodily parts and functions were linked with the powers of the signs of the zodiac. The zodiac and its signs were certainly present in Britain in Roman times (43–410 CE). The signs denote not only the heavenly constellations but also qualities or collections of attributes, so they also have a symbolic function. The Hermetic maxim, "as above, so below" states that the greater world, the Cosmos, is reflected in the lesser world, the human being. The parts of the human body therefore reflect aspects of the Cosmos, and these are expressed through the signs of the zodiac. The relationship to the parts of the body is also symbolic. The meaning of each sign expresses subtle qualities present in the corresponding part of the human body. The human head, vision, and expression are ruled by Aries, the Ram; the neck, throat, and voice by Taurus, the Bull. Gemini, the Twins, correspond with the arms. Cancer, the Crab, rules the chest, breasts, and stomach; and Leo, the Lion, the heart. Virgo rules the abdomen and intestines; Libra, the Scales, the kidneys and the navel; and Scorpio, the genitals. Sagittarius, the Archer, corresponds with the thighs; Capricorn, the Goat, the knees; and Aquarius, the Water-Carrier, with the lower legs. Finally, the two fishes, Pisces, rule the feet.

OPERATIVE MAGIC PRINCIPLES

There are two basic magical practices: direct natural magic and talismanic or sigil magic. Since antiquity, they have been used in parallel with one another. Amulets—actual things, such as a quartz pebble, a sliver of alder wood, the feather of a raven, a wolf's heart, or a toad's bone—contained the particular unique power of that stone, plant, or animal. Each could be used for appropriate magical effects, related to the nature ("virtue") of the animal, plant, or stone. Often these materials were difficult to obtain. Once found, certain rituals were necessary to channel their power for human use. Actual powers present within physical objects could also be accessed through images of the object, by signs that referred to them, and by corresponding powers, such as planetary spirits or zodiacal signs. This is the underlying concept of runic and sigil magic, where magicians use visible marks to embody the power rather than the actual objects. A sigil may denote the power of a stone, tree, animal, planet, star, spirit, or god and particular aspects of them according to the needs of the magician. Of course, it is still necessary that a sigil must have a physical form. It must be written upon something, using a medium, whether blood or inks, so there is still a physical composition of the talisman that must be in concurrence with its meaning in order to work. It must be consecrated ritually to activate its power. Runes are magic sigils that are also letters of an alphabet.

Runic talismans were characters of texts inscribed on particular woods, such as yew, and empowered by blood. The Old English word *teáfor,* meaning red coloring (ochre, red chalk) continues in the English shepherds' word for sheep-marking, traditionally red, *tiver.* This was probably the word used in the past for empowering runes and other magical items with blood. The German word *Zauber,* "magic," is cognate with it, as is the Old Norse *taufr,* "a talisman." Technically, runes are not distinct from other forms of magical sigils. Bind-runes (*bindnar runir*) were used from the earliest times to make composite sigils expressing the combined power of two or more runes. Icelandic magical texts contain talismanic sigils composed of runes combined with other elements: astrological, planetary, metallic, and spiritual. Sigils can be marked upon objects, animals, and people to empower them with the virtues of the thing signified by the sigil. Tools and weapons were inscribed with runes that empowered them with a readable text, whether the name of a feared and famous sword or the use of a talisman against the dangers of the sea. They were also used to ward off illness, dangerous things, hostile magic, and destructive entities such as evil spirits (Old Norse *meinvættir*) and black vessels. Individuals could be marked with permanent sigils, as in 1609 when astrologer Simon Forman inscribed the characters of Venus, Jupiter, and Cancer on his left arm and right breast using an ink made from gold (Rosecrans 2000, 46–48). Enthusiastic writers on ancient skills and wisdom sometimes portray the practitioners of the past as perfect masters who could do no wrong and never fail, but the world is not and has never been like that. It has a built-in failure rate. Inept magic is mentioned in *Egils Saga,* where the eponymous hero finds a supposedly healing whalebone talisman upon the bed of a very ill woman. It has ten runes wrongly inscribed. Egil destroys it, saying, "A man should not cut runes unless he can read them properly, because a false runestave has been the downfall of many." He carves a new stave with the proper runes, and she recovers.

People with the Scottish surnames Freer and Frere claim to be descended from the astrologers of the kings of Scotland. In the Scottish highlands and islands, augury (*frith;* Old Norse *ófreskr*) was conducted to find lost people and animals and determine their location. The *frith* was made on the first Monday of the quarter, just before sunrise. The *fritheir* (diviner, seer) having fasted, with bare head, bare feet, and closed eyes, went to the threshold and put a hand on each doorjamb. Concentrating upon the objective, the *fritheir* opened his eyes and stared straight ahead. From what he saw, he made his augury (Carmichael 1997, note 194). This is a classic example of what in Old Norse is termed *framsýni* (foresight). *Frith* was also conducted in the highlands of Scotland on Hallowe'en at the meeting of three roads; sitting on a three-legged stool, the *fritheir* perceived the names of those doomed to die in the coming year. Also, a *fritheir* could see the spirits of the dead by standing at a crossroads with his chin resting on a forked stick. First to be passing would be the shades of the good, then the shades of those who have been murdered, then the damned (Puhvel 1976, 169–70). On the Isle of Man, people who were born after the death of their father, or who had a cross of hair on their chests, or whose eyebrows met, were reputed to possess second sight. It was a practice of such people to go into a churchyard on the eves of the New Year, of St. Mark's Day, and of Midsummer Day to foretell who was to be buried in it during the ensuing year (Moore 1891, 162). The claim to be able to see otherworldly events and harmful entities was used by some people for personal gain. The man reputed to be the last boggart-seer in Lancashire, northwestern England, died around the middle of the nineteenth century. In 1867, Harland and Wilkinson wrote, "J. W., the last of the ancient race of boggart-seers in the township, used to combat with feoorin' between East End and Droylesden toll gate; but as he died a few years ago without bequeathing his gift, he (happily) carried with him his mantle to the grave" (Harland and Wilkinson 1867, 55). A boggart-seer was a person who could see the evil entities called boggarts, the unquiet spirits of the dead, and knew the techniques of neutralizing them.

Much of northern magic is concerned with illness and healing, combating spirits and other entities that were perceived as the root cause of the symptoms. There is a considerable corpus of these magical charms from Anglo-Saxon England. In his *Anglo-Saxon Magic,* G. Storms asserted that these magical formulae were the oldest relics of Anglo-Saxon and Germanic literature, stemming from ancient traditions. Storms stated that these charms are of outstanding importance because they give us more than a tantalizing glimpse of a "strange world," and emphasise the close connection between Anglo-Saxon magic and religion (Storms 1948, 5–11). In traditional worldviews, untoward events are often ascribed to the visible or invisible action of benevolent or malevolent entities (Storms 1948, 49–50). The Anglo-Saxon charms tell of the elves (*ælf;* plural: *ylfe*) as destructive entities causing illness, and dwarfs were also characterized as disease-spirits (Storms 1948, 50–51).

There was a similar concept in Welsh tradition of destructive entities causing disease. In his *Ancient Cymric Medicine,* Henry S. Wellcome quotes a poem ascribed to the British bard Taliesin. It describes the devastating Yellow Plague of Rhôs as the result of a disease demon, "a most strange creature that will come from the sea-marsh." In the poem "it is concealed because sight cannot perceive it" (Wellcome 1903, 41). Wellcome sees this as "ancient Cymric bacteriology." Some Anglo-Saxon charms are to combat specific disease-spirits that had infected the patient's blood. The charms seek to expel them by letting blood, which will take out the disease-spirits as well (Storms 1948, 51–52). Christianity redefined all of the earlier dwarfs, elves, beasts, and injurious spirits as agents of the devil, but it was essentially the same system given a new theoretical basis (Storms 1948, 51).

HUMAN AND ANIMAL POWERS

Men who had the ability to change shape were *hamramr,* "strong in form." Fighting men who took on battle frenzy were called *Berserkir* or *Úlfheðinn.* They were men who wore bear pelts or wolf skins to acquire the power of these fearsome wild animals. The belief was that these men could actually transform themselves into real bears or wolves. This technique was apparently uncontrollable. Those who went into it experienced possession by the beast. The *Völsunga Saga* tells how the heroes Sigmund and Sinfjötli put on magic wolf skins that took them over, and uncontrollably they became wolves and rampaged, randomly killing people. Finally, they succeeding in removing the skins and burnt them. The terror engendered by these merciless men is evoked in the ninth-century poem *Hrafnsmál:* "the Berserks bayed . . . the Úlfheðnar howled." Viking Age helmet panels found at Torslunda in Sweden show bears, a wolf-headed warrior, and spearmen wearing helmets with boar crests. The tradition of the bear warrior, its frenzy removed by military discipline, continues today in Denmark and Britain, where the royal guards wear bearskin hats as part of their ceremonial uniforms.

Belief that *hamramr* was a physical reality of devilish origin was the basis of many accusations in medieval and later witch trials. A Bull of

Fig. 2.1. Torslunda helmet plates with beast-warriors.

Pope Gregory XI refers to witches' sabbaths at which the devil appeared as a toad or a ghost or a black cat (Burstein 1956, 22). During the witch hunts, women accused of witchcraft were said to have transformed themselves into hares, cats, dogs, toads, bees, flies, and other unlikely animals. Ann Baites, who was tried as a witch in Northumberland, northeastern England, in 1673, was said to have changed into a cat, a hare, a greyhound, and a bee. Belief in supernatural animal helpers and human transmogrification did not die out in the medieval period. Belief in *hamramr* continued in England well into the twentieth century. In 1901 the Lincolnshire folklorist Mabel Peacock wrote of people suspected of "knowing more than they should." One of these "students of unholy lore" could, it was claimed, take on the shape of a dog or toad when he was determined to attack his neighbor's cattle. He worried sheep and oxen in the shape of a dog, and in the shape of a toad, he poisoned the pigs' feeding trough (Peacock 1901, 172; Peacock and Carson, December 1901, 510). Eric Maple recounts a story from Canewdon in eastern England where a witch took on the shape of a toad. Other witches then made visits to her in the shape of toads to renew their power (Maple 1960, 246).

3

Place, Space, and Time

THE PRIMACY OF THE NORTH

Wherever we are, each of us, with our awareness centered in our bodies, is the center of our world. Where we are at any given time is *the* place, our place in the world. The world of our present consciousness is here and now. Each of us is centered upon ourselves, and from this state of centered presence comes the idea that the surface of the earth is centered at a particular place. Socially, ritual, religious, and political centers are based upon this understanding.

The view from the center is inherent in orientation and time-telling. Visible rising and setting points of the sun form markers on the horizon that define directions from the center point from which they are viewed. Of course, these are all apparent phenomena, the result of the rotation of the earth on its axis and its orbit around the sun. Sunrise and sunset at the vernal and autumnal equinoxes is due east-west, and all other rising and setting points of the sun vary day by day and season by season. But these changes are not random; they are progressive. Days lengthen from the midwinter solstice until the midsummer solstice, when they shorten again progressively until the shortest day at the winter solstice.

In the north, calendars evolved from these cyclic sequences of increase and decrease. In the Northern Hemisphere, the most southerly point of the sun on the horizon is at the winter solstice, after which sunrise is progressively farther north, day by day, until the summer solstice, when the sunrise is at its most northerly rising point. Sunsets, too, are the most northerly at the summer solstice and most southerly at the winter one. The only unchanging solar directions are due south, the highest point of the sun in the day, the zenith, and due north, when the sun is at the lowest point (beneath us at midnight), the nadir. These remain the same throughout the year. The conceptual line between the zenith and the nadir is the meridional line, due north-south. This was of significance in the Norse coming-into-being myth, where orientation within space is the precondition for existence to emerge. In *Ginnungagap,* the primeval void, a north-south division arose where ice in the north came into contact with fire from the south, bringing into existence the world and all beings within it.

The concept of four directions emerged from the apparent path of the sun in its daily appearances above the horizon through the year. The sun rises toward the east, whose meaning is "growing bright" and "burning." The south is the direction where the sun reaches its greatest daily altitude and gives its fullest light. The west is the direction of the going down of the sun, and the north is the direction of night, meaning "away" and "below, where the sun is beneath the place where we are." But north does not necessarily mean night, as it does in regions closer to the equator. North of the Arctic Circle at midsummer, the sun does not set at all, remaining above the horizon due north at midnight. This is the famous phenomenon of the midnight sun (Reuter 1985, 4–5).

North was an important sacred direction in pre-Christian times. It was the direction of prayer in the indigenous religions of northern Europe, directed toward the North Pole, the "immovable heavenly seat" that is the axis of the earth, around which the night sky appears to rotate (Reuter 1985, 6). In Viking times, settlements were often built up from south to north, the second settler taking the land to the north of the first homestead. The younger son of the homesteader then had the rights to the southernmost plot of land (Reuter 1985, 5). Farmhouses and halls in that period were oriented east-west so that the owner's high seat on the northern long wall faced due south, the high point of the sun at midday. The high-seat pillars were carved with sacred images and decorated with "god-nails" (*reginnaglar*). On the Moot Hill, the place of the local assembly, the king and the lawspeaker stood in the north, facing south; the assembled people faced north. The plaintiff stood in the south and faced north to seek official justice, but in civil legal proceedings that were not considered to be a contest, such as the conclusion of a contract, one party faced west, and the other east (Reuter 1985, 5).

The early Christian apologist Origen taught that hell was at the center of the earth and the entrance to it was at the North Pole. Interestingly, in common with Greek and Roman geographers of the period, he recognized that the earth was round, a fact later considered heretical by religious literalists. Each time the Northern Lights appeared, Origen claimed, this was a sign that the gates of hell had opened, warning sinners of their impending doom; "the doctrine of fear of the North creeps in everywhere" (Johnson 1912, 335). The Christian missionaries to northern Europe condemned veneration of the north on the grounds that praying northward was evil. The Christian condemnation of the north was taken from Old Testament biblical sources. The books of Job, Jeremiah, and Isaiah claimed that the "sides of the north" were the abode of the Devil (Job 21:6–7; Isaiah 12:12–13; Jeremiah 4:6). The biblical separation of the sheep from the goats sends the goats to the left-hand side. According to Jewish tradition, that is the north. In medieval times, Anglo-Norman heraldry followed this division, the right being called *dexter* and the left, *sinister*. These words still have good and bad connotations today. The understanding that the sun can stand in the north and give light at midnight was unknown in the ancient Middle East, and there the north meant only darkness and evil.

The religious conflict of sacred directions was manifested in royal edicts. Around the year 800 CE, when Frisia was repaganized by King Gotrik of Denmark, doors were cut through the north walls of churches, and Christians were forced to crawl through them facing north. In the eleventh century, the Norwegian king Olaf III (Olaf Kyrre; reigned 1067–1093), who was Christian, had the northern high seat of the royal hall moved to the eastern side (Reuter 1985, 6). In pre-Christian Iceland, burials appear to have been without a significant common orientation (Eldjárn 2000, 285). Norse pagan burials, on the other hand, have a marked tendency to a north-south orientation (Shetelig 1912, 230). Christian burials were always intended to be east-west with their head to the west (and their faces therefore to the east), reflecting the belief that the final summons to Judgment would come from the east. Hence in Wales the east wind was known as the "wind of the dead man's feet." In 1648 in *His Noble Numbers,* the English poet Robert Herrick expressed this as the Christian sacred orientation in his religious poem *North and South:*

> *The Jewes their beds, and offices of ease,*
> *Plac'd North and South, for these clean purposes;*
> *That Man's uncomely froth might not molest*
> *Gods ways and walks, which lie still East and West.*
> (HERRICK 1902 [1648], 363)

Some early medieval churches, which were oriented east-west, had entrance doors on both north and south sides; but at some point the north doors were blocked, except in rare instances where the only entrance was to the north. In 1899 George S. Tyack wrote, "The north was of old mystically supposed to typify the Devil, and a usage prevailed in some places of opening a door on that side of the church at the administration of Holy Baptism, for the exit of the exorcised demon" (Tyack 1899, 66). Tyack gave a specific example of this: "In the Cornish church of Wellcombe is a door in the north wall, locally known as 'the devil's door,' which is opened, at the renunciation in the baptismal service, for the exorcised spirit to take his flight" (Tyack 1899, 171). The location of burials with regard to the direction of the church was significant. In the graveyard, it was customary to bury the dead on the southern side of the church. In his *On Praying for the Dead,* the English bishop Miles Coverdale (1488–1569) wrote, "As men die, so shall they arise: if in faith in the Lord toward the South, they need no prayers; they are presently happy, and shall arise in glory: if in unbelief without the Lord toward the North, then are they past all hope" (Coverdale 1846, 258).

Only those who had transgressed and were considered unworthy of a full Christian burial were interred on the north side. For example, in 1786 at Turlagh in Ireland, Robert Fitzgerald was hung for murder and was buried "on what is generally termed the wrong side of the church, in his clothes without a coffin" (Tyack 1899, 66).

The meridional (north-south) line is also significant in traditional British folk magic. In Cornwall, western England, in 1665, the "Conjuring Parson" William Rudall recorded in his *Diurnall* how he laid a ghost by ritual magic. He describes how he made a magic circle and set up a rowan staff in a pentacle before standing in the south of the circle, facing due north to call up the spirit (Hawker of Morwenstow, quoted by Bottrell 1880). There is a Welsh folk belief that a healing spring should have an outlet toward the south, which means that the water flows from the north (Johnson 1912, 332). A recorded instance of healing using south-running water was noted in the nineteenth century in the north of England in connection with a talisman called the *Black Penny*. When cattle showed symptoms of mad cow disease, the Black Penny had to be dipped in a south-flowing spring before water was taken from the spring and given to the ailing livestock (Henderson 1866, 164). Practices of the *Toadmen* of the east of England recorded in the twentieth century used the water of a stream flowing from north to south to select a particular bone of a toad used for magical purposes (Parsons 1915, 37; Evans 1971, 217–21; Pennick 2011b, 33). Cambridgeshire fenman W. H. Barrett recorded a tradition that brown toads were introduced to Britain by the Romans, who used them as a compass. A dagger blade was placed on the warts on the toad's back, and the toad moved until the blade pointed north (Porter 1969, 51).

Fig. 3.1. Toadman's toad bone, Cambridgeshire, England.

THE EIGHT AIRTS

An Ancient Way of Dividing Up the Land

A fourfold conceptual model of existence is found throughout the European tradition. The geomantic division of towns and cities into four quarters (hence the word quarter for a district) is first recorded in the *Disciplina Etrusca* (Etruscan Discipline), the ancient art of the Augurs of Etruria in Italy in the early years of the first millennium BCE. The Roman surveyors, members of the guild of Agrimensores, used the sixteenfold *Disciplina Etrusca* for laying out the orientation and groundplans of temples, fortresses, and cities. This was a particular skill that embodied Etruscan spiritual principles, divination, and augury. How far it was known outside expert circles is uncertain. Fourfold divisions of countries, especially islands, are also a tradition. The island of Bornholm in the Baltic traditionally has four distinct regions, or quarters; so do Iceland and Ireland. The four provinces of Ireland—Leinster, Munster, Connacht, and Ulster—are the most anciently recorded example of this ritual division.

In agricultural and seagoing societies, people are always aware of the visible horizon as they observe the apparent motions of sun, moon, and stars in relation to their location. This is the essence of traditional European perception, in which no part is isolated from any other part.

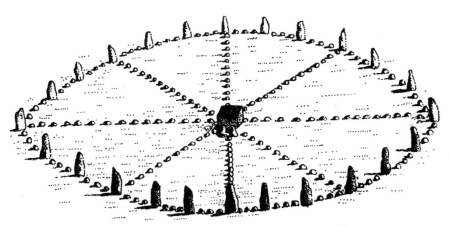

Fig. 3.2. Eightfold stone circle formerly at Solá, Norway.

The conceptual layout of the land was perceived according to natural measure, which divided the circle of the horizon into four quarters by imaginary lines running north-south and east-west. This division derives from the structure of the human body and the structure of the world. Between these two conceptual lines at right angles, the horizon is divided by further lines in the intercardinal directions. The southern quarter is the quadrant between southwest and southeast; the eastern quarter is between southeast and northeast; the northern sector is between the northeast and the northwest; and finally, the western quadrant is between the northwest and the southwest. These eight directions come from the physical structure of the world we live upon: the north-south polar axis and the east-west one at right angles to it, the plane of the earth's rotation.

Recognition of this inherent eightfold division is necessary if one wants to make a square or rectangular structure facing the four quarters of the heavens, such as a traditional building. The four cardinal directions are therefore at the midpoints of the four quarters. The fixed eightfold division of the horizon is a marker of the apparent motions of the celestial bodies, which are cyclic. Depending on latitude, the position of the rising and setting sun at the solstices and at other significant times of the year will be at different places on the horizon relative to the eightfold division. At certain times they will coincide with one or other of the eightfold markers, such as at the equinoxes. These directions played an integral part in traditional ways of life. The traditional reckoning of solar time was used in northern Europe until the arrival of cheap clocks and the imposition of centralized standard time, first by railway companies, then by governments.

TIME AND THE DAY

The word "day" has two different literal meanings. A day can be the period of daylight between sunrise and sunset, as opposed to night. But a day can also mean the period including darkness, the modern 24-hour day (Old Icelandic *dægr*), as defined by the calendar, running from midnight to midnight. Two different interpretations of the same word caused confusion when the Christian religion was introduced. Christian time division originated with the early monasteries in Egypt. It was used to govern the times of their daily cycle of prayers. Their "Temporal Hour" system of time-telling divided the day of daylight into twelve equal hours. There was not a serious difference between the length of the day in summer and winter in Egypt at a latitude around 30°. But in northern Europe, between 24° and 36° north of Egypt, the length of difference between summer days and winter days is enormous. In the northern winter the nights are longer than the days, but in summer they are shorter, so in systems dividing daylight into twelve, the hours are significantly longer in summer than they are in winter. In Egypt the difference was negligible, but in Iceland, for instance, where it is light for three common (modern) hours in winter, but twenty-one hours in summer, the church method of day-division was unacceptable. In winter the church temporal hour amounted to fifteen minutes by modern reckoning, and in summer one hour and forty-five minutes. Temporal hours are not a workable system in the north, but they were used by the clergy, who must have understood that the indigenous system was better suited to practical use.

Because of the considerable differences in day length during the year, awareness of the directions was more highly developed and widespread in the north of Europe than in many other parts of the world, for it was a necessary part of survival. The knowledge of the airts (eight directions) was an integral part of the knowledge of farmers, builders, seafarers, warriors, and magicians. The Tides of the Day are an octaval system. Each Tide is not related to the length of daylight, but to a whole cycle of light and dark, the calendar day. There are eight equal divisions for the modern 24-hour period, reckoned as beginning and ending at 7:30 a.m. These Tides are not the same as, nor are they related to, the tides that ebb and flow in the sea. Markers of the Tides are always the same, so sunrise and sunset vary between the Tides. In winter a certain point in a Tide will be in darkness, when in summer at the same point it will be light.

How long daylight lasts varies with the season. The range between the height of the sun at noon on midwinter and noon on midsummer is also notable. The sun rises due east twice a year at the vernal and autumnal equinoxes, that is 6:00 hours in modern clock time, and when it sets due west, it is 18:00. When the sun stands due south at any time of year, it is 12:00 noon, but the height of the sun varies from day to day. The lowest altitude of the sun at noon is at the winter solstice, and its highest altitude is at the midsummer solstice. The visible rising and setting points of sun, moon, and stars are not the same in different places; one must have local knowledge. Between the southernmost rising of the sun at midwinter and the most southerly sunrise at midsummer, the sun rises due east at the equinoxes, crossing the east-west line southward in winter and northward in summer. This defines the two halves of the year, the dark half and the light half. They are dependent upon the latitude at which the observer stands but also depend on the site from which we are viewing them.

From the viewing point of a farmstead or sacred place, these sunrises were marked by a convenient natural feature such as a mountain or by an installed marker (a post, a standing stone, a cairn, or a tree of notable species planted deliberately) at that point. In addition to sunrises at notable times of year, the markers indicate the time of day when the sun stands at any altitude above them. For convenience, houses were built in relation to the cardinal directions, so that the door faced one of the important directions, and anyone going out could view the corresponding marker. Old Icelandic houses had a "house stone" in front of the door on which the observer stood to view the sky. The Althing in Iceland observed the sun's course, and hence the time, from the lawspeaker's seat (Reuter 1985, 7).

For time-telling, the sun was used by day and the stars by night. The eightfold system could be used for time-telling irrespective of the lay of the land. The height of the horizon above or below our viewing point alters the apparent rising—and setting—places of the celestial bodies. Unless the site has a horizon of equal height all around it, we will not see the celestial bodies rising and setting symmetrically with relation to the cardinal directions. On a level horizon there is an annual solar geometry where the midsummer solstice sunrise is diametrically opposite midwinter sunset, and the winter solstice sunrise is directly

Horologii Iconismus.

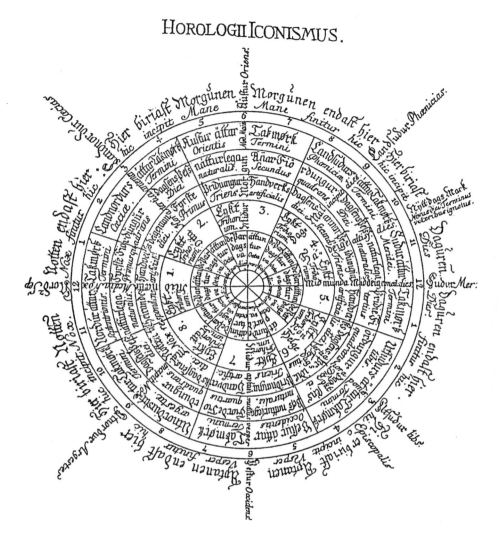

Fig. 3.3. Eightfold wheel of time from Bjornsson's *Rimbegla,* Copenhagen, Denmark, 1780. The Library of the European Tradition

opposite midsummer sunset. But such places are rare. At any time of year when the sun is above the horizon, it will always be above the same horizon marker at the same time of day. This is the principle of the sundial.

Sundials of the Anglo-Saxon era in England are often called "scratch dials," sexton's wheels, and mass clocks. Extant sundials are on the oldest surviving buildings, which are invariably churches. The grammarian Ælfric (ca. 950–1021) records that in Anglo-Saxon England there were professional time-tellers called *tídsceáware* or *dægmæl-sceáware*. The oldest datable Anglo-Saxon sundials, such as the seventh-century one on Escomb Church in County Durham, divide daylight into four parts. So do the oldest dials in Ireland, on standing stone slabs also dating back to the seventh century CE, such as those at Monasterboice and Kells. Later dials have the traditional eightfold day, sometimes melded with the twelvefold hours of the Christian form of time reckoning. Kirkdale Priory in North Yorkshire, England, has a sundial using this system. It dates to between the years 1056 to 1066. Carved next to it is the Old English text that reads, "This is the day's sun marker at every Tide." The eight Tides of the day as observed in Old England, described in the modern 24-hour clock system, are as follows: *Morgan,* from 4:30 to 7:30; *Dæg-Mael,* 7:30 to 10:30 (this is the first Tide of the day); *Mid-Dæg,* 10:30 to 13:30; *Ofanverthr Dagr,* 13:30 to 16:30; *Mid-Aften,* 16:30 to 19:30; *Ondverth Nott,* 19:30 to 21:30; *Mid-Niht,* 21:30 to 1:30; and *Ofanverth Nott,* 1:30 to 4:30. In Wales the equivalent Welsh system named the Tides Bore (equivalent to *Morgan*), Anterth, Nawn, Echwydd, Gwechwydd, Ucher, Dewaint, and Pylgeint.

In the eightfold system the morning mark points are significant in managing the beginning of the working day. *Morgan,* the morning Tide, begins with the sun at the East-North-East point, 4:30 a.m. local apparent time in the current time system. This point was called *rismál,* "getting-up time" in Old Norse. *Morgan* is followed by *Dæg-Mael,* breakfast time, reckoned as the first Tide of the day. The point of transition between these Tides is a significant horizon marker where the sun stands East-South-East, 7:30 a.m. local apparent time in the current time system, called *dagmálastaðr* in Iceland. The South-South-West mark point corresponding to 13:30 was called *miðmundi,* and West-South-West (16:30) *eyktarstaðr.* In the summer half of the year, *eyktarstaðr* was the point where the day's work ended. On the day in autumn when the sun set at *eyktarstaðr,* this marked the beginning of winter (Reuter 1985, 7).

The eight directions were called *ættir* (singular: *ætt*) in Old Norse.

Fig. 3.4. Damaged stone slab with eightfold sundial,
Kells, Ireland.

More generally, the word means "direction," for the verb *átta* means "to orient oneself." The *ættir* of the horizon relate to eight periods of time called in Old Norse *eyktir,* a word apparently linked with the English word "yoke" and the German *joch* (Reuter 1985, 7).

In Scots, *airt* means "a quarter of the heavens; point of the compass; the direction of the wind" as well as having meanings related to transitive movements in a direction, such as "to point out the way to a place; to direct; to turn in a certain direction . . . to aim at" (Warrack 1988 [1911], 4). Similarly, in modern Irish *aird* means a direction or a point of the compass. In northeastern England the directions are referred to as the *airts,* whereas in Lancashire, northwest England, they are *haevers* (Harland and Wilkinson 1867, 149; Warrack 1988 [1911], 4).

In the integrated culture of the north, *ætt* equally refers to lineage, family, clan, and house in the sense of an aristocratic ancestral line. These are traditionally related to the place that family or clan originated and lived. The Old Norse *ætt* is also a group of eight runes in the 24-rune futhark. There is a tradition of the *ættar-fylgja*, "family *fylgja*," which cares for the fortunes of the family and is the property of one or other of the family members. When its owner dies, the *fylgja* finds a place with another relative, if possible. The properties ascribed to this kind of *fylgja* appear to have similarities with the belief that particular angels or spirits rule the directions as well as places.

OTHER SYSTEMS OF TIME

The direct observation of the sun from a particular place is the basis of the eight tides of the day. But in northern Europe there have been numerous ways of dividing the day for secular, religious, and magical purposes. The ecclesiastical way of dividing the day was not into eight tides, but divided daylight into twelve equal parts and the night into twelve equal parts. These hours are called Canonical, Temporal, or Unequal Hours. This came into conflict with traditional northern ways of time-telling when Christianity was brought into northern Europe. From about the ninth century, the church had a fixed system of monastic rituals, "canonical offices" that consisted of eight daily prayer events called Lauds, Prime, Terce, Sext, None, Vespers, Compline, and the Night Office or Vigils, divided into a number of sections called Nocturnes. From the 1300s, starting in Italy, the practice of dividing the day into twenty-four hours became widespread in Europe. Magicians used and still use the unequal hours system known as the Planetary Hours.

There are four main systems of time divisions. *Horæ ab ortu solis,* "hours from the place of the sun," otherwise called Babylonian Hours or Greek Hours, start with sunrise and end at the following sunrise, dividing the day into twenty-four equal hours. This is also called the "Natural Day" (Tupper 1895, 120). Daylight hours are numbered low. *Horæ ab occasu solis,* also called Italian, Welsch, or Bohemian Hours, start the

Fig. 3.5. Versions of time division in northern Europe, Olaus Magnus, 1555.
The Library of the European Tradition

hours at sunset and end at sunset, so daylight hours are numbered high. *Horæ norimbergenses,* Nuremberg Hours, can begin either at sunrise or sunset. Daylight hours are numbered from sunset, as in the Babylonian/ Greek Hours; at sunrise, they are numbered in a new series, as in the Italian/Bohemian system. *Horæ communes,* known as Common Hours, French Hours, and German Hours, divide the day into two periods of twelve, beginning at midday and midnight, 12:00 noon and 12:00 midnight. This is still the most common means of time-telling, with *ante meridiem* (a.m.) and *post meridiem* (p.m.) hours, though the 24-hour clock is used in transport and business to avoid confusion. The medieval sundial and compass makers of Nuremberg called the hours of the 24-hour system *Grosse Uhr,* "great hours," and those of the Common Hours, *Kleine Uhr,* "small hours" (Gouk 1988, 18).

When they had been abandoned for everyday time-telling, the Unequal Hours system survived in use in magic as the Planetary Hours. This method assigns a particular astrological planet to each hour of the day and night through the week (Agrippa 1993 (1531) II, XXXIV). The time from the sun rising to its setting is divided into twelve and the night from sunset to sunrise also divided into twelve. These are the twelve hours of the day and twelve hours of the night, which of course vary in length continuously as the duration of daylight and darkness lengthen or shorten with the seasons. The first hour of each day is ruled by the lord of that day, so the first hour of Sunday is ruled by the Sun and so on. The seven astrological planets are numbered in their traditional sequence in descending order, as in the nine spheres of traditional cosmology: Saturn, Jupiter, Mars, the Sun, Venus, Mercury, and the Moon. So on a Wednesday, the first planetary hour is Mercury; the second, the Moon; the third, Saturn; and so on. The Wednesday sequence begins again with Mercury at the eighth hour, and the twelfth hour of the day is therefore Mars. The planetary sequence goes on into the twelve hours of the night with the first hour being the Sun. It repeats again at the third hour of the night, when Mercury rules. The last (twelfth) hour of Wednesday night (Thursday morning in modern reckoning) preceding sunrise is therefore Saturn. At sunrise on Thursday, the next planet, Jupiter, rules the first hour. It is an ingenious system, which continuously recycles the seven planets in their proper order, day after day.

Counting the day from sunset was a widespread custom whichever system of hours was in use. The eve of a day counted as the beginning of that day, even though now it is numbered on the preceding calendar day. So May Eve is after sunset on April 30 and in Germany is also known as *Walpurgisnacht*. Other festivals, such as St. Mark's Eve, Allhallows' Eve (Hallowe'en), Christmas Eve, and New Year's Eve, are all major eves in customary celebration and magical observance. In ancient Ireland, a night (*oídhche*) was used to measure the days rather than calendar days beginning at midnight. The new day began at sunset, not at sunrise, so that what was called a Monday night would precede the day of Monday, as still used in the eve system. Counting time by nights, not by days, still survives in British English, where a fortnight means two weeks (fourteen nights). The obsolete word *sennight* (seven nights) was formerly used to describe a week.

Traditional time-telling went into decline when clocks were invented and became generally available. The regular machinery of the clock became the norm by which time was measured. But certain remote places and trades retained traditional time lore long after it had been abandoned in most places in favor of clock time. Places without railways were less affected, as there was no timetable to keep to. In the Faroe Islands the traditional system continued well into the twentieth century, and rural workers improvised methods of time-telling well into the twentieth century.

RULE-OF-THUMB TIME-TELLING

Knowing the directions and gauging the height of the sun were the two important factors of telling the time of day. The directions were common knowledge to all, and the sun's height could be determined by common objects, the human body, and local knowledge. O. S. Reuter noted that the method for announcing an agreed time to stop work, or any other time needed to be marked, was by the height of the sun rather than its direction. A common measure in medieval Iceland was the shaft height of the sun. This was in the afternoon when the lower edge of the sun appears to rest on the point of a spear set up nine feet from the observer. This was the observer's own spear, made for him personally according to his physical height. It was set up so that he could still reach comfortably with a shafthand (that is, with the thumb held out from the fist) up to the socket of the spearhead. Because each man's spear was related to his personal size, this technique gives the same sighting angle for any man using his own weapon. This technique removed the necessity to observe the horizon, using a common weapon as the instrument of measurement (Reuter 1985, 8).

In the preindustrial era, precise times were generally not required.* A less rigid schedule was current for everyday needs. In England the day and night were customarily divided into thirteen parts. This "thirteen times of day and night" is a rule-of-thumb way of telling time, practical enough for a life not ruled by the clock (Lawrence 1898, 339):

---

*Exceptions to this were the practice of astrology and magical procedures that required the presence of specific celestial powers.

1. After Midnight
2. Cockcrow
3. Between the first cockcrow and daybreak
4. The Dawn
5. Morning
6. Noon
7. Afternoon
8. Sunset
9. Twilight
10. Evening
11. Candletime
12. Bedtime
13. Dead of night

In the days before mechanical time-telling was readily available, the hours of the day and night were told by the sun by day and by the stars at night. The most basic way to improvise a sundial is to use one's hand. The hand is held out at head height, palm upward. A small straight stick is held in the crook of the thumb at the angle of the latitude,

Fig. 3.6. Shepherd's hand sundial, Germany, sixteenth century.
The Library of the European Tradition

determined by the angle of shadows at noon. The stick becomes a shadow-casting gnomon. Before noon it is held in the left hand, pointed toward the west; after noon, in the right hand, oriented to the east. The shadow cast by the stick shows the time by the position of its shadow against the joints of the fingers and the fingertips.

More substantial temporary turf dials, otherwise known as "shepherds' dials" or "witches' dials" are known to have been made by herdsmen in the rural parts of southern England. The practice was discontinued gradually, and by the beginning of the twentieth century, they were used only in Kent, Surrey, Sussex, and Essex. They seem to have gone out of use completely during World War I. Shepherds used the dials to tell them when it was time to move the sheep from the grazing land to get them to the sheepfold before sunset.

The basic shepherd's dial was made by cutting a circle in the turf about 18 inches (460 mm) in diameter. Then a straight stick about a foot long (305 mm) was pushed vertically into the ground at the center of the circle. North of the vertical stick, another stick, notched to mark the hours, was laid east-west inside the circle at right angles to a north-south line. Each end touched the circle. Having an intimate knowledge of the land on which they worked every day, herdsmen knew what distant landmark, or "farthest beacon" marked north. The stick at the center was the gnomon that cast a shadow upon the notched stick. The hour was indicated where the shadow touched a notch. Some shepherds dispensed with a notched stick and made small ridges in the earth to mark the hours. There is no one way of doing things traditionally, so others made a different dial that was a reversal of the principle of the dial just described. It started with the circle, but a shorter stick was stuck in the center. Into the perimeter of the circle, another stick a foot long was put in the ground, due south of the first stick. More sticks were stuck into the circle at appropriate distances for the hours or tides relative to the first stick. Traditionally, seven sticks were used. All had the function of gnomons, casting shadows across the central stick, which was the marker of the hours (Gossett 1911).

These traditional methods were in use until the availability of cheap clocks and watches, and the imposition of standardized time in time

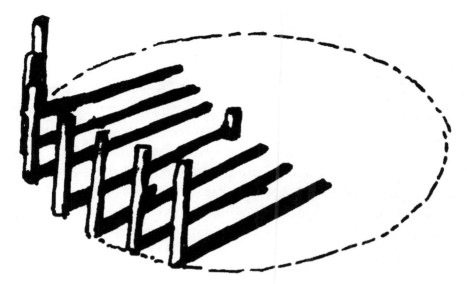

Fig. 3.7. Southern English shepherd's dial.

zones, delocalized time-telling. The need to have the same clock time at different places, rather than the sun-determined local apparent time, so that trains could run safely, led railway companies to standardize their clocks at a main station. Later, government edicts enforced railway time on whole countries. The concept of legal time was created, where the official mean time and later "daylight saving time" determined by central government became the everyday reality. People were forced to use government-defined time rather than the natural real time told from the sun, which thereafter was ignored. After that, ancient traditional methods continued to be used by only a very few people, such as traditional astrologers and practitioners of magic. Almost everywhere on Earth now, real local apparent time is different from official clock time. It is a subtle dislocation whose effects on the human body are ignored.

THE WEEK AND ITS DAYS

The earliest recorded continuously cycling seven-day week was in use among the Hebrews from the fifth century BCE. The Sabbath was the named day, while the others were numbered (Green 1998, 236). The week was transmitted outside Judaism by Greek-speaking Jews, and by the second century BCE the planetary names were being used: Zeus, Thursday; Aphrodite, Friday; Kronos, Saturday; Helios, Sunday; Selene, Monday; Ares, Tuesday; and Hermes, Wednesday (Green 1998, 237–38). Naming the days of the week expresses the magical theory that the particular virtues and powers of each planet are strongest on the day dedicated to them. From the Greeks the week went into the Roman Empire, where the days were named for the Roman gods: Jupiter for Thursday, Venus for Friday, Saturn for Saturday, Sol for Sunday, Luna for Monday, Mars for Tuesday, and Mercury for Wednesday. Use of the seven-day week traveled beyond the borders of the Roman Empire, and the day names were again reconfigured by the *interpretatio Germanica* with the names of the northern gods. In the same period Christian apologists, including Augustine, Philastrius, and Caesarius of Arles, preached that it was sacrilege to use the Pagan names of the weekdays and recommended using numbered days instead. Their recommendations were not followed. In Anglo-Saxon England, for example, the day names became *Tíwesdæg,* Tuesday, named for Tíw (the English god corresponding to the older Germanic Tîwaz); *Wôdnesdæg,* Wednesday, for Woden; *Þunresdæg,* Thursday, for Þunor; and *Frigedæg,* Friday, for Frigga. Saturday appears as a direct import without a significant deity, as the god Sæter or Satern is not among the main gods and goddesses. *Sunnandæg* and *Mónandæg,* Sunday and Monday, are named directly for the sun and the moon. The simple references to the sun and moon reflect the absence of solar and lunar deities in Germanic religion, in contrast with the Graeco-Roman pantheon.

The particular virtues and powers ascribed to each planet are embedded in traditional lore of good and bad days to do things. Each day had a specific quality that enhanced particular tasks and hindered others. Certain kinds of magic performed best on certain days of the week. All over Europe are folk sayings that describe what one must and must not do on a particular day. Because the church adopted Sunday as its holy day, most prohibitions referred to this day. At many times and places, laws prevented business from being conducted on a Sunday. An Irish example will give a flavor of weekday beliefs. In 1887 Lady Wilde wrote that people believed the strength of the fairies' malevolent powers were dependent on the day of the week, "The first days of the year and of the week [Sunday] are the luckiest. Never begin a journey on a Friday or Saturday, nor move from your residence, nor change a situation. Never cut out a dress or begin to make it on a Friday, nor fix a marriage, for of all days the fairies have the most malefic power on a Friday" (Wilde 1887, II, 116).

EGYPTIAN DAYS

Good and bad days known as "Egyptian Days" or "The Dangerous Days in the Year" appear in a number of medieval magical and medical texts. The medieval Welsh book of the Physicians of Myddfai solemnly explains:

> Sound teachers have discovered and written as follows, namely, that thirty-two days in the year are dangerous. Know that whosoever is born on one of those days, will not live long, and whosoever is married on one of them, will die ere long, or will only exist in pain and poverty. And whosoever shall begin business on one of them, will not complete it satisfactorily. (Pughe and Williams 1861, §93, 58)

There is no general concurrence of the actual Egyptian Days in published texts. For example, Myddfai has totally different days from those listed in the Icelandic *Galdrabók*. An Icelandic list of Egyptian Days in the *Galdrabók* gives two bad luck days in each month (Flowers 1989, 67), while the Myddfai list has between one and four bad days per month (Pughe and Williams 1861, §93, 58). So in February, *Galdrabók* warns of the 3rd and the 4th, while Myddfai lists three: the 16th, 17th, and 18th. For May, *Galdrabók* has the 3rd and the 7th, while Myddfai lists four: the 15th, 16th, 17th, and 20th. For October, *Galdrabók* has the 3rd and the 10th, while Myddfai has only one, the 6th. Again, different combinations of bad days appear in a Swedish runic calendar of 1710, published in 1895, February having the 11th, 17th, 18th, and 19th, and May the 7th. It concurs with Myddfai in October with the 6th being the one bad day (Simpson 1895, 236).

These days clearly had an origin in various dire events, but by the time they were promoted in books, their origins were forgotten, and they were no more than superstition, handed on through practical observance and in respected texts. An indication of their origin comes from H. C. Agrippa in his *Three Books of Occult Philosophy* (1531). Agrippa notes that *Penitential* or *Black Days* originated as days when the commonwealth suffered some notable blow. For example, the Romans commemorated the day before the fourth Nones of August because it was the day they suffered heavy defeat by the forces of Hannibal at the Battle of Cannae in 216 BCE. In Jewish tradition June 17 and July 9 are Black Days: the first date was said to be when Moses broke the tables of the law, and Manasseh set up an image; the second date was when both temples of Jerusalem were destroyed (Agrippa 1993 [1531], III, LXIII, 670). They were called Egyptian Days, Agrippa tells us, because in ancient times the Egyptians observed days when bad things had happened, and subsequently every nation took up the practice to commemorate their own national setbacks. In modern times 9/11 is the most recognized of these days. By definition historic lists of Egyptian Days must vary from country to country, hence the lack of consistency.

RUNIC CALENDARS

Runes may have been used in calendars and almanacs in pre-Christian times, as there was always a need for some means of recording the passing of time. In Iceland in 1639, an edict of the church labeled the use of runes as witchcraft. Árni Pétursson was burnt to death in the presence of the Icelandic Althing in 1681 because he had used runic magical formulae. But at the same time, the runes were in everyday use in Scandinavia and Estonia in calendars and almanacs carved on wooden staves. The runic perpetual calendar was called a clog almanac in England, *primstav* in Norway, *rimstock* in Denmark, and *runstaf* in Sweden. Their notation was based upon the Roman calendar enacted by Julius Caesar in 46 BCE. This Julian Calendar became progressively more inaccurate, until it was replaced in 1582 by Pope Gregory XIII and the current Gregorian Calendar came into being.

J. Barnard Davis noted in 1867 that there were two kinds of northern almanacs carved on wood and other materials: the more ancient Runic Calendars, inscribed with runes; and the less ancient, runeless calendars, the Staffordshire clog almanacs.

They were the Primstaves of the Norwegians, so named from the new moon, prima luna, or from the Prime, or Golden Number engraved on them; and Rimstocks by the Danes, from the Icelandic and Anglo-Saxon word Rim, a calendar, and Stock, a staff or stick . . . they were mostly made of wood (treen), but far from exclusively so. Some were of horn or bone . . . and some were inscribed on parchment; the wood itself differed in different examples. Many were of oak, some of box, some of pear tree, some of lime, and so on. Many were constructed in the form of a sword or sabre, or a long staff or baton; all, emblems of power in the hands of priests and rulers. Some of these staves were hexagonal in form . . . more were rectangular; some prismatic staves. Others of these calendars were of tongue-shaped leaves united at one end by an iron pin riveted in, just in the shape and manner of a fan. Another series is formed of thin tablets of wood, each of which has two holes pierced through it, one near either extremity, so that two thongs may be passed through all the laminæ; and when these are tied the instrument closely resembles a modern book. (Davis 1867, 458–59)

These almanacs could also be in the form of a ring. The *messedag* (Mass-day) staff shown in figure 3.8 was depicted in a Norwegian almanac (*Norske Folke-Kalender*) for 1848 (Davis 1867, 471).

The essentially Christian calendar on the runic almanacs carried on the church's complex computations of the date of Easter, depending upon interactions between the vernal equinox and the full moon. The common runic calendar contained seven recurring letters that were the first seven runes of the futhark and another nineteen that indicated the Golden Number cycle. Printed runic almanacs were produced in Sweden until the middle of the eighteenth century. The runes finally went out of use as a practical almanac in Estonia in 1921, when the Julian Calendar was

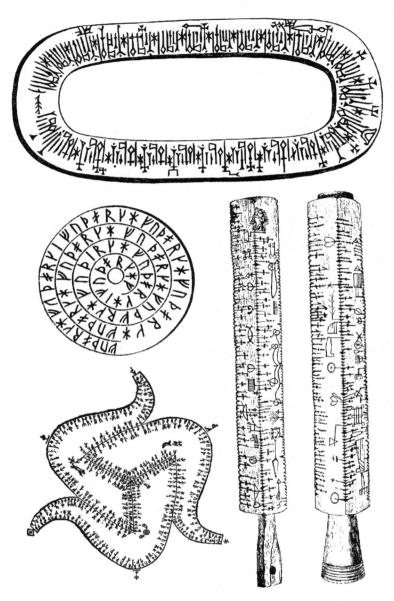

Fig. 3.8. Runic Almanacs. The Library of the European Tradition

finally abolished, and the Gregorian one, already used everywhere else, replaced it. The printed page illustrated here is from the work by Doctor Plot, *The Natural History of Staffordshire*, 1686, where he compared the English clog almanacks with the Swedish *runstaf* and gave the numbers for the runes and their names. A woodcut in the second volume of Olof Rudbeck's *Atlantica* (1702) depicts a mid-seventeenth-century runic calendar from Österbotten "På bräde uti en Treefootz lijkness," in the likeness of a treefoot. The threefold year of the northern tradition marked by *Vintersblót* (Winter's Day, October 14), *Midvintersblót* (Midwinter's Day, January 13) and *Sommarsblót* (Summer's Day, April 14), fits this form admirably. Winter's Day and Summer's Day were marked on Estonian runic calendars until 1921.

Two-sided almanacs were divided on one side from January 1 to July 1 and the other side from July 2 to December 31. They could be read from left to right or right to left. Four-sided almanacs were divided from January 1 to April 3; April 4 to July 1; July 2 to October 12; and October 13 to December 31. Unlucky or "Egyptian" days were marked on some almanacs. Mark days on runic almanacs included days from pre-Christian and Christian systems. This list compiles significant mark days from various runic almanacs with their varied signs (Harland 1865, 126–30; Davis 1867, 468–70; Simpson 1895, 236–40; Schnippel 1926, 39–106; Pennick 2001, *passim*).

January 1, New Year's Day; Kalends of January: a circle

January 6, Epiphany; Twelfth Night: a star, three circles or crowns for the Three Kings

January 13, Tiugunde Day (20th day after Yule); Ides of January; *Midvintersblót:* inverted horn

January 25, St. Paul; Old Disting (*Dísarblót,* festival of the Dísir): sword, ax

February 2, Candlemas: threefold branch

February 3, St. Blaise: binding knot

February 14, St. Valentine: true-love knot

February 24, St. Matthias: fish (commencement of the fishing season), feather

March 1, St. David; Foe-ing Out Day (spring cleaning, magical cleansing): harp, binding-pattern

March 25, Annunciation (Lady Day): threefold branch

April 14, Summer's Day, *Sommarsblót:* leafy bush

April 23, St. George: a sword, spear

April 25, St. Mark's Day: cuckoo ("St. Mark's Gowk"), cross in circle

May 1, May: stylized May tree

May 3, Holy Cross Day: cross

June 11, St. Barnabas: haymaking rake

June 24, St. John the Baptist: sun, ax

July 10, St. Knut: scythe

July 29, St. Olaf: ax

August 10, St. Lawrence: grid

September 14, Exaltation of the Holy Cross: a cross

September 21, St. Matthew: stag, carpenter's square

September 29, Michaelmas: horn, steelyard, pair of scales

October 14, Winter's Day; *Vintersblót:* pine tree

October 28, St. Simon and St. Jude; *Fyribod* (forebode, the onset of winter): knot

November 1, All Saints; Hallowmass; *Helgerne;* Kalends of November: circle, binding knot

November 11, Martinmas; Old November Day: ax, goose

November 23, St. Clement: anchor, pincers (blacksmith's)

November 30, St. Andrew: saltire

December 13, St. Lucy; Ides of December: branches of light

December 21, Yule; St. Thomas; Midwinter: hand, spearhead

December 25, Christmas: semicircle on a straight stroke, drinking (wassail) horn

4

Astronomy and the Winds

In the previous chapter the natural division of the earth into four directions and four quarters was based upon the perceived rotation of the heavens and the positions of sun- and moonrises. The various sorts of calendars were and can be regulated by solar and lunar phenomena without recourse to observing the stars. However, there is a star that stays close to the hub of the Northern Hemisphere night sky as it appears to circle during the night. In modern astronomy this star is called Polaris (*Stella Polaris,* the Pole Star or North Star). This star is an important marker in traditional navigation, both at sea and on land. It is a symbol of constancy and reliability, the unwavering guiding light, which leads us unfailingly to our destination. The mariners' use of the North Star has given it many names: Tir, Stella Maris, the Lode Star, *Leitstern,* the Nave, the Leading Light, and the Nail. The latter name likens the star to a nail, around which the heavens rotate like the hub of a wheel. This star, which in the last millennia has appeared to stand above the terrestrial pole, was a guiding light for those navigating at sea and on land. The Old English Rune Poem tells of it as *Tir,* "which keeps faith well, always on course in the dark of night." Its official astronomical name is Polaris, and a Medieval Latin epithet for it is *"Stella non erratica,"* "the unerring star," and as an emblem it has the motto, *"qui me non aspicet errat":* "He who does not look at me goes astray."

STARS, ASTERISMS, AND CONSTELLATIONS

The names of the asterisms and constellations of the night sky demonstrate a particular worldview, and in northern Europe the etymology of the word "star" relates to "the scattered, strewn" (Reuter 1985, 19). Some Norse and some Welsh constellations are named after mythological objects. The varied names give us an insight into the worldview of people in the past, and the interweaving of the characters of folktales with the everyday world. In recent years many people have attempted to "reconstruct" a northern astronomy as it may have existed in Viking times. The old names of some stars are recorded. Sometimes, too, speculative names from Norse mythology have been attached to constellations of Graeco-Arabic astronomy, which are thought provoking. However, surviving traditional names of asterisms from northern Europe show that at least some of them do not correspond with the classical constellations, which, although they have a venerable history, are essentially arbitrary concepts.

Traditionally, the North Star (Stella Polaris) is bound up with the lore of the asterism close to it, the constellation called "Ursa Major" (the Great Bear) in modern astronomy, which is used as a means of finding it. Like the North Star, the Great Bear has numerous names in traditional northern European astronomy. The North Star can be located in the night sky by following the pointer stars of the constellation of Ursa Major, known by their Arabic names, *Merak* and *Dubhe*. The arrangement of the stars of Ursa Major has been likened to a plough or a wagon in various traditions. In Germanic astronomy the constellation was called either Woden's Wagon or Charles's Wain (Reuter 1985, 19). Traditional Welsh astronomy, recorded in Robert Roberts's *Arweiniad i Wybodaeth o Seryddiaeth* (A Guide to a Knowledge of Astronomy; 1816), calls the asterism *Saith Seren Y Gogledd* (the Seven Stars of the North) by similar names: *Men Carl, Men Charles* (Charles's Wagon), or *Jac a'i Wagen* (Jack and his Wagon). Sometimes in Welsh the name of the Great Bear is translated literally: *Yr Arth Fawr*.

Another common traditional name for Ursa Major is the "Plough"; in Welsh *Yr Aradr* (the Plough) or *Yr Haeddel Fawr* (the Great Plough

Handle); correspondingly, the constellation Ursa Minor is *Yr Haeddel Fach* (the Little Plough Handle). As well as Charles and Jac in their wagons, Peter holds the plough. In Scots a name for Ursa Major is *Peter's Pleugh* (Warrack 1988 [1911], 409). Yet other Welsh names of this constellation are *Llun Y Llong* (the Image of the Ship); *Y Sospan* (the Saucepan/Dipper). In the English tradition, Charles's Wain/the Plough and the Pleiades are confusingly both called the Seven Stars; as also in Welsh where *Saith Seren Y Gogled* (the Seven Stars of the North; Ursa Major) are distinguished from *Saith Seren Siriol* (the Seven Cheerful Stars; the Pleiades). According to Finn Magnussen (1845), the Pleiades were known in winter in Iceland as the Star. This asterism was used at night to tell the time, by noting the compass direction over which the Star was standing, or by its relationship to the landscape tide-markers (Reuter 1934, 185). According to eastern English traditional horsemanry, the seven nails in the horseshoe symbolize the seven stars of the Plough (Tony Harvey, personal communication).

The "belt" of the constellation Orion is a prominent feature in the night sky, being three bright stars apparently forming a line, and notable as a seasonal and nighttime marker. By its early rising, it signified the beginning of the season of harvest (Reuter 1985, 13). In both Welsh and Scottish tradition, this has been named as a measuring rod. In England it was called the Tailor's Yard Band and in Wales it is *Llathen Teiliwr* (the Tailor's Yardstick), and in Scotland the King's Ellwand or the Lady's Ellwand (Sternberg 1851, 126; Warrack 1988 [1911], 157). (An *ellwand* is a measuring rod, a Scots Ell in length, 37.0958 inches.) The latter name dedicated to the Lady recalls the Scandinavian name of Orion's Belt, *Friggs Rocken* (Frigga's Distaff) (Reuter 1985, 19). Another Welsh name connecting it with Our Lady is *Llathen Fair* (Mary's Yardstick). A Scottish name for the asterism is Peter's Staff (Warrack 1988 [1911)], 409). This asterism attracted various other names in northern Europe: the Three Fishers, the Rake, the Three Reapers, and even the Plough (Reuter 1985, 19). Another Scottish asterism, the Ellwand of Stars, denotes three stars in the constellation Lyra (Warrack 1988 [1911], 157). Sirius, called the Dog Star in England and Scotland, was Loki's Brand in Pagan Iceland (Reuter 1985, 19–20).

Several other Welsh constellation names come from mythic characters in the Mabinogi, including *Llys Dôn* (The Court of Dôn), Cassiopeia; *Caer Arianrhod* (Arianrhod's Fortress), Corona Borealis; and *Telyn Arthur* (King Arthur's Harp), Lyra. In the latter constellation, Welsh astronomy differs from the Scottish in expressing the asterism in a classical way as a musical instrument and not a measuring rod. In common with Greek mythology, Norse myth tells of features set in the sky by the gods as memorials of their deeds. Two asterisms are associated with body parts of giants: Aurvandil's Toe and Thjassi's Eyes. O. S. Reuter identifies Corona Borealis as the Old Norse constellation Orendil's (Aurvandil's) Toe. Snorri Sturluson's manual for poets, *Skáldskaparmál*, tells how Thor was carrying the giant Aurvandil in a basket across the ice river Elivagar, and his toe stuck out and was frozen, so Thor broke it off and threw it into the sky, where it became a star. Another giant, Thjassi, was killed by the Æsir, and his eyes were set in the sky as a memorial (Reuter 1985, 19, 20; Jones 1991b, 16). The stars Castor and Pollux appear to be the best candidates for this asterism. T. C. Lethbridge notes an English folktale collected in Horsley, Gloucestershire, which tells how the giant Wandil stole springtime, and winter continued without end. The gods hunted him down, recovered springtime, and cast the giant into the sky as a punishment. His eyes are seen in the night sky as Castor and Pollux (Lethbridge 1957, 71; Jones 1991b, 16–17). The Milky Way is seen as a road in the sky: an old Germanic name is *Iringsweg* (Iring's Way); English tradition calls it Ermine Street, a name of one of the Four Royal Roads of Britain. In Welsh traditional astronomy it is *Llwybr y Gwynt* (the Path of the Wind); it also has the mythological name *Caer Gwdion* (Gwydion's Fortress).

THE FIFTEEN STARS

Although they are known as the Fifteen Stars, they consist of fourteen major stars and one asterism: Aldebaran, Algol, Algorab, Alphecca, Antares, Arcturus, Capella, Deneb Algedi, the Pleiades, Procyon, Regulus, Sirius, Spica, Stella Polaris, and Vega (Wega). Each of the fifteen stars expresses a particular astrological quality. Each star has a

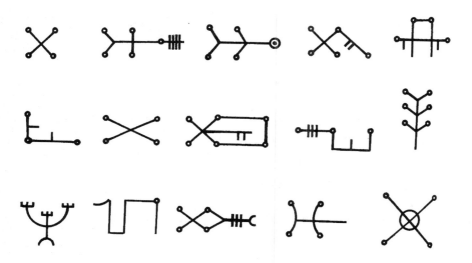

Fig. 4.1. Sigils of the fifteen stars. Top line, left to right: Aldebaran (the Follower); Algol (the Torch); Algorab (the Raven); Alphecca (Aurvandil's Toe); Antares (Fenris-wolf). Middle line: Arcturus (the Day Star); Capella (Goat star); Deneb Algedi (Goat's tail); Pleiades; Polaris (Lode Star, the Nail). Lower line: Procyon (the Torch Bearer); Regulus (the Lord); Sirius (Loki's Brand); Spica (the Sheaf); Vega (the South Star).

corresponding gemstone, stone, or mineral and is assigned a sigil. In astrology the given virtues of these fixed stars combine with the planets to produce harmful or benevolent outcomes. They are rarely used in modern astrology, yet in medieval times their significance was taken into account, their sigils used magically, and as visible stars they assisted orientation and navigation.

Aldebaran (α Tauri), the Bull's Eye, is a red star that was one of the four Royal Stars of ancient Persia (with Regulus, Antares, and Fomalhaut). Astrologically, it was ascribed by Ptolemy to the nature of Mars. It rules over the red gem Carbuncle (Ruby). Algol (β Persei) is a white binary star traditionally malefic, bringing misfortune, violence, and destruction. Its nature is of Jupiter and Saturn. It is considered the most eminent of the stars, ruling over the Diamond. Algorab (δ Corvi) is another double star, purple and pale yellow. Like Algol, the Wing of the Crow, it is a malevolent star, of the nature of Mars and Saturn. Its stone is the Black Onyx. Alphecca (α Coronae Borealis) is a brilliant white star, signifying the knot of the ribbon of the Northern Crown. Its nature parallels Mars and Venus, bringing dignity and honor, artistic and poetic qualities. Alphecca's stone is Topaz. Antares (α Scorpii) is a red and emerald green binary star. Its name means "rival of Mars," and it marks the heart of the Scorpion. It is another malevolent power, bringing ruin and destruction through obstinacy. Its stones are Amethyst and Sardonyx. Arcturus (α Boötis) is a golden-yellow star also known as the "Bear Guard" (Arktouros). It partakes of the natures of Mars and Jupiter, or alternatively Mercury and Venus, bringing wealth, honors, and fame won by self-reliance. Its corresponding stone is Jasper.

Capella (α Aurigae), the Goat Star, is a white star, of the nature of Saturn and Jupiter. A beneficent star, its powers give honor, position, and wealth, and its correspondence is the Sapphire. Deneb Algedi (δ Capricorni), called the judicial point of the Goat (Capricorn), is an equivocal star, about whom various authorities differ widely, hence its attributions of beneficence and destructiveness, sorrow and happiness, life and death. Its planetary correspondences are Mercury and Saturn, and its gemstone is Chalcedony. The Pleiades are an asterism composed traditionally of the seven stars Alcyone, Calæno, Electra, Maia, Merope, Sterope, and Taygete. The position of the main star Alcyone is used in astrological calculations, and the Pleiades have the nature of the planet Mars and are considered to be disastrous, bringing illness, disaster, and death in conjunction with various planets. The Pleiades rule over the metal Quicksilver (Mercury). Procyon (α Canis Minoris) is a yellow and yellow-white binary star, called "before the dog" because in rising it precedes the Dog Star, Sirius. Its qualities are related to anger, carelessness, and violent activity; its planetary correspondences are Mercury and Mars, and its gem is Agate.

Regulus (α Leonis), the King's Star, is a triple star, white and blue-white, also known as Cor Leonis (the Lion's heart), one of the four Royal Stars of ancient Persian astronomy. Its powers are those of Jupiter and Mars, but it brings violence and temporary military success that ends in failure and death. Granite is the stone of Regulus. The Dog Star Sirius (α Canis Majoris) is a brilliant yellow and white binary star of the nature of Venus. It brings faithfulness, honor, and fame, and those born under its influence become custodians or guardians; its gem is Beryl. Spica or Arista (α Virginis), the Grain of Wheat, is a white binary star that partakes of the qualities of Venus allied with Mercury. Its gem is Emerald, and generally, it brings good fortune. Stella Polaris (α Ursa Minoris) is the North Star. It is a double star, pale white and topaz yellow. Its powers are those of Venus and Saturn, and astrologically Stella Polaris brings bad fortune. Its stone is the Lodestone, a natural magnet. This star will reach its nearest point to the true pole in 2095. Finally, Vega or Wega (α Lyrae) is a pale green star. An alternative name for this star is *Vultur Cadens,* the Falling Vulture. Its stone is Chrysolite, and the star's influence is of the nature of Venus and Mercury. Vega will become the pole star around the year 13500 CE (Robson 1969, *passim*).

H. C. Agrippa lists the Fifteen Stars in order of their power and their rulerships, based upon their position in their constellations, beginning with Taurus. Their order is: (1) Algol, (2) the Pleiades, (3) Aldebaran, (4) Capella, (5) Sirius, (6) Procyon, (7) Regulus, (8) Stella Polaris, (9) Algorab, (10) Spica, (11) Alchamech (Acturus), (12) Elpheia (Alphecca), (13) Antares, (14) Vega, and (15) Deneb Algedi (Agrippa 1993 [1531], I, XXXII; II, XXXI). Names ascribed to some of them by Otto Sigfrid Reuter as existing in ancient Germanic astronomy are the Torch (Algol); Alphecca (in Corona Borealis, Aurvandil's Toe); the Day Star (Arcturus); the South Star (Vega); the Torch Bearer (Procyon); Loki's Brand (Sirius); and Thjassi's Eyes (Castor and Pollux) (Reuter 1985, *passim*).

THE FOUR CORNERS OF THE HEAVENS

Although astrological charts are now drawn in a circle, in earlier times a square was used. The square was oriented "foursquare"; that is, with the sides running north-south and east-west. Square talismans are based on this principle, with their sides conceptually oriented in line with the four directions. In this system there are four corners at the intercardinal directions, giving a conceptual eightfold division. The quincunx, an important sigil in magic, is also arranged with four points in the corners of a square and another at the center. In northern household tradition the four corners of the building and those of each room are seen as places where either benevolent or malevolent sprites may dwell. During construction the corners are protected with offerings embedded in the fabric of the building, and when the building is in use, they are periodically reconsecrated with offerings of various kinds.

Medieval astrologers signified the four corners of the heavens as four progressive qualities: rising, midheaven (zenith), falling, and the lowest point (nadir). These correspond to the apparent places of the sun at sunrise, noon, sunset, and midnight at the equinoxes (Agrippa 1993 [1531], II, VII). In northern cosmology the four corners of the heavens were supported by four dwarfs Norðri, Suðri, Austri, and Vestri, who are mentioned in the list of dwarfs in *Gylfagynning*. In European high magic the four corners were ruled over by the four archangels: Gabriel, north; Uriel (or Nariel), south; Michael, east; and Raphael, west. Some medieval churches, such as the former gate guardian St. Botolph's in Cambridge, have guardian figures set at the four top corners of the tower.

The four corners of Iceland were supposed to have supernatural guardians. Sturluson tells a story of how the Danish king Harald Gormsson sent a magician to Iceland in the shape of a whale to report on the island. Along the north coast the magus perceived the land to be populated thickly with *landvættir* (land wights). At Vopnafjörður he tried to go ashore, but a dragon accompanied by other venomous beasts attacked him. On the south side he came to Eyjafjörður and was attacked by a giant bird. At Breiðafjörður, a monstrous bull accompanied by a band of hostile *landvættir* frightened off the magus. Then at Vikarsskeið another landing attempt was thwarted by a mountain giant wielding an iron staff. Apart from the dragon, the guardians closely resemble the evangelical beasts from Christian symbolism.

In Amsterdam in 1913 stone images of the four northern dwarfs were set in the ceiling of the main entrance of the shipping companies' office called Het Scheepvaarthuis, a building that is an archetypal example of the Amsterdam School architectural style. Supporting the heavens, the dwarfs surround a metal image of the Great Bear with the stars, including the mariners' guiding light, the North Star, represented by electric light bulbs (Boeterenbrood and Prang 1989, 101). The building is now an exclusive hotel.

THE EIGHT WINDS

Recorded wind lore from the north is far less coherent than in the Mediterranean mythos. However, a particular place is given as the origin of the winds: a remote island or dangerous, forbidden mountain. According to Roman tradition, the gods set Aeolus to rule the winds under the aegis of the goddess Juno. The winds were kept in caverns on the mountainous isle of Lipari and contained or released at will by Aeolus. In ancient Gaul (modern France), the god of the winds was Vintios, and the winds blew from his holy mountain, Mont Ventoux, in the south of modern France. Aeolus and Vintios were tutelary deities of all things connected with the wind. Sails, windmills, windvanes, weathercocks, washing lines, kites, illnesses carried by the wind, blown musical instruments, and the aeolian harp (whose strings produce harmonic modes) are all under the rulership of wind gods. Around 50 BCE the Macedonian architect Andronikos of Cyrrhus designed the octagonal Tower of the Winds at Athens, which still stands.

The classical tradition has four winds that correspond with the four cardinal directions: Boreas, Euros, Notos, and Zephyros. We receive from Andronikos the mainstream European tradition of the eight winds; the four preceding cardinal winds and four others located at the four corners of the heavens. The eight winds on the Tower of the Winds are, starting at the north and going sunwise, Boreas, Caecias, Apeliotes, Euros, Notos, Lips, Zephyros, and Skiron. These are known in medieval and later cartography, compasses, and maps by their Latin names, described by Vitruvius. The north wind is called Septentrio, the east wind is Solanus, the south wind is Auster, and the west wind is Favonius. The intercardinal winds are Aquilo, northeast; Eurus, southeast; Africus, southwest; and Caurus, northwest. These are the wind names that were adopted across northern Europe. The names of the winds are inappropriate as they are derived from specific qualities of winds perceived at Athens and later refined in southern Italy. The qualities of the classical winds cannot be meaningful outside the places where they were first recognized, yet they were used widely to define the compass rose. Even the Spanish imperial surveyors who laid out new towns in the Americas had the classical wind names on their plans. Old city plans from places as far apart as St. Petersburg, Edinburgh, Stockholm, Lisbon, Milan, and Mexico City show these eight winds. In 1992 at Cambridge University in England, the Maitland Robinson Library, a neoclassical building, was constructed at Downing College. Designed by Quinlan Terry, its octagonal upper section is a reworking of the Tower of Winds at Athens. It bears the names of the eight winds, carved in Greek characters. The classical eight winds are a very tenacious example of mythical continuity.

In practical terms the meanings of these eight winds are useless outside their area of origin. Those who used the wind for their livelihoods—sailors, windmillers, and traditional healers—always had their own names for local winds, which depended on where they were. There are a few records of local wind names in parts of Europe that actually refer to the local wind qualities. The traditional description of winds conserved in certain parts of France and Germany give an indication of how winds must have been perceived all over Europe in former times. In Provence and along the Côte d'Azur, *la rose des vents* (wind rose) is divided into thirty-two winds whose names vary from place to place and from season to season, and even according to strength. Winds recognized with the same name come from different directions in different places as local topography dictates. For example, on the coast at Nice the summer northeast wind *Grégal* has a different character in the autumn, when it is called *Li Rispo*. In winter, again it has a different quality, and it is called *Orsuro*. When it is gale force, the northeast wind at Nice is *L'Aguielon*. There, the south wind is generally called *Marin* (also *Miejournau, Mijournari,* or *Miejour*), but when it is soft and fresh, *L'Embat*, whilst in summer it is called *Li Marinado*. A notable wind recognized in *la rose des vents* painted inside Provençal windmills is called *Ventouresco*. It is a wind held to emanate from Mont Ventoux, the Celtic holy mountain of the winds, upon which Pagan pilgrims left small musical horns as votive offerings to the god.

In Germany, the Bavarian fishermen's tradition of the lake called Ammersee has two parallel descriptors: one is direct descriptions, and the others are based on the places from which the winds are blowing. The principle of naming comes from desired directions of sailing, or from well-recognized places in the wind's direction. The Ammersee is relatively small, so the wind names are less diverse than those of the Provençal winds. A northeasterly wind is called *Vorderwind* (front wind), a westerly is *Hinterwind* (back wind). Another name of the *Hinterwind* is *Schwabenwind*, blowing from Swabia, west of Bavaria. A *Hochwind* (high wind) is a southwesterly *Wessobrunner Wind* in the place-directional terminology. Winds from the south and southeast are called *Sunnenwind*, or the southeastern is called a *Beuberger Wind* after the place it comes from. A northerly is a *Geradeheraufwind*, otherwise a *Donau*, from the River Danube. A *Querwind*, otherwise a *Zwerchwind* (crosswind) is a northwesterly. In general, the widespread Latin names were used to mean particular directions on the magnetic compass rather than to denote actual air and weather qualities, as anyone who had to sail a ship or windmill was well aware.

The Icelandic magical talisman for navigation, called a *Vegvisir* (waymarker) in the *Huld Manuscript,* shows the eight directions denoted by different glyphs that may once have represented the sigils of the eight winds (Davíðsson 1903, pl. VI). According to renaissance writers on divinatory geomancy, the condition of the wind was taken into account before performing a divination. If it was unfavorable, the divination could not take place. Symbolically, the Irish bards assigned colors to the winds: the east was red; the south, white; the west, brown; and the north was black. Traditional medicine took note of the winds, for it was believed that certain winds at certain times brought illness and pestilence. The wind blowing at one's birth also determined one's future life, in complement to the influence of one's natal horoscope. The first breath that a baby takes is the air from whichever wind is blowing at that moment, and this has a lifelong effect. In Wales on *Teir nos ysbrydion,* the "three spirit nights," the wind blowing over the feet of corpses (the east wind) bears sighs to the homes of those doomed to die during the coming year (Puhvel 1976, 170).

In Scots tradition a red wind was an easterly to which plant blight was attributed. A traditional English adage says, "When the wind is in the east, it is neither good for man nor beast"; equivalent Scottish sayings are "When the wind is in the east, the fisher likes it least" and "When the smoke goes west [i.e., when the wind is coming from the east], good weather is past." Another Scots adage tells us, "Everything looks large in an east wind," referring to distant mountains. This one may well have its origin in the writings of Aristotle (*Problems*, 55): "In an east wind all visible things appear larger; in a west wind all sounds are more audible and travel further." The influence of classical texts on folk sayings can never be discounted.

It appears that the effect of the wind indoors was taken into account in traditional society. The wind blowing at birth affected the life of every person, and the wind determined the onset and progress of certain illnesses. An indoor indicator, seemingly irrational, was used in Great Britain. There was a common belief that a dead kingfisher, suspended from a cord, would always turn its bill in the direction of the wind. This is alluded to by Christopher Marlow in his play *The Jew of Malta* (1633): "But how now stands the wind? Into what corner peers my halcyon's bill?" The 1878 book *English Folk-Lore* records stuffed kingfishers hanging from the beams of cottage ceilings to act as weather vanes, "and though sheltered from the immediate influence of the wind, never failed to show every change by turning its beak to the quarter whence the wind blew" (Dyer 1878, 76).

WIND VANES, WEATHERCOCKS, AND WINDMILLS

Wind vanes are finely balanced artifacts that swivel on a fixed upright, driven by the prevailing currents of wind. The wind vane appears as the final rune of the first *ætt* in the Common Germanic Futhark. It is the rune *wunjo* (Old English *wyn*). It signifies the function of a wind vane that moves according to the winds, yet remains fixed in one place. Its reading is "joy," obtained by having a stable base but being in harmony with the surrounding conditions. In the Viking Age, gilded

Fig. 4.2. London St. Mary le Bow church dragon wind vane, designed by Edward Pearce, 1680. Drawing by Nigel Pennick, 2008

metal weathervanes were mounted on ships, and similar ones were set up on stave churches in Norway. A golden wind vane was on the *Mora,* the flagship of William of Normandy, during his cross-channel voyage to invade England in 1066. A traditional motto depicted with a weathercock in seventeenth-century emblem books is, *"Officium meum stabile agitare":* "It is my function to turn while remaining stable."

Structurally related to the wind vane is the vertical windmill, and millers had the most subtle appreciation on land of wind direction and speed. Dutch millers have names for the strongest winds measuring between 7 and 9 on the Beaufort Scale. Force 7–8 winds are called *Blote bienen* (bloody bees). All canvas must be taken from the sails when the wind is this strong. Force 8–9 winds are called *Blote bienen en geknipte nagels* (bloody bees and clipped nails), and a special canvas must be unfurled on the sails to slow them down, for the friction of runaway sails against the bearings runs the risk of fire and destruction of the mill. Although the Beaufort Scale was only devised in 1805, the use of specific names for wind speeds indicates an earlier origin. The craft of sailing windmills has been transmitted unbroken from master to apprentice from the twelfth century until the present day.

WIND MAGIC

There is a very ancient tradition that magicians have the ability to control the weather. H. C. Agrippa ascribed the supposed abilities to the wonderful power of enchantments. With a magical whispering, rivers could be turned back, the sea bound, and the winds controlled (Agrippa 1993 [1531], I, LXXII). These beliefs predated Agrippa by a long time, as he quoted Apuleius, Lucan, Virgil, and Ovid as his sources. In the north it was believed possible that the winds could be controlled by magic. Erik Edmundsson Väderhatt ("Weatherhat," also called Eric of the Windy Hat; ca. 849–ca. 882) was a king of Sweden who was said to own a magic hat that he used to control the winds so his ship would always be able to sail where he wished. By turning his hat on his head toward the direction of a desired wind, it would start to blow. An illustration from Olaus Magnus (1655) shows the king on land, pointing to a ship, while crowned clouds are above, signifying his magical control of the weather. In northern seaports until the demise of sailing ships, sea witches sold ropes in which they claimed they had tied up the winds magically. Seamen who bought the charm received a rope tied with three knots. In the fifteenth century Ranulph Higden wrote that in the Isle of Man "is sortilege and witchcraft used; for women there sell to shipmen wynde [wind] as it were closed under three knottes of threde, so that the more wynde he would have the more knottes he must undo" (Moore 1891, 76). These magic ropes were considered proof against becoming becalmed. Undoing the first knot was supposed to provide a gentle wind. The second knot undone would yield a stiff wind, but the third knot released a gale. Labyrinths were also part of Scandinavian mariners' wind magic, used to call up the wind in the Age of Sail. A

Norwegian labyrinth called *Truber Slot,* beside Oslo Fjord, was activated magically to ensure favorable winds for sailing. The method was to walk to the center and back out again without stumbling. According to labyrinth researcher John Kraft, appeasement of the deity of the northwest wind was associated with labyrinth magic (Kraft 1986, 15).

Magical and Sacred Places in the Landscape

Throughout Europe, legends of the landscape express an understanding that the land is ensouled. Since antiquity, it was taught that a respectful, caring spiritual awareness of the land spirits brought plentiful harvests, healthy and productive livestock, and a peaceful society. The traditional relationship of people to the land depended upon the activities of everyday life. Differing climates and landscapes gave each place its own character. From hunting, farming, fishing, trades, and crafts came the rites and ceremonies, festivals and divinities. Living close to nature brought a keen awareness of all aspects of the world. The ancient northern understanding of the sacred was "organic religion," multiform and polytheistic. This worldview acknowledged spirits of the earth, air, fire, waters, and trees, and the spirit guardians of fields and flocks.

Different human activities had their spiritual protectors, especially those who had to travel on land and sea. The spirits of the ancestral dead were present at certain places. Ancestral holy places—homesteads, grave mounds, tombs, and battlefields—were sites where the ancestral spirits could be venerated and asked for assistance. There was also belief in unseen humanlike beings such as house sprites, elves, fairies, kobolds, boggarts, and trolls. Supernatural beasts such as spectral dogs, water

Fig. 5.1. The Long Man of Wilmington. Chalk hill figure,
Wilmington, Sussex, England.

monsters, and dragons lurked in dangerous places. There were personifications of disease and death, and demons who brought bad luck and
ruin. All of these spirits and entities interacted with human life. Some
were helpful, some required gifts of acknowledgment to perform tasks;
others had to be placated lest they brought disaster. Religious and magical rites served to communicate with spirits and interact with them.
Every place had an innate spiritual quality that the Romans recognized
as the genius loci, the spirit of the place.

Landscape features deemed sacred are hills and mountains, vol-
canoes, springs, rivers and lakes, ravines and caves, notable rocks and
exceptional trees. Each feature has its particular marks of veneration.
Devotees ritually ascended holy hills on days dedicated to sky gods.
Valuable items were thrown into lakes and springs as thanksgiving
or propitiation of the lake spirits. Sacred trees were surrounded by

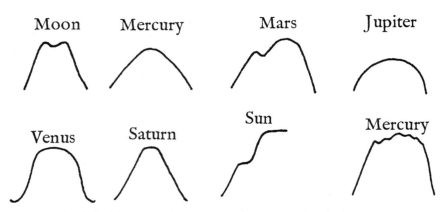

Fig. 5.2. Mountain shapes according to medieval planetary correspondences.

protective fences. They were bedecked with garlands and ribbons, and food was left for their guardian sprites. Stopping places along tracks and roads had shrines to local gods, places where wayfarers could give thanks for having gotten there safely and ask for protection on the road ahead. Stories were—and are still—told about events that happened at particular places, which gave them their names. The names of gods, heroes, saints, and villains, records of magical happenings and accidents, all appear as place names.

Sometimes, the genii loci were not localized at a particular spot on the ground. In ancient times deities of whole forests were venerated, such as Vosegos, Celtic god of the Vosges in Alsace (modern France), and Abnoba, goddess of the Schwarzwald (Black Forest, south Germany). Every river had its goddess or sprite, and many still bear the names. The river Severn in England recalls the goddess Sabrina, while in France the rivers Seine and Saône are named for the goddesses Sequana and Souconna. River deities were honored with festivals and sacrifices. Contemporary folklore tells how the indwelling spirit of certain rivers requires the loss of at least one human life a year. One of them is the River Trent in the Midlands of England, whose dangerous tidal bore is personified as the Eager, a name recalling the Norse sea god Ægir. The river Eider in north Germany was called Ægir's Door (Ellis-Davidson 1964, 128).

ICELAND

A Medieval Pagan Landscape

Because of the unique history of the island, the nature of the pre-Christian northern European sacred landscape is recorded in Icelandic literature. During the ninth and tenth centuries, the previously uninhabited island of Iceland was colonized by settlers. They came mainly from Norway and the Western Isles of Scotland and were predominantly Pagan in outlook. Their spiritual response to the landscape is recorded in *Landnámabók,* the book of settling the land. The settlers were intensely aware of the spiritual nature of the landscape, and certain areas were deemed spiritually inappropriate for settlement. These places were the territories of the *landvættir* (land wights), the spirits of place. Ceremonies were performed in honor of these *landvættir,* and offerings left for them. *Landnámabók* records an example where Thorvald Holbarki went to Surtur's cave and recited a poem in honor of a giant that resided there. The mountain Helgafell was designated as holy, and, before praying facing toward it, devotees washed their faces out of respect. These and other instances of spiritual recognition in Icelandic documents tell much about the religious practices that existed across northern Europe in Pagan times.

The island of Iceland was divided up into religious jurisdictions, ruled over by sacred officials called *goðar* (singular: *goði*) who officiated at religious rites and ceremonies. They were not comparable with later Christian priests, as the office of *goði* was held by a priest of a tribe or clan who had a certain sacred place in common. *Goðar* were never full-time officials, for they were hereditary landowners who had the duty to maintain the ancestral holy places. The *Allsherjargoði,* the high priest of Iceland, was the direct descendent of the first settler, Ingulf Arnarson. He was in charge of the temple at Kialarnes. Iceland was divided into four quarters, each containing three jurisdictions, which were further subdivided into three *goðorð* (the name for the priestly office itself). Each *goðorð* had a *goði* who lived at a particular holy place and was its guardian, but not necessarily its owner. The public temples were sometimes owned by women. The office of *dewar,* keeper of ancestral sacred things, continued in Scotland and Ireland in a Christian context until the nineteenth century and remains as a surname of Scottish origin.

PLACES OF WORSHIP HOFS AND TEMPLES

The ancestral spirits (Old Norse *dísir*) were worshipped collectively at special places, often holy hills recalled today in Germany by names such as Disenberg or Disibodenberg. Offerings were made to the ancestresses at these places for the good fortune of the family and the fecundity of flocks and fields. There were also holy places of Germanic and Norse religion that had no particular natural feature. They were marked by standing stones, poles, wooden images, and semi-open sacred pavilions and spirit sheds. The Anglo-Saxon *wih* was a basic sacred image standing in the open. More substantial was a shrine on "a rocky outcrop" (Old Norse *hörgr;* Old English *hearg*), which may have been covered with a tent or pavilion (Old English *træf*). In Scandinavia and Scandinavian colonies, communal worship took place in the *hof,* an ordinary hall-form farmhouse that had a special extension, the *afhús,* where sacred objects and images were kept. Here, regular festivals to mark the passing of the seasons were observed. There were also purpose-built temples (*höfuð-hof*). Each January, Scandinavians celebrated a collective festival of the *dísir* called *Dísarblót* on sacred hills and at temples erected to venerate them.

The development of Norse temples (and perhaps also Frisian and Anglo-Saxon ones) from the nobleman's hall (*hof*) or farmhouse where sacred rites were conducted is clear. The northern *hof* was a sanctified part of an ordinary farmhouse belonging to the local *goði*. In later times, the religious parallel was the Christian chapel that was an integral part of the castle or larger manor house. The first Norwegian settlers of Iceland (ca. 870–930 CE) transported temple buildings there from Norway. The *Eyrbyggja Saga* tells how, after performing a divination, the *goði* Thorolf Mostur-skeggi dismantled his temple and shipped it, with the earth beneath it, from Norway to Iceland. The earth floor had received the libations and offerings made in the temple, so it had to be taken along with the timber building. The new temple site was decided by divination. As his ship approached the Icelandic coast, Thorolf threw the high seat pillars, on one of which was carved an image of the god Thor, into the sea. Where the tides brought them ashore, there he reerected the temple.

The temple that Thorolf Mostur-skeggi "let be raised" was described as a great house, with the entrance in one of the sidewalls by the far end, the same layout as that in later medieval churches. Inside, before the door, were the high-seat pillars that the sea had brought ashore there. They had "god-nails" driven into them. At the center of the temple, the images of the gods stood on a platform (*Eyrbyggja Saga* 4; *Kjalnesinga Saga* 2). The *Eyrbyggja Saga* is not contemporary with the ritual relocation of Thorolf's temple, but it seems to preserve local tradition reliably, though it was probably written at Helgafell monastery in the late twelfth or early thirteenth century (Ellis-Davidson 1993, 102–3). Many early Christian churches were built over Pagan sacred places when the old religion was destroyed, though the spirit of what went before is still discernable at some of them more than a thousand years later. Places that could not be appropriated by the church had their indwelling spirits redefined as harmful demons and evil spirits and were shunned as dangerous locations.

ROYAL AND SACRED ROADS

In northern Europe, roads are ascribed to great kings of legendary history. This mythos viewed them not as disconnected individual roads but as a systematic infrastructure. Geoffrey of Monmouth's *History of the Kings of Britain* (ca. 1136) recounts how the roads of Britain were constructed on the orders of Belinus, king of the ancient Britons. According to Geoffrey, Belinus ordered four paved roads to be built across Britain that led in straight lines between cities (Geoffrey 1966, 93). These were known as the Four Royal Roads of Britain. They were protected in law against anyone who committed an act of violence upon them, a stricture added to the earlier *Molmutine Laws* that historically were translated from Old Welsh into Latin by the historian Gildas (sixth century) and incorporated into English law by King Alfred the Great in the ninth century (Geoffrey 1966, 93–94). Ireland, too, had royal roads. Tara of the Kings (*Teamhair na Riogh*) was the ancient royal capital of Ireland, and its most sacred and sovereign place. The Five Royal Roads of Ireland radiated from Tara. *Slige Midluachra* ran to Emain Macha near Armagh in the north; to the northwest ran *Slige Asal;* to the mid-west, *Slige Mór* connected Tara with Uisnech, the "Navel of Ireland," where stood the omphalos, and on to Galway on the west coast. *Slige Dála* linked Tara to Tipperary in the southwest, and to the south, *Slige Cualainn,* ran to Bohernabreena, south of Dublin. Like their counter-parts in Great Britain, these Royal Roads had a spiritual dimension that guaranteed royal protection of those traveling along them.

According to the thirteenth-century chronicler Roger of Wendover, the seventh-century English king Eadwin (Edwin) of Northumbria (northern England and southern Scotland) employed an astrologer, Pellitus, to advise him. Eadwin, founder of the city of Edinburgh, was said to have made the roads so safe that even a woman laden with gold could travel in safety. Alongside the roads, he laid pipes to supply trav-elers with drinking water (Giles 1849, I, 79–80). In Sweden the leg-endary King Onund the Land-Clearer was credited with creating the country's roads. In *Ynglingasaga* (37) Sturluson recounts: "Onund had roads made through all Sweden, both through forests and bogs, and also over the mountains; therefore he was called Onund Road-Maker." The time of King Onund, Sturluson tells us, was notable for fruitful seasons, occasioned by his clearing of forests for cultivation. A historic road-making northern king was Harald Blåtand Gormsson (Harald Bluetooth) of Denmark (ca. 935–ca. 986). Around the year 980 CE he ordered the surveying and construction of a highway along the Jutland Ridge, avoiding crossing most rivers. This road was called *Hærvejen* (military road) or *Oksevejen* (cattle road). Narrower roads ran from the Jutland Highway to the main towns. Harald also built six circular for-tresses, laid out by his surveyors and constructed with precise accuracy (Nørlund 1948, 14). The historic King Edward I of England (reigned 1272–1307) followed the mythic image of the great northern king by a systematic roadside clearance of forests to rid the country of the threat of highway robbers.

MOVEMENT

The *Laxdœla Saga,* a thirteenth-century tale of the people of Laxardale in Iceland, recounts the rites and ceremonies of moving from an old farm to a new one. There is a ritual form. The smaller animals make up the head of the procession, then the more valuable cattle, and finally the beasts of burden left the farm. The drove was arranged so that the small animals arrived at the new farm at the time the beasts of burden were leaving the old farm with the household goods (Hasenfratz 2011, 67). The procession had to be on a direct path, and there were no gaps in it, maintaining continuity between the old and the new. A crooked path would serve as a binding knot that would disrupt the success of the new venture. This magical principle of directness is found five hundred years later in the rituals of a powerful Scottish rural fraternity, the *Society of the Horseman's Grip and Word:* here the candidate for initiation was taken deliberately indirectly by the "crooked path," "the hooks and crooks of the road," which severed his contact with his former life as a nonmember (Rennie 2009, 1, 86). Once he was initiated as a horseman, he would no longer be crooked, but always plough his *rigs* (furrows) straight.

PAGAN TRACKWAYS AND SPIRIT PATHS

In certain landscapes local people recognized invisible otherworldly paths that ran across the country between notable features associated with the spirits of the land. These may have been tracks on which religious processions took place in Pagan times. The *Capitularia Regum Francorum,* dating from the days when the Frankish kings were attempting to destroy non-Christian belief and practices, refers to the "Pagan trackway" called *yries* marked by rags and shoes, along which processions were made. These tracks were among "the irregular places which they cherish for their ceremonies." A "Pagan trackway" of the Viking Age exists in Sweden as the "cult road" at Rösaring, associated at its southern end with a stone labyrinth and a burial-ground contemporary with the road. It is about 10 feet (3 m) wide, has a north-south orientation, and running along the top of a ridge for 600 yards (550 m).

In Ireland some people who suffered misfortunes and ill health believed it was caused by living in a house built at a "contrary place." The worst contrary place to be was on a path where the fairy procession traveled. Building on a fairy path is fraught with danger, for the fairies process along it at certain times of the year and will punish anyone who has blocked the way. In Ireland, Paddy Baine built his house with its corner across a fairy path. The house was disturbed, so he consulted a woman who knew about such matters, who advised him to remove the corner, which he did, after which all was well (Michell 1975, 88). Fairy paths sometimes pass beneath buildings constructed across the way, leaving the right of way unobstructed. This feature is called a *closs* in Scotland. On Dartmoor in the west of England, an ancient track called the Mariners' Way runs through the central passage of an ancient traditional longhouse at West Combe. In south Wales it was considered risky to build a cottage in or near the place where an elder tree grew. Elder trees have equivocal magical attributes and are associated with the fairies (Trevelyan 1909, 316). Naturally, fairy trees are located at places on fairy paths. W. Y. Evans Wentz notes that fairies were held to be the spirits of the departed (Wentz 1911, 33). In Scots belief the paths were used by the *Fairy Rade,* the fairies' expedition on May Day to attend their great annual feast (Warrack 1988 [1911], 163).

The fairies' journeys along their well-defined tracks resemble the more frightening appearance of the Wild Hunt (*Wilde Jagd*). It was an appearance of a band of terrifying huntsmen thought to ride through the land on dark, wild horses. Accompanied by hellhounds, the hunt rode in pursuit across the landscape, either in the air or on the ground, especially during the winter months. The hunt is known all over northern and central Europe, and some of the names reflect the being or entity supposed to lead it, or the hounds that run with the hunters. In Old English it was *Herlaþing* (assembly of Herla); in Old French, *Mesnée d'Hellequin* (Hellequin's household); in Welsh, *Cŵn Annwn* (dogs of the underworld; hellhounds); and in later English lore, the Devil's Dandy Dogs and Gabriel Ratchets. The latter hunt is led by the Spectre Huntsman, and the noise of the yelping hounds is a portent of bad luck or death to those who hear it (Harland and Wilkinson 1867, 89).

A Norwegian name for the wild hunt is *jolareidi,* linking it with Jul (Yule), midwinter. A story told in a folksong collected from Telemarken, Norway, in the eighteenth century recalls the wild hunt called *Åsgårdsrei.* The word *Åsgårdsrei* appears to be related to the Old Norse word *öskranligr,* meaning "fearful," and *rei,* a procession on horseback, hence the "fearful procession" or "terror-ride" (Gjerset 1915, II, 97). Also the connexion with Asgard, the abode of the gods, is apparent. This spectral procession consisted of the spirits of the dead who in their lives were not evil enough to be condemned to hell, but who remained unsettled spirits after death. This is one of the ideas held in Celtic countries about the fairies. Thor (seen as an evil spirit), Gudrun, and Sigurd (the slayer of Fafnir) are the leading figures of the *Åsgårdsrei* as it travels through the air to places where fights and murders occur, to fetch the souls of those killed. After dark, people feared to stand outdoors in case the *Åsgårdsrei* should appear and abduct them. The apotropaic sign of the cross on the house door warded off the *Åsgårdsrei* (Gjerset 1915, II, 97).

Coffin paths and roads of the dead are paths along which dead people were carried to the church, especially in mountainous terrain where homesteads and small groups of houses had no consecrated burial ground. The lore of coffin paths has features in common with spirit ways. In lowland areas coffin paths avoided houses and roads and crossed as few fields as possible. This was said to minimize the blighting effect of death on living and growing things (Tebbutt 1984, 17). In Britain road names such as Burial Lane, Corpse Lane, and Lych Way denote these deathly paths. It was a common belief that the act of using a path for a funeral somehow dedicated it as a public right of way. At the funeral of a gardener at Girton, Cambridge, in 1936, the pallbearers insisted that because they had carried a coffin with a corpse through Girton College from one gate to another, the path must now be a public right of way (Porter 1969, 30). A Welsh funeral custom had the pallbearers carrying the coffin put it down at each crossroads they came to and say a prayer (Trevelyan 1909, 275). Over the border in the Golden Valley of Herefordshire, England, Ella Mary Leather recorded the custom in 1912. The coffin was taken on a roundabout way to the church, and it was put down for a few moments at every crosssroads, the mourners standing still (Leather 1912, 122).

THE FAINTY GRUND

People living a traditional, self-reliant life without powered machines and the backup of rescue services have a subtle recognition of all conditions around them. The recognition of debilitating places was a feature of traditional life in Scotland and Ireland. In Ireland such places were seen as a kind of fairy grass. The Scots *fainty grund* and the Irish *fear gortha* ("hungry grass" or "hunger-stricken earth") signified ground where one felt faint. In Scotland it was deemed necessary to carry a piece of bread in the pocket when going to such a place, and in Ireland is a record of a woman who always kept some porridge in a pot ready to help wayfarers who succumbed to the harmful place (Warrack 1988 [1911], 162). In her *Ancient Legends, Mystic Charms, and Superstitions of Ireland,* Lady Wilde said of the *Fair-Gortha,* the harmful "hunger-stricken sod": "if the hapless traveler accidently treads on this grass by the roadside, while passing on a journey, either by night or day, he becomes at once seized with the most extraordinary cravings of hunger and weakness, and unless timely relief is afforded he must certainly die" (Wilde 1887, II, 69).

Wilde also wrote of another herb, or fairy grass, called the *Faud Shaughran* (the "stray sod"):

Whoever treads the path it grows on is compelled by an irresistible impulse to travel on without stopping, all through the night, delirious and restless, over bog and mountain, through hedges and ditches, till wearied and bruised and cut, his garments torn, his hands bleeding, he finds himself in the morning twenty or thirty miles, perhaps, from his own home . . . those who fall under this strange influence have all the time the sensation of flying and are utterly unable to pause or turn back or change their career. There is, however, another herb that can neutralize the effects of the *Faud Shaughran,* but only the initiated can utilize its mystic properties. (Wilde 1887, II, 68–69)

6

Boundaries
and Liminal Spaces

BORDERLINES

Boundaries are primarily about ownership. Property rights—whether private, public, sacred, or otherworldly—define the meaning of areas in culture and in law. Those who claim ownership to areas can bar access to the latter by those whom the owners consider have no right to be there. This principle applies to areas defined as human property as well as those deemed to be in the ownership of spiritual beings. Access to space has always been controlled carefully in all civilizations. Concepts of belonging to the group, ritual cleanliness, personal worthiness, and status are necessary for one to have access to an area, whether it be national territory, a private club, or the inner sanctum of a temple. From antiquity, religious buildings have been made in forms considered worthy to be the indwelling places of gods and goddesses, and the boundaries around them have been policed to prevent access by those considered profane.

Boundaries are lines of division between areas perceived by humans as distinct from one another. Boundaries can be invisible or visible lines of demarcation that distinguish and define relationships between different areas in contact with one another. They can be natural or artificial, passable or impassable. Natural boundaries such as rivers, unclimbable ridges, mountains, and seas are obvious to everyone. They are barriers to everything that moves on land. Only flying creatures may cross them without problems. Because boundaries in themselves are the interface between two distinct areas, they are difficult places. The problems of physical boundaries are self-evident. It is not easy to cross a river without a boat, a bridge over it, or a tunnel beneath it. To cross a mountain range needs a pass, which may be impassable because of snow in wintertime. These natural boundaries are geographical realities with which human beings must deal. Human-made boundaries, though arbitrary, are invested with the characteristics of natural boundaries, usually backed up with violence, implied or actual.

Human-made boundaries are intended to mark the point where the area belonging to "us" becomes the area belonging to "them." So they are always potential places of contention and strife. Many fights between neighbors and wars between gangs, tribes, and nations begin as border disputes. Historically, all boundaries were ill defined and ever changing. The history of the boundaries between clan, tribal, ethnic, religious, feudal, and national areas in northern Europe is so complex that much of it is unknowable. One thing is clear: human-made boundaries are not fixed forever. They are a process rather than a thing; they are essentially arbitrary and transient. In historical terms they do not last long. Even when they are visibly of profane origin, boundaries have a magical function. They form a conceptual barrier against the "other," a line over which the "other" must not cross on pain of physical or supernatural retribution. In this way they are comparable to the circles made by magicians, which theoretically create magic boundaries that enclose and protect the operator whilst preventing any summoned entities from entering and doing harm.

The origin of geometry (*geometria*) in land surveying is apparent in the word itself: *geo-* (earth) + *metria* (measurement). Fixing property boundaries, locating boundary markers, and verifying them required practical methods that would be transparent in their function, easily resolving disputes between neighbors. Ritual redefinition and magical reempowerment of boundaries was necessary, and annual public perambulation of the boundaries of villages and fields was a feature of life. In Pagan times, circumambulation of fields with an image of a god or goddess, stopping at marker points, was continued in a Christian context with the rituals of "beating the bounds" in medieval and postmedieval times. In the fourth century CE, the repaganization of the Gothic lands was accomplished by a perambulation of divine images around boundaries. The Greek Orthodox chronicler Socrates recorded that between 369 and 372 CE the Goths rejected missionary attempts to make them convert to the Arian sect of Christianity, expelling the missionaries and expecting Christians to attend public rites and ceremonies. King Athanaric stated that the Goths' ancestral religion was being debased and ordered the Gothic territories be reconsecrated by a *xoanon* (the Greek word for a carved cult image) perambulated around each settlement. Gothic *xoana* were images consisting of a human head carved on a post, such as those well known from the temples of the Baltic. By making a circuit of the boundary, everything within it was reconsecrated. A

Fig. 6.1. Gothic repaganization of the land by *xoana* carried on camels.
The Library of the European Tradition

Byzantine triumphal arch set up in Constantinople had a carving of this event, showing the *xoana* carried on camels. The image in figure 6.1 is from *Imperium Orientale* by A. Banduri, published in Venice in 1729.

In the north of England, a comparable sacred perambulation was made by Christian monks with the bones of Bishop Cuthbert, who died in 687 CE and was buried at Lindisfarne. In the year 875 the inhabitants of the monastery fled a Danish military invasion, "the wicked army of the unbelievers." Bishop Eardulph and his monks fled with their treasure, books, ritual paraphernalia, and the bones of Cuthbert. Then they carried his bones round the northlands for seven years. Churches were founded at many places where they stopped. This ritual perambulation was first to Elsdon and down the River Rede to Haydon Bridge, then up the South Tyne to Beltinghame, then along the road by Hadrian's Wall to Bewcastle. From there they turned south to Salkeld and went by way of Eden Hall and Plumbland into Lancashire and the River Derwent. Then northward to Whithorn, on the Galloway coast, then southward again across Stainmoor into Teesdale. From Cotherstone the trail ran through Marske, Forcett, and Barton to Craike Abbey near Easingwold. The entourage stayed there four months before they resumed their travels, going to Chester-le-Street. The destroyed monastery was refounded there, Cuthbert was reburied, and Chester-le-Street became the seat of the Bishop of Bernicia.

Boundary markers were always taken seriously, and means enacted to maintain them. There is a biblical curse on boundary movers, and even supernatural sanctions against those who tamper with boundaries. Von Schaewen's *Dissertatio physica de igne fatuus* (1714) tells that in Germany the sprite called Feuermann ("Fireman") appeared carrying a red-hot measuring rod on a chain and riding on a horse of fire pulling a red-hot plough. He came to punish those who moved boundary markers. But even when boundaries are seemingly obvious, there are ways around them. There is an English tradition from Lincolnshire that tells us, "If a person sells his soul to the Devil, to be delivered at a certain specified time, the vendor, if wary, may avoid payment by putting in the contract 'be it in the house or out of the house' and then when the time arrives, sitting astride on a window sill or standing in a doorway" (Peacock 1877,

I, 84). Then the Devil is thwarted. While this is an amusing story, it teaches that one must be precise in definitions, and that being on the liminal space of a boundary is to be neither inside nor outside.

THE MAGIC OF CROSSROADS, BURIALS, MAGIC, AND SPELLS

Crossroads are places of transition, where the axis linking the underworld with the upper world intersects this world on which we walk. As with all liminal places, the crossing of roads is a place of physical and spiritual dangers. Here the distinction between the physical and nonmaterial worlds appears uncertain, and the chance of encountering something Otherworldly is more likely than at other places. In the Roman Empire, crossroads were acknowledged with a *herm,* an image of the god of traffic and trade, Mercury. This god, who indicates the right road and guides the traveler's footsteps, was the generalization of the particular spirit of each individual crossroads. Woden (Odin), as god of the crossroads, was in this aspect similar to Mercury, and later Christians set up stone crosses where the Roman *herms* or posts sacred to Odin had once stood. As *Hangatýr* (God of the Hanged), Odin was the god of the gallows, and often gallows and gibbets were set up at crossroads for the execution of criminals. In England until 1823 the bodies of people hanged there were often buried at the crossroads.

Burials at liminal places, including roadsides, parish boundaries, and crossroads, are common in English folk tradition. Bob Trubshaw noted that many Anglo-Saxon Pagan burials are found near parish boundaries, which may postdate them (Trubshaw 1995, 4–5). Until the nineteenth century, crossroads were favorite places of execution in England, as the crossroads place-name Caxton Gibbet in Cambridgeshire attests. The bodies of the hanged were buried close by, often under the road surface itself, as they were not allowed in consecrated ground. The records of crossroads burials in England go back to the sixteenth century: a parish record from Pleasley in Derbyshire from 1573 tells how a man found hanged was buried at midnight at the highest crossroads in the district with a stake in him

(Roud 2003, 443). Until 1823, under Church of England rules, suicides, Nonconformists, Quakers, Jews, Gypsies, outcasts, and executed criminals were not permitted to be given burial in consecrated ground (Stephen 1868, 152ff). The practice was abolished finally by an Act of Parliament (4 Geo. 4, ca. 52, 1823) that also prohibited the custom of hammering a stake through the body.

People who killed themselves were thought to become earthbound spirits, dangerous to living people (Tebbutt 1984, 17), and a stake was driven through a suicide's body to prevent the person from walking as a revenant. In his *Historia rerum Anglicarum* (ca. 1190) William of Newburgh tells how the corpses of the dead could come forth from their graves, wander about to terrorize and attack the living, and return again to the grave. He tells of a case in Buckinghamshire, England, where a dead man left his grave and attacked his widow, then her family and neighbors. The revenant was laid by a Christian cleric, who wrote a text and put it upon the corpse to bind it in the grave (William of Newburgh 1861, 5, 24). In Iceland is a tradition that a magician could activate a *draugr* (revenant) and send it to attack someone (Solheim 1958, 298). A magical text published almost 700 years later in 1903 by Ólafur Davíðsson gives a remedy using a magnet for those suffering from *draugablettir,* "ghost spots" caused by the touch of a *draugr* sent to get them (Davíðsson 1903; Flowers 1992, 102).

The custom of driving a stake through the body as binding magic to prevent the *draugr* from walking and doing harm to the living is recounted in the thirteenth-century text *Eiríks Saga Rauða.* It tells how in the Norse colony in Greenland bodies were buried provisionally at the place where they died until they could be taken for burial in Christian sacred ground. The provisional burial involved a stake being hammered through the chest as a magical precaution against the deceased's becoming a *draugr.* When the corpse was exhumed so it could be taken for Christian burial, the stake was removed, and consecrated water poured into the space where it had been (Hasenfratz 2011, 70). In ancient Germany, Iceland, and England, the corpse of a criminal was treated in the same way, with a stake through the body, and *Grettis Saga* tells that heavy stones were laid upon it and also other magical bindings, including wicker hurdles and binding knots of wool to bind the ghost (Tacitus 1959, 28–29). A typical example from nineteenth-century England is from *The Peterborough Weekly Gazette,* July 30, 1814: "an unknown man found dying of poison, self administered, in Godmanchester, was buried at the crossroads leading to Offord." Suicides and executed criminals were often buried at the same crossroads, as an account from Norwich in *Norfolk and Norwich Notes and Queries* (August 15, 1896) attests: "R. M. L." tells how his father remembered "seeing a suicide carried past his house at twelve at night, to be buried at the cross roads at Hangman's Lane. An immense crowd followed, to see the stake driven though the body."

In England trees growing at crossroads were reputed to have grown from stakes driven through the bodies of murderers and suicides. A typical example was at Redenhall, Norfolk, where a willow tree called Lush's Bush, said to have grown from a stake, marked the grave of a suicide. In 1813 another suicide, Mary Turrell, was buried there and had a stake hammered through her heart by the parish constable (Halliday 2010, 84). The Cruel Tree at Buckden in Huntingdonshire, felled in 1856, was much feared as a place of bad luck. It was reputed to have grown from a stake driven through the body of a murderer who suffered burial at a classic liminal place: the crossroads of the Great North Road and Mere Lane on the parish boundary of Brampton and Buckden (Tebbutt 1984, 18). Another sort of outcast buried in the road in England was women reputed to be witches. In 1915 Catherine Parsons reported that in Cambridgeshire the Horseheath woman known as Daddy Witch was buried in the middle of the road opposite the hovel where she had lived. The place was marked by an unusual dryness of the road, reputed to be caused by the heat from her body (Parsons 1915, 39). The Horseheath Women's Institute *Scrapbook* for 1935 states that one must nod one's head nine times for good luck before passing over Daddy Witch's grave (Porter 1969, 163). At nearby Bartlow was a bump at a crossroads where a witch was said to be buried (Porter 1969, 161).

Crossroads were places of divination. A custom to ask questions of the dead was practiced in Denmark. One had to go to crossroads at midnight on New Year's Eve and stand inside the square made by the intersection of cart tracks. Then the querent had to call out the name of a dead person, and he or she would appear and answer three questions (Kamp 1877, 390). It was believed in Wales that on each of the *teir nos ysbrydion* (the "three spirit nights": May Eve, St. John's Eve, Hallowe'en) one could go to a crossroads and listen to what the wind was saying. It was a way of finding out the most important things that would happen during the forthcoming year (Trevelyan 1909, 236). The same rite existed in Germany, where, as in Denmark, the individual had to go to a crossroads on New Year's Eve, sit on an animal skin, and listen for what was to happen (Grimm 1888, III, 1115). This recalls the ancient Norse practice of *útiseta* (sitting out) where a person sat out at night under the stars on the skin of a sacrificed animal to hear inner voices or the voices of spirits. Sacrifices at crossroads also appeared in the trial of Dame Alice Kyteler as a witch in Kilkenny, Ireland, in 1324. Among other accusations, "they offered in sacrifice to demons living animals, which they dismembered, and then distributed at crossroads to a certain evil spirit of low rank, named the Son of Art" (Seymour 1913, 27). In the nineteenth century black cats were still being sacrificed at crossroads in Denmark. The animal was buried there and dug up again when decomposed so that a neck bone could be recovered and worn as a ring that supposedly conferred invisibility (Kristensen 1885, III, 72).

The crossroads is a "favorite place to divest oneself of diseases or other evil influences" (Crooke 1909, 88). In northern magic it is customary to rid oneself of used *materia magica* at the crossroads. Objects believed to be bewitched were burned at crossroads (Stracherjan 1867, 358). Among other dangerous powers, the crossroads conducts away the baneful energy of the evil eye, dispersing it to the four quarters of the world, so preventing it from injuring the person or object of its focus. The ague, warts, and other diseases have been the object of rites and spells at crossroads. A tradition recorded in Shropshire is that a person suffering from warts must rub an ear of wheat against each wart, wrap the wheat ears in a piece of paper, then throw it away at a crossroads. The warts would disappear, being transferred to whoever found the piece of paper and picked it up (Burne 1883, 200).

Under Christian influence, despite the cross's being a Christian emblem, the crossroads became associated with the evil spirits and the Devil. In the Alps the entity called Schratl was called up magically by a crossroads ritual. One had to write one's name on a piece of paper, sign it with one's own blood, put it in a box, catch two black beetles, imprison them in the box with the paper, and take it to a crossroads. Then Schratl would appear in the form of a huntsman and offer to fulfill one's desires (Puhvel 1976, 172). Welsh folk belief asserted that on May Eve witches dance at crossroads with the Devil (Trevelyan 1909, 152). The crossroads Devil appears in an Irish spell titled *How to have money always*, as recounted in 1887 by Lady Wilde: "Kill a black cock, and go to the meeting of three crossroads where a murderer is buried. Throw the dead bird over your left shoulder then and there, after nightfall, in the name of the Devil, holding a piece of money in your hand all the while. And ever after, no matter what you spend, you will always find the same piece of money undiminished in your pocket" (Wilde 1887, II, 82–83).

Tales of the German magician Doctor Faustus say that he went to a crossroads in a forest near Wittenberg to raise the Devil: "toward evening, at a crossroads in these woods, he drew certain circles with his staff; thus in the night between nine and ten o'clock he did conjure the Devil." The crossroads features as the locus of a central European magical tradition of making magic bullets that are certain to hit the target. The rite also involved summoning the Devil (or another infernal spirit) there and casting the bullets under his supervision. Carl Maria von Weber's 1821 opera *Der Freischütz*, based upon genuine folk tradition, includes a scene where magic bullets are cast at a crossroads. Like much of northern magic, it has a numerical element:

Now the blessing of the bullets! [Bowing to the earth in each of three pauses] Protect us, you who watch in darkness! Samiel, Samiel! Give ear! Stand by me in this night until the spell is complete! Bless for me the herb and lead, bless them by seven, nine and three, that the bullet be obedient! Samiel, Samiel, to me!

It is clearly the demon Samael that Weber intended to portray. According to Heinrich Cornelius Agrippa, Samael is the Prince of the

Accusers, the devil of fire in the infernal world. In Jewish magic he is one of the three princes of Gehenna, the place in the north that stores all fire, ice, snow, hailstones, violent winds, and darkness (Agrippa 1993 [1531], II, VII; III, XXIV).

THE GOODMAN'S GROUND

In northern Europe in medieval and later times was a tradition of setting aside pieces of land that neither spade nor plough was allowed to touch. Typically, they were triangular corners of fields, dedicated by the farmer who promised never to till the earth there. Inside the boundary the pristine condition of the earth prior to its tilling by man is preserved. There, the land wights still have a place to be, and the former "wilderness" is remembered. In England uncultivated triangular pieces of ground at a trifinium, the center of the junction of three country roads, were frequently called no-man's-land, inferring their ownership by nonhuman entities. Some of them still have stone crosses that may denote the Christianization of a place considered to be eldritch.

There were forerunners of this practice in Pagan times; the Scandinavian sacred enclosure called a *vé* is an example. The *vé* was a triangular enclosure, set aside from the everyday world by a row of *bautasteinar* (uninscribed standing stones) or a fence called the *vébond*. The Danish royal sanctuary at Jelling was such a *vé* (Dyggve 1954, 221ff.).

The *vé* was primarily a place for rites and ceremonies. After the Christian church became dominant, these were deemed heathen practices and were forbidden. In northern Europe early Christian legislation forbade people specifically from worshipping at groves, at stones, in sanctuaries, and at places designated *stafgarðr* (fenced enclosures) (Olsen 1966, 280). Elder trees (*Sambucus nigra*) often grow in such places, such as the grounds containing Siberian "spirit sheds," and veneration of this kind of tree was specifically prohibited as a "heathendom" in England by a law of King Edgar (reigned 959–75 CE). Helmold's *Chronicle* (1156) records that the sacred grove of the Slavonic god Prove at Stargard (Szczeciński) in Pomerania, was enclosed by a fence (Vána 1992, 178, fig. 44). In the Polish countryside to this day,

Fig. 6.2. Runestone in the *vé* at Jelling, Denmark.

one can see crosses by the roadside and at "no-man's-land" triangles, with fences around them.

Under Christian influence these tracts of sacred land became associated with the Devil. Eldritch field corner triangles in Scotland are called the *Old Guidman's Ground*, the *Gudeman's Croft*, the *Halieman's Ley*, the *Halyman's Rig*, the *Black Faulie*, the *Auld Man's Fold, Clootie's Croft*, and the *Gi'en Rig*. The plethora of recorded names shows how widespread the practice was; in Scots all but the latter are "eke-names" or bynames of the Devil. Sir Walter Scott, in his *Letters on Demonology and Witchcraft*, noted "though it was not expressly avowed, no one doubted that 'the gudeman's croft' was set apart for some evil being; in fact, that it was the portion of the arch-fiend himself . . . this was so general a custom that the Church published an ordinance against it as an impious and blasphemous usage." Scott continued:

This singular custom sunk before the efforts of the clergy in the seventeenth century; but there must still be many alive who, in childhood, have been taught to look with wonder on knolls and patches of ground left uncultivated, because, whenever a ploughshare entered the soil, the elementary spirits were supposed to testify their displeasure by storm and thunder. Within our own memory, many such places, sanctified to barrenness by some favorite popular superstition, existed, both in Wales and Ireland, as well as in Scotland; but the high price of agricultural produce during the late war [Napoleonic War] renders it doubtful if a veneration for greybearded superstition has suffered any one of them to remain undesecrated. For the same reason the mounts called *Sith Bhruaith* were respected, and it was deemed unlawful and dangerous to cut wood, dig earth and stones, or otherwise disturb them. (Scott 1885, *Letter* III, 78–79)

Another Scottish name for these places is *Aplochs*, corners of cornfields or meadows left uncultivated for the supposed benefit of the warlocks, to keep their favor (Warrack 1988 [1911], 8).

In Lincolnshire, eastern England, trees grow in the triangular corners of some fields. These are called Devil's Holts. The folklorist C. B. Sibsey noted in 1930 that the belief was still current that they were left for the Devil to play in; otherwise he would play in the fields and spoil the crops (Rudkin 1934, 250). Daddy Witch, the nineteenth-century Cambridgeshire wise woman, was said to own a grimoire called *The Devil's Plantation* (Parsons 1915, 39). The name of this book refers to the local word for uncultivated corners of fields, deliberately left fallow by farmers because they are no-man's-land, places where the *yarthkins* or *hytersprites* dwell. In the west of England, this kind of "waste piece of land" is called a *gallitrap*. Folklorist Theo Brown viewed gallitraps as transdimensional gateways, artificial entrances to the underworld (Brown 1966, 125), for the word "gallitrap" was also used to describe a magic circle, pentacle, or triangle made by a conjuring parson to lay a ghost or entrap a criminal. An eighteenth-century account of ghost laying in Cornwall, southwestern England, by the Reverend Corker, a famed "conjuring parson," refers to just such a magic triangle:

The parson, assisted by Dr. Maddern and the miller, drew the magic pentagram and sacred triangle, within which they placed themselves for safety, and commenced the other ceremonies, only known to the learned, which are required for the effectual subjugation of restless spirits (Rees 1898, 255).

Related to these set-aside areas are clumps of pine trees that stand isolated from other trees. They can still be seen in many places in England and Wales. These plantations are generally Scots pines (*Pinus sylvestris*), which grow closely together and are dark, tall, and visible from a long way off. They were planted as markers on trackways and drovers' roads along which sheep and cattle were herded. Athough driving herds had existed for thousands of years, by the Middle Ages the business of driving herds of animals long distances had developed. By the seventeenth century major routes from Wales into southeastern England and from Scotland to East Anglia and London became established. When the drove was stopped each night, the beasts needed to graze, and stances where this could happen were established, where drovers could pay to pasture animals overnight. Drovers' stances were marked by plantations of a few Scots pine trees, located to be visible from afar in open country. Many remain today, untouched in the manner of the eldritch field corners and Devil's Holts.

HOLMGANGA, BATTLE, AND TRIAL BY COMBAT

Related to the Norse *vé* is the enclosure created in ancient Iceland for *hólmganga* (single combat, literally "going on an island"). Such judicial combats (duels) were conducted formally in places separate from the everyday world: either on an island (the meaning of the word), in a special enclosure such as a circle of stones (*Egils Saga,* chap. 64), or on a "cloak" pegged down by *tjösnur,* ritual pegs with round heads reminiscent of household images (*Kormáks Saga,* chap. 10). The cloak on which they fought was a piece of fabric or animal skin five ells long. The pegging down was done with a rite called "The Sacrifice of the *Tjösnur*" (Collingwood 1902, 67). *Hólmganga* was banned in Iceland in the year 1004. In medieval times the formal *lists* used in chivalric combats are a descendant of this tradition, and the boxing ring continues it today.

In Anglo-Saxon England temporary enclosures for judicial single combat and even full-scale battles were cut off from the everyday world by a fence of hazel (*Corylus avellana*). All around the battlefield, hazel poles were set up, marking the ground where the battle was to be. This was called "enhazelling the field." The poles were erected by the heralds in charge of the proceedings. Once a battlefield had been enhazelled it was considered a shameful act for an army to scour (pillage) the country until the battle was won (Hull 1913, 67). The decisive Battle of Brunanburh (937 CE), in which English forces under King Æthelstan defeated the much larger Confederation army composed of Scottish, Welsh, Irish, Danish, and Norwegian units, was a formal challenge held upon an enhazelled field. A medieval Arthurian text, *Sir Gawain and the Lady of Lys,* tells of the adventures of Sir Gawain at Castle Orgellous, where a delineated field of combat was laid out: "At the four corners of the meadow were planted four olive trees, to show the bounds of the field, and he was held for vanquished who should first pass the boundary of olives" (Weston 1907, 66).

Trial by combat was an ancient legal method of determining guilt or innocence. Medieval laws, including the *Capitularies* of Charlemagne, the French *Laws of St. Louis,* and the crusader-era *Assizes of Jerusalem,* set the rules for duels fought for the settling of property rights, or for avenging crimes. The *Assizes of Jerusalem* list murder, manslaughter, rape, wounding, treason, neglect of feudal service, and deprivation or exclusion from rightful possession as grounds for trial by combat. Even witnesses at court and judges could be required to fight a duel with the accused or plaintiff. Only ladies, men older than sixty years, and disabled people could appoint a champion to fight in their place. Duelists fighting according to the rules of the *Assizes of Jerusalem* fought in *lists* surrounded by trenches and palings as in *hólmganga*. Before the combat, each duelist had to swear an oath on the Bible that neither his person nor his horse was secretly guarded (by magic) and that he had used no witchcraft. The defeated duelist, if he was not killed in combat, was hanged. If a champion lost the duel, both champion and plaintiff were hanged. A woman whose champion failed was burned at the stake, and he was hanged. In France the final trial by combat took place in 1547 (Kottenkamp 1988, 105–7).

LABYRINTHS

There are over five hundred ancient stone labyrinths documented in Scandinavia and Iceland, and a few cut in the turf in England, Germany, and Poland. Stone labyrinths are made of rounded stones ranging in size from pebbles to boulders, laid on the earth or on rock surfaces. Some are close to prehistoric burials or grave fields, and it is claimed

Fig. 6.3. Turf labyrinth formerly at Sneinton, Nottingham, England, 1797.
The Library of the European Tradition

that some may date from the Bronze Age, though most are thought to be less than nine hundred years old (Kern 1983, 391; Kraft 1986, 14). There are numerous folktales and folk practices recorded about these labyrinths, and their names are evocative of ancient cities and turning pathways. For example, the Russian labyrinth name Vavilon (Babylon) derives from the old Russian word *vavilonistyy* ("twisting, curved"). A Welsh name, *caerdroia*, literally means "city of turnings" but is also associated with another famous ancient city, Troy, hence one of the English names for labyrinths, "Troytown." Scandinavian names include *trøborg* and *trælleborg*, with allusions to both Troy and trolls. German names also refer to Troy, such as *Trujaburg*, but others include *Windelbahn* ("winding way"), *Schlangengang* ("snake path"), and *Zauberkreis* ("magic circle"). An Icelandic name, *völundarhús* ("Wayland's house"), associates the labyrinth with the legendary blacksmith Völundr, a myth parallel with the tale that the labyrinth was invented by the metalworker Daedalus on the island of Crete (Meyer 1882, 290). The apotropaic power of iron to shield against and bind evil and bad luck is shared by the labyrinth pattern.

In 1684 the Swedish antiquarian Johan Hadorph, who catalogued over one thousand runestones, wrote about the Troijenborg at Rösaring, where, he commented, there had been much sacrifice to the gods in olden days. The labyrinth at Rösaring is part of a "cult site" that has ancient cairns and what appears to be a ceremonial roadway running a north-south alignment along the ridge for 590 yards (540 m). In 1872 S. Sörenson wrote about a labyrinth called Truber Slot that existed in former times at the mouth of Oslo Fjord, Norway. Said to have been built by a virgin, it was activated to ensure favorable winds for sailing. Appeasing the deity of the northwest wind was given as the functionality of labyrinths in a newspaper article in 1945 (Kraft 1986, 15). John Kraft notes that the fishing village of Kuggören in northern Sweden retained knowledge of labyrinth magic into the 1950s. A fisherman from Södermöja recalled visiting Kuggören in 1955, where he saw an old man run through the labyrinth. As he ran, he spit in his hand, or on something he held, and threw it backward over his shoulder. This was for luck in fishing. This man was known locally as the Kuggören cunning man who used steel to heal people and livestock and practiced magic in the labyrinth. He died in 1963 without transmitting his magical knowledge to his sons, who were not interested.

In Sweden in 1973 Eva Eskilsson from Härnösand recounted that a former ship's pilot had told her that when mariners were delayed by bad weather and could not sail, they would build labyrinths of stone so that the wind would get caught up in them and so reduce in strength (Kraft 1986, 15). The same story has been collected by folklorists from Husum, Germany, and Haparanda and Luleå in northern Sweden. As turning magic, labyrinths were used to trap harmful sprites. Kraft reported in 1986 that Gösta Janssen from Rådmansö parish told him that he had heard that fishermen used to walk a labyrinth near Stockholm when they laid their nets. This was to exorcise evil ghosts to guarantee a good catch (Kraft 1986, 15). The Swedish fishermen used them to prevent *smågubbar* (little people), malicious land wights, from coming on board ship to disrupt the haul. The *smågubbar*, it was believed, would follow the fishermen around until they boarded their vessel. So the fishermen would go into the center of a labyrinth, and the *smågubbar* would follow them in, getting confused in the process. Then the fishermen would run from the labyrinth to the ship and cast off before the *smågubbar* could reach it.

It is possible that labyrinth fishing magic has a prosaic origin. Fish weirs and fish traps on rivers and in tidal areas made from stones, sticks, wattles, basketwork, and timber, either with or without nets, were used widely in Italy, France, England, Scotland, Wales, Poland, Estonia, Norway, Sweden, Hungary, and Germany, where they were called a *Fischzaun* (fish fence) or a *Fischirrgarten* (fish maze) (Buschan 1926, 322). Coastal magical labyrinths for the entrapment of fishing with nets from ships may follow on from the construction of actual coastal fish labyrinths (*Fischirrgärten*), using the form of the unicursal labyrinth rather than the shapes suitable for catching fish. The labyrinths on the coast of the White Sea in Russia are in the area of the spawning grounds where seasonal fishing was carried out (Gurina 1948, 33). In northern Sweden and Finland, labyrinths were used by Sámi herdsmen as a means of magical protection of their reindeer from attacks by wolverines (Kraft 1986, 19).

CHURCHYARDS AND GRAVES

The Houses of the Dead

An ancient Germanic custom was to bury bodies in *Totenbäume,* "trees of the dead." They appeared in the Alamannic period (213–496 CE). A *Totenbaum* was made from a hollowed-out trunk of an oak tree, with a lid that was carved with a scaly serpent with a head at each end. The last known burial in a *Totenbaum* was Graf von Buchaw in 1151 (Paulsen and Schach-Dörges 1972, 21–22). Some hogback tombstones of the Viking Age in Scotland have serpentlike roof ridges that resemble the *Totenbaum,* although these tombstones did not contain the body. Beds of the dead made of planks slotted into cornerposts were used in Merovingian times along with *Totenbäume* in Germany (Paulsen and Schach-Dörges 1972, 23–25). Grave chambers made from jointed planks had existed in Celtic burials in mainland Europe in pre-Roman times. From the late seventh century similar "box shrines" were made in Ireland from thin slabs of stone whose form was derived from carpentry (Herity 1993, 101–94).

FUNERAL CUSTOMS

The lykewake is the tradition of watching over a corpse until it is taken away to be buried. The period between death and burial was believed to be dangerous, as the spirit of the deceased remained close to the body. The sight of the dead was considered dangerous. The corpse's eyes were shut, and coins were placed over them. The old Norse death rites (*ná-bjargir*) were conducted from behind the corpse so that the one performing them could not fall under the gaze of the deceased, who could then claim the living person and bring him or her over to the side of the dead (Hasenfratz 2011, 69). When the cause of death was uncertain, there were particular rites to ask the spirit what was the cause of death.

Churchyards and graveyards are special tracts of land ritually set aside for the dead. They are places of dread because everyone knows that one day we will die and end up in one. They were also feared because the spirits of the dead resided there and could affect people unfavorably if they happened to go there. Traditionally, there are apotropaic amulets, talismans, and sigils that ward off evil spirits from a place, or pin them down, and the graveyard is no different from anywhere else they are used. A cross upon a grave, apart from being a marker that someone is buried there, also serves a magical function to prevent his or her spirit from manifesting. Graves and tombs contain the remains of individuals who led particular lives. Because the spirit was once present in the body, the grave is not just a meaningless place where the corpse is disposed of, but a meaningful location associated with the individual buried there. Graveyards contain the remains of famous and infamous people, saints and criminals, and their graves are resorted to by relatives, descendants, pilgrims, tourists, and those who believe some benefit will accrue for visiting any particular grave. Traditionally, the tomb or grave is the house of the shade or ghost of the individual. It must be kept clean, adorned with flowers and other offerings in order that the memory of the deceased be kept up, and also that the shade might not wander from the grave and do mischief. In the Catholic tradition there is a special day, November 2, on which family and ancestral graves are swept, cleaned, and tended, thereby maintaining the protective power. This day is observed in some countries as the Day of the Dead. It is close to the old Celtic festival of Samhain, and the Hallowe'en ghosts and demons of the modern festival continue the observance in a commercialized manner.

THE FIRST BURIAL

The actual location of the first grave in a new cemetery is also significant, for tradition asserts that the spirit of the first one buried becomes the guardian of the graveyard. An ancient Norwegian belief about the *haugbonde* (Old Norse *haugbúi,* mound dweller), which haunted burial mounds near farms, was that it was the ghost of the first owner (founder) of a farmstead, and its supernatural guardian. Offerings of food and drink were left for it. Animals (and people) sacrificed at the foundation of buildings were deemed to remain as ghostly apparitions that guarded the place, such as the *Kirk-grim* or the guardian of churches, and the graveyard belief is clearly the same (Howlett 1899, 31). In Somerset this being was called the Churchyard Walker (Tongue 1958, 44). Writing in England in 1899, George Tyack noted:

> There is a superstition in many places that it is something worse than unlucky to be the first corpse buried in a new churchyard; the Devil, in fact, is supposed to have an unquestionable claim to the possession of such a body. In Germany and in Scandinavia the enemy is sometimes outwitted by the interment of a pig or a dog, before any Christian burial takes place. For a long time the people were unwilling to use the churchyard of St. John's, Bovey-Tracey, for this reason; and only began to do so after a stranger had been laid to rest therein. The same idea prevails in the North of England and in Scotland. There can be little doubt that in this we have a relic of the Pagan custom . . . namely, the offering of an animal, or even of a human, sacrifice at the foundation of a new building." (Tyack 1899, 80)

In 1958 Ruth Tongue noted that the sexton (gravedigger) was often appealed to "behind the parson's back," so a person would not be the first to be buried. She tells how in one instance a large black dog belonging to a local farmer had mysteriously disappeared, and the sexton was said to have killed it and buried it in the graveyard before the funeral of the person (Tongue 1958, 44). A Breton tradition is that the last person buried any year becomes the Ankou, a grim reaper who drives a spectral cart that comes for the dead. He or she remains the Ankou for a year, when the last person of that year is buried (Simpson 1987, 41).

A rare account from the English West Midlands in the mid-twentieth century concerns the customs of traveling showmen who were accustomed to lay out fairgrounds. The custom recorded was sufficiently notable that a national newspaper reported it (*The Sunday Express*, December 12, 1943). The funeral of Pat Collins, "The King of the Showmen," took place at Bloxwich in December 1943. The location of Pat Collins's grave was ritually divined by his son:

There was a strange incident at the cemetery when the old man's son visited it accompanied by Father Hanrahan, of St. Peter's Catholic Church, Bloxwich, to select a site for the grave. When he came to seek a site for his father's last resting place it was found that the Catholic portion of the cemetery was full. The adjoining land which belongs to the cemetery was specially consecrated. When Mr. Collins went to select a place for the first grave, he brought his foot forward, raised it and brought his heel down sharply on the turf, making a deep dent in it, exclaiming as he did so, "This is the spot. I want the exact center of my father's grave to be over that mark." He explained to the priest: "My father used those words and that gesture for 60 years every time he inspected a fairground site to indicate where the principal attraction, usually the biggest of the merry-go-rounds, was to be erected. He never measured the ground, but the chosen spot was always in the exact center of the show ground. It was a ritual with him."

Pat Collins was duly buried at the center of the new graveyard as the first interment. Whether or not a dog had preceded him was not mentioned.

Divination of a gravesite in open country, that is, ground not consecrated by the church, appears in the ballads of Robin Hood. Medieval outlaws like Robin Hood and Little John were refused Christian burials, and the reputed graves of both men were in unconsecrated ground. Whoever the original Robin Hood was, there are two extant old ballads telling of Robin Hood's death, *Robin Hood His Death* and *Robin Hood's Death and Burial*. The first appears to suggest an outlaw's road burial at "yonder streete" with a grave "of gravel and greete (grit)." The second tells how Robin Hood lies dying from blood loss at Kirkley-hall. He summons Little John to his deathbed and asks him for his bow. With his last strength Robin shoots an arrow out of the window to divine the place where he will be buried (Dobson and Taylor 1997, 134–39). Divination by arrow shot also appears in folktales about the location of medieval churches, including Salisbury Cathedral.

EVOCATION OF THE DEAD AND
GRAVEYARD MAGIC

The Norse magic for summoning the dead, a "death charm" or "death song" (*val-gardr*), is a waking song, beginning with "Vaki!" ("Awake!"), such as is described in the Eddic poem *Svipdagsmál*. If the awakened dead is not a relative, then the information obtained may be a curse, the spirit telling of the necromant's doom, for instance. The *Indiculus Superstitionum et Paganiarum,* from the era of St. Boniface (Winfrith) in Germany (seventh–eighth century), is an index of forbidden "superstitions and heathen customs" that includes *dadsisas,* "sacrilege committed over the dead" (Boudriot 1964, 51). The oldest known northern death magic talisman is a bracteate found in the mouth of a skeleton in a Swedish grave. It bore an anagram of the Latin letters *SISU* (Düwel 1988, 75, 77, 90, 105). The *sis* component of *dadsisas* is clear.

In the north of England, malevolent entities that emerged from graveyards in the shape of the vicious bar guest, boggart, or bogey man were believed to be the spirits of those who were not honored as worthy ancestors, but instead ignored or vilified. One belief about the bar guest was that he was the ghost of a suicide or murderer, an unjust oppressive landlord, or a murder victim. This shunned outcast was denied rest in the proper place in the spirit world, but instead was aimlessly wandering the earth, doing mischief and physically attacking people. They were not vampires like those described by William of Newburgh. Magicians called boggart-seers were employed to deal with these dangerous apparitions. The last one died around 1850 (Harland and Wilkinson 1867, 49, 55).

Churchyards and cemeteries are also places where the *materia magica* used for certain purposes can be obtained. Practitioners of graveyard magic who intended to contact spirits used bones, graveyard earth, and fragments of coffin. Churchyard materials are deemed to possess magical and physical qualities; for example, coffin dust is said to be toxic (Newman 1948a, 127). The fear that one's bones may be used in necromantic conjuration or for other magical purposes was always an argument for cremation. In his *Hydrotaphia* (1658), Sir Thomas Browne wrote, "to be gnawed out of our graves, to have our skulls made drinking bowls, and our bones turned into pipes, to delight and sport our enemies, are tragical abominations escaped in burning burials" (Browne 1862, 152).

Digging in graveyards for human bones for magical purposes has always been prohibited. But people did take human bones from churchyards and use them magically. There is a considerable literature from Scandinavia of such human bone magic. In his Northamptonshire folklore Sternberg (1851) mentions one instance he found of someone who possessed a human kneecap to ward off rheumatism (Sternberg 1851, 24–25). In 1895 W. B. Gerish published an East Anglian churchyard charm taught by the Chedgrave Witch to a Loddon girl at the beginning of the ninteenth century. The rhyme or charm gave a graveyard rite for a woman to gain a husband, seemingly with a form of evocation of the dead. She had to go alone to the burial ground and make three crosses from "graveyard bits," then choose a gravestone to hold them between the "finger slits" over the stone. One cross represented the girl, another the would-be husband, and the third stood between them. If both crosses leaned across the middle one, the man's name would come to the girl. But in performing the ritual, she would lose a year of life, and the person who was buried in the grave over which the rite was conducted would somehow be able to use the "last year on earth-life" that she would have had (Gerish 1895, 200). The widespread belief that everyone has a particular fixed time to live is implicit in this rite.

Another kind of marriage magic used churchyard toads. According to Mabel Peacock, using toads found in churchyards were recommended by witches to women who wished to entrap men who would be "compelled to accept the yoke of wedlock." A woman who wanted to marry a particular man had to go to Holy Communion at eight o'clock. She should take the communion bread but not swallow it. Then, "after you come out of the church, you will see a toad in the churchyard." She had to spit the host out so that the toad would eat it. After that, her man will be magically compelled to marry her (Peacock 1901, 168). In

Ireland, a spell to cause hatred rather than love between partners made use of graveyard materials. It involved taking a handful of clay from a new-made grave and shaking it between the couple, saying, "Hate ye one another! May you be as hateful to each other as sin to Christ, as bread eaten without blessing is to God" (Wilde 1887, II, 82).

7

Materials and Crafts

THE SPIRITUAL NATURE
OF CRAFTSMANSHIP

To live, humans everywhere have to deal with the same fundamental constraints of existence. In different places the outward appearance of how people dealt in the past with necessities has its own characteristic cultural forms. All visible and invisible manifestations of existence emanate from true principles. The outward forms of human artifacts vary according to culture, place, and time. But each material used in human culture has its own innate character, and each technique used to work that material brings its own particular way of working, thinking, and feeling. Every new piece of handwork renews the freshness of experience of the craftsperson. The act of making is primal when it expresses the fullness of being. The craftsperson is in touch with the life of nature through a process of reorigination that accesses the source of existence. The creative act is a transposition from the spiritual realm to the sensory; the fixing of a visible form of something that previously did not exist. Tradition recalls the old English craftsman's principle of "simplicity and singleness of purpose," that anything we make or do must be as perfect as circumstances permit, embodying usefulness, meaning, and spirit. Ensouled artifacts are timeless in that no further degree of wholeness or presence can be reached beyond their present state. Spiritually, there is a unity between the maker and the thing made.

CRAFTSMANSHIP

Attention to Detail: The Life of Materials

There was, and is, always progress. Tradition has never been static, conserving everything totally unchanged over centuries. Tradition evolves to accommodate changes, but the changes fit in with what went before through adaptation and reinterpretation. New insights and methods can evolve continuously within tradition. In traditional society, in metalwork, music, and magic alike, the student learned by example rather than precept. There were no schools, no professional teachers, no instruction manuals. Most of those who became masters were born into an environment where it was natural to learn one's family craft. Learning was by being there, watching, then doing it when one was ready. Today, some sit beside a master and watch, and know they are learning true principles and techniques from him or her; some go to school and pay to be taught by those who share their knowledge; and some are self-taught, finding out how to do it by trial and error, examining the remnants of lost arts and bringing them back into contemporary practice. However we may learn the techniques, an understanding of true principles is a fundamental necessity in the European craft tradition. The craftsperson transforms raw materials into beautiful artifacts, making the world a better place in which to live.

THE QUALITIES OF TREES AND WOOD

Birch (*Betula pendula*) is a white hardwood with grey or white bark. Magically, it signifies purification, and birch branches inside or outside a house resist malevolent influences and bring good luck. Maypoles made from whole birch trees are common in northern European tradition. Birch is the first letter of the Irish Ogham script, *beth;* it is also the Common Germanic Futhark rune *berkano* and the Anglo-Saxon rune *beorc.* Birch wood was used to make cradles for babies, because of both the characteristic of the wood and the tree's nascent spiritual virtues. A birch-bark hat was worn by the Celtic lord buried in the grave mound at Hochdorf, Baden-Württemberg, Germany, ca. 550–500 BCE. Birch hats worn by the dead are mentioned in an old Scots ballad, *The Wife of Usher's Well,* dating from well over two thousand years later. Until the early twentieth century, birch boxes were used in Estonia for offerings to the household spirit, Tönn. In the Finnish epic the *Kalevala,* Väinämöinen made the second of his stringed instruments called kantele from the wood of the birch tree.

The ash (*Fraxinus excelsior*) is a magically powerful tree. In Norse mythology the world tree Yggrassil is usually depicted as an ash, and the first man, Askr, was made from an ash tree. Ash is the Anglo-Saxon rune *æsc.* The wood was used in divination and making spears, staves, and traditional broom handles. The Irish Druids carried ash staves, and it was believed that ash warded off poisonous snakes and other vermin. In Britain ash tree leaves are carried as lucky charms, especially when they have an even number of divisions on each side (the "Even Ash").

Elm (*Ulmus* spp.) was the wood of choice for coffins for the dead, as it was valued for its resistance to splitting. The inner bark was used for making the seats of chairs. Elms were devastated in northern Europe in the second half of the twentieth century by a fungal disease.

The elderberry tree (lady tree, bourtree, *Sambucus nigra*) has some positive and negative magical aspects, being connected with witches and fairies. Elder twigs hung in sheds, stables, barns, and garages protect against lightning. In the Isle of Man, elder trees were grown next to cottages to protect against sorcery and witchcraft. But it is unlucky to bring elderberry branches inside a house, or to burn the wood, as that summons unwanted entities (Roud 2003, 169). Whistles made from elder wood are used to summon spirits, and mouthpieces for the Dutch *Midwinterhoorn* (Midwinter Horn trumpet) are made from elder.

The most venerated of all trees in Europe is the oak (*Quercus robur*). In Pagan times oaks were venerated in groves sacred to the wielders of thunder: Zeus, Jupiter, Taranis, Thunor, Thor, Pehrkons, and Perkūnas. Magically, wood from a lightning-struck tree is especially effective, and oak sprigs are talismans against lightning. The Anglo-Saxon rune *ac* signifies oak. Oak is a very strong and durable wood, used in timber-frame buildings and in shipbuilding. The evergreen oak (*Quercus ilex*), like the holly (*Ilex aquifolium*), is special because it is not a conifer, yet it does not lose its leaves in the wintertime. In the Baltic countries perpetual fires were kept burning in the sacred precincts of evergreen oaks, dedicated to the god of lightning and the goddess of fire. An enormous sacred oak tree that was revered at the holiest place of the Old Prussians at Romowe was felled by the Grand Master of the Teutonic Knights (*Deutsche Ritter*) during the crusade against the heathen religion in the 1200s.

All through Britain and Ireland, rowan (mountain ash, *Sorbus aucuparia*) is an important magical protective against bad luck, ill wishing, and supernatural attack. Crossed rowan twigs, taken from the tree without using a knife and tied with red thread, were set up on May Day to protect stables, cowsheds, and garages. There is an old Scottish saying describing the protective magic of rowan, "rowan tree and red thread gar the witches tyne their speed" (rowan tree and red thread make the witches lose their energy). In the Shetland Islands it was noted that a small piece of rowan wrapped with red thread and sewn into the clothes, protected the wearer against the evil eye (*New Statistical Account* 1845, 142). Cattle drovers had whip handles made of rowan, as the Yorkshire adage tells us: "If your whip-stock's made of rowan, you may gan [go] through any town" (Nicholson 1890, 125–26). Magically defensive heck posts in northern English farmhouses were sometimes made of rowan (Hayes and Rutter 1972, 89). Branches of rowan were set up over house-door lintels to bring good fortune. Renewed four times a year, they were placed there on a Quarter Day and replaced with new ones on the next Quarter Day. Rowan crosses also protected newly planted seeds in the garden. The rowan tree appears as the savior of Thor in the tale of Aurvandil, whose toe ended up as a star. Washed away by the powerful river Elivagar, Thor seized an overhanging rowan branch and pulled himself out of the torrent. The adage "Thor's salvation, the rowan" refers to this myth.

The evergreen yew (*Taxus baccata*) is the longest-lived tree indigenous to Europe, and some are believed to be over two thousand years old. The yew grows in holy ground, graveyards and churchyards, and it is a very poisonous tree. So it is viewed as a tree of life and death, and its wood has been used in magic since early times. Horn-shaped amulets of yew wood bearing incised runes are known from Lindholm in Sweden and in Friesland from Wijnaldum (both sixth century CE), as well as runic yew staves from Britsum and Westeremden, the first dating from ca. 500–650 and the latter around the year 800. Also found at Westeremden was a rune-bearing yew implement used in weaving, also ca. 800. There are runic inscriptions on the Britsum and Westeremden amulets, the first of which reads "always carry this yew in the press of battle," and the second gives the possessor power over the waves of the sea (Elliott 1963, 67, figs. 19–23). There are two runes that take the yew for their names, and they represent different artifacts made from yew wood. The Germanic yew rune *eihwaz* and the Anglo-Saxon rune *éoh* take the form of the pothook, while the Younger Futhark rune *ýr* signifies a bow made of yew wood. A traditional German adage conserves the ancient belief in the protective magical virtues of yew demonstrated in these ancient staves: *"Vor den Eiben kann kein Zauber bleiben"* (before the yews, no [harmful] magic can remain).

Evergreens are special trees because they are green in winter when most broad-leafed trees have lost their leaves. So they symbolize the continuity of life through hard times. Magically, they bridge the boundary between life and death. The yew is highly toxic, and no part of it should be used as incense or medicine. In the 1980s a British Druid died after ingesting yew tree leaves. It is very dangerous to breathe the vapor of the red resin that oozes out from the bark in hot weather, though this is said to have been done in the past by those who wanted to see visions. This is not recommended. No part of a yew tree should ever be burnt on a ceremonial fire, for its smoke is lethal.

Fir and pine trees are linked together because they are resinous evergreens whose wood burns with a strong light. The European silver fir (*Abies alba*) is a magically protective tree that wards off ghosts and other harmful beings, while the Scots pine (deal, *Pinus sylvestris*) is a tree of indication and illumination. Slivers of resinous conifer wood from various species of pine and fir were used as a source of lighting in former times. In Germany they were called *Kienspan* and in Scotland, fir (fire). Pine is the Anglo-Saxon rune *cén*, meaning a flaming torch, signifying literal and figurative illumination. The deal apple, the cone of the pine, was used ritually, and it was the sacred emblem (*Stadtpyr*) of the Swabian goddess Zisa, whose shrine was at Augsburg, Bavaria. In Britain, the Scots pine was planted as a way marker on cross-country tracks, to show cattle drovers where they could pasture their herds for the night. Fiddlers use its resin as rosin on their bows. Strasbourg turpentine, a product of the silver fir, was used in the past as a remedy against rheumatism and wounds. The spruce (*Picea abies*) is best known as the Christmas tree. Pine, fir, and spruce are resonant woods, so they have an important use for making the soundboards of musical instruments. These conifers grow in harsher environments than the larger broad-leaved trees, so they were timbers of choice for building in lands where they were abundant. The juniper (Savin, *Juniperus communis*) provides twigs that are talismanic against the evil eye. Its smoke has a number of distinct qualities. It was believed to combat evil spirits, and so was used in sickrooms in the days before chemical antiseptics were developed. In Germany juniper sprigs are sometimes laid ceremonially in the foundations of a building to protect the future inhabitants against disharmony.

The various species of willow (*Salix* spp.) have exceptional powers of regeneration and are symbolic of purification and strong binding forces. The thin flexible withies cut from pollarded willow trees are used to make baskets and hurdles, and for binding in general, both on the physical and magical levels. Willow withies are used to bind the Dutch Midwinterhoorns together, and the noose of the gallows tree was made of plaited willow. "The willow has a mystery in it of sound," wrote Lady Wilde in 1887, as ancient Irish musical instruments were made of the wood (Wilde 1887, II, 117). Hazel (*Corylus avellana*) is the tree of bards and heralds, denoting wisdom and authority. The Ogham character *coll* signifies the hazel, and bardic abilities. Hazel poles (Old Norse *hoslur*) were used to mark out sacred enclosures as the enhazelled field for judicial combat. Hazel wands were used as shooting marks by medieval English archers, as recounted in the legends of William of Cloudesly and Robin Hood.

Like the willow, alder (*Alnus glutinosa*) grows in damp areas. Its wood after cutting withstands wet conditions. So it was used for piling foundations of buildings in lake villages and crannogs, as well as for later towns on unstable ground, such as Amsterdam. Alder was used for structures that remained permanently wet, where some woods would rapidly rot away; the wheels of watermills, water pipes, and buckets. For hundreds of years Sámi in Lapland who had been forcibly baptized by Christian priests chewed alder bark, sacred to the reindeer god Leib-Olmai, and used its power to reverse the effects of baptism. There was also a tradition in Finland of making an image of a horse from alder wood for magically protecting stables. A Celtic tradition asserts that aerial spirits can be called up with alder whistles.

The linden (lime tree, *Tilia platyphyllos* and other related species) has a fine-grained hardwood used for shields in the Viking era and for making intricate wood carvings, especially for religious images. In the Netherlands, Germany, Austria, and Switzerland, where they exist, the *Dorflinde* (village linden) marks the exact center of the settlement. They serve as the centerpiece of public gatherings and celebrations. In former times these linden trees were "trained" so the branches made platforms where festive music and dancing took place. Some trees had two or three platforms, resembling the levels of the cosmic axis. In Central Europe the otherworldly serpentlike *lindwurm* is said to reside in linden trees for the middle 90-year period of its 270-year life span.

There are three sorts of thorn tree, all of them protective: blackthorn (sloe, *Prunus spinosa*), whitethorn (hawthorn, May, *Crataegus monogyna*), and sea buckthorn (*Hippophaë rhamnoides*). All three are powerful talismans against harm. The Anglo-Saxon rune *þorn* (thorn) signifies the defensive power of thorns. In Great Britain and Ireland, thorn hedges were laid around sacred places, and lone thorn trees were feared as the dwelling places of sprites and fairies. The whitethorn is particularly associated with the rites and ceremonies of May Day, its white flowers being called May blossom. In England, May blossom was not brought indoors, as a warning rhyme from Warwickshire informs us: "Hawthorn bloom and elder flowers will fill a house with evil powers" (Langford 1875, 15).

Blackthorn staves were used by Scottish warlocks, and in eastern

England a *sway* (wand) made from blackthorn or hazel was part of the cunning man's paraphernalia. Although sea buckthorn's twigs are difficult to obtain, its bright orange berries were strung together to make magically protective necklaces partaking of the power of thorn. The bramble (blackberry, *Rubus fruticosa*) is a trailing thorny plant whose stems are useful in physical and magical binding. In the "Nameless Art" (East Anglian rural magic), nine lengths of bramble were tied together as a Sprite Flail and used to spiritually cleanse (exorcise) little-used paths and tracts of ground believed to be infested by dangerous spirits. As well as lone thorn trees, Fairy Trees come into being when oak, ash, and thorn trees naturally grow so closely together that they join with one another through ingrowth. Fairy Trees look unusual, and the places that they grow take on a special character.

The apple (*Malus* spp.) bears a fruit that has been taken to symbolize eternal life. In Norse mythology Iduna kept the "apples of life," which prevented the gods from aging. Apples are used in divination, especially concerning love. In England at midwinter, apple trees are wassailed: honored in a ceremonial way with gifts and songs, so that they will bear abundant fruit at the following harvest. Mazer Bowls turned on a lathe from maple (*Acer campestre*) wood are used traditionally to serve drink at wassail ceremonies in honor of apple trees.

The wood of the aspen or shiver tree, which is a kind of poplar (*Populus tremula*) is magically protective, used to in former days for magic shields and measuring sticks. The Anglo-Saxons planted aspen trees as markers of boundaries of farms and parishes, as their white-backed leaves that tremble in the wind are visible from afar.

The rare wild service tree (*Sorbus torminalis*) was used magically to protect people against dangerous wild things, and its wood was used for talismans. The wood of another small and infrequently encountered talismanic tree, the wayfaring tree (*Viburnum lantana*), provides magical protection for travelers.

The beech tree (*Fagus sylvatica*) is the tree of letters. In former times it was the wood of choice for written talismans, for magically, the beech stores and protects knowledge. The traditional Irish drum (*bodhrán*) has a beechwood frame.

Holly (*Ilex aquifolium*) is the magic tree of the Yule celebrations of midwinter. After Yule a sprig of holly kept at home will continue its protective powers. In Ireland in former times, pothooks were made from holly if iron was not available (Evans 1957, 68). The very hard wood was good for clubs and cudgels, used in personal defense.

Mistletoe (*Viscum album*) is special because it does not have roots in the earth but grows semiparasitically up among the branches of other trees. Green, ball-shaped mistletoes are easily seen in winter when the leaves of the host tree have fallen. Mistletoe is best known as a luck-bringing Yuletide decoration, with the custom of kissing beneath it. Although people kiss beneath cut boughs that have been hung up, kissing beneath a living tree on which the mistletoe is growing is the luckiest of all.

IRON

Like everything in human existence, the development of traditional skills has its own history that retains its archaic origins within its very nature. In traditional handicrafts there is no distinction between magic, religion, and artisanry, for the craftsperson has a subtle rapport with the material world much more than mere manipulative skill. In traditional society, people who made things were seen as transformers of the world, performing magical acts for the benefit of all members of the family, clan, tribe, or nation. The smith, predominantly seen as a worker of iron, but also a maker in general, had a mythical status. In his *Deutsche Mythologie,* Jacob Grimm explained how the Old Norse word *smiðr* meant not only a handworker with metal, but also a master builder. Similarly, the Estonian words for carpenter, potter, and wheelwright are all versions of the word for smith. In Germany and the Netherlands, Schmitt, and in Estonia the name Sepp (smith) and its variants, are common surnames, as is Smith in Great Britain and among those of British descent. Old English and Norse mythology honors the smith Wayland (Völundr) as a figure with semidivine powers.

Iron is a magic material with extensive lore in every culture. As a skilled worker of iron, the smith was always viewed as a man of magical abilities, practitioner of a technology that has the potential to overcome nature. The early technique of making iron, introduced to the north around 500 BCE, involved heating iron ore with charcoal, made from part-burnt wood. This makes a "bloom" of iron, containing impurities that must be removed by repeated heating and hammering. The final result of this is wrought iron. It is a completely malleable material, ideal for forging into intricate shapes. Master blacksmiths can bend, stretch, split, twist, and make hammer welds with iron to create the master-works of wrought iron in their typical shapes, many of which have a magical meaning. These shapes, emergent from the "virtue" or innate qualities of the material, have been conserved from ancient times into the present day. Iron was viewed as a material imbued with magical virtue, too. It was recognized that if a blacksmith hammered an ingot of iron held in a north-south direction, the iron would become empowered as a magnet. Then it would have the power to attract other pieces of iron and, if floating on a piece of wood, would turn toward the north.

Fig. 7.1. Blacksmith hammering iron north-south to magnetize it (*Auster,* south; *Septentrio,* north). The Library of the European Tradition

At an early point it was realized that iron could be shaped and nailed to the hoofs of horses and oxen to improve traction and prevent wear. Horseshoes in particular acquired a magical lore.

The only drawback with iron is that it rusts, meaning that the ancient pieces still in existence have been preserved through some lucky chance where rusting has been inhibited. In the north, very ancient iron items are rare, but some have been discovered. In Wales an ancient firedog dating from around the first century BCE was discovered in a peat bog at Capel Garmon. Preserved in the National Museum of Wales in Cardiff, it is a work of skill with loops, knobs, and animal-head finials. In the British Museum in London is a fourth-century wrought-iron window grille found at the site of the Roman villa at Hinton St. Mary, Dorset, England. All across northern Europe, despite centuries of repeated wars and depredation, churches, cathedrals, and secular buildings retain their original iron fittings. At Durham in the north of England, the west door of the Norman cathedral retains its twelfth-century wrought iron hinges and strap work. The strap work of doors and heavy oak chests frequently bears magical sigils hammered into the iron when it was hot. The act of striking the pattern into the metal is in itself a magical act of will.

Other essential artifacts made by blacksmiths were nails and chains. Both of these possess magical lore beyond the innate magical virtue of the metal itself. In the late Roman Empire, iron nails marked with images and inscriptions were used in magical rites. "God nails" are part of the sacred array of Viking Age halls and temples, and the old English expletive "God's nails!"—whether or not it refers to the nails with which Jesus was nailed to the cross—is an expression of the magical power of nails. Nails driven into doorposts for good luck can be seen at many old inns in Great Britain. Magic nails made especially by blacksmiths were used to nail horseshoes to beams, doorposts, and beds in order to bind spirits. Pins, also made of iron, feature strongly in northern European folk magic as well as in American hoodoo.

Folklorist Camilla Gurdon noted a spirit-nailing story from eastern England (Suffolk). Her informant, "Mrs. H.," told her: "I once lived in a curious old house—The Barley House, out Debenham

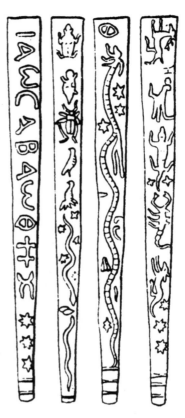

Fig. 7.2. Magic Nails with Greek inscriptions, beasts,
and sigils. The Library of the European Tradition

way—and that were haunted. There were a great horse shoe nailed
into the ceiling on one of the beams and they say that were to nail in
a spirit so as he couldn't get out: a lot of clergymen done it" (Gurdon
1893, 559). A story of the same period from western England (Dorset)
recounts:

> A woman was sure that she was in the power of a witch. Her soap
> would not lather at the washing. She was advised to nail up a horse
> shoe (there were special nails for this) and to lay a besom across the
> threshold, for when the witch came she could not pass over it, and
> must ask for it to be removed, and so would be detected. Also evil
> spirits could be kept from coming down a chimney by hanging a bag

in it containing salt. The bag must be hung on one of these special nails. (March 1899, 480)

The hammer is the essential tool of the smith, and the short-handled hammer of the god Thor (Þórr) was called Mjöllnir (mell or maul, "the crusher"). The hammer is a symbol of power that was used in Norse religion as an instrument of consecration. Figures from European mythology such as Hephaistos, Daedalus, Wayland, Vulcan, and Thor all relate to the magic powers of the hammer. In Viking times, fathers made the sign of the hammer over the family meal, ploughmen made the sign over the fields, and *goðar* made it over couples in the marriage ceremony. Thor has a number of attributes that identify him with smiths. Some altars in temples of Thor are reported as being made from a block of metal, clearly an anvil. The heavy leather belt worn by all blacksmiths is repeated in Thor's belt of power, Meginjörð, and another blacksmith's attribute is his iron-gripping glove, Járngreipr. As a Christian sigil, the Tau cross resembles Mjöllnir. It refers to Anthony of Egypt, who is depicted iconically with his sacred pig and a bell, holding a Tau cross as a staff. St. Anthony lived in ancient Egyptian tombs and conjured up the old gods so he could defeat them in spiritual combat. This is the theme of *The Temptation of Saint Anthony* in art. Identically with the Hammer of Thor, the Tau cross is a magical protection against powerful hostile spiritual forces. Hammer-shaped bones were prized as "lucky bone" amulets in parts of England (Sternberg 1851, 150, 154).

Hammer magic was being conducted in Victorian England and came to the attention of folklore collectors. A well-known Lincolnshire wise woman, Mary Atkin, was the wife of "a most respectable farm bailiff, who did not hold with her goings on, although he dared not check them." A famous spell she used in the late 1850s, often misquoted, tells of her hammering horseshoe nails already attached to a bed as a remedy for the ague: "she took me into his room and to the foot of the old four poster on which he lay. There, in the center of the footboard, were nailed three horseshoes, points upward, with a hammer fixed cross wise upon them." She explained to her visitor in her local dialect that "when the Old 'Un comes to shake 'im" this action would fix him and he would not be able to pass on. The charm was

> *"Feyther, Son and Holy Ghoast, Naale the divil to this*
>   *poast.*
> *Throice I smoites with Holy Crok, With this mell Oi*
>   *throice dew knock,*
> *One for God, An' one for Wod, An' one for Lok."*

Mary Atkin took a mell (hammer) in her left hand and tapped the shoes' nails, at the same time incanting the charm, which invokes "the three holy names": Father, Son, and Holy Ghost, to nail the Devil to the post, binding "The Old 'Un" who was deemed to be the cause of the shaking of the ague patient (Gutch and Peacock 1908, 125). A nail ritual recorded in Suffolk in 1893 was used to transfer the ague to another person. It instructs:

> You must go by night alone to a crossroads, and just as the clock strikes the midnight hour, you must turn about thrice and drive a tenpenny nail up to the head in the ground, then walk away backward from the spot before the clock ends striking twelve, and you will miss the ague; but the next person who goes over the nail will catch the malady in your stead. (Gurdon 1893, 14)

KEEPING THE WILD HORSE AWAY

The Wild Horse or Night Mare (German *Mahrtenritt*) was believed to be a supernatural mare of irresistible power that would attack people by night. The Night Mare gains entry to the sleeping place through tiny cracks in the door or wall. The mare pins down her victim with an oppressive weight upon the chest or throat. She tramples or rides the sleeping one and thrusts her tongue into the victim's throat to prevent him or her from crying out. The victim is tormented heavily and may become ill or even die from the visitation. The mare can only leave by the same way that it came in. If someone stops up the opening, it is caught. Naming the mare's name will also trap it. It was believed that the Night Mare could be conjured up and sent to attack or kill the magician's adversary. The *Ynglinga Saga* recounts how King Vanlandi, who had betrayed Drifa, his Finnish bride, suffered magical retribution. He was trampled to death by a magically summoned mare. Vanlandi suddenly became sleepy and lay down to rest, but when he had slept a little he cried out that a mare was trampling him. The king's servants ran to his assistance, but when they turned to his head, the mare trampled his legs so that they were nearly broken, and when they went to pull the mare off his legs, she was treading on his head, and so the king died.

In 1894 folklorist George Day saw a horseshoe nailed to the door of a cow house in Ilford, eastern England, and asked the lad there the reason for it. He was told, "to keep the wild horse away." "Good fortune will follow you if you pick up a horse shoe," he explained (Day 1894, 77). That was in the days when almost all transport was by horse,

Fig. 7.3. Horseshoe as protection, Hengrave Hall, Suffolk, England.

and "cast" shoes could be found by the roadside. Folklore collectors all over Great Britain and Ireland have noted the old custom of nailing a horseshoe over a door or upon it, and this of course continues today, even when horseshoes have become rare items. The horseshoe must be nailed with its horns pointing upward. Then bad luck or a witch cannot pass the threshhold (Glyde 1872, 50).

THE NINEFOLD COSMOS IN
ENGLISH HERALDRY AND COLOR SYMBOLISM

An ancient system of the spiritual meaning of materials is the color symbolism of heraldry, which remains in use in Great Britain today. Heraldry emerged out of the early medieval use of emblems upon the shields of armored warriors as identifying marks in battles and tournaments. They were systematized under the feudal system, and a set of rules governing patterns and colors was developed by colleges (guilds) of professional heralds who controlled heraldic usage. Written around 1300, the earliest treatise *De Heraldrie* emphasized the importance of standard colors. In 1417 the Duke of Clarence, Constable of England (chief of staff of the army), ordered his heralds to study the properties of colors and their relationships to precious stones, herbs, and other connections so they could be used properly to symbolize the personal qualities of the owner of the coat of arms (McFadzean 1984, 19–20). Around the same time another significant work on the theory of heraldry was *Les Blazon des Couleurs en Armes,* written before 1437 by the herald Jean Courtois from Mons (in modern Belgium). He was herald to King Alfonso V of Aragon and Sicily. Courtois's work gives the connection between the colors and the planets, later detailed by Dame Juliana Berners in England in *The Boke of St. Albans.*

A ninefold system reflecting the symbolic structure of the Cosmos was systematized by the medieval heralds. As well as in Courtois's text, it is described by Anselm in his *Palais de'Honneur;* in a manuscript of the time of King Edward III, *Einseignemens Notablez aulx poursuivans;* and by Dame Juliana Berners in her *Boke of St. Albans.* The cosmological origin of the color system is archetypal, Berners

Fig. 7.4. Heraldic coats of arms, Schwäbisch Gmünd, Germany.

tells us: "The lawe of arms the which was effigured and begun before any lawe in the worlde, both the lawe of nature and before the commandments of God. And this lawe of arms was grounded upon the IX diverse orders of angels in heaven encrowned with IX diverse precious stones of colors and of virtues diverse also of them are figured the IX colors in arms."*

There are nine permissible heraldic colors, of which there are two variant forms. The first and older system uses two metals, five tinctures, and two furs, whilst the second system replaces the furs with two additional tinctures. Confusingly, the word "tincture" is used sometimes as a general term to describe all nine heraldic colors, but strictly a tincture is a color, not a metal or fur. The two heraldic metals are Or (gold) and Argent (silver). For practical purposes, yellow and white are permissible substitutes for the actual metal. The five tinctures are Azure (blue),

---

*I have partially modernized the spelling.

Gules (red), Sable (black), Vert (green) and Purpure (purple). The two furs are Ermine and Vair (imitating the pelts of the stoat in wintertime and the blue-gray squirrel, respectively).

Ancient European cosmology envisages the cosmic structure as nine distinct spheres that surround the earth like concentric shells. The outermost is the *Primum Mobile* (Prime Mover), Empyrean or Ninth Heaven, which is the realm of God. Inside this is the sphere of the Fixed Stars, or Stellar Heaven. Below this sphere are the Spheres of Saturn, Jupiter, Mars, the Sun, Venus, Mercury, and the Sphere of the Moon. Beneath all, in the sublunary realm, is the Earth. Originating in archaic Europe, these nine heavens appeared later both in Christian cosmology and the Nine Worlds of Norse myth. According to Aristotelian precepts, each of the metals and tinctures possesses a spiritual virtue related to a particular planetary sphere. Or signifies and relates to the Sun; Argent, the Moon; Sable, Saturn; Azure, Jupiter; Gules, Mars; Vert, Venus; and Purpure, Mercury. The later tincture scheme, which is also ninefold, omitted the two furs, Vair and Ermine, and in their place introduced two new colors, Tenné (tawny) and Sanguine or Murrey (blood red). The exact tint of Sanguine is described as midway between Gules and Purpure. The color known as Tawny was later renamed Orange in popular usage, though it remains in the name of a British species of owl, the Tawny Owl.

In the text *Einseignemens Notablez aulx poursuivans,* preserved in the College of Arms in London, the heraldic colors are related to the heavenly hierarchy. This originated in the writings of the Christian theorist, Dionysius the pseudo-Areopagite. His system ranked the powers of the various denizens of heaven in terms of military organization. So in the heralds' text, the silvery Argent Seraphim are "full doughty and glorious," and the "unfaint and durable" Cherubim correspond with the dark Sable tincture. Then come the Thrones, who are "wise and virtuous in working," with the loyal tincture Azure. Next are the Principalities, "hot of courage," corresponding with the ruddy Martian Gules. The Dominations, of the blood-red Sanguine, are "mighty of power," and the Tawney Powers are "fortunate of victory." The Virtues are "knightly of government," with their imperially rich tincture Purpure, while the

Archangels, who bear the verdant Vert tincture, are "keen and hardy in battle." Finally, the angels, who are classified as "sure messengers," bear the noble solar metal Or.

According to Dame Juliana Berners, the seven planetary gems relate to the heraldic metals and tinctures. Or is topaz; Argent, pearl; Sable, diamond; Gules, ruby; Azure, sapphire; Vert, emerald; and Purpure, amethyst. In English heraldry there are different color names for the jewel-like roundels. Golden roundels are called Bezant; those of silver, Plate; and red, Torteaux. Blue roundels are Hurts; black, Pellet; green, Pomeis; and purple, Golpe. The final two, Tawny and Sanguine, are called "Orange" and "Guzes," respectively. The name of the color "Tawny" declined in use as the round citrus fruit called oranges became widely available in the north.

In addition to the planetary powers of traditional cosmology, heraldic colors are emblematic of particular virtues, elements, and physical bodily humors. *Einseignemens Notablez aulx poursuivans* lists them. The first color, Azure, signifies loyalty and the sanguine humor; the second, Gules, valiant action, fire, and the choleric temperament. Sable, the third color, represents the Devil and the Earth, and in man, the melancholic humor. Sinable (green) signifies the plants and trees and, in a man, love and courtesy. Purpure indicates riches, abundance, and largesse. The first metal, Or, denotes the golden sun and noble goodwill in a man, while the second, Argent, signifies water, humility, and the phlegmatic temperament.

Sir John Ferne's *The Blazon of Gentrie,* published in 1586, explains that the colors most commonly used in tournaments have spiritual correspondences with particular numbers, human age groups, seasons, humors, and herbs.

Azure (blue) corresponds with the planet Jupiter, the metal tin, and the weekday Thursday. It expresses the virtues of justice and loyalty, or purity; the zodiacal signs of Taurus and Libra; the month of September; the blue lily; the element of air; the season of spring; the sanguine humor; the numbers four and nine; and, in the Ages of Man, boyhood (seven to fourteen years).

Gules (red or vermilion) corresponds with Mars, iron, and Tuesday; charity and magnanimity, or power; Aries and Cancer; March, June and July; the gillyflower; fire; summer; choler; three and ten, and virility (the ages of thirty to forty).

Sable (black) has Saturn as its planet and Saturday as its day; prudence and constancy as its virtues. Its corresponding metal is lead. The Sable zodiac signs are Capricorn and Aquarius, with December and January its months. Its flower is the Aubifaine, its element earth, and its season, winter. The black humor is melancholy, its age decrepit or crooked old age, and its numbers five and eight.

Vert or Sinable (green) is the coppery planet Venus and Friday; love, loyalty, affability, and courtesy; Gemini and Virgo; August; all kinds of green plants; spring, water, the number six, and lusty green youth (twenty to thirty years of age). The green temperament is phlegmatic.

Purpure (purple) corresponds with the planet Mercury, the metal quicksilver, and Wednesday. The purple virtues are temperance and prudence; its zodiacal signs, Sagittarius and Pisces. The violet is the Purpure flower. Elementally, it corresponds with water and earth, while its season is winter. It partakes of the choleric humor and signifies the age of gray hairs in human life. It rules the numbers seven and twelve.

Or (gold or yellow) signifies the Sun and Sunday, the metal gold, the virtue of faith and constancy; the zodiac sign Leo; the month of July; the marigold flower; the element of air; the season of summer; the sanguine humor; the numbers one, two, and three; and, in the Ages of Man, the young age of adolescence (fourteen to twenty years).

Argent (silver or white) is the Moon, silver, and Monday; hope and innocence or, alternatively, joy; Scorpio/Pisces; October/November; the white rose and lily flowers; autumn; the phlegmatic humor; the numbers ten and eleven; and human infancy, the first seven years of life.

By means of these colors, the heraldic artists were able to express certain virtues and convey particular meanings that other heralds could recognize immediately. They remain today as a traditional symbolic language. The seven tinctures are a symbolic system with magical overtones well beyond heraldry. The concept of seven colors is recorded from ancient Ireland, where one's rank in society was shown by how many colors one was allowed to wear. When in the seventeenth century Sir Isaac Newton shone sunlight through a prism, he described seven colors of the rainbow, even though medieval artists had never distinguished blue and indigo when painting rainbows. It was for mystical—rather than perceptional—reasons that Newton defined the number of colors as seven. The heavy agricultural horse breed from East Anglia called Suffolk Punch has seven shades, defined in 1880 when the first Stud Book was published by Herman Biddell. All horses must be a shade of chesnut (spelled that way) and of one of seven shades: dark liver, dull dark, light mealy, red, golden, lemon, or bright (Chapman 2007, 87).

8

The Spirit of Craftsmanship

TRADITIONAL TIMBER
BUILDINGS AND THEIR MAKING

The act of making is an essential human activity central to our being. The craftsperson's work ethic generates a harmonious relationship with nature and other people. The master craftsperson has gained the insight to see beyond the outer form of the material into its inner essence. This ability was explained by English master craftsman William Morris in a lecture delivered in 1881, titled *Art and the Beauty of the Earth:* "try to get the most out of your material, but always in such a way as honors it most. Not only should it be obvious what your material is, but something should be done with it which is especially natural to it, something that cannot be done with any other." Aesthetic rightness and beauty is expressed in practical, personal ways. We attempt to emulate what is worthy in whatever spiritual climate we find ourselves. The function of the spiritually made artifact is to disclose the sphere of the sacred in human society. Making artifacts spiritually makes the self knowable and gives us the possibility of attaining personal integrity. To achieve this, the maker requires a mindful awareness of the nature of reality, an understanding of being that comes from an organic way of life.

Buildings have no meaning without human interaction. They are wholly the product of human ingenuity and skill. Human activities are personal: whatever form they may take, they come directly from specific individuals, acting at a specific place, a specific time, and a specific cultural moment. This is essentially local, even when it claims to be otherwise. Historically, each of the traditional elements of architecture came about through practical usage by the assemblage of components, each with a more or less natural form. Most basically, they are the frame of timber; the roof of bark, thatch, or wooden shingles; and the wooden door. More advanced concepts were derived from practical necessities; for example, the concept of proportion arose through the necessary repetition or alteration of structural components. In the development of European traditional architecture, the so-called ornamental parts of the assemblage either derive directly from the constructional techniques, as a skillful development of them, or as the result of rites and ceremonies that are also essential elements in the use of buildings.

Fig. 8.1. Timber-frame building patterns, making sunwheels, Shrewsbury, Shropshire, England.

The Latin verb *ornare,* from which the word ornament is derived, meant to prepare something in such a way that it was fit for sacred use. Traditional ornament often makes permanent the remains of otherwise transient adornment. Garlands, flowers, fruit, leaves, flags, birds, bones, and skulls adorn buildings in the form of carved stone and metalwork on temples, churches, and public buildings, while wood, pargetting, and paint serves the vernacular. These are formalized in such a way that they enhance the buildings' function, in a physical, cultural, and symbolic way, reinforcing collective belief and identity.

TIMBER SHRINES AND TEMPLES

Food supply is a matter of life and death, and safe storage guards against shortages. Food-storage structures must be raised off the ground to prevent vermin from gaining access and eating the contents. From Ireland and Britain to western Siberia, traditional granaries and provisions stores were small wooden buildings raised off the ground on posts, stones, or pillars. Particular rites and ceremonies were performed traditionally to magically safeguard these food stores, and it is probable that wayside shrines of spirits and deities were developed from raised storehouses. In Scandinavia the traditional storehouses of the Sámi were log structures supported on poles, accessed by ladders (Pareli 1984, 116). Until the late nineteenth century, the Ob-Ugrian (Khanty or Ostyak) people in Siberia built similar "spirit sheds" to house their holy objects. These were wooden structures raised off the ground by six pillars. They were clearly derived from storehouses (Kodolányi 1968, 103–6). These sheds were located in groves of elder trees (*Sambucus nigra*). In Estonia images of the gods Tönn, Metsik, and Peko were kept in off-ground storehouses standing upon stones (Moora and Viires 1964, 253). The Ob-Ugrian shrines housed boxes containing sacred objects and clothing, and in Estonian granaries, the images of the house spirit called Tönn were kept in special oval boxes, resembling the traditional Russian oval birch-bark bread boxes. A late record of veneration of Tönn in Estonia was in Vändra parish in the early years of the twentieth century. In England and Wales mushroom-shaped staddle stones, which supported long-vanished granaries, are used as garden ornaments. I have been told on a number of occasions that they have a magical function to ward off bad luck.

The great temples of the north were timber buildings. Little remains except written accounts, for they were destroyed by Christian crusaders between the eleventh and the thirteenth centuries. The temple at Uppsala in Sweden was the greatest Pagan sanctuary in Scandinavia. Adam of Bremen (ca. 1070), who lived when the temple was in existence, described it as "completely adorned with gold." To his manuscript a scholiast later added a note (*scholium* 139) telling of a golden chain running around the temple. This chain appears in a woodcut of 1554 illustrating the works of Olaus Magnus, made 450 years after the temple was destroyed. Traditional timber buildings of northern Europe, including the surviving Norwegian stave churches, are made completely of timber with no metal fittings except door hinges and sometimes shingle nails. So the chain seems an unlikely description. If it is a misreport, it might refer to gilded or painted carvings on the *takfot,* the beam at the top of the wall that supports the tie-beam rafters known as *bindbjalke* or *stickbjalke.* Carvings of the *takfot* exist from remaining medieval longhouses and churches in Scandinavia, including the Swedish churches at Hagbyhöga, Kumlaby, and Väversunda. The *takfot* carvings depict animals, dragons, and interlace patterns (Sjömar 1995, 219, 222). In northern England and southern Scotland, the form of hogbacks (stone monuments of the Viking Age) recall shingle-roofed buildings with the richly carved *takfot* beneath.

Temples of the west Slavonic gods in what is now Germany and Poland were also ornate timber buildings. Many were in towns built on islands in rivers, strongly defended with ramparts of earth and timber. Rügen was a holy island in the Baltic Sea with two major temple complexes, Karentia and Arkona. The temple at Arkona had an earth floor, into which the legs of the four-headed image of Svantovit were set. That temple had a single entrance, and the roof was supported by four columns. The west Slavonic name for a temple was *continen,* the modern Polish *konczyna,* meaning an "end" or "gable," for, according to Herbord, the Pomeranian temples were buildings with gables (Herbord

1894, II, 31). At Gozgaugia the building was described as "a temple of wonderful size and beauty" (Herbord 1894, III, 7). The main *continen* at Sczeczin (Stettin), enshrining the three-headed image of the god Triglaus or Triglav, was "rich in ornament and art," having painted sculptures on the wall. Sczeczin had a religious complex containing four separate temples and halls where the nobles gathered for sacred feasts served on dishes of silver and gold.

A basic understanding of the construction of some Slavonic temples has been obtained from archaeological excavations. The temples appear to have been constructed from vertical timbers, and they were roofed with shingles. An idea of what their walling was like can be seen in England in the remaining parts of one of the oldest timber churches in existence at Greensted-Juxta-Ongar, Essex (Clucas 1987, 29). Dendrochronologically dated to 845 CE, the Anglo-Saxon church is composed of oak trees cleft in half. They are grooved on each side and set vertically, joined by narrow wooden strips set in the grooves. Structurally, the Greensted church must have been very close to the contemporary Pagan temples farther east. Comparable staves of oak with human faces carved at the top were found in remains of the ninth-century temple at Ralswieck-Scharstorf on Rügen (Váňa 1992, 171, fig. 39). Similar humanoid knobs existed at the top of the vertical planks that formed the walls of the Slavonic temple at Gross-Radern in eastern Germany. The heads of the *tjösnur* used to delimit the fighting area in *hólmganga* resembled these.

CRAFT FRATERNITIES AND GUILDS

Traditionally all crafts were acquired by novices learning directly from highly skilled masters through personal contact. The most able novices eventually progressed through a journeyman stage to become recognized as masters in their own right. Because of this continuity through the generations, craftspeople have banded together in groups for mutual support and the continuance of the craft. These traditional organizations were self-reliant and self-governing and had some spiritual and moral teachings. The antiquity of guilds in Britain is uncertain.

Undoubtedly, when much of western Europe was part of the Roman Empire, various Roman craft guilds operated here. A craft legendarium tells how, around 715 BCE, Numa, king of Rome, codified rules for the Collegia, guilds of craftspeople. The Roman Collegia honored tutelary gods who ruled the craft. Members conducted collective rites and ceremonies in honor of their deity. The craft guilds of post-Roman times, when the empire had disintegrated in the west, may well have continued some of the characteristics of the older Roman Collegia, honoring the corresponding Christian saint in place of the Roman god.

In most European cities in the medieval period were crafts and tradesmen's guilds, each with a religious connection to a patron saint. The word guild (Old English *gild*) itself has an early origin, for in Anglo-Saxon England the *frith-gild* was a mutual-protection society organized by family groups. Craftsmen's guilds undertook to do the best work possible, and the quest for excellence was inherent in their work. The motto of an ancient Norwich guild expresses the material and spiritual aspirations of all guilds: "to do well, and to have continuance in well doing." The master does not overturn the accepted norms:

Fig. 8.2. Coopers' (barrel makers) guild shrine,
Antwerp Cathedral, Belgium.

they are created anew. Pride in one's work was paramount. In the medieval period, any work of skill was called a "mystery," and the craft guilds that maintained and transmitted the tradition were called "mysteries." It was the guilds that staged the mystery plays enacted on holy days. Bards in medieval Wales were known by the kenning "carpenters of song," for craftsmanship is a state of being that is independent of the type of materials upon which we work. Once Protestantism split the church, the overt connection in Protestant lands with tutelary saints was broken, and the organizations became secularized as companies and brotherhoods, though their internal myths and legends were not forgotten. Trade guilds in towns and cities were fully recognized legally, serving local business interests defending the interests of their members.

Journeymen traveling from place to place and rural fraternities tended to be less regulated officially and were often clandestine, with secret passwords, handshakes, signs, tattoos, and other means of recognition. In traditional trade guilds there are standard questions and answers, accompanied by particular words and gestures that are taught to initiates and used by members to determine whether an unknown person claiming to be a member actually is one. In France the builders' guilds were prohibited in 1189 because of their use of secret words and actions, and in 1326 the Council of Avignon reaffirmed the ban. "The Horseman's Grip and Word" was actually the name of the fraternity of horsemen in Scotland. So the emphasis on magic is among rurally based trades, such as journeymen, millers, horsemen, and drovers, as well as people who went to sea.

The traditional form of organized craft practice has three stages: apprentice, journeyman (outwright), and master. These correspond to the three stages of learning. First, the novice has spontaneity without control. The next stage is to have control, but with consequent loss of spontaneity. Finally, masterhood consists of regaining spontaneity and having control with spontaneity. Traditionally, a journeyman had served his full apprenticeship and was qualified to practice the trade as an employee of a master. For this, he or she was entitled to the going rate of pay. The journeyman would travel from place to place, recognized by his knowledge of the secret signs and words of his craft, until he found a master to work for. Since ancient times, there has been a religious dimension to crafts, under the tutelage of gods, founding fathers, or saints, and their *legendaria* and foundation myths were recalled in the rites and ceremonies of the guilds. In France three grand masters of old are honored in Compagnonnage: King Solomon, Père Soubise, and Maître Jacques. Freemasonry, unlike Compagnonnage, which is no longer operative, honors Solomon and the Phoenician architect of the Temple of Jerusalem, Hiram. Compagnonnage and Freemasonry are institutions where spiritual symbolism plays a major part in the rites and ceremonies. Similarly, the mutual societies that grew up in Britain in parallel with trade unions in the nineteenth century—organizations such as the Oddfellows, the Britons, and the Foresters that promoted ideals of fellowship—have or had rites, ceremonies, symbolism, and regalia with origins in the medieval or earlier religious guilds. Some contemporary trade unions still use the religious terms "chapel" or "chapter" to denote a local division. This is the last remnant of the former spiritual nature of workers' associations.

TOOLS AND GUILD LEGENDS

Tools are magical objects. Pagan divinities and Christian saints were often depicted with craftsmen's tools or weapons that signified the nature of their skills, powers, or symbolic deaths. In Scotland all men who worked trades using a hammer were deemed to be members of the Hammermen's Guild. In 1694, for example, the hammermen of Selkirk included blacksmiths, coopers, a coppersmith, stonemasons, and wrights. Makers of larger objects from wood and metal were wrights, such as wheelwrights, wainwrights (wagon makers), shipwrights, and arkwrights (box makers). The sign of the guilds of hammermen is the crowned hammer, and it can be seen on old tombstones in Scotland. An instance of the magical and symbolic nature of tools comes from the British shoemakers' legendarium. St. Hugh's Bones are emblematic of the "Gentle Craft of Shoemaking." According to the story, Hugh was son of a Pagan king, Arviragus of Powisland (Powys, Wales). He married a Christian princess, Winifred of Flintshire, who converted him to Christianity. For this he was disinherited and cast down into poverty, so he was compelled to learn the trade of cordwainer (shoemaker). Hugh then preached the gospel by day and made shoes by night. Both he and Winifred were put to death during the persecution of Christians by the Roman Emperor Diocletian. Winifred was beheaded, and Hugh was forced to drink a cup of her blood, mixed with cold poison, after which his body was hung on a gallows. But he bequeathed his bones to his fellow shoemakers. After the bones had been "well picked by the birds" some shoemakers took them down from the gallows and made them into tools. From then on their tools were named St. Hugh's Bones and described in a guild rhyme, *The Shoemakers' Shibboleth,* learning of which was part of the initiation into the craft guild. Before the availability of steel, the finest needles used by shoemakers were made from bone. Hence each tool the shoemaker uses is symbolically a certain part of the body of the founder.

Craft guilds had their own rites and ceremonies, many of which were conducted at special places. In Shrewsbury, England, from 1598, the ground called Kingsland, now a park, was the venue for the Shrewsbury Show, a trade guild festival. The guilds built temporary "arbors" at Kingsland in which they conducted their rites and ceremonies and made merry. The Patriotic Company of Shoemakers of Shrewsbury had the symbolic images of their patron saints, Crispin and Crispianus, on the entrance to their arbor, and next to it was an octagonal enclosure with a labyrinth cut in the turf. It was called The Shoemakers' Race. It was destroyed in 1796 when the guild sold the land for a windmill to be put up there. Another shoemakers' labyrinth, the *Windelbahn,* existed at Stolp in Pomerania (Słupsk, Poland). The festive day of both the English and the Pomeranian shoemakers' guilds was the first Tuesday after Whitsunday. At Stolp an elected *Maigraf* (May Lord) oversaw the festivities (Sieber 1936, 83–86). Guild rites and ceremonies all over northern Europe included the staging of miracle plays, sword dancing (Corrsin 1997, *passim*) and feasts on the day of their spiritual patrons or founders.

Another guild legendarium concerns *The Miracle of Bread.* According to one horsemen's catechism from eastern England, "the

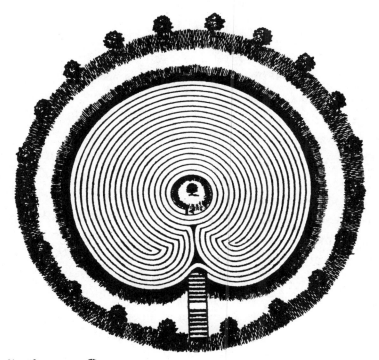

Fig. 8.3. Słupsk shoemakers' labyrinth in Pomerania, Poland.
The Library of the European Tradition

word" was imprisoned between black boards and chained and pad-locked in the pulpit of the church. It was impossible for it to get free among the plough and the nets, so the season of famine could be at an end. So the "lesser world" of the fiddle, the rune, the word spoken, must by necessity work the miracle of bread. The ploughmen prepare the ground and sow and harrow in the grain. The seeds germinate, grow, and produce ears of grains. They are harvested by the laborers, trans-ported and threshed, then taken to the mill, where the miller grinds the grain into flour. This Miracle of Bread links the society of horsemen with the millers, another group in possession of the "word."

The first magical act of *The Miracle of Bread* is plowing the fields, forming straight rigs (furrows) in which to sow the grain. The rite of "setting the rig" uses two willow sticks, each called a *dod,* which are set up at each end of the furlong to be plowed, and both activated magically and made visible by wisps of straw tied near the top. The ploughman lines up his horses in front of one dod and looks toward the other dod at the end of the furlong, noting what is visible behind it, a back mark called "the farthest beacon." The first furrow is drawn straight toward the second dod, keeping the farthest beacon in sight. The rest of the furrows are plowed parallel with the first one.

The Miracle of Bread centers upon the cycle of the growing grain, just as the traditional English ballad *John Barleycorn Must Die* tells of the emergence of the barley plant from the seemingly dead grain buried in the earth and its seasonal development in time until the cycle is completed and begins once again. In the larger, more organized lodges there were degrees based upon various progressive states of the growing grain, as in the song, as *The Miracle of Bread* has six stations or stages: the Plough, the Seed, the Green Corn, the Yellow Corn, the Stones, Rising Again. The primary function of any craft is to be effective, and like other handicraft skills, ploughing was an art tried and tested in the harsh world of physical reality. If it had not worked, it would soon have faded into oblivion.

9

Natural Measure

We are so used to counting in tens, using decimal coinage and metric measurements, that it is difficult sometimes to think in other ways. The decimal system is not the natural way of measuring; it comes from a mathematical rather than a practical worldview. Traditional measure is totally practical. It is based upon the requirements of cooking, handicrafts, agriculture, and trade. It emerges directly from the characteristics of the materials being measured, and not from mathematical theory. These weights and measures are physical; they relate to the human body and natural objects, and they are interconnected in subtle ways. Traditionally, length, weight, and capacity is divided by halving. A unit of anything is divided into two halves, then halved again to produce four quarters, then halved again to produce eight eighths, and so forth. This can be done by eye, or by folding anything foldable. Three such divisions cut the item into eight equal parts, and in natural measure 3, 4, and 8 are significant numbers. Traditional weights and measures as well as time were based on an eightfold system. Eight is significant also because it occurs in the eightfold division of space into the eight airts, the octave of the musical scale, and the thirty-two divisions of the compass rose (8 × 4). Norse weighing used a system of measure that existed until 1971 in the traditional coinage of Great Britain and Ireland: 1 Mark = 8 Ører = 24 Ertogar = 240 Penningar (from which the coin called a penny is derived, though now it is one-hundredth of a pound Sterling). This is a 1 × 8 × 3 × 10 sequence.

Common measurements were necessitated by trade, so that some meaningful exchange of value could take place, or critical quantities of materials could be determined repeatedly. A characteristic traditional system of measure conserved into modern times is recorded in the medieval Welsh medical text *Meddygon Myddfai* (The Physicians of Myddvai), whose contents include herbalism and forms of magical treatment. Legend places the origin of the Myddfai physicians' knowledge, famed throughout Wales, in an otherworldly gift of a bag of medicines from the Lady of the Lake (Pughe and Williams 1861, xxiii–xxx). After giving the standardized "weights and measures of proportion" that include the common Apothecaries' Measure, the writer gives fluid measures, which clearly are arranged according to the principles of natural measure. Fluid or liquid measure is based on a fourfold principle. Four podfuls made one spoonful. Four spoonfuls make one eggshellful. Four eggshellfuls make one cupful. Four cupfuls make one quart. Four quarts make one gallon. Four gallons make one pailful. Four pailfuls make one *grenn* (a large earthenware vessel). Four *grenns* make one *mydd*. Four *mydds* make one *myddi* (hogshead barrel) (Pughe and Williams 1861, 458). "All the measures of solids and fluids should be of warranted [i.e., standardized] weight and measure, so that they may afford warranted and just information in order that the medicines administered to the sick may neither be ineffective nor poisonous, and that every dose may be of the proportion intended" (Pughe and Williams 1861, 458). However, traditional measure of weight is also given, "conjectural measures, dependent upon the Physician's judgement." This traditional measure is as follows: four grains of wheat = one pea; four peas = one acorn; four acorns = one pigeon's egg; four pigeon's eggs = one hen's egg; four hen's eggs = one goose's egg; four goose eggs = one swan's egg.

THE NORTHERN CUBIT AND ITS DERIVATIVES

Natural measure is a system used between the Iron Age and the Middle Ages, having its origins in the oldest known measures. It continues today in the mile, used in the United Kingdom and the United States, and its traditional submultiples. The mile is a multiple of the ancient and consistent measure known as the Northern Cubit and its half, the Northern Foot. This existed prior to 3000 BCE, being used in ancient India, Mesopotamia, Europe, North Africa, and China (Skinner 1967, 40). It was associated in Europe with the Germanic peoples, and was taken to wherever they migrated, so in that context the Northern Foot is known as the Saxon Foot. This unit measures 13.2 inches (335.3 mm).

Artifacts found in remains of the Indus civilization at Mohenjodaro (dating from around 2500 BCE) have this measure incised upon them, as do the XIIth dynasty (ca. 1900 BCE) Egyptian cubit measures from Kahun. Royal Cubit measuring rods of the XVIIIth dynasty (1567–1320 BCE) have the Northern Foot marked at the 18th *digit*. In twelve BCE Nero Claudius Drusus, Roman governor of Lower Germany, had to adopt the Northern Foot as the official measure for the province, rather than the *Pes,* the shorter Roman Foot. The Northern Foot was defined as two *digits* longer than the *Pes.*

Primarily a land measure, the Northern Foot is part of an interlinked system of measures. It is the base unit of the Rod, the Rood, the Acre, the Furlong, and the Mile. The Northern Foot has a 4:3 relationship to the Natural Foot (or Welsh Foot). They are both submultiples of the Rod (16 feet 6 inches; 5.0292 metres); the Northern Foot is one-fifteenth of a Rod and the Natural Foot, one-twentieth. Both Northern and Natural Feet are subdivided into palms or Shafthands (Scots *shathmont* or *shaftmon*), 3.3 inches (83.8 mm). Three of these make a Natural Foot and four a Northern Foot. Each Shafthand subdivides into three Thumbs of 1.1 inches (27.9 mm), and each Thumb is divided into three Barleycorns of 0.37 inches (9.4 mm). So the Natural Foot measures 9 Thumbs (27 Barleycorns) and the Northern Foot 12 Thumbs (36 Barleycorns).

Measurements used in handicrafts and building construction take these measures up using mainly the 8/3 pattern. An Ell is 2 Northern Feet long (8 Shafthands). A Fathom consists of 3 Ells, 6 Northern Feet (24 Shafthands). A Rod (otherwise Perch or Pole) is 2½ Fathoms, 15 Northern Feet, 20 Natural Feet (60 Shafthands). One Furlong is 40

NATURAL MEASURE

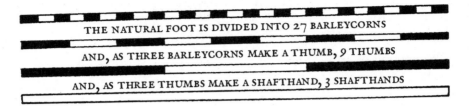

THE NATURAL FOOT IS DIVIDED INTO 27 BARLEYCORNS

AND, AS THREE BARLEYCORNS MAKE A THUMB, 9 THUMBS

AND, AS THREE THUMBS MAKE A SHAFTHAND, 3 SHAFTHANDS

THREE SHAFTHANDS MAKE A NATURAL FOOT

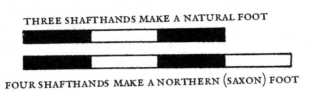

FOUR SHAFTHANDS MAKE A NORTHERN (SAXON) FOOT

Fig. 9.1. Natural measure.

Rods, 600 Northern Feet, 800 Natural Feet. (In the eighteenth century, for surveying purposes, the Furlong was subdivided into ten units called Chains). The Mile measures 8 Furlongs, 320 Rods, 4,800 Natural Feet, and 6,400 Natural Feet. In England a longer Mile was sometimes reckoned, 10 Furlongs in length. This is the Country Mile or Derbyshire Mile, 6,000 Northern feet and 8,000 Natural Feet; the Cheshire Mile was 7,680 Feet. The Scots Mile is 5,952 Feet; the Irish 6,720 Feet (Michell 1981, 21).

Measuring the land and setting up landmarks is a magical act that brings stability to society. Traditional area measure is derived from squares based on the Rod of 15 Northern feet. A Rood of land is one Rod wide by one Furlong in length, 15 by 600 Northern Feet, 20 by 800 Natural Feet. Its area is 9,000 square Northern Feet and 16,000 square Natural feet. One Acre is an area measuring 10 by 100 Fathoms; four Roods make an Acre, measuring 60 by 600 Northern Feet; 80 by 800 Natural Feet. A Ferlingate or *ferdelh* is one square Furlong, 600 by 600 Northern Feet, 800 by 800 Natural Feet. Four Ferlingata make one Townyard or Virgate, a quarter of a Mile square measure, 1,200 by 1,200 Northern Feet. Four Virgata make one Hide of Land, half a Mile by half a Mile, 2,400 by 2,400 Northern Feet. Hyde Park in London, England, is a relic of this traditional land measure, and the customary four quarters of medieval towns reflect the Townyard of four Ferlingata. When the United States was surveyed for settlement from 1785, the Mile was taken as the unit for the grid with which it was laid out (Johnson 1976, *passim*). The grid was subdivided into Sections of land subdivided into four square Quarters of 160 Acres with sides half a mile long, the old English Townyard. The Quarters were again subdivided into 40 Acre Quarter Quarter Sections, the old English Ferlingate. The landscape of the United States is the largest example of natural measure.

Traditional land measure is thus a completely integrated system. The present Foot commonly used is not the Northern one, though the Northern Foot is embedded in the measured landscape. It is a compromise originating in 1305 in *The Statute for Measuring Land,* part of the reforms of King Edward I of England (33 Edward I, Stat. 6, 1305). Until then, different parts of the king's realm had used different measures. In former Saxon areas the Northern Foot was used; the Natural Foot was used in predominantly Celtic parts. Versions of the Roman Foot were used in building along with the Norman Foot and the Greek Common Foot. *The Statute for Measuring Land* abolished these local variants and set up a standard Foot, which is the current standard. Land-measure units from the Rod upward were not changed. The Rod was defined as 16 feet 6 inches in the new measure, which subdivided the new Foot into 12 inches and abolished the old subdivisions. This made the new Foot (304.8 mm) in a 10:11 ratio with the old Northern Foot, which is the reason that the Mile is an odd figure of 5,280 feet. Edward I's statute introduced a new measure; three of the new Feet became the Meter Yard (Yard, 914.4 mm) to which later mete wands conformed. This was subdivided into 16 units, the Nail of 2¼ inches, used in Britain until the twentieth century in cloth measure. Four Nails of cloth measure made one Quarter; three Quarters made one Flemish Ell. Four Quarters made one Yard, and five Quarters made one English Ell. Another measure related to the Yard is the Hand used to measure the height of horses, one Hand being 4 inches, one-ninth of a Yard. In The Nameless Art (East Anglian rural magic), a sway (magic wand) made from blackthorn or hazel should measure an old Ell in length (26.4 inches; 67.06 cm).

Fig. 9.2. Measures of the city of Augsburg, Bavaria, Germany.

In the Holy Roman Empire in medieval times, each city had its own standards of measure, based on local needs. In England and Scotland there were national measures valid across the countries. The standards were displayed in public for everyone to check measures against them. Standard measurements were made in durable metals, generally iron or bronze, and fixed to stone structures near the marketplace, so that their measure could be taken and used according to law. The measures of Augsburg in Bavaria, Germany, are shown here.

In Dunkeld, Scotland, the Ell Shop (built in 1757) is called that because there is an eighteenth-century iron ellwand fixed to one corner. It was the standard for cloth merchants in the marketplace. Also in Scotland, in the square of Fettercairn, Kincardine, is the remains of the Mercat Cross, which has an ell measure cut into the stone. Measures were transferred from place to place by taking a measure from one of these public standards. It can be seen in the case of weights, too, such as the practice of using Ouncle Weights, recorded in Scotland but clearly of much wider application. These were large stones, usually taken from the seashore, that were checked for weight against known weights, then used as weights in their own right (Warrack 1988 [1911], 392). (The Stone is still a weight used informally to weigh people in Britain. It is 14 pounds, so someone weighing 140 pounds is 10 stone.)

Publicly displayed official measures were the legally enforceable standards of the city or nation. Many local Feet and Ells for measuring cloth, however, inside and outside the Holy Roman Empire, were derived from the Northern Foot. Cities as far apart as Lyon, Moscow, and Verona, and the island of Sardinia, used Feet clearly northern in origin. As far away as China, the *Revenue Ch'ih* was the same as the Saxon Foot until it was abolished in the twentieth century (Skinner 1967, 43). The Ells of cloth weaving and trading cities in the Low Countries, such as Antwerp, Namur, Nijmegen, Leiden, Oudenarde, and Maastricht were the Northern Cubit. In the Empire the cities of Aachen, Nuremberg, and Berlin used the measure, as did the Italian cities of Ferrara, Padua, Ravenna, Venice, and Trieste.

CAPACITY MEASURES

English traditional capacity measures, too, are based on the system of halving divisions. The Gallon is divided into eight Pints, each of which is subdivided into four Gills or Quarterns. The Quartern is one-sixteenth of a Gallon. Four Gills equal one Pint; two Pints are a Quart, one quarter of a Gallon; two Quarts are a Pottle, half a Gallon; two Pottles are a Gallon. Two Gallons equal one Peck; four Pecks (eight Gallons) make one Bushel; two Bushels, one Strike; two Strikes, one Coomb (Sack); two Coombs, one Quarter. Thirty-six Bushels make one Chaldron. The capacity of a cube with sides measuring one Shafthand is very close to the Pint. In the 1497 standard, the Pint was defined as equal to 12½ Troy Ounces of wheat; the Quart 25, the Pottle 50, and the Gallon 100, making the Bushel 800 Troy Ounces of wheat. Measures of ale and beer were also based upon the Gallon, but in a ninefold system. The smallest beer keg was the Pin, equal to four and a half Gallons, 36 Pints. Two of these make a Firkin, nine Gallons; two Firkins are a Kilderkin, 18 Gallons (144 Pints); two Kilderkins make a Barrel, 36 Gallons (288 Pints), and two Barrels are a Puncheon, 72 Gallons. Additionally, there are intermediate beer measures. Three Firkins make a Half Hogshead; two Half Hogsheads, of course, make a Hogshead; and two Hogsheads make a Butt of 108 Gallons.

This system of division was applied to the Winchester Standard of King Edgar (reigned 959–975 CE). In 1340 under King Edward III, it was made the universal standard in England: "It is assented and accorded that from henceforth one Measure and one Weight shall be throughout the realm of England, and that the Treasurer cause to be made certain standards of the Bushel, the Gallon, of weights made of brass, and send the same into every county where such standards be not sent before this time" (14 Edward III, Stat. I, Cap. 12, 1340). In Edward III's statute, the Pound was defined as 6992 Grains, with an Ounce of 437 Grains for a 16-Ounce Pound. In 1824 in the United Kingdom, the standard was altered to the Imperial System by an approximately 3 percent increase in volume. The ratios and names of the units remained the same. The tenth-century Winchester Standard still applies in the U.S. Gallon and its derivatives. All of these systems of measure allow numerous whole-number divisions of measure, more practical and convenient than systems based on ten.

METE WANDS, THE "DRUID'S CORD," AND TAKING ONE'S MEASURE

The eighth-century Anglo-Saxon military surveyors who built Offa's Dyke and Wat's Dyke, which formed the border between England and Wales, had precise systems of measurement (Fox 1955). Clearly, these were based upon standardized measuring rods. Similarly, the tenth-century Danish earthwork called the Danevirke and the Trelleborg-type ring fortresses demonstrate precise surveying and layout of military fortifications. At Trelleborg all the main dimensions were precisely related, and the houses inside the ring fort were all the same size. Although the exact nature of the measures is disputed, the ratios are precise. If the main buildings are taken to be 100 units (feet) long, two small houses in the middle of the blocks measure 30 × 15 units, the houses in an outer ward 90 units, and the circular rampart is 60 units thick. The radius of the inner edge of the circular rampart is 234 units, as is the distance between the inner and outer ditches (Nørlund 1948, 14).

The "druid's cord" is a string or rope with twelve knots equally spaced, making thirteen equal units. In East Anglian tradition this measuring cord is called a *snor* and the marker knots are *snotches*. Druid's cords can be of any length, so they can be a way of using different measures, depending on distance between knots, so long as they are equally spaced. It is not primarily a form of measurement, but a geometrical tool. The primary function of a druid's cord is the production of right angles on the ground, as in laying out a garden or building plot. The cord can be used to construct Pythagorean triangles (right-angle-containing triangles with whole-number side lengths; e.g., 3, 4, 5). Nineteen different triangles with whole-unit sides can be made with the druid's cord, producing forty different angles at the vertices. It is possible that this basic tool was used to lay out stone circles and enclosures, Norse triangular sacred plots, labyrinths on the ground, and "mystic plots" for ritual use. The druid's cord also facilitates various other shapes to be laid out (Morgan 1990, 109–13; Pennick and Gout 2004, 52–55, 111).

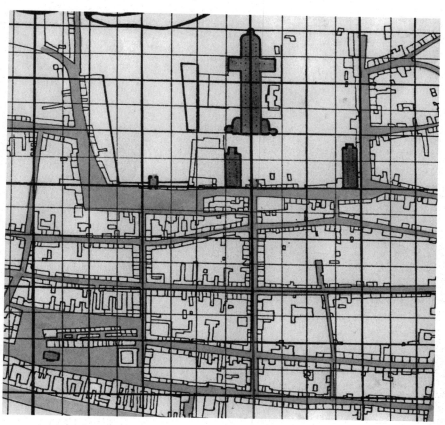

Fig. 9.3. Grid layout of the streets of Bury St. Edmunds, Suffolk, England, on a modular measure, based on the orientation of the Abbey church, ca. 1050.

"Taking someone's measure" is considered to give the measurer power over that person. It is associated with death because the coffin maker always needed to measure the dead person's body to make a coffin the right size for burial. If an evil person should have one's measure, then one was doomed. But measurement was also an element of traditional healing. An accusation of measurement witchcraft from northern England is preserved in a Durham *Book of Depositions* from the year 1565 to 1573 (vol. xxi of the Publications of the Surtees Society). The alleged witch was Jennet Pereson, who was accused of using witchcraft in "measuring belts to preserve folks from the fairies" and taking payments to heal people "taken with the fairy." She was said to have sent for south-running water to heal a sick child whom they believed had been taken with the fairy and thus fallen ill. Her antifairy magic was condemned as witchcraft (Henderson 1866, 140–41). Three hundred years later in Wales, Marie Trevelyan recorded measurement used as a form of medical diagnosis:

Old women who were skilful in making herb-tea, ointments and decoctions of all kinds, professed to tell for certain if a person was consumptive. This was by measuring the body. They took a string and measured the patient from head to feet, then from tip to tip of the outspread arms. If the person's length was less than his breadth, he was consumptive; if the width from shoulder to shoulder was narrower than from the throat to the waist, there was little hope of cure. The proper measure was made of yarn. (Trevelyan 1909, 317)

This practice appears to be based upon a belief that the ideal proportions of the human body are concomitant with health.

10

Traditional Buildings and Practical Magic

BUILDERS' RITES AND CEREMONIES

Omens and Portents

The foundation of sacred buildings, especially when done by Celtic Christian priests, often used divinatory methods to determine the site. Wild pigs were ostenta for building several churches in what are now England, Wales, and France. St. Dubricius (Dyfrig, ca. 450–ca. 530) owned an estate called Inis Ebrdil in south Wales. Seeking the place to build a monastery, he found a white sow and her piglets, which he took as an ostentum to build there. They called the monastery Mochros, "the swine moor" (Baring-Gould and Fisher 1907–1913, II, 366). In Alsace around the year 660, St. Arbogast (whose name means "swine spirit"), founded the monastery of Ebersmünster in the Forêt de Haguenau, because of the same ostentum. In the sixth century the Welsh king Gwynllyw was converted to Christianity and decided to build a church. He searched around and found a white ox with a black spot on its forehead. This was the omen, and there on the hill where it stood, the church of St. Wooloo was built (Baring-Gould and Fisher 1907–1913, III, 238).

According to old chronicles, also in sixth-century Wales the Celtic saints Cadoc, Dunwyd, and Tathan loaded their building materials onto a wagon and yoked up a pair of oxen. The location for their church was to be determined by where the ox wagon stopped. So they started the oxen off and allowed them to wander, pulling the wagon. It stopped on a high point between two woods, *Pen y ddau lwyn* (Pendoylan), and there the new church was built (Baring-Gould and Fisher 1907–1913, II, 386–87). In the Norse tradition the *Vatnsdœla Saga* tells how the Norwegian wise woman Heid told Ingimund, whose *hlutr* (portable sacred image) of the god Freyr had disappeared, that it would be found in Iceland. Ingimund sent two Finnish magicians there to locate the *hlutr*, which they did. But as they were unable to recover it for him, Ingimund emigrated to Iceland and founded a new hall called Hof on the site.

Fig. 10.1. Wolf with the head of St. Edmund, St. Edmundsbury Cathedral.

Locating the best place for a building was not restricted to churches and temples. There are spiritual house-site location practices recorded from all over northern Europe. Once the actual site was determined, it had to be tested to see if it was suitable. A person with "land wisdom" (Old Saxon *landwísa*) had to be consulted. Methods used by the practitioner included asking permission from the earth spirits, fairies, *landvættir, jordvättarne,* and so on. A south Slav divination used a wheel-shaped bread, rolled onto the site. If it fell on its upside, then the earth sprite had agreed it was a good place to build. If it fell upside down, then no building took place (Bächtold-Stäubli 1927–1942, III, 1558). The haunts of local spirits, such as standing stones and ancient mounds, had to be recognized and avoided. Houses were not to be built blocking fairy paths or spirit paths, or where the Wild Hunt was known to ride, so a local knowledge of these was necessary for the locator. There were prohibitions against building at places where predators ate their prey or where animals were slaughtered, sites where bones had been dug up, or where there was a boulder too large to move. Places where once houses had stood, but had burned down, were avoided. Locations where livestock lay down to sleep, or where a lucky object had been found, were considered favorable. Places where strong crosswinds were prevalent (wind corners) were avoided. Building over a spring of water was not recommended. The locator had to camp out on the site for a Thursday or Friday night to determine what the nature of the place was (Honko 1962, 189).

An Estonian custom placed stones on the site. If, after three days, there were worms beneath them, then the site was viable. In Iceland the site of a new house was measured three times. If the measures were the same each time, then building could proceed. In the Faroe Islands a magnetic compass was taken to the site. If the compass gave a false reading, "out of line," this was an indication that the *huldu* (hidden) spirits there had refused permission to build (Bächtold-Stäubli 1927–1942, III, 1558). Direction was important. Traditional houses took the prevailing winds into account, if possible. Of course, a new house that was a continuation of a row of houses followed the orientation of the others, whether or not the first house had been oriented properly or not.

Certain evil spirits were associated with certain winds at certain times of the year, and it was best not to have to contend with them.

In some places the site of the house and garden was marked symbolically and magically by ploughing a single furrow sunwise between four corner markers right around the boundary. The boundary ditch was a deepening of the *sulcus primigenius,* the primal furrow. In Estonia and Finland a cross was dug in the earth on the site before building commenced (Honko 1962, 190). A tradition in eastern England is that after the ground where the house is to be built has been cleared of vegetation, it should first be swept with a nine-bramble sprite flail, then again with a besom of birch twigs on an ash stave made especially for the purpose. After use, both flail and broom must be burnt, for once a broom has swept away harmful influences, if it is not destroyed, it can be used magically to cause harm. In many cultures a sacrifice was made when a building was commenced, and the remains of the sacrifice buried in the first posthole or beneath the foundation stone.

Fig. 10.2. Carving of bound sacrificial victim beneath the font of Castle Frome church, Herefordshire, England.

Foundations laid in blood were believed to make the building stand firmly (Howlett 1899, 30). In his *Deutsche Mythologie* Jacob Grimm noted that in former times it had been considered necessary to build living animals, even human beings, into the foundations of buildings. Such foundation deposits have been discovered in places too numerous to list. Horses were significant in the north, as detailed below. Not only animals were put down at the foundation ceremonies. Excavations of the sites of ritual centers in Scandinavia unearthed foundation offerings in the form of pieces of gold foil embossed with images. In Sweden at Helgö, twenty-six gold pieces were found, while at Maere in Norway nineteen were found in the postholes of a building that existed on the site before a Christian church was built there (Lidén 1969, 23ff.). Similar embossed gold foil images are known in Germany as far south as Konstanz. Clearly they were sacred offerings placed in the earth during the rites and ceremonies of foundation to give the building spiritual protection. In the thirteenth century the Grand Master of the Teutonic Order placed a golden cross in the ground at Romowe in Old Prussia as the foundation of the church built where the felled sacred oak of the Pagans had stood. There is a tradition in Germany that sprigs of the juniper tree (Savin, *Juniperus communis*) should be laid ceremonially in the foundations of a building to ward off future disharmony among the people living there. The day of the week and the phase of the moon were also taken into account. In Germany building should not start on a Monday, nor should one begin to build a chimney on a Friday (Bächtold-Stäubli 1927–1942, III, 1562).

HORSE BURIAL, HORSE REMAINS, AND BONES IN BUILDINGS

The horse had preeminence as the most sacred animal in the northern tradition. The oldest Norse law texts indicate that the horse was the most important sacrificial animal in public rites and ceremonies (Carlie 2004, 124). Human burials containing horses and parts of horses took place widely in northern Europe in Pagan and later times (Cross 2011). Horsemen and horsewomen were accompanied to the grave by their sacrificed horses, and certain medieval aristocratic funerals featured the slaughter of the deceased's horse. Such was the case in 1216 at the funeral of King John of England and in 1378 for the funeral of the Holy Roman Emperor Karl IV. When the French nobleman Bertrand du Guesclin was buried at St. Denis in 1389, his horses were sacrificed after being blessed by the Bishop of Auxerre. The tradition continued in military circles. In 1499 *Landsknechte* mercenary soldiers sacrificed a horse to mark the end of the Swabian Wars. At Trier in the Rhineland in 1791, the horse of General Friedrich Kasimir was buried with him in his grave, and at the funeral of Charles Davis, Queen Victoria's leading huntsman at Sunninghill in England in 1866, his horse was shot and its ears cut off and buried with the huntsman in the churchyard of St. Michael and All Angels.

It is notable that Saxo Grammaticus (ca. 1200) recorded the northern practice of setting up the head of a horse: "so he first put on a pole the severed head of a horse that had been sacrificed to the gods, and setting sticks beneath displayed the jaws grinning agape" (Saxo 1905, 209). This was the *niðstöng* (scorn pole), set up with the horse's head facing the house of the magician's enemy. Functionally, the *niðstöng* is the same as the apotropaic carved heads on ships' prows. On land the intention of the *niðstöng* was to drive away the *landvættir* and render the land of one's enemy *álfreka* (defiled, spiritually dead; literally a "driving away of the elves"). According to Icelandic Pagan belief and much later tradition in East Anglia, it was recognized that at places where helpful sprites of the land (e.g., the Icelandic *landvættir*) have been driven away deliberately, the land is spiritually dead. In Pagan Iceland the word *álfreka* was used, and this is the common technical term used today in English (in East Anglia, it is *gast* land, "ghost land"). When such places are no longer tended by their spiritual guardians, inevitably they will become barren; animals and people living there will decline and die.

Traditional buildings in lower Saxony have gables in the form of two opposed horses' heads that are an overlapping continuation of the barge boards (*Windbretter*) beneath the roof at the gable end (Von Zaborsky 1936, 279–87). A horse's head was used in Germany to prevent witches from entering a house (Bächtold-Stäubli 1927–1942, 1, 143ff.). Horse skulls were deposited beneath and inside many buildings in northern

Europe, sometimes in large numbers (Hayhurst 1989, 105–7). For example, forty horse skulls were neatly laid in ranks under the floor in a seventeenth-century house in Bungay, Norfolk, England (Mann 1934, 253–55), and in Helsinki Old Town, Finland, a horse skull was discovered in 1993 beneath the north wall of a sixteenth- or seventeenth-century outbuilding (Hukantaival 2009, 350–56). In eastern England, W. H. Barrett recalled in the 1960s a foundation rite his uncle performed when building a chapel in the remote fenlands in the 1890s. During the digging of the foundations of a Primitive Methodist chapel at Black Horse Drove, Barrett was sent to buy the head of a horse from

Fig. 10.3. Primitive Methodist Chapel, Black Horse Drove, Cambridgeshire, England, site of the last known horse-head foundation rite.

a knacker's yard. It was brought to the site, and Barrett's uncle located the center of the site with a stake, dug a trench, opened a bottle of beer, and put the head in the trench. Then he poured some beer over the head, and the builders all had a drink of beer before burying the head under bricks and mortar to make the foundation (Porter 1969, 181). The function was to bring good luck and keep the witches away.

A practice of stable-building magic was recorded in the nineteenth century at Kiiminki, Finland. A horse made from alder wood was made when a new stable was built. It was covered with a blanket belonging to a woman who had recently given birth, The horse's eyes were marked by the woman's blood. A mixture of barley grains and quicksilver (mercury) was placed in front of the alder horse in a basket, and the whole assemblage was buried under the threshold of the new stable to protect the building and its horses. If the alder horse is inverted, it will kill the horses in the stable. If a thief steals the alder horse and puts it under his or her stable, the protection and luck is transferred. A means of destroying the good fortune of the stable is to steal the alder horse, carry it around the perimeter of the pasture, then bury it upside down by an anthill to the north of the field. Then the horses pastured there will die, and the only remedy is to abandon the stable and build a new one in a different location (Hukantaival 2009, 350–56).

The Museum of Cambridge has a number of horse fragments recovered from old buildings, both from Histon: half a jawbone found bricked into a chimney and a leg bone from another chimney. Another horse leg bone was found in 1959 in the building that houses the museum, the former White Horse Inn. In the nineteenth century, beneath part of the Norman gatehouse of Bury St. Edmunds Abbey, twenty-one skulls were found. Twenty were wolf skulls, and one was that of a wolfhound. Bones were a building material in former times, and floors were made from them, such as in a house at Fulbourn, Cambridgeshire, whose hall floor was of sheep bones (Evans 1971, 200). But clearly cats, dogs, chimney bones, and horse skulls were not structural materials.

From early times, however, the bones of large whales were used to build houses. In his 1655 description of the north, Olaus Magnus wrote that people constructed houses erected from whole whale ribs. After the whales had been defleshed, the skeletons were left to the weather until they were totally disarticulated, cleaned, and whitened. Then they were taken to a suitable place and erected like a cruck house, where the walls and roof are integral. The structural bones were covered with suitable material and smoke holes left in the roof ridge or at the sides. Internally the house was divided up into separate rooms. Doors were made from whale skin leather. The remains of a few houses of whalebone existed until recently in Greenland, Ireland, England, and Germany, mostly at ports where whaling had been a major concern (Redman 2004, *passim*).

TOPPING OUT AND CONSECRATION

The completion of the roof is the magical act of enclosure. There are traditional rites and ceremonies for this still performed in many parts of Europe. In Germany, Switzerland, and Austria, it is the *Richtfest* or *Hausräuchi,* which is best performed on a Saturday. Before the final topping out, the timbers were hit with tools, chains were rattled, and a general *Hillebille* (hullabaloo) was made to chase away evil spirits. A fir tree covered with ribbons or a garland of flowers was raised to the roof with singing and rejoicing. The *Bauherr* (master) of the carpenters, dressed in ceremonial clothes, hammered in the last nail. At the end a glass or a bottle was thrown from ground level over the roof. If it did not break, this was a bad omen (Bächtold-Stäubli 1927–1942, III, 1564, 1570–1571).

From ancient times, topping out involved the completion of the roof ridge and the installation of any sacrificial or apotropaic objects. Gable ends and roof corners of traditional buildings are protected by various talismanic images, such as carved dragon's heads on Norwegian stave churches, gargoyles on stone churches, and hip knobs, horse's heads, and roof-ridge figures on vernacular buildings. They are said to ward off the evil spirits of the air, and keep the building safe. In the year 517 Pope Gregory I gave an edict against exhibiting the heads of sacrificial animals in the Germanic lands, but the custom of setting up animal heads on buildings was never abolished. There is a record of a sheep skull erected on an upper corner of a house at East Baldwin on

Fig. 10.4. Heads of livestock and figure of Béél, Belsen,
Baden-Württemberg, Germany.

the Isle of Man to overlook a chapel opposite (Hayhurst 1989, 106). Skulls with antlers are still set on buildings in districts where hunting takes place. Ancient stone buildings incorporate the heads of animals, a practice that appears to be a reminiscence of the use of sacrificial beasts. The early medieval church at Belsen, Baden-Württemberg, Germany, shown in figure 10.4, has heads of cattle, sheep, and pigs, and the image of a being known as Béél.

Christian rites were incorporated into the rite of entry, with a priest saying prayers and using salt and holy water. Salt, pepper, and sometimes bread was strewn upon the window ledges. Moving in should not take place during a waning moon or a new moon, and an animal such as a cat, rabbit, or hen was sent in first. This was because of the common belief that the first to enter a new house would die within a year, or in the second year at the latest. People had to enter with full hands, so they would never be short of food, and in the state of Baden, the rhyme *"Glück ins, Unglück raus!"* (In with luck, bad luck—get out!) was recited (Bächtold-Stäubli 1927–1942, III, 1566).

BUILDING DEPOSITS

Artifacts and Animals

Despite the relatively large number of artifacts found within the fabric of old buildings and reported, they have all been random discoveries. They are few in number, and often their provenance is poorly documented. Perhaps the largest class of objects is shoes. There is a very large collection in Northampton of old shoes discovered in this way. Above a fireplace in the seventeenth-century Long House at Walsworth, Hertfordshire, were deposited a mummified cat and rat, and in the ceiling of a ground-floor room, a shoe, a shoe iron, three marbles, two buttons, two coins, and a pair of scissors. In 1981 at Billericay Hospital, Essex, a cache of magical items was discovered in the roof. It contained two human figures made from rags, a notched wooden tine, a piece of coal, and ruminant bones, including part of a jaw with teeth and the head of a thigh bone. The items appeared to date from the 1850s, when the hospital was a workhouse (Simon Walker, personal communication). Around 1940 a human figure made of clay or putty was discovered on a beam in the Cambridge University Anatomy School, a building completed in 1938. M. Hume told Cambridge folklorist Enid Porter that the senior laboratory men knew of the figure and were protective toward it as a safeguard. It was still there in 1962 but subsequently disappeared (Porter 1969, 397–98).

Whole animals were deposited in places where they dried out and became naturally mummified. In a study the author conducted in the 1980s (unpublished), more than fifty examples of dried cats were found in England alone, though there were also examples from Ireland, France, Germany, the Netherlands, and the United States. Oral tradition explains that dried or naturally mummified cats were tied up and put in place alive and left there to die. They were put there to ward off fire and vermin. To remove them from their resting place brings bad luck on the house. A cat found in 1971 in the roof of an 1820 watermill at Sudbury, Suffolk, had its feet bound together with string. The press recounted the trail of bad luck that followed in the wake of its travels before being replaced (Groves 1991, 69). Another dried cat with bound legs was found in a boarded-in part of the roof space at Compass Cottage in Baldock, Herfordshire (Simon Walker, personal communication).

In the early 1980s a mummified cat found in the Eagle Inn in Cambridge was shown to the author by the craftsman who discovered it during refurbishment work. Another mummified cat was in the author's possession, having been discovered in an eighteenth-century barn at Newport, Essex. It was kept in the workshop of Runestaff Crafts and disintegrated in 1996 when the workshop was blown down in a storm.

Fig. 10.5. Mummified cat from the roof of a barn in Newport, Essex, England.

The skull, recovered subsequently, showed a puncture wound that appeared to indicate that the cat was killed by a blow to the head before being deposited on a roof beam. It is clear that far more cats than dogs ended up as building deposits. An unusual instance was at the Carlton public house in Leigh-on-Sea, Essex, in 1984, when a mummified whippet dog was discovered beneath the floor of stables built in 1898. The belief that it is bad luck to move such an animal led to its ceremonial reburial in a wood-lined grave, with sprigs of yew and thyme, and a message to the dog apologizing for disturbing it (Saward and Saward 1984).

BONES

Toad and Frog Magic

There is a large body of magical lore about toads and frogs. Pliny, in his *Natural History* (ca. 77 CE) mentioned the *rubetiæ*, toads that lived among the brambles and briars, whose bones could be used magically. If the little bone in its left side was put into boiling water, Pliny claimed, it could procure love and cure mad dogs. If the little bone from the right side was put into the water, it would become cold and could never be made hot again unless the bone was taken out. If the right-side bone was bound to a sick person by a snakeskin, it cured the quartan, and restrained love and lust (Pliny 1989, bk. 32, chap. 18). A ritual for finding the magic toad bone is the central feature of British toadmanry. It is mentioned in connection with witchcraft in *The Discoverie of Witchcraft* by Reginald Scot (1584). Medieval bestiaries asserted that the toad is a venomous animal, fatal to humans. Its head was believed to contain a talismanic stone with the power to heal all kinds of venomous bites and sores upon the human body (Simpkins 1912, 357). The stone was boiled in water, then applied to the afflicted part. What passed for toadstones were identified in modern scientific taxonomy as the palatal teeth of the fossil fish *Lepidotus* (Ettinger 1939, 151). In German tradition, the *Krotenstein* ("toad-stone") is a fossil echinoid.

Toad and frog bones played a significant role in British country magic. A person who had performed the ritual for finding the magic bone was called a toadman or toadwoman. Possessors of the toad or frog bone claimed magical powers over fellow creatures, both animal and human. It was particularly associated with horsemanry, the bone giving a man the power to control any horse, however vicious it might be (Burn 1914, 363–64). The magic bone was obtained by a specific ritual. The would-be toadman or toadwoman would catch a frog or toad and kill it. Then it was defleshed, either by allowing it to rot naturally or by burying it in an anthill. Once it had decayed, leaving only the skeleton, the bones were carried to a stream running north–south. The bones were floated in the running water, and a bone that appeared to turn against the current and float upstream was the magic bone (Scot 1584, 6, 7; Parsons 1915, 37). Different accounts of the ritual specify different times and days to perform it: on the full moon (Porter 1969, 56; Evans 1971, 217–19), on the new moon, or on St. Mark's Eve (Burn 1914, 363–64; Roper 1883, 794). A version of the rite was called *The Water of the Moon* by the Norfolk horseman Albert Love (Evans 1965, 217–18). A person who has conducted this ritual "has been to the river." This was said of visiting ploughmen who performed unexpectedly well in ploughing matches, or a surprisingly accurate visiting darts player in a pub.

The toad bone was said to give toadmen power over not only horses, but also cattle, pigs, and women, and the toadwomen power over horses, cattle, pigs, and men. Lincolnshire folklorist Mabel Peacock noted that the toad bone could hypnotize all sorts and conditions of creatures at the will of its owner (Peacock 1901, 169). The bone also gave the power to steal without getting caught, because toadmen and women could gain entry to places that were closed to others. There was a saying from the Fenland of eastern England, "No door is ever closed to a toadman" (Pattinson 1953, 425). There are a number of accounts of toadmen gaining access; one from 1911 tells of a head horseman who claimed the ability to make locked doors fly open by throwing his cap at them (Randall 1966, 110–11). Another used the heart of a frog to enable him to go through the small holes cut in barn doors to allow cats access, so that he could steal corn (Rudkin 1933, 199). Going out of the sight of men—invisibility—was another attribute of the bone owner. A related technique of invisibility using animal parts was published by William Singer in Scotland in his 1881 book about the Miller's Word and horsemanry. This "coat of darkness" involved shooting a black crow over the shoulder and taking certain objects from the crow's brain (Singer 1881, 12). Black cats and crows featured in invisibility magic in other parts of Europe.

BOTTLES, HEARTS, AND PINS

Magically trapping and binding someone's spirit into a bottle or another sealed container, thereby stealing his soul, makes him dispirited. We say that someone has "lost her spirit," or that someone "drove his spirit away." Techniques for conjuring and imprisoning people's spirits are a universal theme in European witchcraft, American hoodoo, and other magical traditions. There are traditions of trapping spirits and sealing them in a container so they can do no more harm, or so they can be used for magical purposes by their owners (Thompson 1934, 138). The bottle is the most common instrument of this. This concept seems to underlie the apotropaic use of sealed jars and bottles deposited beneath thresholds and in buildings for magical purposes. In England they are known as "witch bottles," and the most characteristic is the "Greybeard" or "Bellarmine." The latter name refers to Cardinal Bellarmine (1524–1621), a Roman Catholic persecutor of Protestants in the Spanish Netherlands, though the bottle jugs were being made for a generation before the cleric ran the Spanish Inquisition in Holland. They were made from around 1500 to 1700 in the Rhineland and shipped to England. They are squat, brown, salt-glazed, round-bellied stoneware vessels, commonly five to nine inches in height. On the front of the neck, a bearded face is imprinted.

Witch bottles contained pins or nails and urine in addition to other organic materials (see Bunn 1982, 5; Massey 1999, 34–36). One found at Ipswich, Suffolk, contained a heart-shaped piece of felt, stuck with pins. A large proportion of discovered witch bottles came from old inns, possibly because the large numbers of people constantly coming and going made additional magical protection necessary. In 1908 the folklorists Gutch and Peacock reported an example of bottle magic from Lincolnshire:

A few years ago, in pulling down an old house in a neighboring village,* a wide-mouthed bottle was found under the foundation, containing the heart of some small animal [it was conjectured a hare], pierced as closely as possible with pins. The elders said it had been put there to "withstand witching." Some time after, a man digging in his garden in the village of Yaddlethorpe came upon the skeleton of a horse or ox, buried about three feet beneath the surface, and near to it two bottles containing pins, needles, human hair, and a stinking fluid, probably urine. The bottles, pins, and so forth came into my possession. There was nothing to indicate the date of their interment except one of the bottles, which was of the kind employed to contain Daffy's Elixir, a once popular patent medicine. The other bottle was an ordinary wine pint. At the time when these things were found, I mentioned the circumstance to many persons among our peasantry; they all said that it had "summut to do with witching"; and many of them had long stories to tell, setting forth how pins and needles are a protection against the malice of the servants of Satan. (Gutch and Peacock 1908, 96)

The nails and hearts found in witch bottles are part of a wider magical practice, as they were put in chimneys along with other magical objects. H. C. Agrippa noted that images were sometimes hung in a chimney over the smoke (Agrippa 1993 [1531], II, XLIX). For example, in a chimney of Shutes Hill Farmhouse at Chipstable in Somerset, England, a bullock's heart pierced with nails and thorns was discovered in 1892. With it was "an object, said to be a toad, also stuck with thorns" (Ettinger 1943, 246). The function of this kind of magic was described by a writer in *The Times* (March 5, 1917), who noted, "a sheep's heart pierced with pins and nails to break the spell of a black witch . . . was prepared by an old woman who practiced in London as late as 1908." It was hung in the chimney to carry out its function. A number of unusual and even unique artifacts used in building magic are in the possession of private individuals. In the author's possession

---

*This was probably the village of Messingham.

Fig. 10.6. Magical artifacts: Cambridgeshire witch bottles and ceramic model church found in chimney at Histon, Cambridgeshire, England.

is a ceramic model church, roughly finished with a dark brown glaze, measuring five by four by two inches (127 × 102 × 51 mm). It was discovered up a chimney of an old house in Histon, Cambs. The model church fell upon a chimneysweep who was cleaning the chimney, so was reputed to be unlucky. It is likely that it was made as an apotropaic object, the church representing sacred power, put in the chimney to prevent entry of evil spirits and bad luck.

11

The Craft and Magic of Buildings

In 1210 the poet Geoffrey de Vinsauf wrote in his *Poetria Nova*, "If a man has to lay the foundations of a house, he does not set his hands to work in a hurry. It is the inner line of the heart that measures out the work in advance. The inner man works out a definite scheme of action. The imagination designs everything before the body performs the act. The pattern is first the idea, then the physical reality." Successful construction of anything can only be achieved through harmonious cooperation. There is no place for destructive competition in the achievement of the work. For through peace and concord small things increase; through discord great things diminish. Traditional crafts always take the time necessary to accomplish the task. Apprentices are taught not to hurry or skimp the work just to finish the job quickly. Something that is nearly right is wrong.

Timber-frame buildings were not made on site, but as prefabricated frames made by carpenters working in a yard at a saw pit. As the timbers were measured, cut, and planed to size, they were assembled on the ground as individual frames. Four types of frames (plates) were created: ground frame (sill), wall frame, floor frame, and roof frame. When frames were assembled at the carpenters' yard, care was taken that the side intended

Fig. 11.1. Timber-frame buildings, Shrewsbury, England.

to face outward was laid facing up, not touching the ground. The outer face of the timbers of a building should never have touched the ground. Also, all vertical timbers were erected in the direction they grew.

The only exception to this was the "dragon post" supporting an overhanging corner, which was erected with the lower part of the tree uppermost. Overall measurements in traditional northern carpentry were taken over the outside "face edges." Unlike the craft of stone masonry, whose internal dimensions define the geometry, the distances between edges define carpenters' techniques.

Design and production of a timber-frame building is not a simple matter. The early art of line involved drawing out the pattern to be cut, full size, upon a flat surface. Outdoors, this is called the framing ground; indoors, the tracing floor. In France this surface is called *épure* (Faucon and Lescroart 1997, 77–79). Each shape is drawn simply with a straightedge, line, and compasses. By these means, basic geometries and harmonic proportions can be achieved. One or the other of the two basic geometrical systems of building—known by their Latin names of *ad triangulum* (geometry according to the triangle) and *ad quadratum* (to the square, in German *acht ort*)—is selected as appropriate. The timber is worked directly from the pattern on the ground, without any drawing on the wood itself. The timbers were numbered, and special carpenters' marks indicated where they fitted in the frame and how they were to be jointed to the adjoining timbers. Then they were transported to the building site and erected. The remains of timber buildings excavated at Trelleborg in Denmark show the high level of geometric accuracy of the late-tenth-century carpenters who built the castle (Nørlund 1948).

A medieval example of *ad triangulum* design is the Rathaus (town hall) at Markgroningen, Baden-Württemberg, Germany, circa 1450, is constructed in *Allamannic fachwerk*. Its ruling geometry is based on equilateral triangles. The ground plan is based on two equilateral

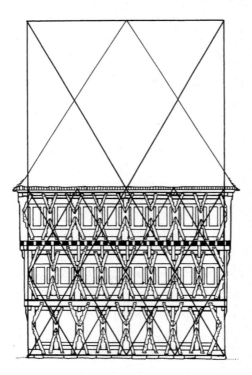

Fig. 11.2. *Ad triangulum* geometry of the timber-frame Rathaus at Markgroningen, Baden-Württemberg, Germany, ca. 1450.

triangles centered on the outside of a central pillar. The height of the Rathaus is equal to half its external length, measured from the outside faces of the sill (ground frame) (Rohrberg 1981, 82–83). The placement of significant features, such as the center line of the middle story, are determined by the art of line. In the same region as Markgroningen, the medieval fachwerk town halls at Besigheim, Esslingen-am-Neckar, Kaye, and Strümpfenbach all have the same geometric ruling principles (Rohrberg 1981, 53–55).

For over eleven hundred years in northern Europe, buildings have been transported by ship over long distances. In the early medieval period, the first Norwegian settlers of Iceland (870–930 CE) shipped prefabricated holy buildings across the North Atlantic. *Eyrbyggja Saga* tells how the *goði* Thorólf Mostur-skeggi dismantled his temple in Norway, dug out the earth beneath it, and had them shipped to Iceland. When the ship drew near the coast, Thorólf ordered the high-seat pillars to be thrown overboard so that the location could be divined where the temple would be reerected. On one of the pillars was an image of the god Thor. The tidal currents carried the pillars ashore, and at that point Thorólf had the carpenters reerect the dismantled Norwegian temple (*Eyrbyggja Saga,* chap. 4). The *Laxdæla Saga* (chap. 74) recalls that at Trondheim in the reign of King Olaf (1015–1030), Thorkel Eyjólfsson made a church for transportation to Iceland.

The Norse practice of making large prefabricated timber structures was carried on by the Normans in their invasion of England in 1066, when the forces of William of Normandy shipped a timber castle across the English Channel. They assembled it at a strategic position shortly after they began their conquest of England. The prefabricators of the Norman castle in 1066 were clearly master carpenters of the highest order, skilled in geometry and measurement. In later times it was commonplace to move timber frame buildings from one site to another. Because they were prefabricated structures, fully numbered and marked, they could be disassembled and reassembled (see West and Dong, 177–79). The Postgate Farm heck post (see page 187) dated 1664 in a building of 1784 indicates transference of timbers considered to be important from building to building, similarly to what is described in

Eyrbyggja Saga. In the nineteenth century, two medieval stave churches were dismantled and exported from Norway: the church from Vang was taken to the Sudeten Mountains region (now in Poland) and reerected at Karpacz, and another timber church was removed to Hedared in Sweden. Three other stave churches were relocated inside Norway: one was removed from Fortun to Fantoft by the Kjøde family, and two others, from Gol and Holtålen, were dismantled and reerected at the open-air museums of Borgund and Trøndelag (Gielzynski, Kostrowicki, and Kostrowicki 1994, 133; Valebrokk and Thiis-Evensen 1994, 75, 89).

WINDMILLS

Water mills existed in the north long before the invention of windmills, which was a major technological breakthrough. Vertical windmills—mills with sails that rotate in a vertical direction on a horizontal wind shaft—appeared first in the north of France during the twelfth century (Notebaart 1972, 96). The original windmills were post mills, timber-frame structures pivoted on an upright mast, which in turn was supported by a ground frame in the form of a cross connected to the post by supporting struts. The whole body of the mill (the *buck*) is supported at a single point on a crossbeam called the crown tree, upon which the mill can be turned to face the wind. The idea of the supporting mast may have been derived from shipbuilding, or from stave-church construction. With the new windmills, the old water-mill cosmology was still evident with the millstones, and to this was added a second cosmological element, the vertical post that supported the mill, arising from crossbeams supporting a trestle that supported the whole structure. To withstand the considerable forces upon the structure during operation, windmills must have a very robust structure. Hardwood timber is an ideal material, flexible enough to transmit stress without breaking the joints. The wind shaft transmits the energy from the rotating sails to the millstones through gearing. Like the water mill, a windmill cannot be run backward, because the sails are constructed to operate in one direction. The physical form of the buck may be derived from earlier timber storehouses and granaries, raised off the ground on posts to keep out vermin.

Millwrights built their mills at places specially chosen for optimal operation, and each mill was built specifically for the place where it was set up. The earliest extant windmills are designed to enable the miller to make the best use of the wind under all conditions. In the Netherlands, where the Dutch millwrights refined traditional windmills to their greatest level of sophistication, some mills were fitted with indicators of wind speed and direction. These were not the mechanical gauges later invented by engineers of the industrial revolution, but from the tradition of direct experience. They are practical tools that enable millers precisely to judge the prevailing conditions without any need to read an instrument. Experienced millers can determine changes in wind direction by the alterations in sound that the wind makes blowing through specially designed apertures in the sides of the mill, enabling them to turn the mill to face the wind when the wind direction alters.

Some mills have a small vane with rotating blades, called a *spinnertje* or *spinmolen,* a "spider mill" or "whirligig" that indicates both wind direction and speed. Often, it carries the name of the mill, for all windmills in the Netherlands and Flanders have names. Also, the gable ends of some post mills and most *wipmolen* and *paltrokmolen* (saw mills) have a hip knob called the *makelaar* (agent) at the opposite end of the roof from the sails. This is a carved post with apertures that make a whistling sound in the wind. The miller can estimate the wind speed from the sound coming from the *makelaar* and adjust the sails accordingly. The *makelaar* is related to some medieval weathercocks in England that had built-in whistles (Mockridge and Mockridge 1990, 35, 57). Winds are always unpredictable, and very strong winds such as the gale force winds called *blote bienen* (bloody bees) and *geknipte nagels* (clipped nails) by Dutch millers pose a material threat to windmills.

There is a code of sail positions in milling in Holland and Friesland. Of course, wind pump drainage mills had to operate at all times, especially when water levels were high. Mills milling corn or for other industrial purposes, such as sawmills and color-grinding mills, had a code by which the stopped position of the sails indicated the status of the work. Vertical sails indicated the working day was over. An X-form indicated that the miller had nothing to do and needed work. Other subtle

Fig. II.3. *Paltrokmolen* (sawmill) *De Gekroonde Poelenburg,* Zaanse Schans, Zaandam, the Netherlands, showing the *makelaar* on the rear gable.

positions from the vertical indicated the mill was out of service from malfunction, or because of a family event such as a wedding, death, or funeral (Notebaart 1972, 145). Deaths in the Dutch royal family are marked in the Netherlands to this day with black fabric on the sails of working windmills, and with stopped mills at the death position.

Mills and milling are not unexpectedly a repository of magical lore. Mills were the first heavy machinery that worked without animal or human power driving them. To people with no idea of how they worked, they must have appeared to run by magic. Mills are viewed almost as living entities, as the naming of them suggests. Both water mills and windmills are traditionally inhabited by a certain kind of house sprite, in Swedish called the *kvarngubben* (the old man of the mill). In Norway and Sweden these mill spirits were evil and controlling; they could stop a mill if it was operated against custom, such as at night or on a Sunday or another holy day.

In Britain there are nineteenth-century documents that deal with the magical powers of the Miller's Word, transmitted to those belonging to a secret grain-millers' guild. Those having the Miller's Word were said to have the power to stop or start a mill at will without touching it as well as stopping horses, influencing women, and becoming invisible (Singer 1881, 11; McAldowie 1896, 309–14). As with other craftsmen's mysteries, entry to the guild was by a terrifying initiation, and as in horsemanry, a man impersonating the Devil appeared to frighten the novice (Hutton 2001, 62). In 1920 Glasgow police superintendent John Ord wrote that the millers "taught their members nothing but evil." They were reputed to have powers to cause telekinetic phenomena; "members of the 'Millers' society claimed the power to raise and stop such proceedings at will," but, Ord commented, "So far as I could learn, there was nothing in their senseless tricks that could be attributed to the supernatural" (Ord 1920). Scottish magical rituals to stop a water mill from working had been revealed by William Singer in Aberdeen in 1881 in his book titled *An Exposition of the Miller and Horseman's Word, or the True System of Raising the Devil.* One rite was empowered by graveyard dirt and another by a bone from a man who had committed murder (Singer 1881, 10).

THE HOLY CORNER

A tradition that continues into the present day in house interiors is the holy corner. In central and eastern Europe and Scandinavia, the traditional living room of farmhouses is arranged on a diagonal axis. This is having the corner diagonally opposite the stove with built-in benches and the family table. Russian lore teaches that one must not sleep in the path used by the *domovoj* house spirit, which runs diagonally across the room (Ivanits 1989, 54). Archaeological evidence from Poland shows this to be a pre-Christian room division (Pokropek 1988, 46). The triangular sacred corner indoors parallels the eldritch land triangles such as the Scottish *Halyman's Rig* (see Scott 1885, 78–79; McNeill 1957–1968, I, 62). The rectangular, parallel system of room division is more recent. In Poland and Scandinavia the traditional layout was gradually overtaken by the parallel system between the seventeenth and twentieth centuries (Nodermann 1973, 328). In Sweden the diagonal arrangement was abandoned when standardized factory-made furniture superseded local carpenter-made furniture. Later the introduction of television sets effected a major reorganization of room layout.

But in Roman Catholic south Germany and Austria the diagonal tradition continues in the twenty-first century, where the built-in house shrine called *Herrgottswinkel* and *Herrgottseck* (Lord God's corner) or *heilige Hinterecke* (holy back corner) is located in the corner of the living room. In it are holy images, religious texts, crosses, and offerings. Salt and pepper are kept in a cupboard beneath the niche. In many modern houses, the *Herrgottswinkel* is represented by a crucifix attached in the corner near the ceiling on the diagonal. The equivalent in traditional Scottish farmhouses was the corner cupboard, protected by charms, such as bundles of rowan twigs (Corrie 1890–91, 76).

MAGIC OF THE HEARTH AND FIRE

The fireplace and the fire burning in it were considered to be the center and soul of the house. In building a house, particular care had to be taken of where the fireplace or stove was to be. The chimney required caution, too, even down to the day of the week it should be built (Bächtold-Stäubli 1927–1942, III, 1562). Objects were deposited beneath the hearthstone when it was laid, horse skulls having been found in Ireland and Wales (Hayhurst 1989, 106). The hearthstone on which the fire burned was protected with spiritual glyphs, crosses, circles or binding patterns to bring good fortune and ward off harm. In 1991 Alan Dakers reported a tradition from Shropshire on the border of England and Wales that such signs were made to prevent the Devil from coming down the chimney (Dakers 1991, 169–70). The Scots word for fire, *ingle,* recalls the rune name *ing.* In Scotland the ingle end of a room is the end where the fire is and the corner by the fireside is the *inglenook,* a name also used in England.

Tending the fire was a ritual practice in the past, and in more recent times some of these traditions have continued on as customs and superstitions, such as the belief that a fire should be kindled by only one person. If two people were to kindle a fire together, they would quarrel (Burne 1883, 275). In Kildare, Ireland, it was reported that

> during the whole month of May no fire was allowed to leave the house under any pretext not even "a live coal" could be handed over the half-door to light a passer-by's pipe, nor could anything be lent or given away out of the house; even if a neighbor or a stranger called for a drink of water, he or she would have to enter the house, help themselves, and then replace the vessel on the "dresser." (Omurethi 1906–1908, 446)

At Yule (midwinter) a special log was burned in the fireplace. In volume II of *The Book of Days* (1869), R. Chambers wrote:

Fig. 11.4. Yule Log 1869. The Library of the European Tradition.

"The burning of the Yule log is an ancient Christmas ceremony, transmitted to us from our Scandinavian ancestors, who, at their feast of *Juul*, at the winter solstice, used to kindle huge bonfires in honor of their god Thor. . . . This venerable log, destined to crackle a welcome to all comers, was drawn in triumph from its resting place . . . in the woods." The log was lit from the remains of the previous year's log, stored away for the purpose. So continuity was maintained (Chambers 1869, II, 735).

THE POTHOOK

The pothook is an implement from which pots, kettles, and cauldrons can be suspended over the household fire. Before the invention of stoves, this was the only way of boiling water and cooking food. Other English names for the pothook are *hanger, hake, chimney hook,* and the Scots *lum cleek.* In the German and French traditions, it is called *Hausherr* and *le maître de la maison,* both meaning "the master of the house." It is the locus of the house spirit (Bächtold-Stäubli 1927–42, IV, 1271). It is a very ancient implement, made of wood in very poor households that could not afford iron, and indeed all were wooden before the production of iron improved its effectiveness. It appears that yew (*Taxus baccata*) wood was very good for making pothooks, being hard, with a good tensile strength and durability (Johnson 1912, 362–63). The shape of the pothook is the Anglo-Saxon yew rune *eoh* (ᛇ), or *eihwaz* in the Common Germanic Futhark, so the pothook partakes of the runic meanings and powers. In Ireland pothooks were made from holly (*Ilex*) (Evans 1957, 68). The form of the pothook is linked in rune magic with the vertical axis of the world, the Norse cosmic tree Yggdrasill, which appears in some accounts as an evergreen yew tree (Thorsson 1984, 44).

The chimney is a vertical axis that links the interior of the house with the air above, the abode of aerial spirits that are warded off other parts of the house by apotropaic devices such as animal figures on the roof ridge, gable patterns, and hip knobs. Above the fire, at the place where the chimney enters the living space, the pothook serves to protect the interior of the house against the entry of harmful sprites down the chimney.

Fig. 11.5. Blacksmith-made pothook.

The shape of the pothook is also an apotropaic device for house protection. It appears in the English craft of pargetting patterns on the external plaster of house walls in East Anglia. There is a swastika made in pargetting work by a pothook pressed into the plaster on an old timber-frame house in Dunmow, Essex. The power of the pothook was used to empower the protective glyph.

Fig. 11.6. Pothook swastika in pargetting work. Great Dunmow, Essex, England.

Blacksmiths use the same form for wall anchors whose S shape is sometimes made in the form of a snake, or crossed to make a swastika. The noted folklorist Ella Mary Leather noted that at Garway in Herefordshire, western England, a blacksmith had asserted that they were made in that form to prevent lightning from striking the house (Leather 1912, 14–16). The pothook is a symbol of ownership of the house, and it was an implement of such spiritual meaning that oaths were sworn upon it (Lecouteux 2013, 73). In the Languedoc, the Eifel, Rhineland, Siebenbürgen, and Westphalia, the pothook played an important role in weddings, as the bride and groom had to make a threefold turn around the hook to ensure good luck. Where the hearth was against the wall, as in later buildings, and it was impossible to circle the pothook, the bride was swung at it three times (Bächtold-Stäubli 1927–42, IV, 1274; Lecouteux 2013, 74). The pothook was an emblem used in the heraldry of the Holy Roman Empire. The original function of the shield in combat is protective, and the emblem of the pothook upon it is an eminent symbol of ownership and protection. The arms of the von Bidenfeld family in Hessen; Schenk von Wetterstetten in Swabia; and Komanski in Silesia have the pothook (Appulm 1994, 95, 159, 131).

HORSESHOES, WALL ANCHORS, AND SPEER POSTS

Another archetypal object manufactured by blacksmiths is the iron horseshoe. In 1894 the folklorist George Day recorded the saying, "Good fortune will follow you if you pick up a horse shoe" (Day 1894, 77). That was in the days when almost all transport was by horse, and lost horseshoes could be found in everyday travels. Folklore collectors all over Great Britain have noted the tradition of setting up a horseshoe over a door or upon it, and this of course continues today, even when horseshoes have become rare items. The horseshoe must be nailed with its horns pointing upward, then bad luck or a witch cannot pass the threshold (Glyde 1872, 50). George Day saw a horseshoe nailed to the door of a cow house in Ilford, Essex, England, and asked the lad there the reason for it. He was told it was "to keep the wild horse away" (Day 1894, 77). In Dumfriesshire, Scotland, John Corrie noted, "A horse shoe nailed over the threshold was supposed to afford perfect immunity, neither witch nor warlock being able to enter a dwelling where this mode of protection had been adopted. By some a branch of rowan was looked upon with equal favor, and bundles of small rowan tree twigs were constantly kept suspended over the doorway, or attached to the box bed or the corner cupboard" (Corrie 1890–91, 76). The seven holes hammered in the classic design of horseshoes to take the nails were seen by members of the horsemen's society as the seven stars of the north (Rennie 2009, 160).

The analysis of signs considered magical and apotropaic in old buildings and artifacts is fraught with problems. Certain simple glyphs are used in most parts of the world, with varying origins and different accepted meanings. Apart from any magical significance, the character X stands for at least eleven different phonetic meanings in various western alphabets, as well as a Roman numeral, so context is crucial. In any particular identified system, then the meaning of signs is given in a "code of symbols, accompanied by traditions which explained them" (Lethaby 1974 [1891], 2). This applies in recognized religious iconography, heraldry, astrology, alchemy, certain currents of magic, and the working marks of particular trades and crafts. But signs and marks that appear in other contexts—such as on ironwork, pargetting, and brickwork, in knitwear and threshold patterns—are not always so readily interpreted unless they are in regions with a strong and well-understood tradition. Many such sigils in northern Europe are recognizable as runes.

A traditional door is the result of the combination of two crafts, carpentry and blacksmithing. The hinges, strap work, studding, and bolts of old outer doors often carry the blacksmiths' magical sigils hammered into the iron when it was hot. The act of striking the pattern into the metal is in itself a magical act of will, especially when accompanied by an incantation, such as when runes are "sung" into an artifact. The most frequently encountered blacksmiths' sigil is composed of crossbars enclosing an X shape. Sometimes they are accompanied by dots hammered in with a punch. These signs can be found on old

Fig. 11.7. Wall anchor with blacksmith's marks, Caister, Norfolk, England.

tools, weapons, and armor, as well as on door and window fittings. In Lithuania the X sign is apotropaic against lightning, as it is the sigil of Perkūnas, god of lightning and fire (Trinkūnas 1999, 70–71).

Wall anchors are the external anchor points of iron bars that bind the walls of old brick buildings and support internal floors. Frequently, they run from gable to gable and along floor lines. In Britain, the Netherlands, and Germany were specialized anchor smiths whose trade was to make the bars and end plates. The outer fittings are made from wrought iron, commonly S or X shaped, and sometimes two Ss were overlapped to make a curved swastika, which the folklorist Ella Mary Leather noted was apotropaic against lightning. The S-shaped ones resemble the pothook, though frequently the ends are forked, and sometimes the S had a head at one end in the form of a snake.

Fig. 11.8. S-form wall anchor. St. Ives, Cambridgeshire, England.

In Great Britain X- and S-form wall anchors are reputed to ward off lightning. Some wall anchors are in the form of characters, such as the initials of the owner, numbers for the date the building was constructed, or—in a few cases—merchants' and owners' marks. The port of Great Yarmouth on the coast of East Anglia was particularly noted for them.

Internal posts, known as speer posts or heck posts, with an X carved on them, are known from traditional houses in northern Yorkshire, England. They form the end posts of wooden screens next to the fireplace.

As with much of traditional art and magic, artifacts were just made without fuss and without record, so there is little information on how these apotropaic posts were made and empowered. Dated heck posts include one from 1664 (Postgate Farm, Glaisdale). However, the building where it is found dates from 1784, so if the year marked on the post is authentic, it may have come from an earlier building, perhaps

Fig. 11.9. X carved in the top of a speer post,
Ryedale, Yorkshire, England.

transferred there to maintain continuity with the old one. While there is no connecting evidence, heck posts clearly recall the high-seat pillars (*öndvegissulur*) in Norse halls and temples, marked with sacred signs, which were taken from place to place and installed in new buildings (see *Eyrbyggja Saga,* chap. 5). There is a record of a second cross being incised in an old heck post from Low Bell End. It was done by a local cunning man known as the Wise Man of Stokesly (Hayes and Rutter 1972, 93). In 1927 Bugle Cottage at Egton was rebuilt with a heck post reputedly made from rowan wood, a replica of an older one (Hayes and Rutter 1972, 89).

Today heck posts with incised X glyphs are generally called "witch posts," but this name is not traditional. There is no record of the name before 1936, when a heck post from an old house at Egton, Yorkshire, was presented to Whitby Museum as a "witch post." In 1870 and again in 1893, Canon Atkinson had donated heck posts to the Pitt Rivers Museum in Oxford, and they were not referred to as "witch posts," for the term does not appear in Atkinson's writings (Hayes and Rutter 1972, 87).

Related apotropaic signs on the roofs of houses can be found on timber hip knobs in England, the Netherlands, and Germany. In the former Dukedom of Minden in north Germany, the house *Geck* or *Geck-Paol* has three-dimensional X carvings, sometimes topped with a wooden "egg" (see Wirth 1934, VI, pl. 268, 3). Painted on farmhouse doorposts, sometimes incised as well, is the X pattern called *Stiepel* (Wirth 1934, VI, pl. 269, 1). In the Netherlands a similar form called *Steepelteeken* was traditional in the Ostmarsum district of Twente province (Propping 1935, 143). Today this pattern is often called the *Dag* sign, a name given it by Walter Propping in 1935 (Propping 1935, 144).

These signs are close to the magical blocker made of sticks or slivers of wood used to block paths to humans and spirits alike. Known as the *Schratterlgatterl* or *Schradlgaderl,* it was used in south Germany, and in the Tyrol (Austria and Italy).

Apotropaic patterns always interlink with each other, being made from available materials. Related sigils painted on door frames were recorded in Germany at Wietersheim-an-der-Weser and in Norway at

Fig. 11.10. Dag-rune shutters, Middelburgh, The Netherlands.

Fig. 11.11. *Schratterlgatterl*, Baden, Germany.

Frille, dated 1573 and 1788 respectively (Propping 1935, 145; Weiser-Aal 1947, 146). A traditional magic sigil called *Old Scratch's Gate* was used in East Anglia for the same purpose, but it was always chalked on doors or above openings in buildings.

OTHER APOTROPAIC DEVICES

It is a widespread folk belief that mirrors reflect not only visible light but also intangible spirits and energies. All over Europe are traditions of straight "spirit paths" along which, at certain times, travel dangerous inhabitants of the Otherworld. Like light, spirits travel in straight lines and unless something is done to stop them, they will enter dwellings whose entrances (windows and doors) are approached by lines of sight. To prevent this happening, various techniques are employed by those whose expertise it is to remedy bad places and ward off harm. Mirrors, often in the form of silvered glass balls, are placed at strategic points to reflect the perceived intrusion.

Fig. 11.12. Geomantic mirror made by Runestaff Crafts, England, 1990.

Witch balls are lustrous blown glass spheres around a foot (304.8 mm) in diameter, usually blue or green, but also of silvered clear glass. Their reflective quality comes from silvering the inside glass sphere with a metallic mercury mixture, the traditional ways of making mirrors. To prevent evil spirits entering the house, witch balls are hung in a window or in the window above the door in houses without leaded glass. In recent years, with a renewed interest in Chinese feng shui, octagonal *ba gua* geomantic mirrors have in some cases taken their place, having the same apotropaic function (see Lip 1979, 109–13). But mirrors and other reflective devices have one weak point. During thunderstorms they are believed to attract lightning, which was viewed in the past as a material thunderbolt. In Britain wall anchors in the form of an S were believed to ward off lightning from a building. In Normandy houseleeks were planted on the roof ridges of farmhouses for the same purpose. An eastern English way to try to keep lightning away from one's dwelling is to bury a toad in the middle of the garden, with others at the four corners. This is quincunx magic, covering an area by treating to four corners and the center. Bay trees planted around the garden, the skin of a seal, and eagle feathers are also antilightning charms (Jobson 1966, 112).

THE PENTAGRAM

The pentagram is an ancient apotropaic sign. It is also called pantacle, pentangle, pentagramma, Solomon's Seal, *Drudenfuss,* and the rempham. It is known from Lombardic and Alamannic sources before the year 700. Medieval and later folk magic gives the pentagram protective power over thresholds. Goethe, in his *Faust,* makes the demon Mephistopheles gain access to Dr. Faustus's house because the *Drudenfuss* is drawn inaccurately upon the threshold. A traditional English counting song known as "The Twelve Apostles" tells "Five for the symbol at your door," which was interpreted by folk song collectors Broadwood and Maitland as the threshold pentagram (Broadwood and Maitland 1893, 154–59). The pentagram has an important place in sacred geometry because the fivefold division of the circle is the starting point for the Golden Section ratio. Before the nineteenth century,

Fig. 11.13. Medieval gothic pentagrams carved on choir stall in St. Botolph's church, Boston, Lincolnshire, England.

the direction in which the pentagram pointed was not considered to be significant. The concept of the evil inverted pentagram was invented by followers of French magus Éliphas Lévi. The medieval choir stalls in St. Botolph's church at Boston, Lincolnshire, England, illustrated in figure 11.13 show the medieval use of the pentagram in this orientation, certainly not with evil intention. The pentagram at the centerpiece of a medieval rose window in Paderborn Cathedral in Germany is also oriented in that manner. The starfish is pentagrammic in shape and was used as a magical protection. The fish called *stella* (starfish) was to be fastened with the blood of a fox by a brass nail to the gate as a preventive against "evil medicines" (Agrippa 1993 [1531], I, XLVI).

HOUSE GLYPHS, SIGILS, AND SPELLS

When bricks began to be used in buildings, they were handmade and fired in wood-burning stacks, so they were not all the same color. Bricklayers made patterns in the walls they built, and a popular design was the diamond or *ing*-rune shape. The protective pattern called *God's Eye* and *Godsoog* on English and Dutch fishermen's ganseys (sweaters) is an array of five diamonds. The sigil was painted on wall plaques in fishermen's inns, with the motto "God sees you," warning the fishermen to behave properly when away from home. Traditional knitters from Arnemuiden used diamond motifs symbolizing prosperity that came from the brickwork of the buildings in the fishing port (Van der Klift-Tellegen 1987, 19, 36). In eastern England in the nineteenth century, bricks were being made on a large scale in different colors, so bricklayers chose contrasting colored bricks to make diamond and *ing*-rune patterns. A house in St. Ives, Huntingdonshire, is shown in figure 11.14.

Fig. 11.14. *Ing* runes in brickwork on Victorian house, St. Ives, Cambridgeshire, England.

On Twelfth Night in German-speaking countries, the Sternsinger ("star singers") go around to houses carrying a paper or wooden star on a pole. They sing an Epiphany carol, then one of them writes in chalk over the door a formula consisting of the initials of the Three Wise Men in the Nativity story, Caspar, Melchior, and Balthasar, with crosses between them and the year date on either side; for example: 20 C+M+B 15. This is said to protect the house and its inhabitants until the next Epiphany. Another German tradition is that if one draws crosses on the doors before Walpurgisnacht (May Eve, after sunset on April 30), the house is protected against witchcraft (Schmidt 1988, I, 93).

Fig. 11.15. C+M+B inscription 1999,
Schwäbisch Gmünd, Germany.

Written talismans and charms were attached to doorposts and lintels or hidden inside them as an alternative. In sixteenth-century Wales, clergyman Lewis Morgan of Aberedw was imprisoned for writing charms and putting them over doors (Simmonds 1975, 19). In England door charms were "supplied for a consideration by the fortune-tellers, astrologers, or 'wise men' of a neighborhood." Harland and Wilkinson recorded a text found over a door of a house near Burnley, northwest England. It read "Sun, Moon, Mars, Mercury, Jupiter, Venus, Saturn, Trine, Sextile, Dragon's Head, Dragon's Tail, I charge you all to gard this hause from all evils spirits whatever, and gard it from all Desorders, and from aney thing being taken wrangasly, and give this family good Ealth & Welth" [*sic*] (Harland and Wilkinson 1867, 62–63). Some charms were more literate, being written in Greek or Latin, or with magical alphabets, magic squares, and seals of planetary spirits. The Scots expression Arsé-Versé (English Arsy-Farcy) denotes a magic spell on the side or back of the house to ward off fire (Warrack 1988 [1911], 9). The dialect word "arsy" means "backward" so the spell refers to something written backward (as with wend-runes) or on the back side of the house. In Scotland an evil spirit called Quhaip was nevertheless protective, for it was supposed to haunt the eaves of houses on the lookout for evildoers (Warrack 1988 [1911], 436).

12

Magical Protection against Supernatural and Physical Attack

VIKING AGE MARITIME FIGUREHEADS

Early medieval ships in northern Europe carried removable images on the prow and stern posts. The dragons on Norse and Norman ships are the best known, serving to protect the ships against sea monsters and other evil denizens of the deep. Figureheads were removable so they could be taken from ships before docking or being dragged on shore, so that the land wights *(landvættir)* would not be frightened by them. Several old texts record the form and nature of these ships' figureheads, and they can be seen on the Bayeux Tapestry as well. They appear in the account of the death of the Norwegian king, Olav Trygvason, in the maritime Battle of Svolder in 1000 CE by Adam of Bremen (ca. 1080) and Saxo Grammaticus (ca. 1200) in his *Gesta Danorum* (ca. 1200) and in Snorri Sturluson's *Heimskringla*. These accounts tell of ships called the *Crane,* the *Long Serpent,* the *Short Serpent,* and the *Iron Ram.* The king's flagship had formerly belonged to a Pagan martyr tortured to death by Olav for refusing to become a Christian. This ship's prow had a gilded dragon's head and a crook shaped like a tail on the stern.

Before the sea battle in which the king's navy was defeated and Olav died, his enemies, the earl of Lade, Eirík Hákonarson, and the Swedish king Swein Forkbeard, were on their flagship and looking out for the flagship of Olav. King Swein is reported to have said that Olav was afraid of them so much that "he dare not sail with the dragon head on his ship." As well as their figureheads, important ships were identified by colored sails. The *Saga of Olav Tryggvason* recounts Eirik Hákonarson's attempts to identify the king's ship, in which he notes a ship with striped sails as belonging to Erling Skjalgson as opposed to the dragon's-wing sails of the king's vessel (*Saga of Olav Tryggvason,* chap. 101–111). Sixty-six years later, Duke William's ship *Mora* had a red sail.

The *Mora* was the flagship of Duke William of Normandy's invasion fleet in 1066. It had a special figurehead, and on top of the mast flew *Gonfanon,* the consecrated banner given to William by the pope to empower him in his attempt to overthrow the English king, Harold Godwinson. The figurehead of the *Mora* was a brass figure of a boy, holding a bow and arrow in his right hand, and blowing a horn with his left. The Bayeux Tapestry shows this figure set astern, but Wace's account sets it on the prow (Bruce 1856, 93). Removable figures could be set at either end of the ship, it seems. Other ships of the Norman invasion fleet had figureheads in the form of dragons, lions, and bulls. The Bayeux Tapestry shows the ships of the Norman invasion fleet drawn up on the shore of England at Pevensey, with all the figureheads removed. A ship shown still on the sea has its figurehead in place; another has it already removed. The sockets for the figureheads are clearly shown in the beached ships. The eleventh-century makers of the Bayeux Tapestry knew of the northern maritime practice, which was observed by Pagan and Christian alike.

MAGIC BATTLE FLAGS AND STANDARDS

Military flags and standards served to identify the army or unit in combat situations. They embodied the power, spirit, and ethos of the fighting force and were believed to bring it good fortune in battle. To capture the enemy's standard was a sign of victory; to lose one's standard, defeat. As long as the flag was flying, there was still fight left in the troops. A standard that became influential in the north was the dragon. This *draco* standard was adopted by the Romans from tribal warrior horsemen: the Alans, Sarmatians, and Dacians. The Persian and Parthian cavalry also flew dragons. It was described by Arrian of Nicomedia in *Ars Tactica* (137 CE) as a long sleeve made from pieces of dyed material sewn together. At the front was a hollow metal dragon's head, supported on a staff. The mouth faced into the wind, and the fabric body trailed behind and filled with air, giving the appearance of a dragon in flight. Trajan's Column in Rome depicts several Dacian examples of this standard. The Romans copied their enemies and introduced the *draco*. Cavalrymen carrying the banner were called *draconarii*. They are depicted in the *Strategikon,* a military manual of the time of the eastern Roman emperor Maurikios (reigned 582–602 CE). The legendary King Arthur was said to have a dragon banner of this kind; his father was Uther Pendragon, whose surname meant "head of the dragon." Anglo-Saxon kings also had dragon banners, such as the white dragon of Wessex. The flag of Wales today is a *Y Ddraig Goch,* a red dragon on a green-and-white background. It was made official in 1959.

Between the ninth and eleventh centuries, the Raven Banner was the standard of Viking Age forces. The *hrafnsmerki* was a flag that depicted a black raven. From contemporary images, it appears that the banner was triangular or semicircular. Its edge was adorned with tassels or ribbons. The *Orkneyinga Saga* tells how, in the wind, the raven appeared to flap its wings and fly. There are extant descriptive accounts of the Raven Banner, both its appearance and its use in battle. The *Anglo-Saxon Chronicle* for the year 878 records the capture from a Viking force of a *guðfani* (battle flag), called "Raven" by the army of Wessex in Devon, western England. The *Orkneyinga Saga* (chap. 11) tells how the Norse earl of Orkney, Sigurd the Stout, had a Raven Banner made by his mother, who was a *völva*. The magic banner would bring victory to the man it was carried before in battle, but the magic came at a price, for it would bring death to the actual standard-bearer.

At the Battle of Ashingdon in England in 1016, the army of King Cnut (Canute) had a white silk raven banner for their standard. Sturluson's *Heimskringla* recounts that Harald Hardrada's raven banner was called *Landøyðan,* "Land Waster" (destroyer of lands). It was clearly a magic banner, promising victory to those who carried it (*Haralds Saga Sigurðarsonar* 22). The banner's luck failed in 1066, when Harald Hardrada's invasion of England met with crushing defeat at the Battle of Stamford Bridge. The Bayeux Tapestry, commemorating the Battle of Hastings, the other famous battle of the fateful year 1066, has a depiction of a Raven Banner carried by one of Duke William's cavalrymen. For his invasion of England, Duke William of Normandy had the *gonfanon,* a personal banner that was given to him by the pope. Heraldically it was *argent,* with a cross *or* in a bordure *azure:* a gold (yellow) cross on a silver (white) background, surrounded by a blue border. This is shown on the Bayeux Tapestry, and it was carried in the Battle of Hastings, in which William was victorious.

A battle in which no fewer than four consecrated standards protected the warriors was fought at Alverton (now Northallerton) and was recorded by Richard of Hexham. It was fought "between the first and the third hours" on Monday, September 22, 1138. Northern England had been invaded by King David I of Scotland's army augmented by Pictish and Cumbrian contingents. They had devastated the northern part of England. The Archbishop of York called a crusade against the invaders, and a sacred standard was set up to call upon divine assistance and to serve as a rallying point. The carpenters brought a timber frame on wheels and erected a ship's mast on it. This magic vehicle was the "Standard." On the top of the mast they hung a silver pyx containing a consecrated host, and from cross arms four magic flags taken from the churches where they were kept: the banners of St. Peter the Apostle, St. Cuthbert of Durham, St. Wilfrid of Ripon, and St. John of Beverley. The latter had been carried in battle two hundred years earlier in 937 by King Æthelstan's English army at Brunanburh. At Northallerton, William of Aumale commanded the English forces, and the outcome was a total rout of the invaders, and the survivors of the battle were hunted down and killed. After taking possession of the booty, which was found in great abundance, the English warriors returned home and "restored with joy and thanksgiving to the churches of the saints the banners which they had received." Because of the wheeled mast, the battle has always been called the Battle of the Standard.

Some magic flags were reputed to have an eldritch origin that invested them with special powers. In Scotland the Mackays possessed an otherworldly flag presented to the clan by a fairy woman, and the Macleods preserved the *Fairy Flag of Dunvegan,* which was given to an ancient Macleod of Macleod on a visit to elfane (Carmichael 1911, 86). In eleventh-century England, Earl Siward of York was given a banner named *Ravenlandeye* by a spectral being whom he met on the seashore. Wearing a wide-brimmed hat, the mysterious being had the attribute of Odin. Siward, who fought against the Scottish king Macbeth, finally committed ritual suicide. On his deathbed he ordered his servants to dress him in his coat of mail and, holding his sword, take him up upon the walls of York. From there, he leapt to his death so that he might die like a man, not like a beast on a bed of straw. For many years the Raven Banner hung in St. Mary's church in York. The retired standards of the

Fig. 12.1. Apotropaic beasts around the door of Kilpeck church, Herefordshire, England, ca. 1150.

British military are hung up in churches today. Once its use in battle is over, the magic flag should be returned to its place of keeping, on sacred ground.

WIND VANES AND WEATHERCOCKS

Wind vanes are finely balanced artifacts that swivel on a fixed upright, driven by the prevailing currents of wind. The wind vane appears as the final rune of the first *ætt* in the Common Germanic Futhark. It is the rune *wunjo* (Anglo-Saxon *wyn*). It signifies the function of a wind vane that moves according to the winds, yet remains fixed in one place. Its reading is "joy," obtained by having a stable base but being in harmony with the surrounding conditions. A traditional motto depicted with a weathercock in seventeenth-century emblem books is *"officium meum stabile agitare"* ("it is my function to turn while remaining stable"). In the Viking Age, gilded metal weathervanes were mounted on ships, and similar ones were set up on stave churches in Norway. The Raven Banner had a similar form.

The origin of weathercocks in the north is uncertain. They may have a southern origin. Early records are few. A ninth-century weathercock is known from Brescia, Italy, where Bishop Rampertus had one erected on the San Faustino Maggiore church in 820 CE (Novati 1904–1905, 497). They were in use in Anglo-Saxon England, as in 862 CE when Bishop Swithun set a weathercock on Winchester Cathedral. (In England, St. Swithun's Day, July 15, is connected with the weather, as it carries folklore that warns of a rainy period of forty days afterward, if it should rain on that day.) According to Ekkehard IV's chronicle *Casus sancti Galli* (chap. 82), in 925 CE the monastery of St. Gallen had its weathercock stolen by Magyar invaders who climbed the tower to remove it. In France in the year 965, a gilded weathercock on the abbey church of St. Pierre at Châlon-sur-Sâone was struck by lightning (Martin 1903–1904, 6). Westminster Abbey in London is depicted in the Bayeux Tapestry, showing a man setting a weathercock on the top at its completion in 1065. Vanes and cockerels are not the only forms of traditional wind markers. A medieval saying from France tells us there are lions, eagles, and dragons on top of churches (Martin 1903–1904, 10). Swans are features of churches in parts of Germany, especially in Oldenburg and East Frisia (Goethe 1971, 7–19).

WOUND-PROOF MAGIC JACKETS AND BLOOD STANCHING

In the medieval history of the Norwegian kings, the *Heimskringla,* the *Saint Óláfs Saga* recounts an event in the Battle of Stiklastad (Stiklarstaðir) in Norway in 1031. The Norwegian farmers had risen in rebellion against King Óláf Haraldson's arbitrary rule and his religious policy, under which he had tortured several Pagan martyrs to death for refusing to become Christian. One of the ringleaders of the uprising, Thorir Hund, a devout Pagan, wore a magic reindeer-skin coat obtained from the "troll-wise Finns," which rendered him wound-proof; that is, invulnerable to edged weapons. In the battle the rebels led by Harek of Tjøtta (Hárekr ór Þjóttu) and Thorir fought their way through to the king and tried to kill him. The king struck Thorir Hund over the shoulders, but his sword appeared blunted and would not cut, and it seemed that smoke came out of Thorir's reindeer-skin coat. Björn, the king's marshal, then attempted to hit Thorir and, knowing he was wound-proof, turned his battle axe so that he could strike Thorir with the hammer end instead of the sharp edge. Thorir fell back injured but ran his spear through Björn. Then the king was killed (*Óláfs Saga Helga,* chap. 226–28). Scottish folklore tells of a magically protective jacket worn by magicians, the *warlock fecket,* that had to be woven from the skins of water snakes at a certain phase of the March moon (Warrack 1988 [1911], 656). A magical way of destroying a wound-proof man that features the number nine repeatedly is described in the legend of Lord Soulis, which is recounted in chapter 13.

The bloodstone is a traditional English remedy to stanch bleeding. According to East Anglian custom, one is hung around the neck on a red silk ribbon, tied with three knots at three-inch spacings. To activate a man's bloodstone, nine drops of women's blood are dripped onto it, and for a woman, nine drops of men's blood (John Thorne, personal communication). English bloodstones are not actually gemstones, but specially made glass beads. In the author's possession is an old bloodstone from King's Lynn, Norfolk, made of blood-red glass. A bloodstone recorded in 1911 was of dark green glass containing white and orange twists (Porter 1969, 83). Similar glass artifacts have been found attached to scabbards of Germanic swords dating from the first millennium CE. The magical function of a scabbard is recorded by Sir Thomas Malory in *Le Morte D'Arthur* (Malory 1472, bk. I, chap. XXIII), where King Arthur receives the sword *Excalibur* and a scabbard for it. But although the sword is invincible, the scabbard is even more valuable, because so long as he has it, he can never die from wounds. In 1865 George Rayson noted an East Anglian remedy against nosebleed, to wear a skein of scarlet silk around the neck, with nine knots tied down the front. The knots should be tied by a man for a woman, and vice versa. He made no mention of the bloodstone (Rayson 1865c, 217).

HLUTR AND ALRAUN

Images are part of many religions, and the Celtic, Germanic, Nordic, and Slavonic peoples had sacred images in households, at important places in the countryside, such as crossroads, in wayside shrines, and in temples. In Pagan times, devotees of gods and goddesses also possessed and venerated small images. Portable humanoid images were being made in the Palaeolithic era, but whether or not they were goddesses cannot be known. Small images of *Lares* (household deities) were certainly in existence in northern Europe in Roman times, along with other figurines. The *Lares* were kept in a house shrine, the *Lararium*. In what is now France, the seventh-century Christian *Capitularia Regum Francorum* condemned images made from rags, "the image which they carry through the fields." In Old Norse a portable image was called *hlutr*. The *Vatnsdæla Saga* mentions Ingimund's *hlutr* of the god Freyr, which disappeared and finally turned up in Iceland. Images such as these were destroyed or hidden when the Christian religion became dominant. Roots of humanoid form may have taken over from actual images as less obviously Pagan in nature.

Fig. 12.2. Alraun, from the author's collection.

There is a saying in Franconia, Germany, that if someone has unexpectedly good fortune he or she must "own an *areile*" (an *Alraune* or *mannekin*) (Lecouteux 2013, 134), a natural or artificially altered root of humanoid form, of which the mandrake is the best known.

The magic mandrake (*Mandragora officinarum*) is a member of the botanical family that includes the potato, tobacco, and woody nightshade species. It possesses a root that appears to resemble the human form, and in former times this was believed to shine at night like a lamp. The roots have two genders, man and woman, mandrake and womandrake. Because such a root resembles the human form, it is considered to be an earth sprite whose magical powers can be harnessed for the magician's use. Womandrake roots were used as charms by women to promote childbearing, to bring prosperity, and to bring lovers the objects of their heart's desire. Mandrake roots were also used in ceremonies to find out secrets and to locate lost property. The root of the mandrake resembles the roots of other plants, including deadly nightshade, white bryony, and bramble (blackberry). The white bryony

(*Bryonia dioica*) has a much dug-for root that was used magically in the same way as the much rarer and far more expensive mandrake root. In Norfolk, England, white bryony is actually called mandrake.

Because they were much sought after for their magical properties, artificial mandrake roots were made. In Germany they were called *Erdmannekin* or *Alraun,* and in Great Britain *mannikin.* In medieval Germany, carved wooden alrauns were made that had grains of barley inserted in the places where hair or a beard should be. The alraun was buried in sand for three weeks, after which it was dug up and the grains had sprouted, making the appearance of hair. In Britain a more sophisticated method was used. In *The Universal Herbal* (1832), we are told:

> The roots of Bryony grow to a vast size and have been formerly, by impostors, brought into a human shape, carried about the country, and shown for Mandrakes to the common people. The method which these knaves practised was to open the earth round a young thriving Bryony plant, being careful not to disturb the lower fibres of the root; to fix a mould, such as used by those who make plaster figures, close to the root, and then to fill the earth about the root, leaving it to grow to the shape of the mould, which is effected in one summer. (Green 1832, 201)

In 1832 this technique was seen as faking, but it appears to have been an old means of making a root effigy for magical purposes. Magic employs images of things and symbols of them to accomplish what the real thing can do (Agrippa 1993 [1531], II, XLIX). In his 1934 book *The Mystic Mandrake,* C. J. S. Thompson noted a report of a "manikin" made from a dried frog, with its head replaced by a root of *Alpina officianarum* (Thompson 1934, 122).

Real mandrake was used medicinally as an anaesthetic. Mandrakes were reputed to have the powers of rejuvenation and were used in love potions. In Britain, by the twentieth century the mandrake was obtained by the Wild Herb Men (the English rural fraternity of root diggers) only for horse doctoring (Grieve 1931, 510–12; Hennels 1972, 79–80). A medieval belief about the mandrake warned that it was dangerous to uproot the plant because to do so would bring certain death within the year. So magicians devised a technique to overcome this. They tied a dog to the plant and caused the dog to uproot it. But during the procedure, it was necessary to stop up one's ears, because when uprooted, the plant gave a hideous shriek, and hearing this horrendous sound was dangerous. Magically, an alraun gave the owner protection against bad weather, warded off the nightmare, and assisted women during childbirth. Like the pothook, the alraun was seen as the protector of the family. However, possession of the magic root was also dangerous, for at some point its luck would run out.

Alrauns had to be treated well, housed in a box, and wrapped in white linen or silk. If an alraun was not respected, it would shriek its disapproval. This is part of the tradition that "no mascot will bring good fortune to one who is unworthy of it" (Villiers 1923, 1). It was believed that if an alraun was put into a glass bottle, it would transform into a spider or scorpion. It was supposed that the "imp" within the bottle could perform magical services for the owner, but if he or she should die possessing such a bottle, then the Devil would take his or her soul (Thompson 1934, 138). An alraun could not be disposed of easily, because it would inevitably return to the owner no matter what had been done to it. Places where people had made a futile attempt to dispose of an alraun gained an on-lay that brought misfortune to others who went there. In 1630 in Hamburg the possession and sale of alrauns was prohibited, and three women were executed for possession (Thompson 1934, 135–36).

HOLED STONES

A stone with a natural hole through it is called a hagstone or holeystone. They have been recognized as magical since ancient times. It was a tradition to hang one on the back of the door in stables to keep the horses calm at night (Glyde 1872, 179; Evans 1971, 181–82), and over beds to ward off bad dreams. The customary thread in Great Britain is a string of flax. Especially magically powerful are holeystones taken from the beach and threaded together into a chain. A holeystone chain from Great Yarmouth on the east coast of England is illustrated here.

Fig. 12.3. Chain of holeystones from the seashore, Great Yarmouth, Norfolk, England.

They are closely related to magic cords containing knots. Strings of magical talismans and amulets are worn as necklaces in many cultures; charm bracelets, called *Wendekette* and *Friesenkette,* in south German and Austrian tradition.

Holed flints were used by the Arts and Crafts architect Edward Schroeder Prior at strategic points on the exterior walls of Henry Martyn Hall in Cambridge. Holed standing stones and holes through stones in buildings are traditionally held in reverence as places of healing and foresight, and oaths were taken on them, a form of binding between two individuals. A holed stone called the Odin Stone stood at Croft Odin on Orkney until it was destroyed by a farmer in 1814.

Oaths were sworn on the stone, and an offering of bread, cheese, or cloth left there. In 1791 a young man was brought before the Elders of Orkney as an oath breaker, "breaking the promise to Odin"; that is, an oath sworn on the stone.

MAGICAL BINDINGS

The Web of Wyrd is likened metaphorically to a woven fabric made on a loom; equally it can be visualized as a series of threads knitted together. Knots are the means by which garments are knitted, and people use knots to tie things up magically as well as physically, bringing them to a full stop. The way to ravel (tie up, or bind) things magically as well as physically is to use a knot to entangle and entrap the designated target. Binding spells are intended to be the magical equivalent of physical knots, nets, and ropes. In mythology, powerful, dangerous beings are captured and bound by the godly powers of proper orderliness. The Old Icelandic text *Gylfaginning* (34, 51) tells of the binding of both the Fenris-Wolf and Loki, and Christian eschatology in the *Book of Revelation* (20:1–3) describes the bondage of the Devil in chains for a thousand years. The conjuring parsons of eighteenth-century Cornwall would "lay" troublesome spirits and imprison them inside objects such as the pommel of a sword or a barrel of beer, or banish them to the Red Sea (Rees 1898, 266–67). In Manchester in 1825 a boggart was trapped and bound under the dry arch of an old bridge over the River Irwell for 999 years. Other magical binding legends and folktales from northern Europe follow the same theme. A traditional carving of the chained Devil exists in Stonegate, York, England.

In folk tradition the most feared power of the witch was the evil eye, "a magical and occult binding." Magicians and witches claimed to have the power to use binding spells against merchants, so they could not buy or sell; against ships, so they could not sail; and against mills, so they would not grind corn. They were supposed to bind wells and reservoirs, so that water could not be drawn from them. Magically, they bound the ground, so that nothing could grow and be fruitful there, and neither could any building be put up. Writing about magicians in 1621,

Fig. 12.4. Bound devil, Stonegate, York, England.

Robert Burton mentions knots among other methods of performing magical acts upon people: "The means by which they work, are usually charms, images . . . as characters stamped on sundry metals, and at such and such constellations, knots, amulets, words, philtres, and so forth, which generally make the parties affected melancholy" (Burton 1621, I, ii, I, sub. III). A person magically bound to do something, as in the expression "she is bound to die" is said to be spellbound. In his influential magical text of 1801, *The Magus,* which was largely plagiarized from H. C. Agrippa, Francis Barrett wrote:

> Now how is it that these kind of bindings are made and brought to pass, we must know. They are thus done: by sorceries, collyries, unguents, potions, binding to and hanging up of talismans, by charms, incantations, strong imaginations, affections, passions, images, characters, enchantments, imprecations, lights, and by sounds, numbers, words, names, invocations, swearings, conjurations, consecrations, and the like. (Barrett 1801, 50)

A binding spell usually employed knots of some kind, but not always. An accusation of binding magic took place in 1662 in the Scottish highlands, when Isobel Gowdie of Auldern was tried for witchcraft. She made a long and detailed confession that led to her being sentenced to death: "Before Candlemas we went by east Kinloss, and there we yoked a plough of toads. The Devil held the plough, and John Young, our Officer, did drive the plough. Toads did draw the plough as oxen, couchgrass was the harness and trace chains, a gelded animal's horn was the coulter, and a piece of a gelded animal's horn was the sock." The sock is the ploughshare. Using the horns of castrated animals to form the coulter and share of the plough would have been a magical act employing parts of infertile animals to bind the ground and render the earth infertile. This is analogous to the Old Norse magical procedures of driving out the land wights and thereby rendering the ground *álfreka*. Of course, it is impossible to plough a field using toads.

In *Welsh Witchcraft* (1975), L. Simmonds tells of a quincunx ritual of binding performed at Llanfechan, Wales. No date is given. A farmer lost several sheep, dead for no apparent reason, so he sent for a wizard from Welshpool to sort it out. The wizard asked the farmer to lead him to the exact center of the farm, and there he set up an ash pole. Then four more were set up, each twenty-five yards from the first, to the north, east, west, and south of the center. Then they walked round the center pole and went to each of the other four poles in order. At each direction they stood in silence as the wizard stared into space. With "will to do . . . bid to do," the rite was over, and afterward no more sheep died (Simmonds 1975, 20). A nineteenth-century magical manuscript by Frederick Hockley is indicative of the areas magicians believed themselves capable of dealing with. It has a spell "to bind the ground, whereby neither mortal nor spiritual beings can approach within a limited distance." This was achieved by making a magic circle of enormous dimensions. The diameter of these circles could be one hundred feet, more or less, according to the operator's desire, or even larger with the intention of keeping all earthly or spiritual beings away from the place by between a quarter of a mile and a mile. Like the Llanfechan ritual, it involved the four quarters, north, east, south, and west, with a magical talisman containing the Seal of the Earth buried at each spot.

KNOT MAGIC

The thorn-bearing, winding, and tangling shrubs bramble (blackberry, *Rubus fruticosus*) and blackthorn (sloe, *Prunus spinosa*) both have turning-related names in Irish, *dreas* and *draion*. They are plants that form barriers in thickets and hedgerows and turn back or entangle animals and people who try to go through. Becoming entangled in thickets of thorns is a physical example of what was believed to happen to spirits when encountering magically charged knots and patterns. Nowadays, Cat's Cradles made from string are seen as a children's game, although identical string-knotting patterns are part of the repertoire of binding magic. In Scandinavia they are called *trollknutar* ("magic knots"), part of the northern circumpolar tradition of string-magic linked to shamanic practices. The northern English and Scots word *warlock,* meaning a cunning man or practitioner of spellcraft, is rarely used today except pejoratively. Because dictionaries have given it meanings such as "liar" and "deceiver," the word has fallen from use. Magically, the power of warlockry is the ability to shut in or enclose; that is, a person who can perform binding spells. A warlock can make a *warlock brief,* binding knots, physical or psychic, intended to ward off evil spirits and to lock up or bind their effects.

There is a large body of lore from the north linking nine knots with healing and warding off illness as well as ill-wishing. The nine knots tied in the silk thread for English bloodstones have been mentioned above. A charm from the Orkney Islands, recorded in 1895, which used a thread of nine knots as a cure for an injured wrist or ankle, is typical. It was put on with this spell:

> *Nine knots upon this thread*
> *Nine blessings on thy head*
> *Blessings to take away thy pain*
> *And ilka tinter of thy strain fire*

(MACKENZIE 1895, 73)

Knots made in rope, cord, and netting for practical and magical purposes, as well for women's hair-braiding, and interlaces made during performances such as sword dancing, are transitory, and there are few surviving examples from ancient times. But as the tradition continued into the present day, we have an understanding of some of their meaning in the unrecorded past. Certain kinds of knots played a part in magical tradition. The *witch knot* was a particular charm worn in a woman's hair, while the triple knot called a *St. Mary knot* was a raveling used to hamstring animals and, by association, prevent actions magically. Sea witches also sold the winds in ropes tied with three knots. In his 1827 short story "The Two Drovers" in *Chronicles of the Canongate,* Sir Walter Scott recorded a Scottish knot custom associated with livestock: "It may not be indifferent to the reader to know that the Highland cattle are peculiarly liable to be *taken,* or infected, by spells and witchcraft, which judicious people guard against by knitting knots of peculiar complexity on the tuft of hair which terminates the animal's tail" (Scott n.d. [1885], 171).

Fig. 12.5. Dragons and binding knots on corner of timber-frame building, Limburg, Germany.

This was known as *St. Mungo's knot,* and a knot known as the *meltie bow* was tied on the cudgels used by herd boys to protect the cattle from harm (Warrack 1988 [1911], 354). In the late nineteenth century, Arthur Moore noted an account from the Isle of Man in which a young man found a woman performing a ritual at a crossroads near Regaby. She was sweeping a circle with a besom (twig broom). He took the besom from her and found that it had "17 sorts of knots" on it. He burned it at midday, and "soon after its destruction the woman died" (Moore 1891, 91).

In Great Britain and Ireland, ancient examples exist of interlaced knotwork carved in stone and wood, tooled on leather, engraved on metal, and drawn in manuscripts. Today, this artistic knotwork is called Celtic Art, after the books of J. Romilly Allan, John G. Merne, and George Bain publicized the ancient art form under that name in the first half of the twentieth century. Many patterns are common to Ireland, the Isle of Man, Wales, Scotland, England, Scandinavia, and Germany. The ninth-century gritstone cross of Hywel ap Rhys, ruler of Glywysing, south Wales (d. 886), is shown in figure 12.6.

Fig. 12.6. Celtic Cross of Hywel ap Rhys, 886 CE, Llantwit Major, Wales.

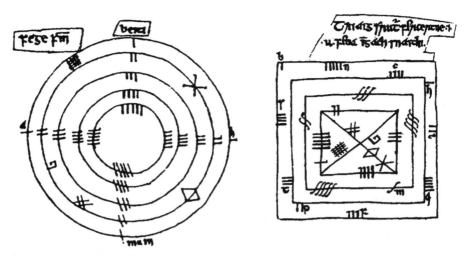

Fig. 12.7. Fionn's shields, Irish Ogham. The Library of the European Tradition

Patterns called *liuthrindi* are known from ancient Ireland, used in a military context to disorient enemies. The Irish Ogham sigil *Feisifín,* Fionn's Shield, can be in a circular or square form. It served as a protective talisman, and its form also resembles certain Icelandic sigils.

The simplest interlaced knot, the fourfold loop, is a very ancient magical sigil. It exists in Roman mosaics of the Imperial period, and early Lombardic and Romanesque churches in Germany, Switzerland, and Italy have the sign carved in stone on column capitals, fonts, and stone screens, where they appear among other interlace patterns. In the north, one survives on a memorial stone on the island of Gotland in the Baltic Sea (Havor II, Hablingbo parish). Dated between 400 and 600 CE (Nylén and Lamm 1981, 39), it appears also on bracteates from Denmark of similar date (Wirth 1934, VIII, pl. 424, fig. 1b; pl. 427, 7b). This and other protective glyphs were carved by the shipwrights on the pivoted wooden oar covers of the Viking Age ship excavated at Gokstad. On the Isle of Man, it exists on the Andreas Cross. It can be found widespread in medieval graffiti in Great Britain (see Pritchard 1967, 133). This simple knot is called *Sankt Hans Vapen* in Sweden, and in Finland and Estonia it is *Hannunvaakuna* (Strygell 1974, 46). One is shown on a 1673 engraving of a Sámi shaman's drum in Johannes

Schefferus's *Lapponia*. In 1901 the Arts and Crafts architect W. R. Lethaby used the pattern in the tracery of the north transept window in his symbolic church at Brockhampton, Herefordshire, England (Mason 2001, 14).

With an additional central cross loop, this fourfold loop was used on traditional English clog almanacs to mark All Saints' Day, November 1 (see Schnippel 1926, pl. II and III). In the Country Calendar, it represents the midpoint between autumn and winter, and from this it has become the sigil for Samhain used by present-day Pagans (see Pennick 1990, 35, figs. 8, 13, 26, 35). A sigil composed of three interlaced equilateral triangles is seen frequently today as a symbol of northern religion. It is the Valknut (*Valknute, Valknut,* or *Valknútr*), the "knot of the fallen" (i.e., the slain). Among the earliest known examples of the sigil are found on some memorial stones on Gotland and on rings and other Viking Age metalwork. It is associated with the god Odin (Thorsson 1984, 107; 1993, 11; Aswynn 1988, 15–54).

A different form of triangular knot, with a superimposed cross, is known as *Sankt Bengt's Wapen* (Strygell 1974, 46). In the Alps some people called up the demonic entity called Schratl by magic at crossroads, but the apotropaic device called *Schratterlgatterl* or *Schradlgaderl* is a means of warding off evil spirits, blocking their paths with a physical

Fig. 12.8. Valknut.

binding knot. This device was made from seven slivers of wood, interleaved to hold together without binding with cords. It was hung on doors or gates considered at risk from spirit attack (von Alpenburg 1857, 369; Bächtold-Stäubli 1927–1942, I, 297). Old Scratch's Gate is a similar magical binding pattern used in East Anglian magic. Old Scratch is a byname for the Devil, and the sigil was chalked on doors and shutters to block the entry of evil. Every form of magic has a magical antidote, and a story told by the Anglo-Saxon chronicler Bede (*Historia ecclesiastica gentis Anglorum*, IV, 22) tells of a runic antidote to binding. In the year 679, Bede wrote, the shackles fell off Imma, a Northumbrian prisoner, every time his brother said Christian prayers for his soul, believing he was dead. Imma was asked "whether he knew loosening runes and was carrying staves with him written down." Loosening runes had a Latin name, *litteras solutorias*.

13

Practical Magic
Patterns and Sigils

THRESHOLD AND HEARTHSTONE PATTERNS

In parts of Great Britain was a custom of marking the threshold or hearth with knotlike patterns to bring good luck and ward off harm. The expert on traditional buildings Sidney R. Jones noted in 1912, "Villagers throughout the north of England make a practice of sanding the steps to doorways. It is an odd custom, many years old, which still survives. The stone step is run over with water, partly dried, and to the damp surface is applied dry sand or sandstone. Varied are the patterns that are worked on risers and treads" (Jones 1912, 114, 116). In various parts of England and Scotland where the practice survived long enough to be recorded, they were drawn with chalk, pipe clay, or sand (Canney 1926, 13). They were made every year on particular meaningful days. In Cambridge this was Foe-ing Out Day, March 1. Some are illustrated in figure 13.1.

There is a pattern seemingly local to the town of Cambridge, called the Cambridge Box. In Newmarket and Cambridge, a continuous loop pattern was also chalked around the edges of floors in stables and outhouses. Clearly an apotropaic pattern, it is called the "running

Fig. 13.1. Threshold patterns from England and Scotland.

eight." This pattern had to be made in a single movement without stopping during the process. Ella Mary Leather describes threshold patterns of chalk in the English West Midlands villages of Weobley and Dilwyn: "The stone would be neatly bordered with white when washed, with a row of crosses within the border" (Leather 1912, 53).

North of Herefordshire, in Shropshire, patterns were made by rubbing bunches of elder, dock, or oak leaves on the stone. In Eaton-under-Heywood in Shropshire, patterns were "laid" on thresholds, stone steps leading to bedrooms, and the hearthstone. Their function was to prevent the Devil from coming down the chimney (Dakers 1991, 169–70). Comparable to these temporary patterns are permanent flooring patterns made from traditional materials: bones, cobbles, bricks, and tiles, and in some places they are related to patterns in brickwork and clothing (Van der Klift-Tellegen 1987, 36–38). The patterns of traditional bit mats or rag rugs resemble those made in brickwork and drawn on hearthstones and thresholds. Patterns often have a diamond in the center, a border and triangles at the corner. Bit mats are made of recycled fabric from worn-out old clothes cut into strips and attached to a fabric base (Dixon 1981, 46–47).

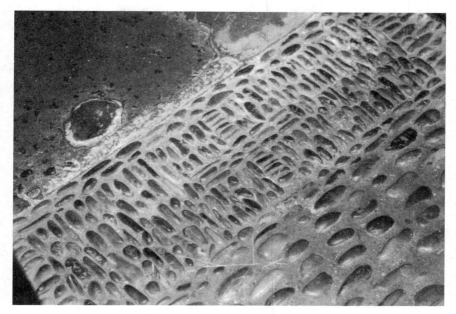

Fig. 13.2. Threshold cross of pebbles, Welshpool, Wales.

THE BINDING OF LORD SOULIS

The story of Lord William Soulis contains many elements of traditional northern magic, and a border ballad composed by John Leyden preserved an older legend in rhyme. Hermitage Castle where Soulis lived was a key fortress on the borderlands of England and Scotland. According to the ballad, Soulis was a cruel and treacherous tyrant who oppressed his vassals and slaves as much as he did his enemies. But he was also a practitioner of magic who had a familiar sprite called Old Redcap. Redcap made Soulis magically wound-proof, so he could not be harmed by edged weapons, neither could he be bound by chain nor rope, but only by sand, which cannot be made into ropes:

> *While thou shalt live a charmed life,*
> *And hold that life of me,*
> *'Gainst lance and arrow, sword and knife,*
> *I shall thy warrant be.*
> *Nor forged steel, nor hempen band,*

Shall e'er thy limbs confine,
Till threefold ropes of twisted sand
Around thy body twine

(HALL 1867, 147–48)

Soulis's enemies finally ambushed him, but their weapons would not bite. But still they succeeded in forcing him to the ground. But when they bound him with ropes, they broke. Then they used chains, and these too would not hold. Only magical ropes could bind him, and the magic number nine appears in the formula. Sand was taken from the stream called Nine-Stane Burn. Nine handfuls of barley chaff were added and threefold plaited ropes made from it. The ropes of sand were contained inside tubes of lead, and it was these with which Soulis was bound. Then, wrapped in leaden bonds that disempowered his magic, he was thrown into a cauldron. They set it upon a fire at Nine Stane Rigg, the ridge separating Teviotdale and Liddesdale, on top of which was a megalithic circle of nine standing stones. Then Lord Soulis was boiled to death in the cauldron inside the circle.

STRAW BINDINGS, KNOTS, AND FIGURES

Straw, the by-product of grain farming, has many uses. Straw rope or netting was used in the western seaboard of Europe to tie down roof thatch, which itself is often made of straw. Traditional bee skeps are made from straw rope, in the form of a spirally wound dome, stitched together. Straw is also woven into hats and shoes, sometimes for temporary and ceremonial use (see Evans 1957, 278; Bärtsch 1998 [1933], 59–82). Special straw crosses are made in Ireland in celebration of St. Brigid's Day (February 1). Straw plaits are most associated with the termination of the harvest, where making special items by plaiting straw was a common practice. In many parts of Europe, the final sheaf of corn to be cut was made into a humanoid figure that was carried ceremonially with the harvest being taken to the farmyard and took an honored place in the harvest feast that followed. An account of the harvest in Norfolk in August 1826 tells how "the *last* or 'horkey load' . . . is decorated with flags and streamers, and sometimes a sort of *kern baby* is placed on the top at the front of the load" (Hone 1827, II, 1166). A visitor to the Cambridge Folk Museum in 1951 told the curator Enid Porter of a tradition from his grandmother's early years in Litlington; how the farmer held up the last shock of corn, then one of the men made a humanoid figure with head, arms, and legs from it. At the horkey supper, the figure sat in a special chair during the feast. After the meal, it was set on top of the corner cupboard, in the holy corner (Porter 1969, 123).

Nowadays, the name "corn dolly" is used to describe any of the numerous forms of straw plaiting formerly connected with the harvest in Great Britain, whether humanoid or not. But the name "corn dolly" is of recent origin; the contemporary names of straw plaits when they were in use being "kirn maiden," "kirn baby," "neck," "ben," and "fan."

The origin of "dolly" as their name comes from a meeting of the Folk-Lore Society in London, February 20, 1901, when "Mrs. Gomme exhibited and presented to the society a Kirn Maiden or Dolly, copied by Miss Swan from those made at Duns in Berwickshire" (*Folk-Lore* 12, 1,

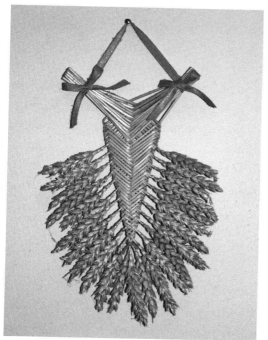

Fig. 13.3. Border Fan straw plait, Melverley, Shropshire, England.

June 1901, 11, 129). In a letter to Gomme, Swan wrote: "I am sure that there was a good-luck superstition attached to the making and preserving of it, although it was not much talked about. The Kirn I sent you, though a modern dolly, is a faithful reproduction of those I have seen and helped to dress 'lang syne'" (*Folk-Lore* 12, 1, 215–16). The image that Mrs. Gomme showed the folklorists was not made from the last sheaf for the harvest but was a replica. Not being an actual Kirn Maiden used in harvest rites and ceremonies, it was called a dolly, just as a dolly represents a real baby but is not one. From the 1950s onward the generic name "dolly" became the norm. Like the name "witch posts," it has no historic authenticity.

In 1951 the organizers of the Festival of Britain in London commissioned masters of straw plaiting to make masterworks of the genre to celebrate the ancient craft. Old and new designs were put on show side by side; the Essex straw plaiter Fred Mizen made a straw lion and unicorn (Cooper 1994, 62), while Arthur "Badsey" Davis made a crown-shaped plait from forty-nine straws, a design now known as "Badsey's Fountain" (Sandford 1983, 56). It is likely that this form originated as the crown of the hay rick (Lambert and Marx 1989, 88). Davis came from a Worcestershire family that had handed down the craft's secrets through the male line for generations. George Ewart Evans notes a man from north Essex who made straw plaits at Blaxhall, Suffolk. He did not put them on the last load, but they were used in the church as decoration during the time of the Harvest Festival (Evans 1965, 214). Traditionally, straw plaiting was done by men until the 1951 Festival of Britain, when the Women's Institute took it up. Now, mistakenly, it is seen as a traditional women's craft, and some who make corn dollies throughout the year view their work as worship of the Goddess.

TRADITIONAL PATTERNS, SIGILS, AND GLYPHS

The skills of self-making are essential in traditional society. The rural poor, and those whose work was independent of masters, or in some way not allied to the urban collective—such as carters, drovers, boatmen, and fishermen and fishwives—retained personal craft skills that were downgraded in towns by the industrial revolution. Their home-crafted clothes, self-made tools, and utensils were often considered rustic or rural by urban dwellers and inferior to manufactured goods. Knitwear is strongly associated with the areas bordering the North Sea, where hardy sheep have been herded for thousands of years. The patterns on traditional woolen knitwear have customary meanings, containing a vast repertoire of symbolic patterns that vary from place to place. Embedded in traditional country and coastal crafts are techniques and patterns that go back perhaps thousands of years. In them the meaningful symbolism and magic of making and the artifacts made affirms the positive values of continuity and self-reliance. The individual designs on traditional fishermen's knitwear from Scotland, England, and the Netherlands are assembled from a repertoire of symbolic patterns that include the cable, flag, tree of life, fishbone, waves, and lightning bolt or zigzag.

Each pattern has its own lore, some of it magical. The *ing*-rune-related pattern of five diamonds called "God's Eye" in East Anglia has the same name in Dutch, *Godsoog*. A woman in IJmuiden told knitting researcher Henriette van der Klift-Tellegen that the *Godsoog* on the sweater looks after the seamen in strange ports, and also that the pattern enables men to find the front in the dark and put it on the right way round. In the Netherlands it is viewed as essentially an English pattern (van der Klift-Tellegen 1987, 19). On the east coast of Britain, the decline of the fishing industry in the late twentieth century broke up many of the communities that had sustained the knitting tradition. Those that still exist now continue as emblems of local identity. Various patterns from Amble, Cullercoats, Flamborough, Newbiggin, Patrington, Seahouses, Scarborough, Staithes, and Whitby are preserved, and new ganseys are knitted according to these traditions. Also extant are the jersey patterns of the Keel and Sloop men on the inland waterways around the River Humber, inland from Hull as far south as Lincoln and Nottingham. They include moss stitch, chevron, hexagram, diamond, tree of life, and chequers.

MAGIC IN MAKING EVERYDAY THINGS

There is no distinction between religion and magic in traditional societies. It is only a matter of semantics how we describe the saying of prayers, incantations, and making signs when something is done. There are many small acts taught as integral with making and doing, such as making the sign of a cross over food. In brewing and baking, for example, the sigil known as "two hearts and a crisscross" was traditionally used to protect the mash or dough. It is composed of two hearts with a cross in between. In 1895 F. T. Elworthy noted that an old man in Somerset had told him that in brewing, before the mash was covered up to ferment, the sigil was drawn to ward off the pixies (Elworthy 1895, 287).

Robert Herrick in his *Hesperides* (1648) alludes to this in a Charm:

> *This I'll tell ye by the way,*
> *Maidens, when ye leavens lay,*
> *Crosse your dow [dough], and your dispatch*
> *Will be better for your batch.*
>
> (Herrick 1902 [1648], 298)

In addition to the invoking of the intrinsic magical powers of the cross and the hearts, bakers used a pin to prick the emblem into biscuits, the "pricking" mentioned in the British nursery rhyme *Pat-a-cake, Pat-a-cake, Baker's Man.*

Fig. 13.4. German ring bread with crosses.

ICELANDIC SIGIL MAGIC

Icelandic sigil magic is extant in medieval magical manuscripts such as the *Hlíðarendabók,* the *Huld Manuscript,* the *Galdrabók,* the *Kreddur Manuscript,* and a number of other original texts preserved in the National Library in Reykjavik. This sigil magic is not unique, as is often claimed, but part of the European mainstream magical use of seals, talismans, and magical warding signs. Sigils of similar form and construction appear in numerous mainland Euopean grimoires, including *The Lesser Key of Solomon* (see Waite, 1911; Mathers, MacGregor, and Crowley, 1997). But in Iceland the sigils appear to have been widespread in folk magic and, more importantly, were collected together and written down, so we have records of many sigils, along with their names and accompanying spells of empowerment. In classical European magic, such complex sigils represent and give access to particular spirits, which then are commanded to do the magician's bidding. General warding signs and magical sigils not intended to invoke spirits are used in traditional trades and crafts. These are known in many other parts of Europe. In Icelandic sigil magic all human necessities are provided for.

The *Ægishjálmur* ("helm of awe," cover or shield of terror), is the best known of all Icelandic magical sigils. Ruling over the eight directions, it is the sigil of comprehensive, irresistible power. Its function is to induce fear in one's opponents, thereby dominating them. In the

Fig. 13.5. Helm of Awe. Painting by Nigel Pennick, 1993

Nibelungenlied legend, the helm of awe was gained by Sigurd Fafnirsbane when he slew the dragon Fafnir. After Christianization, Sigurd was said to be one of the spectral riders in the *Åsgårdsrei* along with Thor, who had been relegated from the status of god to that of evil spirit. But the *Ægishjálmur* remained as a powerful magical sigil. Another Icelandic magical symbol, the *Salomons Insigli* (the "Sign of Salamon," named for the Jewish king Solomon), does not refer to the common hexagram or pentagram, but rather to a sigil that is a form of the *Ægishjálmur.*

In Anglo-Norman heraldry, this sigil is the Escarbuncle, and in German heraldry, Glevenrad or Lilienstapel. Technically, the pattern arose in the armorers' craft as a means of strengthening a shield (Fox-Davies 1925, 64, 290–91). The image of the Helm of Awe and the heraldic Escarbuncle and Glevenrad is that of a blinding light dazzling the onlooker. As its Anglo-Norman name tells us, the heraldic emblem represents the carbuncle, the fiery red gemstone that we call a ruby. The characteristic of the carbuncle was to shine in the dark "like a live coal," for the Latin word *carbunculus* means "a little coal." Albertus Magnus wrote that the carbuncle was ascribed the powers of all other gemstones (Albertus Magnus 1569, II, ii). It possessed a virtue against all airy and vaporous poisons (Agrippa 1993 [1531], I, XIII). The carbuncle is ruled magically by the red star Aldebaran, the eye of Taurus the bull. The Old French saga *Le Pélérinage de Charlemagne* (The Pilgrimage of Charlemagne) tells that Charlemagne's bedchamber was reputed to be lit up by a carbuncle.

Charlemagne features as the emblem of power and stability in the Icelandic sigil called *Karlamagnúsar Hringar* (The Rings of Charlemagne). This sigil purports to represent nine rings of help sent by God with his angel to Pope Leo to be given to Charlemagne to protect him against his enemies. The Roman, Byzantine, Carolingian, and Ottonian emperors, as well as many early medieval kings, had their own monograms composed of the letters of their names (Weber 1940, 334–42). They may well have been tattooed upon slaves as a sign of ownership (Gustafson 2000, 17–31). It is possible that magicians used these emblems of imperial power as sigils in their magical operations. It is clearly part of mainland European magic connected with a strong

Christian orientation. Charlemagne was the Holy Roman emperor who suppressed Paganism in Saxony and resisted Islamic invaders in France, so he was the epitome of a defender of the faith. Charlemagne's sigil is threefold, three rings of three, and the accompanying spell is empowered by the three holy names: "In nomine Patris et Filio et Spiritu Sanctu Amen" [*sic*]. It is therefore a ninefold charm, composed of nine rings, each with a corresponding power. Nine is the ancient northern magic number, and although ascribed to Pope Leo and Charlemagne, the nine rings are redolent of the tale of Draupnir, "the dripper," a magic artifact made by two dwarf artisans for Odin. Draupnir's magic was that from it every ninth night, eight new rings dropped.

The first ring of Charlemagne protects against the wiles of the Devil, attacks by enemies, and troubles of the mind. The second ring prevents collapse of the will, fear, and sudden death. The third turns back the hatred of one's enemies upon themselves so that they are fearful and retreat. The fourth ring is against wounds from swords; the fifth against being disorientated by magic and losing one's way; while the sixth wards against persecution by powerful, evil men. The seventh circle brings triumph in legal disputes and general popularity; the eighth suppresses fear, and the ninth wards off all vices and debauchery. When expecting the enemy to come, these nine circles of Charlemagne are intended to be worn on the chest or on either side of the body. In

Fig. 13.6. Anglo-Saxon magic rings. Top: gold ring with runic magic inscription from Kingsmoor, Cumbria, England. Below: gold ring with sigils at each end, Peterborough, England. The Library of the European Tradition

its form, this sigil also resembles the seal of the evil spirit Forneus, a sea monster who teaches all arts and sciences and reconciles enemies (see Waite 1911, 204–5).

Icelandic magical staves protected against everyday problems: *Kaupaloki* helped merchants to close deals and enjoy prosperous businesses; *Þjófastafur* warded off thieves, or exposed their deeds; *Angurgapi* was carved on the ends of barrels to prevent leaking; *Veiðistafur* gave luck to fishermen; *vegvísir* helped mariners keep on course and ride out bad weather, while farmers used *Tóustefna* to keep foxes away. This was the magic used to get by in everyday life. *Varnarstafur Valdemars,* "Valdemar's Protection Stave," was used to augment the user's status and happiness. Gambling and sporting contests are uncertain pastimes, and every culture has magical spells and practices to give the contestant an edge over the opposition. In 1905 Willard Fiske noted a charm: "If thou wishest to win at backgammon, take a raven's heart, dry it in a spot on which the sun does not shine, crush it, then rub it on the dice." Another talisman used a different part of a bird: "In order to win at *kotra,* take a tongue of a wagtail, and dry it in the sun; crush and mix it afterward with communion-wine, and apply it to the points of the dice, then you are sure of the game." A *kotruvers* (spell) for winning at backgammon was recorded by Jón Arnason. It called upon the power of famous Norse kings. "The *kotrumenn* (backgammon players) should call 'Olave, Olave, Harold, Harold, Erik, Erik.' The one wishing to win must write this formula in runes and either carry it somewhere on him, or let it lie under the backgammon board, on his knees, while he is playing. He must also recite the Lord's prayer in honor of St. Olave, the king" (Fiske 1905, 346).

Contestants in *glíma* (wrestling) used the sigils *Ginfaxi* and *Gapaldur.* Written on parchment, *Ginfaxi* and *Gapaldur* were put in the wrestler's shoes so they would operate during the bout. *Ginfaxi* was worn under the toes of the left foot, while *Gapaldur* was put beneath the heel of the right foot. *Dunfaxi,* carved on a piece of Oak, was used to win in legal cases. There were also magical sigils and formulae used to call up evil spirits and awaken *draugr* revenants (*stafur til að vekja upp draug*); ones against harmful magic (*stafur gegn galdri*); and ones

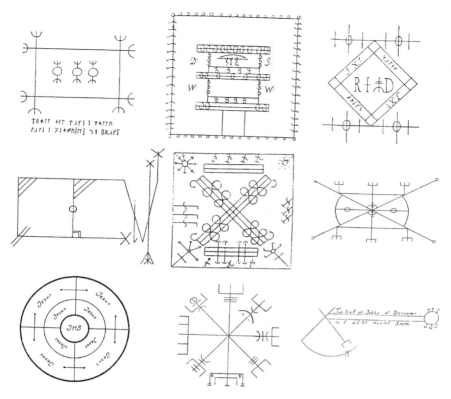

Fig. 13.7. Icelandic talismans and magical sigils from the *Galdrabók*, *Huld Manuscript*, and so forth. Left to right, top row: *Lásabrótur*, lock-breaker; *Drottníngar* signet, against all spirits; *Jósúa insigli*, protective power of Joshua. Middle row: *Dreprún*, livestock death sigil; *Astros*, disempowerment of detrimental runes (see British threshold patterns); *Thjófastafir*, thieves' sigil. Lower row: Cross of Óláfr Tryggvason (ninefold names of Jesus), protective; *Vegvísir*, direction knowledge; *Vatrahlífir*, protection in water. The Library of the European Tradition

using magic against other people, such as the fear-inducing *Óttastafur;* and *Dreprún,* the Death Rune, which is actually a sigil and not a rune (Davíðsson 1903, *passim;* Flowers 1989, 59–103). The housebreaking sigil and spell *Lásabrjótur,* the "lock-breaker" or "castle-breaker," evoked the power of trolls to move the bolt inside the door, pulling it so the Devil's squeak would be heard (the bolt sliding open). It was to be laid on the lock and breathed upon. One of the powers ascribed northern

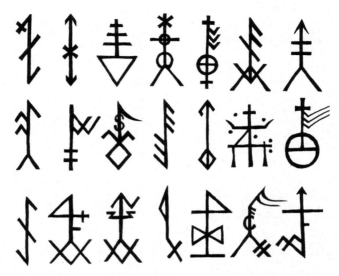

Fig. 13.8. Medieval housemarks and owners' marks from eastern England, to identify property, but also with a magically protective function, many being derived from bind-runes.

European folk magicians is the ability to get through locked doors. In East Anglia, eastern England, the adage "no door is ever closed to a toadman" expressed the belief that someone who possessed the toad bone had the power of invisibility and unauthorized entry.

LOTS

St. Peter's Game

The interface of randomness and the determinate occurs in the throwing of dice. When a particular number turns up, it is a moment of irreversible change. War veterans often talk about a bullet "with your number on it" that inescapably dooms one to die. Numbers and counting appear to be embedded in the selection of sacrificial victims. In the fifth century CE, Sidonius Apollinaris noted the custom of Saxon pirates who sacrificed each tenth captive to the god of the sea as a thanksgiving for a successful voyage before setting sail for home (Dalton 1915, VIII, 6, II, 150). This is the Roman custom of decimation. The means of selection of victims for sacrifice is often described as "drawing lots," but a number sequence recalled in Finnish and Swedish labyrinth traditions may be a surviving example of a particular means of selection. Two small rock-cut labyrinths on the island of Skarv in the Stockholm Archipelago, Sweden, are accompanied by a long rectangle in which the sequence is carved (Kern 1983, 411). This sequence is also known from runic calendars from Norway (Davis 1867, 472).

The number sequence is called St. Peter's Game, *Pietarinleikki* (Finnish), *Sankt Päders Lek* (Swedish), or *Sankt-Peters-Spiel* (German). In ancient rock carvings, medieval clog almanacs, and primestaves this sequence is depicted as a series of crosses and uprights, drawn between two parallel lines. It is a method of dividing 30 into two equal parts, picking out every ninth one. This is the sequence XXXXIIIIIXXIXXXXIXIIXXIIIXIIXXI (4, 5, 2, 1, 3, 1, 1, 2, 2, 3, 1, 2, 2, 1).

Fig. 13.9. Sámi world pillars with rods and *Pietarinleikki*. Eighteenth-century engraving. The Library of the European Tradition

Hermann Kern states that this "game" is widespread in northern Europe and known as far back as the tenth century in Germany, where it was called *Josephsspiel* or *Judenersäufespiel* (Kern 1983, 411). According to the explanatory tale, a ship carrying Christians and Jews was overtaken by a storm that threatened to sink it. St. Peter was on board, and he resolved that it was necessary to throw half of the passengers overboard to save the rest. It was agreed that as there were thirty people on board, fifteen Jews and fifteen Christians, fifteen would have to die, and they would stand in line and every ninth one would be thrown overboard. St. Peter arranged them so Christians and Jews were in the sequence, then picked out every ninth person. This meant that only Jews were thrown overboard (Davis 1867, 472). While this tale is framed as a pro-Christian, anti-Semitic polemic, the connection of the sequence with throwing people overboard is redolent of Sidonius's account of the practices of Saxon pirates (Ahrens 1918, II, 118–68).

14

The Magic of Music

SOUND AND NOISE

Since time immemorial, it has been recognized that rhythm and harmony impart grace to the inner parts of the soul. The human soul, it appears, being one with the cosmos, responds to the same cosmic harmonies. Aristotle wrote that music has the power to lead the soul back from states of unrest to that of harmony, to relieve mental illnesses and to rectify the character. Sound has a significant effect on the environment, and noise-making devices are used throughout the world at rites and ceremonies that serve to drive off bad luck and evil influences. Shouting and singing, clapping hands, and stamping feet need no instruments, but for continuous loud noises something more is required. Rattles, clappers, buzzers, drums, bells, and fireworks all have their part in ceremonial and magical performance. In preindustrial times before ubiquitous machine-made noise was everywhere, there was real silence. The Scots expression *howe-dumb-dead* describes the dead silence in the middle of the night, and "the dead of night" is a comparable English expression (Warrack 1988 [1911], 274). But silence in the night, let alone the day, is a rare thing in industrialized countries now.

In former times, before machine noise was everywhere, calls from instruments such as the *lur,* the *alphorn,* the *Midwinterhoorn,* and the highland bagpipes would carry for significant distances under the right conditions, for there was no extraneous noise to obliterate them, as is the case today with incessant motor traffic and aviation. Similarly, church bells could be heard miles away, and the state of the weather could be inferred by the varied sound qualities of the ringing. Church bells especially were considered to suppress all spirits and eldritch beings that were within their sound range. As Arthur William Moore wrote in 1891, "It is well known that all Fairies and their like have a great objection to noise, especially to the ringing of church bells" (Moore 1891, 41). In ancient Ireland and Scotland distances were often roughly calculated by the distance sound travels. In the *Senchus Mór,* "*magh*-spaces" appear in the law governing going to someone's aid in distress. A *magh*-space was as far as the sound of a bell (an ecclesiastical handbell) or the crow of a rooster could be heard. The *magh*-space was also the feeding range for bees (North 1881, 56).

Rocking stones, boulders naturally perched on others but able to move, were revered as special. They were not seen as natural features, but rather ones that had been placed there by gods, giants, heroes, or saints. They had a connection with the winds, as many of them were so finely balanced that they moved in the wind. In his poem *Argonautica,* Apollonius Rhodius (ca. 100 CE) wrote that Hercules erected a stone over the grave of one of the sons of Boreas, the north wind. It moved in the slightest breeze, seeming to hover above the rock below. Rocking stones that generated sounds were held in awe. The Roulter Rocks on Stanton Moor in Derbyshire were kept in almost constant motion, grinding against the basal stone on which they perched, making an eerie noise. One of these Derbyshire rocking stones was called the Minstrel of the Peak. Its sound, attributed to otherworldly spirits, could be heard from many miles away. Most rocking stones of the British Isles were destroyed by religious fanatics, who considered them to be objects of superstition. Those that survived religious conflict were knocked off their perches by deliberate vandalism once the stones had been made famous by antiquaries and became the focus of tourism.

INCANTATION

Spoken and Sung Charms

Priests of the Celtic Church in Ireland, Great Britain, and Brittany composed protective charms that could either be chanted or sung. They circulated widely for many centuries, and some of them are still in use. The *Lorica* of St. Gildas was composed against the devastating Yellow Plague in 547 CE, and *Sen Dé* by St. Colman mac Ui Cluasaig was against the plague of 697 CE. These charms, originally composed to magically ward off specific plagues, took on a more general protective character (Baring-Gould and Fisher 1907–1913, III, 129). A legend of the Breton saint Hoernbiu tells how his hen was stolen by a fox, so he prayed, and the fox brought it back unharmed. The prayer was written down and became a general charm against foxes in poultry yards (Baring-Gould and Fisher 1907–1913, III, 279).

Enchantment is literally weaving a magic spell by singing a song. Most religions have hymns and chants that appear during rites and ceremonies. There are numerous extant Pagan hymns from southern European antiquity, including those attributed to the musician-prophet Orpheus. In the north, too, are a few notices of religious and magical incantations and songs from ancient times. The Icelandic word for invocational magic, *galdur,* is associated with the verb *gala,* "to chant, sing, or call." It is equivalent to the English word "enchantment," which refers to a magical effect brought about by chanting or singing spells. The Icelandic *Þorfinns Saga Karlsefnis* tells how a female magician performed *galdur* with a beautiful voice. *Galdur* appears to have usually been performed alone, but it is possible that a group of people may have performed some of the incantations. The technical terms for Icelandic magical staves and sigils are *galdrastáfur* (staves) and *galdramyndir* (sigils), which indicate that incantation was part of making them. *Éiríks Saga Rauða* tells of an instance of incantation from the time in Greenland after the Christian religion became dominant. A *völva* (seeress) conducted a ceremony that reached the point where a hymn or incantation called a *varðlokkur* needed to be sung to continue. None there knew it, except a young woman on a visit from Iceland. She was a Christian but had learned it from a woman who looked after her when she was a child. She did not want to sing it but eventually was talked into singing the *varðlokkur,* which enabled the ceremony to be completed.

Incantations were associated with later European witchcraft, too. In his *The Masque of Queens,* performed at Candlemas in 1609 by the queen of Great Britain and her ladies, Ben Jonson notes that the witches in the play have "these shouts and clamors, as also the voice *har, har,* are very peculiar with them." For example, the seventh charm of Jonson's theatrical witches:

> *7 Charm, "Black go in, and blacker come out;*
> *At thy going down, we give thee a shout.*
> *Hoo!*
> *At thy rising again, thou shalt have two,*
> *And if thou dost what we would have thee do,*
> *Thou shalt have three, though shalt have four,*
> *Thou shalt have ten, though shalt have a score*
> *Hoo! Har! Har! Hoo!"*
>
> (JONSON 1816, VOL. 7, 118).

Jonson's notes to the masque detail numerous sources for his characterizations, including ancient and contemporary literature and what would now be called folklore. There are similar calls in the traditional German Fastnacht carnival processions, many of which can be dated back to medieval times. Much later accounts of witchcraft also record incantations and calls. James Wentworth Day records an account by Alfred Herbert Martin, a farm laborer who worked on the Mersea Island in Essex for more than forty years in the early twentieth century. Martin claimed to have seen Mrs. Smith, known by the witch name of Old Mother Redcap, crossing the water to the island on a hurdle as if it were a boat. Martin claimed that as she peeled potatoes in her kitchen, Old Mother Redcap would chant the invocation "Holly, holly, brolly brolly, Redcap! Bonny, bonny" (Day 1973, 39).

MAGICAL INFLUENCES

In ancient Irish tradition, there were three different kinds of music: *golltraidheacht,* a festive and martial measure; *geanttraidheacht,* the sorrowful measure; and *suanttraidheacht,* a soothing measure. The latter had such power that it sent its hearers to sleep for a day or two (North 1881, 40). According to Lady Jane Wilde (1887), there was a beautiful description in one of the ancient manuscripts showing the wonderful power of Irish music over the sensitive humans: "Wounded men were soothed when they heard it, and slept; and women in travail forgot their pains" (Wilde 1887, I, 53). Music can bring joy and lift the spirits, a form of magic if ever there was one. The Old English Rune Poem has the following verse for the rune *Peorð:*

> *Byð symble plega and hlehter wlancum*
> *Þar wiggan sittaþ on beorsele bliþe ætsomne.*
> *"A lively tune means laughter and play*
> *Where brave men sit in the mead hall*
> *Ale-drinking warriors blithe together."*

The shape of this rune (ᛈ) clearly signifies a lyre or harp. A lively tune, conserved into the twenty-first century by the modern Irish word *port,* which means a tune, more particularly among traditional musicians, a jig, or *port béil,* a lilt. In an Irish idiom, the *port* is seen as life, as in the saying *"tá mo phort seinnte"* ("I am done for"): the tune of life is finished. It seems to have had a magical use. A 1670 French grimoire, *Magic Secrets and Counter-Charms,* written by Guidon, "practitioner of occult healing," deals mainly with shepherds' and horsemen's magic. It refers specifically to the jig in a charm ritual that is intended to give protection against all firearms, bewitching the star that guides the firearm by means of a jig. The jig is followed up by a command in the name of the Father, and the Son, and Satanatis, finished with the sign of the cross (Guidon 2011 [1670], 49). In some way the jig binds the power of the star that rules the specific day, thereby disempowering the gun.

Incantations unintelligible to those not in the know are associated with particular trades. They are, of course, part of the same tradition as the incantations magicians or witches use in their rites and ceremonies and in the preparation of active substances. Sea shanties are well known nautical work songs. But there are other, more magical, traditional songs and incantations employed by fishermen. One of the author's ancestors, Shepherd Pennick (1820–1885), spent his working life as a master mariner sailing out of Brightlingsea, Essex, England, fishing for oysters. Oyster-dredgers were known for their special incantations, unintelligible to outsiders, uttered during the process of trawling the seabed for the shellfish. It was a widespread tradition on both sides of the Atlantic, noted by the American esoteric writer Astra Cielo in 1918: "During oyster dredging, fishermen often keep up a monotonous chant to charm the oysters into their net" (Cielo 1918, 144).

Other fishermen catching different things also chanted specific words and songs that were used only at sea. In Shetland these were called *lucky words* (Warrack 1988 [1911], 341). There is a fishing tradition in the Appalachian Mountains in the United States stating that fish bite best at night, and if you play a fiddle or guitar, the fish love music so much that they cannot remain in the water but will come to the surface where they can be caught. This may well have been an ancient belief in Europe. Generic boat songs are well known from the Scottish tradition, the *jurram* being a "slow and melancholy boat song" and the *eeran* an oar song sung during rowing (Warrack 1988 [1911], 155, 297).

There are fascinating old stories of how sounds and music affect animals. The prophet Orpheus is depicted in ancient Greek and Roman images charming the animals with his lyre playing. H. C. Agrippa stated that the sound of a drum made of the skin of the rotchet fish (red gurnard, *Trigla cuculus*) would drive away all creeping things, as far as it can be heard (Agrippa 1993 [1531], I, XXI). The legend of the Pied Piper of Hamelin gives his music the power to charm both rats and children. A curious note in *Fenland Notes and Queries* (vol. IV [1899], 242) claimed that "when the Earl of Bedford determined to drain the land he adopted the strange device of training six of the largest deer and keeping them shut up some time he tamed them by the constant sounding of drums harps and other instruments then harnessed them like a set of coach horses and presented them to the King Charles I."

In the Western Isles of Scotland, when driving the cattle to pasture in the morning, the herdsman or herdswoman sang a song with a pleasant melody. It was sung in slow, measured cadences, and the measured walk of the older cattle was in time to the singing. Going to bring the cattle home in the evening, on approaching the herd, the herder sang *fàilte a' chruidh,* the song of welcome to the cattle, and they responded by making sounds (Carmichael 1997, n. 364). The use by horsemen of particular unusual sounds in the language for controlling horses was noted by the English folklorist Gertrude Jekyll in 1904. In her *Old West Surrey,* she noted that they were not pronounced words, but uttered with a rumbling, hollow resonance, perhaps produced from the stomach by an open throat (Jekyll 1904, 166).

OTHERWORLDLY MUSIC

From the ninth century at the latest, labyrinths made of turf or stones were used in the rites of spring, for ceremonies for the dead and weather magic. Folklore of certain labyrinths in the British Isles identifies them as dwelling places of fairies. The turf labyrinth at Asenby in Yorkshire, England, was in a hollow atop a hillock called the Fairies Hill, where those who ran the maze would kneel when they reached the center "to hear the fairies singing" (Allcroft 1908, 602). Fairy music and song heard at such places is a theme in Celtic folk tales, and certain tunes played today are said to have a supernatural origin. A motif in story telling is of the musician who considers himself not good enough to be taken seriously, who encounters the Otherworld, then returns empowered as a fine musician admired by all. In Ireland and Gaelic Scotland there is a tradition of *ceol-sidhe,* the "fairy music" gifted to musicians by otherworldly beings. Flannery, the legendary bagpiper of Oranmore in Galway, Ireland, became a virtuoso when he was taught piping below ground by a subterranean being.

Similarly, on the island of Skye in the Scottish Hebrides, a tale is told of Iain Òg MacCrimmon, who was depressed because he was not considered a good enough piper to compete in a contest called by the clan chief, MacLeod of Dunvegan Castle. Iain Òg MacCrimmon went into a cave at Harlosh Point to play the pipes alone, and there a fairy woman appeared to him, produced a silver chanter for his pipes, and taught him how to play it. "Your handsome looks and sweet music have brought you a fairy sweetheart. I bequeath you this silver chanter: At the touch of your fingers, it will always bring forth the sweetest music." This was the famous *sionnsairairgid na mna sithe,* "the silver chanter of the fairy woman." Iain Òg MacCrimmon went to Dunvegan Castle, entered the piping contest, and was judged to be the best of all. The enchanted chanter of fairyland gave him abilities denied to others (Carmichael 1911, 86). The cave is known today as the Piper's Cave.

According to the ancient Celtic tradition, he was appointed as the hereditary piper to the MacLeods, and for many generations MacCrimmon's descendants were renowned pipers and composers of new pipe music. At Borreraig Farm, across Loch Follart, opposite Dunvegan Castle, Iain Òg MacCrimmon founded a piping school to which advanced students came from all over Scotland and Ireland to perfect the art of piping. The highest standards of *ceol mor* or *piobaireachd,* the characteristic music of the Scots highland bagpipe, were attained at Borreraig, for the course to mastery of the pipes took seven years. The school existed from around 1600 to 1770. Another otherworldly musical piece connected with Dunvegan Castle is "The Dunvegan Lullaby" or "The Dunvegan Cradle Spell," reputedly sung by a fairy woman who comforted an unhappy baby when its nurse was away for a while. The nurse listened and recalled it.

St. Patrick is said to have heard the *ceol sidhe* played on the *timpán* and stated that it would equal the very music of heaven if it were not for "a twang of the fairy spell that infests it" (Wentz 1911, 199–200). This account mentions the playing of the *timpán* at *Samhain* (*Lá Samhna,* November 1) by "The Wondrous Elfin Man," when the fairy music would make all that heard it fall to sleep (Wentz 1911, 200). Turlough O'Carolan, the celebrated seventeenth-century blind Irish harper, was said to have slept out one night in a fairy rath (fairy hill or fort) and received the gift of *ceol-sidhe* in his dreams. When he awoke, he remembered the music and played it. Lady Wilde recounts the story of an Irish piper, who, walking through the hills one evening, heard a fairy piper play an exquisite tune called "Móraleana." The fairy told him that he could only play "Móraleana" three times in his life before an audience. If he played it a fourth time, a curse would befall him. He played it only three times and never again until he found himself in the final round of a piping competition. He knew he would win if he played "Móraleana," so he played it and won the prize as best piper. At the moment the garland of Bardic mastery was placed upon his head, he collapsed and died upon the stage. One must not use a fairy gift for worldly gain. There is a story told today among traditional musicians in Ireland and Britain that if the tune "King of the Fairies" is played through three times in a row, the king of the fairies will appear. If the musician has played well, he or she will be rewarded; but if the tune was played badly, some unspecified otherworldly punishment will befall the player. "King of the Fairies" is in the "eldritch key" of E minor.

In his *Carmina Gadelica* (1900) Alexander Carmichael noted an *òran sìdh* (fairy song) that a man heard when searching for sheep at Creaga Gorma, Hèathabhal, on the isle of Barra in the Western Isles of Scotland. A fairy woman was grinding a quern (hand mill) and singing the song. Carmichael published this song and four others, recalled by girls and women from Iochdar, Sandray, and Mingulay. Three were heard at fairy mounds and another was part of a traditional story about Roderick MacDonald, a man who had built his house on a fairy site where a fairy woman sang as she ground her quern, so he was forced to move elsewhere (Carmichael 1997, 478–80, 663). The music of the Manx song called "Bollan Bane" (The White Herb), "a plant known to the Fairy Doctors, and of great healing virtues," was noted around 1840 one evening on the mountains by a person who heard it being sung by the fairies (Moore 1891, 41). In her introduction to the section on the Isle of Man in *The Fairy Faith in Celtic Countries* (1911), Sophia Morrison recounted a twentieth-century tradition of otherworldly music. William Cain, a fiddler from Glen Helen (formerly called Rhenass), was known as "Willy the Fairy" for his knowledge of fairy music. He sang and played airs he said he had heard the fairies playing

(Morrison 1911, 118). Once he saw a great glass house like a palace, all lit up, in a glen beneath the mountains at Brook's Park, where the fairies were playing. He stopped and listened to a tune until he got it, then went home to practice it on the fiddle. William Cain later played that fairy tune at Manx entertainment staged in Peel by Sophia Morrison (Wentz 1911, 131).

ANCESTRAL MUSIC

Bardism in the past tended to be hereditary, and at certain times hereditary scalds and bards were attached to royal and noble families. There was an Irish tradition that the bardic families possessed secrets, which they transmitted from generation to generation. In 1887 Lady Jane Wilde wrote of the "herb of which a drink was made, called The Bardic Potion, for the Bards alone had the secret of the herb, and of the proper mode of treatment by which its mystic power could be revealed. This potion they gave their infant children at their birth, for it had the singular property of endowing the recipient with a fairy sweetness of voice of the most rapturous and thrilling charm. And instances are recorded of men amongst the Celtic Bards, who, having drunk of this potion in early life, were ever after endowed with the sweet voice, like fairy music, that swayed the hearts of the hearers as they chose to love or war, joy or sadness, as if by magic influence, or lulled them into the sweet calm of sleep" (Wilde 1887, II, 67).

In Scotland there were hereditary pipers retained by the chief of the clan, of which the Borreraig School MacCrimmons are the most famous. Others include the MacArthurs, pipers to MacDonald of Sleat; the Rankins, pipers to the MacLeans of Coll, Duart, and Mull; and the MacGregors, pipers to Campbell of Glenlyon. Hereditary bards and pipers in ancient Scotland had a piece of land given to them by the clan chief to farm or graze animals upon, and various payments for attending official events and celebrations. Instruments are handed down in the family, and generations of descendants may be playing the same instrument that their ancestors played. As an old Scots saying tells us, "shared gold goes not far, but a shared song lasts a long time."

15

Northern Instruments

THE *KANTELE*, LYRE, AND ALLIED INSTRUMENTS

In the Finnish *Kalevala* epic, the shaman-craftsman Väinämöinen had a magical genesis. He crafted the first *kantele* harp out of the skull of an enormous pike fish and strung it with strings spun from a woman's hair. The original instrument was lost at sea, so Väinämöinen fashioned a new one from the wood of the birch tree. Traditional kanteles are made from a hollowed-out block of wood and have five horsehair strings, but

Fig. 15.1. Finnish *kantele*, twentieth century.

metal strings superseded horsehair when wire began to be manufactured industrially. Later instruments have more than five strings, and a classically oriented concert kantele with key-altering levers like the classical concert harp was devised by Paul Salminen in the 1920s.

The related northern lyre was a bardic instrument in ancient times. This instrument consisted of a flat soundbox connected to two side pieces joined at the top by a yoke that supported the strings. At the lower end of the soundbox was a tailpiece that anchored the strings, which passed over a bridge resting on the soundboard. At Paule, Saint-Symphorien, in the Côtes-du-Nord region of France there is a Celtic stone figure dating from the second century BCE that depicts a musician holding a lyre and wearing a torc round his neck (Dannheimer and Gebhard 1993, 278). In Ireland there are depictions of lyres on Celtic crosses. Remains of lyres from the sixth and seventh centuries have been found in Anglo-Saxon royal burials in England, as at Sutton Hoo and Prittlewell. Gaelic harps in Ireland and Scotland were strung with bronze or brass wire from early times, but it is likely that comparable instruments in Britain and continental Europe were strung with hair or gut.

There are two ways of playing the northern lyre and kantele. One is to play them like a plucked psaltery, with the left hand supporting the body and the right hand picking individual strings. Another way uses a plectrum held in the right hand. This strikes the strings, strumming across all of them. The left hand is held behind the instrument and uses the fingertips to stop strings that the player does not want to sound. In this way different chords can be played. The modern autoharp is based upon this principle. Some versions had a fingerboard between the two supporting arms. This permitted the musician to stop the strings with his or her fingers, as on a fretless instrument such as the violin. The bowed northern lyre with a fingerboard appeared around the eleventh century in Wales as the *crwth,* and England where it was called a *crowd.* In Ireland a twelfth-century depiction of this instrument is carved in stone at St. Finan's church at Lough Currane, County Kerry. In Scotland in the twelfth and thirteenth centuries the word *cruit* (otherwise *crott*) meant not a northern lyre but the Gaelic harp, a triangular frame harp. From the fourteenth century, the Gaelic harp was called *clàrsach* in Gaelic and *cláirseach* in Irish.

A tradition of making one's own instruments from available materials existed in country districts in eastern England well into the twentieth century. During World War I, soldiers improvised instruments from salvaged materials. In the region around Cambridge, a local instrument, a kind of plucked psaltery called the Anglia harp, related to the Finnish kantele, was made and played. Locally, a hammered dulcimer with single instead of multiple courses of strings was called a harp, even though it had bridges unlike an Anglia harp (Wortley 1938–1975, 20). Most Anglia harps are more basic, without bridges and usually with fifteen strings made from piano wire. The Midwinterhoorns of Twente province in the Netherlands are not manufactured, and all are different, not being tuned to a particular pitch. As with many traditional musicians up to the middle of the twentieth century, it is likely that instruments were tuned relative to the player's singing voice, rather than standard pitch. Medieval instructions (ca. 1123) exist for casting tuned bells (*cymbal*), made in sets of eight or nine. They were cast from wax that was divided by weight according to proportions that would produce a diatonic musical scale. They were tuned relative to one another by weight, and not tuned from a determinate concert pitch (Theophilus 1979, 176–79).

DRONES

Traditional instruments originating at various historical times have been used to produce a hypnotic droning sound, such as buzzers, bagpipes, bumbass, Jew's harp, *Scheitholt*, *Hommel*, mountain dulcimer, and hurdy-gurdy (Old Nick's birling box). Ritual music predominantly employed the drone as a major element. The Scots word *droner* can mean a player of the bagpipes, as well as a bumblebee (Warrack 1988 [1911], 147); the same sort of "buzzing-bee" name is given to the Dutch and German drone-based fretted stringed instruments called *Hommel* and *Hummel*, respectively. The single-stringed musical instrument devised by Pythagoras, the Monochord, is an image of the cosmos, as Robert Fludd noted in 1617. This instrument, used from Pythagoras onward, became, with the addition of strings, the German *Scheitholt* and *Hummel;* in France the *épinette des Vosges* and *épinette du Nord;* in the Netherlands, the *Hommel;* in Friesland, *Noardische Balke,* and in Norway, the *langeleik*. The oldest known *langeleik* comes from Vardalsåsen near Gjøvik in the Oppland district. It bears the date 1524. From mainland Europe, versions of these instruments were taken to the United States. There in the Appalachians it was standardized as the mountain dulcimer. This diatonically fretted instrument is now played widely in European folk music, including by the present author. Another related drone instrument is the string drum, sometimes called a timbrel.

It was also referred to as the *chorus* and has the French names

Fig. 15.2. String drum timbrel made by Nigel Pennick, 2009.

tambourin á cordes and *tambourin Béarnais* (Munrow 1976, 33–34). It is a rhythmic drone instrument with tensioned strings along a rhomboidal sound box. The strings are beaten with a stick, and as an accompaniment to a three-hole pipe, it is tuned to the keynote of the pipe and its fifth. The Scots verb *to drum* means to repeat something monotonously, to drone (Warrack 1988 [1911], 148).

THE BUZZER

The buzzer is a simple drone instrument consisting of a piece of hard material attached to a string and whirled around to make the sound. It is frequently called by the anthropologists' name "bullroarer," though this name was never employed anywhere by its actual users. It is an archaic instrument. One found in 1960 at Kongemosen in Sjælland, Denmark, was dated at around 6000 BCE. It is a piece of bone shaped as a pointed oval, with a hole bored through one end, through which a piece of string could be threaded. Swinging it in the air produced a humming sound. This instrument is simple to make, and disposable.

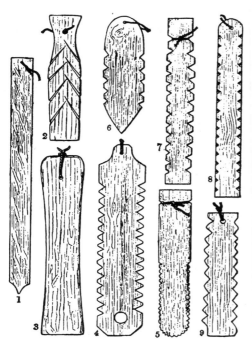

Fig. 15.3. Buzzers from England. The Library of the European Tradition

The Danish word for it is *brummer;* in English the names were mainly bummer, hummer, humming buzzer, or buzzer. Various designs were collected in England in the nineteenth century and, according to the custom of the time, classified by county. Haddon wrote in 1908 that the ends were usually square, but the string end could be rounded; the sides could be serrated or simply notched along both surfaces of each side (Haddon 1908, 278).

In the 1850s the young weavers of Belfast liked playing what they called the *boomer* or *bummer,* described as "an oblong piece of wood, pierced with two holes, and serrated all round" (Haddon 1908, 284–85). The Scottish *bummer* or *bum-speal* was described in 1911 as "a thin piece of serrated wood attached to a string," swung to give a booming sound. In Scotland the tambourine was called a *bumming duff.* The Scots word *bum* means "to drone, as in a bum note, a note misplayed in a tune" (Warrack 1988 [1911], 62). Haddon's informant in north-eastern Ireland stated that once when, as a boy, he was playing with a *boomer* an old country woman said it was a "sacred" thing (Haddon 1908, 283–84). In the Schwarzwald of south Germany, the instrument was called *Schlägel* or *Brummer.* Sometimes, one was attached to the end of a whip and whirled round at ceremonial events; this is called a *Schwirrholz* (Seidel 1896, 67).

In Scotland the instrument is also known by a name that associates it with thunder; generally as a thunder-spell, and in Aberdeen as a thunderbolt (Haddon 1908, 280–81). Alice Gomme in her *Traditional Games of England, Scotland, and Ireland* gives this definition:

> Thun'er-Spell. A thin lath of wood, about six inches long and three or four inches broad, is taken and rounded at one end. A hole is bored in that end, and in the hole is tied a piece of cord between two and three yards long. . . . It was believed that the use of this instrument during a thunderstorm saved one from being struck with "the thun'er-bolt." (Gomme 1894 and 1898, II 291)

The Scots dictionary compiler Alexander Warrack describes the *thunder speal* being "whirled round the head to mimic thunder"

(Warrack 1988 [1911], 612). Gomme noted that the more rapidly the instrument is swung the louder is the noise. Haddon noted that when swinging more rapidly, the high note of a buzzer passes into a low harmonic. In Galicia this tuning effect was called *bzik* (Haddon 1908, 285).

Related to the buzzer is the *sneerag*, made of one of the larger bones of a pig's foot connected to two worsted strings, used to produce a snoring sound (Warrack 1988 [1911], 540). A wooden version is the "buzz," made from a small, flat, rectangular piece of wood through which two holes are pierced. A long, continuous piece of string is passed through the holes and tied in a loop. The loops are held in the two hands, and the wood is swung around to twist the string. Then the hands are strongly and steadily drawn apart, causing the wood to spin rapidly, producing a buzzing sound. The momentum makes the string twist itself up again, and it can then be pulled, reversing the spinning "buzz" (Haddon 1908, 284–85).

ROTATORY RATTLES, *WALDTEUFEL*, JACKDAW, AND *ROMMELPOT*

Another type of traditional noisemaker consists of a handle with a circular ratchet at the top, onto which is pivoted a framework holding flexible wooden slats that overlap the ratchet. When the instrument is whirled around, the slats interact with the ratchet to make a rattling sound. This is the *Rärre* used by Devil guisers in the Swabian-Alemannic Fastnacht tradition of south Germany. Rattles of this sort were used as a warning of poison gas attacks in World War I. In his exposition of the buzzer, Haddon describes "a child's toy well known in Germany as the *Waldteufel*" (Woodland Devil). He described it as a small cardboard cylinder, open at one end and closed at the other like a drum. To the middle of the drum a horsehair or fiber was fastened, and the other end was tied to a piece of wood. The wood at this spot is coated with resin to produce a grating sound that was transmitted along the fiber, the cylinder acting as a resonator (Haddon 1908, 284). A related English instrument was the jackdaw, which was made of about an inch of the top part of the neck of a wine bottle. Over this was stretched a bit of parchment, which was tightly tied under the projecting rim of it. A long horsehair, with a knot at the end, was then put through the parchment, the knot being inside the neck. By wetting the forefinger and thumb and drawing the horsehair between them, the player could produce sounds by moving the hand rapidly or slowly or in jerks.

A related friction drum played in the Low Countries is known by its Dutch name, *rommelpot* (rumble pot), from the Dutch verb *rommelen,* meaning "to produce a low, dull noise, to rumble." In Germany it is called *Brummtopf* (Munrow 1976, 34). The sound of the *rommelpot* is produced by the vibration of a membrane stretched tightly across the neck of an earthenware pot, jug, or soup bowl. Traditionally, the membrane is made from the bladder of a pig or cow, and a wooden stick is inserted through the middle. Rubbing the stick with moistened fingers produces the sound, and variations in pressure control the pitch. The sound was considered unearthly or diabolical, especially when the pot contained dried peas or was half-filled with water. In Flanders the *rommelpot* is an instrument played traditionally on various festive days (De Hen 1972, 105–10). In Brabant there is a traditional dance called "Rommelpot," which of course should be accompanied by the instrument. Like the *bodhrán* (see below), after almost falling into disuse the *rommelpot* was given a new lease on life through the efforts of Paul Collaer and Felix van Eekhoute. There is an unbroken tradition of playing it in the Belgian village of Kessenich.

THE FRAME DRUM

The frame drum is well known as the sacred instrument of the shaman. It has a mystique because it enables the shaman to enter altered states of consciousness and practice soul-flight (Old Norse *hamfarir*). It was rare in Europe outside areas where shamanism was practiced.

In nineteenth-century Cornwall a sea witch called Kate "the Gull" Turner possessed a frame drum or "tambourine" with which she performed divinations. Orientation of the drum according to the cardinal directions appears to have been part of the ritual. In Britain and Ireland

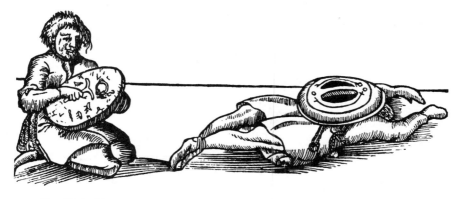

Fig. 15.4. Sámi shamans' drums, Finland, from Johannes Schefferus's *Lapponia* (1673). The Library of the European Tradition

the frame drum was traditionally seen as a ritual instrument and played only during the rites and ceremonies on May Day and Hallowe'en, and by the Wren Boys at Midwinter. In the west of Britain and Ireland, the frame drum appears to have been identical with an agricultural implement called the *wecht, wight,* or *dallan,* used for winnowing, separating the chaff from the grain (Evans 1957, 211). Structurally, the implement is like a sieve, but instead of having interwoven cords to screen out large from small objects, it has a base made from an animal skin, so it can easily double as a drum. An English frame drum in a rare photograph taken of Jack-in-the-Green at a traditional May Day performance in Oxford in 1886 is much larger than a *wecht* or a *bodhrán.*

An indication of the tradition of calling upon things to grow is in the Scots expression "deaf grain," meaning grain that has lost the power to germinate (Warrack 1988 [1911], 127). The name of the Irish frame drum, *bodhrán,* is derived from the Old Irish word *bodhar,* meaning "deaf" or "haunted" (James 1997, 78). Materials matter both acoustically and magically. For the bodhrán, makers prefer to use goatskin or deerskin, giving a good sound, but calf, sheep, donkey, and greyhound skins were also used to stretch across the frame (James 1997, 80). Goatskin is considered to produce the authentic bodhrán sound (Driver 1994, 4). H. C. Agrippa commented that a drum made from wolf's skin causes a drum made of lambskin not to sound (Agrippa 1993 [1531], I, XXI). With both the shaman's drum and the bodhrán, the skin is stretched across the frame with its outside facing outward; that is, the surface that is played. The bodhrán frame is made of ash, bent green and lapped at the joint (McCrickard 1994, 20). It has crossbars at the back made of wood or metal, which stabilizes the frame and provides a handhold. Some shamans' frame drums also have crossbars, while others have a metal ring suspended by thongs, or a rod carved into a humanoid form.

In former times the bodhrán was associated with the west of Ireland, parts of the counties of Clare, Cork, Kerry, Limerick, and Tipperary (McCrickard 1994, 21). At one time it was played only during ritual performances by the Wren Boys on St. Stephen's Day (December 26), in a rite that involved hunting and killing a wren and parading it from house to house. In the 1960s it was played notably by Seán Ó Riada (1931–1971) and adopted by other Irish traditional musicians as a viable instrument for music at all times. In 1986 the Irish playwright J. B. Keane wrote a play titled *The Bodhrán Makers*. In the early twenty-first century, the Irish bodhrán is widespread among traditional and folk musicians in Ireland, Great Britain, and the United States.

THE CLAPPERS

It was formerly customary to make percussive sounds at Eastertime. There is a German tradition of hitting walls with hammers in springtime (*Sonnenvogelklopfen*). In Wales children used clappers to make a noise to alert householders to give them eggs for Easter (*clepio wyau'r pasg*). There are two known forms of egg clappers from Wales. The simpler clapper is a wooden instrument shaped like a cooking spatula to which two other flat pieces of wood are tied tightly by strings threaded through two holes. When the handle is shaken, the tied-on pieces clap against the flattened end. A larger kind of clapper is a wooden board with a hole at the center through which a handle protrudes. A double-headed wooden hammer is hinged into the top of the handle, and rapid movement makes the hammer swing back and forth, hitting the board (Owen 1987, 86). There is an English saying, "to go like the clappers," derived from the speed with which the clappers can be played. Related in structure is the Lithuanian *skrabalai*. The instrument consists of a trapezoidal wooden trough hollowed out from a block of oak or ash, with wooden or metal small clappers hung inside. The *skrabalai* is shaken so that a clapper knocks against the side of the trough, making a hollow clapper sound. It can also be played as a drum using sticks.

BONES

Bones make good percussion instruments. A pair of cow ribs rattled together was a traditional instrument everywhere there were cattle. Rib bones were called knicky-knackers in seventeenth-century Britain, where, not surprisingly, they were associated with butcher-boy rituals and pastimes. It was traditional for butcher boys to serenade newlywed couples with marrowbones and meat cleavers. "Formerly, the band would consist of four cleavers, each of a different tone, or, if complete, of eight,

Fig. 15.5. *The Butchers' Serenade,* 1869.
The Library of the European Tradition

and by beating their marrowbones skilfully against these, they obtained a sort of music somewhat after the fashion of indifferent bell ringing. When well performed, however, and heard from a proper distance, it was not altogether unpleasant. A largesse of half-a-crown or a crown was generally expected for this delicate attention. The butchers of Clare market had the reputation of being the best performers" (Larwood and Hotten 1908, 358). An illustration of this from Chambers's *Book of Days* (1869) is shown in figure 15.5.

The bones, smaller than full cow ribs, are a folk instrument that in the nineteenth century became associated with blackface minstrels. But they were never exclusively a minstrel instrument, for they are played in performances and pub sessions of traditional music of Britain and Ireland. Two or more bones are held loosely in one or both hands, which then are shaken in rhythm to produce percussive sounds. Sometimes they are played by step dancers in accompaniment to their dance steps. Bones players consider the best material to be whales' bones, very hard yet easily worked like wood (Driver 1994, 25).

BELLS

Bells are closely connected with religious rites and ceremonies, as well as being an adjunct to dance and as a warning in transport. They signify and amplify the presence of desirable spiritual powers, while suppressing unwanted intrusions. Bells transmit the virtue of the metal of which they are made. In ancient Greece resonant metal instruments were called "the bronze" (*chalkos*). A scholiast of Theocritus remarked that the *chalkos* was sounded at eclipses of the moon "because it has power to purify and to drive off pollutions." Sounding the bronze in ancient Rome was instrumental in rituals. Ovid noted that the annual visits of the spirits of the departed to their former homes were brought to an end by sounding a bronze plate and ordering them to leave.

The particular resonance of a bell depends upon the material it is made of, its dimensions, and its shape. Its sound is a manifestation of these qualities. Early bells were made by bending sheet metal to shape and riveting the join, and cowbells are made in this way now. This kind of bell is still hung around the necks of herd animals to ward off evil. The other kind of ancient bell is the spherical bell used from early medieval times on horse harness. Bells like these are similar to the ceremonial bells worn by some shamans, guisers, and Morris dancers. They ring as the performer walks, runs, or dances. Town criers in England ring a handbell to attract people before making their official announcements. From the early medieval times, large church bells were cast in foundries. It is not known whether bells were introduced into northern Europe by the Romans or by Christian missionaries, but the clergy of the Celtic Church certainly recognized the sanctity of bells. Bells that had belonged to revered priests were preserved in ornate reliquaries. They were no longer capable of being sounded, but considered magically powerful objects in their own right. The bell of the ninth-century Irish priest, St. Cuilleann, is a typical relic used for ritual purposes. For many years it was kept in a hollow tree at Kilcuilawn at Glenkeen, County Tipperary. In the eighteenth century it was taken out so that oaths could be sworn upon it. Bells like this were in the keeping of *dewars,* hereditary relic keepers, and handed down through the generations in families. For example, on the island of Inishkeel, County Donegal, the O'Breslan family kept the Bell of St. Conall. In the Christian tradition, bells were baptized and given names.

BELLS IN HORSEMANRY

The Scots ballad "Sir John Gordon," collected by John Ord in his *Bothy Songs and Ballads,* tells how Sir John encountered the Queen of Faerie and was taken away to the Otherworld where he had to serve her. The horse ridden by the Queen of Fairyland was bedecked with a particular number of bells:

> *Her gown was o' the green, green silk,*
> *Her mantle o' velvet fine,*
> *And from the mane of her milk-white steed*
> *Silver bells hung fifty and nine.*

(Ord 1995, 423)

In England it was a medieval custom to give a golden bell to the winner of a horse race. An annual race with this prize was run on St. George's Day (April 23) at Chester. Racing for a bell led to the expression for being the winner, "bearing off the bell" (Larwood and Hotten 1908, 174–75). *The Carter's Health,* noted in Nuthurst, Sussex, England, 1812–13, refers to the custom of "the wild stud," and the best mare.

> *Of all the horses in the Merry Green Wood*
> *'Twas the bob-tail mare car'd [carried] the bells away.**
> (CLARK 1930, 797)

In the British Isles, packhorse gangs were a common form of transport before the construction of turnpike roads, canals, and railways. A number of horses (a train) proceeded in single file along unpaved trackways or across open moorland along customary routes. Each horse in the train was fitted with packs or panniers. The train was led by a lead horse that was fitted with bells. In 1790 Thomas Bewick noted that the packhorses,

> in their journeys over the trackless moors . . . strictly adhere to the line of order and regularity custom has taught them to observe; the leading Horse, which is always chosen for his sagacity and steadiness, being furnished with bells, gives notice to the rest, which follow the sound, and generally without much deviation, though sometimes at a considerable distance. (Bewick 1790, 14–15)

The bells on the lead horse also gave warning to other travelers that a packhorse train was coming, so they could take avoiding action. According to the mythos of the Scottish Horsemens' Society, taught to new members at the time of initiation, the names of the first mare and stallion were Bell and Star. There was a bell on her brow and a star on his brow (Rennie 2009, 111). This, of course, is symbolic. The bell and

---

*The author was taught a slightly different version in Cambridge in the 1960s (Pennick 2011a, 51).

the star are both symbols of guidance. The lead horse's bell guided the packhorse train, while the leading star whose position in the sky never changes allowed navigation at sea and on land.

THE NORTHERN HORNS: *LUR, NEVERLUR, BARKLUR,* AND *MIDWINTERHOORN*

Surviving ancient horns from Ireland, circa 500 BCE, were made of bronze. Some were up to eight feet long, made from smaller pieces riveted together. The largest ones were side blown. A similar Scandinavian horn was the *lur* (cf. Old Norse *luðr,* a "hollow log"). The earliest known instruments came from the Bronze Age and were actually made of bronze. There were once two ceremonial horns bearing figures and runes, fashioned out of sheet gold and dating from the early fifth century CE, which were found at Gallehus, north of Møgeltønder in Jutland, Denmark, in 1639 and in 1734. As they were not intact when found, and have since been destroyed, it is not certain that they were musical instruments, but the banded construction resembles known musical horns made in Scandinavia and the Netherlands from various species of wood.

The most well-known Bronze Age lurs are the Brudevælte lurs, discovered by Ole Pedersen in 1797 in a bog near Lynge in North Zealand, Denmark. They are different from the Viking Age battle horns found in Germany, Denmark, and Norway, which were straight, end-blown wooden instruments about a yard long, bound with willow withies. Bronze lurs have an S-shaped curve reminiscent of aurochs' horns. Battle horns known from sagas had the same function as bugles in later military use. A lur was buried in the Oseberg ship burial of a Norwegian noblewoman dated 834 CE. It was a conical horn enclosed in a richly decorated oak box, one of the earliest musical instrument cases known. Later medieval horns made of pine or fir bound with birch bark (*neverlur*) were used by peasants in Scandinavia. The *barklur* or *barkhorn* (Finnish *touhitorvi*) was made from spirally wound strips of alder, ash, spruce, or willow.

Similar in construction to the ancient horns described above, the

Midwinterhoorn is an instrument used in ceremonial tradition in the Dutch provinces of Overijssel and Twente and the Achterhoek district of Gelderland province. As its name suggests, it is played outdoors around the winter solstice between the beginning of Advent (December 6) and Driekoningen (Twelfth Night) January 6. It is a wooden instrument of archaic appearance, with a special form of construction. They are overblown horns with no finger holes, producing natural harmonics. There are two kinds of horns made according to this technique: *natte hoorns* (wet horns) and *droog hoorns* (dry horns). Dry horns are not traditional. They are a modern version of the Midwinterhoorn, with the wooden halves glued together. Traditional Midwinterhoorns are made usually from curving branches of alder or birch trees, measuring from about four to six feet (1.2 to 1.8 m). The longer the horn, the easier it is to play higher notes. A horn made of alder is called an *elsenhoorn,* and one made of birch is a *berkenhoorn.* The narrow end where the mouthpiece is set can measure from one to two inches (25–50 mm), and six inches (150 mm) at the wide end.

The maker of the *natte hoorn* shapes the branch, then puts it in a well, where it is left to soak for a period. When the wood has soaked sufficiently, the horn maker cuts off the bark using a draw knife. When it is thoroughly wet, it is hauled out and split longitudinally. The two halves are hollowed out and made smooth, and a hole is drilled in the narrow end to take the mouthpiece. When ready, the two halves are put back together. Bulrush leaves are put in the join, and the horn is lashed together tightly with *brummel,* willow, or bramble (blackberry) stems coiled round the horn six times, their ends being tucked beneath the last coil. Then wooden wedges are hammered under the bindings from the narrow end of the instrument. There are at least six bindings on each horn. Then the Midwinterhoorn is put back into the well until the bulrush and bindings have swollen in the water and made the horn airtight. The wedges are hammered farther in, and the *hap* (mouthpiece) is made of elder wood and fitted into a hole at the narrow end of the horn.

Midwinterhoorns are not tuned to any common pitch, as they are essentially solo instruments used in calling and answering when played with others at a distance. The Midwinterhoorn player holds the horn laterally, though it is blown straight down the tube. The shape of the mouthpiece allows it to be blown straight down the tube, although it appears to be across like the classical flute. Some ancient images of horns resemble those made today, and many medieval images of celestial horn blowers show lateral blowing like the Midwinterhoorn, such as in the early fourteenth-century wall painting in Schleswig Cathedral, Germany, of a horn-blowing woman riding a tiger, possibly an image of the goddess Freya. The *natte hoorn* is blown wet, and it is customary to blow the Midwinterhoorn over a well. This amplifies the sound of the horn. When the horn freezes in winter, it produces a particularly brilliant sound that is said to enhance the fertility of the soil and promote an abundant harvest (Montagu 1975, 71–80; Thijsse 1980, *passim*). The Midwinterhoorn may have survived in this region because Twente province was a Catholic enclave in a Protestant country. The Calvinist prohibitions on music did not reach there, and during the sectarian wars of religion it was used as a warning signal of the approach of Protestant military forces.

PRACTICAL AND MAGICAL MATERIALS

Writing "on sound and harmony," H. C. Agrippa noted that some sounds go well together, while others can never be harmonious. One of his examples was that strings made of sheep's gut can never be tuned together with those of wolf's gut. Although this may not technically be true, it clearly was a tradition among instrument makers that certain materials would not work with certain others, so they were avoided (Agrippa 1993 [1531], II, XXV).

Traditional stringed instruments need to be made from combinations of particular woods if they are to sound good. The back and sides of instruments such as fiddles must be made of a stiff and resonant wood, such as ash, beech, maple, sycamore, walnut, and willow, or rarer woods from fruit trees such as pear and cherry. The main soundboard of the instrument must be made with a thin, stiff, strong wood, cut on the quarter. Conifer wood is ideal, and pine, cedar, fir, and spruce are favoured. The neck must be made from a strong, durable wood that can be carved freely, such as sycamore, maple, or beech.

Some ancient ballads and sagas give material descriptions of how to make things. The Finnish *Kalevala* details the materials of the kantele made by Väinämöinen from the wood of the birch tree, the materials of the tuning pegs, and the strings. In Ireland *Cormac's Glossary* (ca. 900 CE) tells that the instrument called the *timpán* was made of sally wood, and the tone of its bronze strings was soft and sweet. The *timpán*, upon which the *ceol sidhe* heard by St. Patrick was played, appears to have been a kind of lyre or psaltery played with a quill plectrum. "The willow has a mystery in it of sound," wrote Lady Wilde, and according to Irish tradition the harp belonging to the eleventh-century King Brian Boru was made of willow wood (Wilde 1887, II, 117). Some Perchtenlauf bands in Austria, the *Holzmusik*, play special wind instruments made entirely from wood, some of which are versions of those customarily made from brass.

DISORIENTATION BY SOUND

One can be disoriented by noise, and in Scots there is the word to describe it: *gallehooing*, a stupefying senseless noise (Warrack 1988 [1911], 202). "Nor do they want music, and in a strange manner given them by the Devil. . . . Where everyone sung what he would, without hearkening to his fellow; like the noise of divers oars, falling in the water," wrote Ben Jonson of the witches in his notes to *The Masque of Queens* (1609). In the early twentieth century, the Dadaists produced the same chaotic, disorienting effect with their "simultaneous poetry." There is a tradition of disempowerment of spirits by music; for example, the seventeenth-century English tune "Stand Thy Ground Old Harry" was said to ward off the Devil.

Evil spirits are believed to be frightened away by sound, as in the German custom of the *Richtfest*, topping out the roof of a new house. The hullabaloo (*Hillebille*) is made with hammers, chains, shouting, and singing and is intended to drive away any evil spirits that would bring bad luck to the new house (Bächtold-Stäubli 1927–1942, III,

Fig. 15.6. Whip-cracking on horseback at New Year,
Pongau, Austria.

1564). Noisemaking is also part of the "charivari" or "skimmington," a near-riotous gathering in public to express disapproval of an unpopular individual. In England this is the "tin can band," or "rantantanning." In Germany it is called *Katzenmusik* (a "caterwaul"), with people banging improvised instruments such as cooking pots and pans, and is intended to drive away evil spirits or run people out of town. In Austria horsemen crack whips at the New Year to purify the air from evil. Noisy fireworks let off at New Year all over the world can also be viewed as driving away the evil spirits from the celebration of the new beginning.

16

Keeping Up the Day

MARK DAYS AND TIMES OF THE YEAR

Traditional festivals held on specific days are often called Calendar Customs, but in actuality they are related to the time of year; the calendar only marks their place in the year. They celebrate either important days in the annual day-length cycle, the changing of the seasons, or religious festivals, many of which relate to the particular season. Aspects or fragments of various old traditions are incorporated in certain festivals: Some are initially pre-Christian in origin, such as Yuletide and May Day; some are derived from Roman Catholicism, such as the holy days of St. Valentine's and St. George's Day. Some are national festivals with a political origin, such as various Independence Days, National Days, Guy Fawkes' Night, and Remembrance Sunday. Some are to do with the annual cycle of agriculture, such as the harvest. Others are festivals of local veneration of official or unofficial saints. They have countless local customs connected with them all over northern Europe, and a few characteristic ones are detailed here. The very diversity of origins and syncretic practices of the year cycle make it futile to assign these mark days to a particular religion, sect, or nation.

They have reached their present state through many changes and additions, and they continue to evolve as new people find new ways

262

of interpreting them. Each individual performance will differ in some way from the previous one, and from others happening in other places at the same time, yet to "keep up the day" in whatever relevant way is to carry on the tradition. Some festivities that continue in the twenty-first century owe their survival to local societies who kept them going against official opposition. In Scotland, lodges of trade guilds such as the Horsemen's Society and the Oddfellows preserved the old forms of festivity when they were dying out from universal observance. This is one of the functions of traditional unadvertised groups in "keeping up the day," making their appearances only during their rites and ceremonies of the appropriate day, whether they are expected or not.

WAYS TO DEFINE THE YEAR

The solar year can be defined in four different traditional ways: the vegetation year, the flower year, the harvest year, and the maritime year. There are ten possible year cycles:

Solstitial solar years:	December–June–December; June–December–June
Equinoctial solar years:	September–March–September; March–September–March
Vegetation Years:	November–May–November
Flower Years:	May–November–May
Harvest Years:	August–February–August; February–August–February
The Maritime Year:	April–October–January–April; October–January–April–October

Between the two solstices, the traditional rural calendar in Britain and Ireland marked the end and beginning of winter by the festivals of May Day (Beltane) and All Saints' (Samhain), respectively May 1 and November 1 in the modern calendar. In medieval times the agricultural year was regulated by the church's "red letter days," particular saints' days that either continued pre-Christian practice or coincided with it. Practically, these days were only an indication, as the fluctuations in the weather that might lead to an early or late harvest, for instance, were the real events that mattered.

THE ANGLO-SAXON YEAR

In the north the physical fact of long days in the summer and short days in the winter is the common feature of the traditional observances. The different ways of life—pastoral, agricultural, industrial, mercantile, and military—all have their contribution to make to days that mark the passing of the years. In England the ancient year-cycle is known in detail. The fervent faith of the early Christian missionaries drove them to obliterate local ancestral traditions and impose the new religion on them instead. Although early Christian chroniclers hated the traditional rites and ceremonies of the country people around them, in their attempts to discredit the elder faith, they wrote about them, in horror. Fortunately, they recorded what our spiritual ancestors did, and because of this, we can understand the meaning of their rites and ceremonies.

The seventh-century chronicler Bede tells us that the ancient Angles divided the year into two halves, defined by the solstices. Each solstice was bracketed by a preceding and following month. In the winter there was *Ærra Geóla,* "Before Yule," the month before the winter solstice, and *Æftera Geóla,* "After Yule," the month after it. Similarly, in the summer time, two months bracket the summer solstice: *Ærra Líða* before Midsummer, and *Æftera Líða* after it. The Anglo-Saxon months had names descriptive of their qualities. January was *Æftera Geóla;* February was *Sol-mónaþ,* "Mud Month" (later called "February fill dyke"); and April *Eóstre-mónaþ,* which was the first month of spring. Eostre was the Anglo-Saxon goddess of the dawn and of springtime, and she gives her name to the festival of Easter, though its actual date is reckoned according to a modified version of the ancient Jewish calculation of Passover. May was called *Þrí-milce,* "Three Milkings," an abundant time when cows have plenty of milk. *Ærra Líða,* "Before the Summer Solstice," was equivalent to June; July was *Æftera Líða.* August was *Weód-mónaþ,* "Weed Month," and September *Hálig-mónaþ,* "Holy Month," the month in which the harvest festival was celebrated. The church banned the name *Hálig-mónaþ* and the new month-name *Hærfest-monaþ,* "Harvest Month," was invented. October was *Winterfulleþ,* the month that began winter. November was *Blót-mónaþ,* "Sacrifice Month," when slaughtered animals were dedicated to the gods. Finally, December, the month before Yule, was *Ærra Geóla.*

YULE

Throughout northern Europe, religious festivals are linked with the seasons, and related folk customs reflect the character of the time of year when they are performed. In the north, winter darkness is more protracted than farther south, and the midwinter solstice, celebrating the return of the light after the longest night of the year, is the major festival of the year. Celebrated with feasting and fires, disguise and games, it is the Old Norse Yule, the "yoke of the year," December 21, the shortest day. This festival was celebrated all over northern Europe, and Christmas is its continuation. It was the Norse *Jul,* Slavic *Kračun,* and the Lithuanian *Kūčios* and *Kalėdos.* The festivities of Yule went on for twelve days, the Twelve Days of Christmas, a time of respite from the hard labor of everyday toil.

YULETIDE GUISING

All over Europe, in the same way that the church sought to extirpate Pagan worship at an earlier period, repeated attempts were made to stamp out the unregulated festivals of the common people. The medieval church was especially ardent in its attempts to wipe out midwinter rites and ceremonies. Records of the attempted suppression of performance traditions, especially those involving animal and other disguises, give us some idea of the nature and content of these events. Clearly, the church suppressed performances when it could; the documentary record is fragmental, but repetitive. There was an especial hatred or fear of people wearing masks and putting on ritual animal disguise. One of the bynames of Odin is Grimnir, interpreted literally as "the one with the grimy (blackened) face," or "the masked one." *Grime* means frost or dirt, and a grim face is one frozen in a forbidding expression. The Old Germanic words *isengrim,* a mask covering the head, or *egesgrîma,* a "terrifying mask," refer to this.

The continuity of masked guisers and those wearing ritual animal disguise is recorded in the history of their prohibition. In what is now Spain, the Bishop of Barcelona banned the stag play in 370 CE (Alford 1968, 122–23). There is a fourth-century calf mask (*vetula*) from Liechtenstein preserved in the Österreichisches Museum für Volkskunde in Vienna. In France in 543 CE, Bishop Caesarius of Arles attempted to suppress mumming in ritual animal disguise in the likeness of calves and other beasts (Bärtsch 1998 [1933], 34). Similarly, in 643 the Lombard king Rotharius ordered that those who wore a mask (*masca*) or a disguise impersonating dead warriors were to be punished. Around the same time, Bishop Eligius of Noyes (died 659) issued edicts against mumming. In 578 CE a church Council at Auxerre, Burgundy, forbade disguisings, and another Council, in the year 614, stated it was "unlawful to make any indecent plays upon the Kalends of January, according to the profane practices of the pagans." In the ninth century Hincmar of Reims told his parishioners that "one must not allow reprehensible plays with the bear, nor with woman dancers, to be performed." Hincmar used the word *talamasca,* also used by prohibitionists Regino of Prüm (ca. 900) and Burchard of Wurms in 1020. It appears that Christian missionaries to Pagan territory sometimes mistook the outings of guisers and mummers as an apparition of the *Mesnée d'Hellequin.* Ordericus Vitalis recorded in his *Ecclesiastical History* that in January 1091 a priest out in open country at Bonneval near Chartres in France came across the Wild Horde, led by a giant carrying a club followed by a horde of demons. This outing of the *Mesnée d'Hellequin* is the earliest known literary reference to the Harlequin disguise. The description tallies with contemporary demonic guisers who appear now around midwinter in events such as the *Perchtenlauf* (Perchten procession) of south Germany and Austria.

Saxo Grammaticus (ca. 1200) recorded the practice of setting the severed head of a sacrificed horse on a pole for magical purposes, and

Fig. 16.1. *Perchtenlauf* at St. Johann, Pongau, Austria.

the horse appears as a major theme in ritual disguisings at midwinter (Saxo 1905, 209). In Iceland at the same time, between the twelfth and fourteenth centuries, successive bishops condemned people who sang ceremonial songs called *Vikivakar,* man-to-woman and woman-to-man. The performances involved animal disguise, the *hestleikur* ("horse game"), a man covered with red cloth guising as a horse (Alford 1968, 132). In twelfth-century England the Bishop of Salisbury, Thomas de Cobham (died 1313), condemned all kinds of actors, especially those who transformed their bodies by contortions and those who wore masks. In thirteenth-century England prominent clerics issued edicts attempting to suppress various practices. Around 1240 the Bishop of Lincoln, Robert Grosseteste, and the Bishop of Worcester, Walter de Chanteloup, both made "disciplinary pronouncements." Chanteloup's Constitutions (1240) and Grosseteste's prohibitions (1236–1244) condemned most folk customs, including some of Christian origin. Among them were miracle plays, "scot-ales," "ram-raisings," and May Games and other athletic competitions, together with craftsmen's "guild-ales" and the ceremonies of *Festum Stultorum* and the *Inductio Mali sive Autumni*. Around 1250 the University of Oxford authorities thought it necessary to forbid the routs of masked and garlanded students in the churches and open places of the city.

In the following centuries the *Orders* of the city of London for 1334, 1393, and 1405 forbade a practice of going about the streets at Christmas *ove visere ne faux visage* (wearing masks) and entering citizens' houses "to play at dice therein," and in 1417 "mumming" was specifically prohibited. In 1418 it was enacted in London "that no manner of person, of whatever estate, degree, or condition that ever he be, during this holy time of Christmas be so hardy in any way to walk by night in any manner mumming, plays, interludes, or any other disguisings with any false beards, painted masks, deformed or colored faces in any way . . . except that it is lawful for each person to be honestly merry as he can, within his own house dwelling"* (Riley 1868, 669). In Germany they were still trying to stop Yuletide guisers appearing. Fear of magic and witchcraft went well beyond the persecution of those who were believed to practice magic. In 1452 masks were banned again in Regensburg, having been banned previously in 1249 (Schwedt, Schwedt, and Blümke 1984, 10; Bärtsch 1998 [1933], 34). The Bavarian *Tegernsee Manuscript* of 1458 recorded that women led by Frau Percht approached human habitations during the Christmas period, and in 1480 the *Discipuli Sermones* also in south Germany condemned people who believed in the goddess "Diana, commonly known as Percht," who wandered in a throng through the darkness. In Nuremberg in 1496 blackening or reddening faces was prohibited. Like so many official prohibitions, all of these edicts seem to have had little effect.

The ragged *Yuillis Yald* (Yule Horse) was mentioned by the royal bard of Scotland, William Dunbar, in the late fifteenth century. In 1543 the Bishop of Zealand in Denmark warned his flock not to observe "unholy watch night" (New Year's Eve) because the *Hvegehors,* a man guising as a horse, was part of the observance (Alford 1968, 132). In 1545 in Rottweil, Germany, *"larven"* (carnival masks) were

---

*I have modernized the English of the original.

Fig. 16.2. Krampus, Austria.

prohibited. Masked performers in the *Perchtenlauf* and carnivals of Germany were repeatedly subject to punishment. In Bavaria, bans were enacted in 1582, 1596, and 1600. In Berchtesgaden, the spiritual home of Frau Percht, the *Perchtenlauf* was banned in 1601. In Riedlingen in 1745 there were prosecutions of people who wore masks. The revolution of 1848 in Swabia gave all citizens the right to wear masks again legally. The longest suppression of all was in Biberach, where guising was banned in 1599 and did not return until 1987 (Wiesinger 1980, 31). In the twenty-first century, ritual disguise still appears in many parts of Europe, not least in Santa Claus costumes (with false beards). The *Perchtenlauf* runs, the Krampus terrifies, straw bears jostle in the streets, the festival of fools rolls on, and in Britain pantomimes with cross-dressed main characters are put on in many city theaters around the Christmas season.

THE OLD HORSE

The mummers' horse using a real horse's skull was significant in British country rites and ceremonies. It is still used in various mummers' plays of the Old Oss (old horse), from whose knockabout antics comes the word *horseplay,* and where the horse kills a blacksmith who is then brought back to life by a doctor. In Derbyshire the old horse appears at Yuletide, sometimes alongside the Old Tup, a mummer guising as the Derby Ram. The oldest known photograph of an English mummers' team, taken in 1870 at Winster Hall, Derbyshire, has a "horse" made from a horse's skull. At Eckington a skull was dug up from a horse's grave especially for the play. "It seems as if the old horse," wrote S. O. Addy in 1907, "were intended to personify the aged and dying year. The year, like a worn-out horse, has become old and decrepit, and just as it ends, the old horse dies. The time at which the ceremony is performed, and its repetition from one house to another, indicate that it was a piece of magic intended to bring welfare to the people in the coming year." Addy also noted that "guising was known among the old Norsemen as skin-play (*skinnleikr*)" (Addy 1907, 40–42; Cawte 1978, 112–18).

In 1850 a correspondent using the pen name "Pwwca" wrote to *Notes and Queries:* "A custom prevails in Wales of carrying about at Christmas time a horse's skull dressed up with ribbons, and supported on a pole by a man who is concealed under a large white cloth. There is a contrivance for opening and shutting the jaws, and the figure pursues and bites everybody it can lay hold of, and does not release them except on payment of a fine. It is generally accompanied by some men dressed up in a grotesque manner, who, on reaching a house, sing some extempore verses requesting admittance, and are in turn answered by those within, until one party or the other is at a loss for a reply. The Welsh are undoubtedly a poetical people, and these verses often display a good deal of cleverness. This horse's head is called Mari Lwyd, which I have heard translated 'grey mare'" (vol. 1 [1850], 173). A similar Twelfth Night custom on the Isle of Man was recorded by Arthur Moore in 1891:

During the supper the *laare vane,* or white mare, was brought in. This was a horse's head made of wood, and so contrived that the person who had charge of it, being concealed under a white sheet, was able to snap the mouth. He went round the table snapping the horse's mouth at the guests who finally chased him from the room, after much rough play. (Moore 1891, 104–5)

Horse-mask customs continue to this day in Mecklenburg and the Harz Mountains of Germany, as well as the Innviertel region of Austria.

In Britain and Ireland, the day after Christmas, St. Stephen's Day, or Boxing Day saw a ritual wren hunt. The wren is a bird that according to custom was left alone except on December 26, when the local Wren Boys went out to hunt one. When they tracked down a wren among the hedges and brambles, it was killed and brought back processionally to the village tied on top of a pole bedecked with fine ribbons. In Wales some Wren Boys made wooden cages to carry the wren around. It was taken from house to house and inn to inn, where special songs about the wren were sung, with titles such as "Please to See the King" and "The Cutty Wren." In Ireland the *bodhrán* was the ceremonial instrument of the Wren Boys. Killing an otherwise protected bird is an instance of reversal in the Yuletide period, which included a feast overseen by a person designated the Lord of Misrule, who permitted card playing and other forms of gambling and performance that were prohibited at other times of year. In Denmark there is a particular card game called *Gnav,* which was only played at Christmastime. Yule was a time of license.

TWELFTH NIGHT

The end of the festival of Yule/Christmas was Twelfth Night, the Christian festival of Epiphany. The custom of wassailing apple trees in England and Wales is observed traditionally around Twelfth Night. Wassailing began as an Anglo-Saxon drinking custom, centered on the loving cup and the wassail bowl, brimming with spiced alcoholic drink. The custom of groups of people visiting houses with a wassail bowl and singing for largesse had become established by 1600, and a

rich tradition has come down to us, involving drinking, singing, dancing, guising, and processing from place to place (Cater and Cater 2013,
15–50). Wassailing was and is conducted in fruit orchards, to charm
the trees to bear plenty of fruit in the coming season. There are special
wassail songs. In his *Hesperides* (1648) Robert Herrick encouraged the
wassailing of fruit trees:

> *Wassaile the trees, that they may beare*
> *You many a Plum, and many a Peare;*
> *For more or lesse fruits they will bring,*
> *As you doe give the Wassailing.*
> (HERRICK 1902 [1648], 251)

SPEED THE PLOUGH

Plough Monday is the Monday after Twelfth Night, when the fieldwork
began again after the twelve days of Christmas. It is an ancient custom
observed mainly in the eastern half of England that continues today,
bringing out the plough to magically ready it for the work ahead. There
are several theories about the day's origin, assuming that it has a single
origin. One theory is that it was brought to England in the ninth century
by Danish settlers as *Midvintersblót,* the day marking the middle of the
winter season twenty days after Yule. The day also commemorated the
victory of the Danish army over the forces of Wessex in the year 878 that
occurred "at midwinter after Twelfth Night," which was *Midvintersblót*
or *Tiugunde Day,* January 13. The Danelaw was established in that year,
and eastern England was under Danish rule thereafter.

Another theory is that Plough Monday was established by the
Archbishop of York in the eleventh century. But it is clear that, whatever other festivals have been attached to it, it is related to the return to
work after the twelve days of Yule. There is an inscription dating from
the late fourteenth century on a beam in the gallery called the Plough
Rood of Cawston Church, Norfolk: "God spede the plow, And send us
all corne enow, Our purpose for to mak, At crow of cok, Of the plwlete
of Lygate, Be mery and glade, Wat Good ale this work mad" [God

speed the plough and send us ale and corn enough, our purpose for to
make at dawn at the plough light of Lygate. Be merry and glad, what
good ale this work made]. At the beginning of the nineteenth century,
F. Blomefield wrote: "Anciently, a light called the Plough Light was
maintained by old and young persons who were husbandmen, before
images in some churches, and on Plough Monday they had a feast, and
went out with a plough and dancers to get money to support the Plough
Light. The Reformation put out these lights, but the practice of going
about with the plough, begging for money remains, and the 'money for
light' increases the income of the village alehouse" (Blomefield 1805–
1810, 9, 212).

In England, Plough Monday was the traditional beginning of
the New Year's ploughing. It was marked by a procession of ploughboys and ploughmen around their local villages, dragging a plough. In
nineteenth-century England, there were two parallel Plough Monday
traditions, coming from regions where ploughing was done by oxen or
by horses. In eastern England at Helpston, north of Peterborough, in
the 1820s the peasant poet John Clare recorded that on Plough Monday
the Plough Bullocks (from the oxen tradition) all blacked their faces,

Fig. 16.3. Plough parade at Whittlesea, Cambridgeshire, England.

while only some of the Plough Witches did. The "She Witch" had his face "raddled," a mixture of colors. In 1873 a newspaper reported what it hoped was the end of Plough Monday observance in Ramsey, which it called "this licensed system of begging and the attendant foolery of disguised villagers in the bloom of red ochre, the sickly pallor of whiting, or the orthodox demoniacal tint of lampblack" (*The Peterborough Advertiser,* January 18, 1873, 3). A record from Eye, to the east of Peterborough, in 1894, tells how then on Plough Monday "a large number of plough boys attired in the most grotesque manner, having faces reddened with ochre or blackened with soot, waited on those known to be in the habit of remembering the poor old ploughboy" (*Peterborough and Huntingdonshire Standard,* January 13, 1894, 8).

A correspondent to *Fenland Notes & Queries* in 1899 records how "the custom on Straw Bear Tuesday was for one of the confraternity of the plough to dress up with straw one of their number as a bear and call him the Straw Bear. He was then taken round the village to entertain by his frantic and clumsy gestures the good folk who on the previous day had subscribed to the rustics' spread of beer, tobacco, and beef, at which the bear presided" (*Fenland Notes & Queries* IV [1899], 228). At Ramsey, Huntingdonshire, where the Straw Bear presided over the festivities, there was an element of tolerated misrule. It was the custom to settle personal scores on Plough Monday by playing practical jokes. This might involve ploughing up the garden or the front step, moving the water butt so it would flood the house when the front door was opened, taking gates off their hinges and throwing them in the nearest dyke (Marshall 1967, 200–1). At Great Sampford in Cambridgeshire around 1890 on Plough Monday the Accordion Man was accompanied by the Pickaxe Man, who used his tool to dig up boot scrapers when requested, "up with the scraper, Jack!" At West Wratting, Billy Rash told folklorist-performer Russell Wortley in 1960 that on one occasion when money was refused them, the ploughboys ploughed a furrow across the lawn of the big house in the village. In Whittlesea in Eastern England (also spelled Whittlesey), the custom was actively suppressed in 1907 by police action (Frazer and Moore Smith 1909, 202–3), though a straw bear was made on later occasions even after World War I and ran

Fig. 16.4. Straw Bear and attendants at Wilflingen, Germany.

clandestinely from house to house avoiding police patrols (Gill Sennett, personal communication). The Whittlesea Straw Bear reappeared in 1980, and now in the early twenty-first century it presides over a major festival attended by thousands. Straw bears appear in various parts of Germany around the same time of year, marking the beginning of the carnival period. One from Wilflingen is shown in figure 16.4.

FEBRUARY AND THE END OF WINTER

St. Brigid's Day and Candlemas, February 1–2 are often conflated, as they coincide with the old Celtic festival called Imbolc or Oimelc. The first is St. Brigid's Day (*Feil Brighde* in Irish). Traditionally it was reckoned as the first day of spring in Ireland. On St. Brigid's Day an effigy called the *breedhogo* was carried around by young people from house to house, where collections of food and money were made "in honor of Miss Biddy." The *breedhogo* was an effigy made from straw in the form of a human figure. It had a head made from a ball of hay, and the figure was clad in a woman's dress and a shawl. A straw plait called

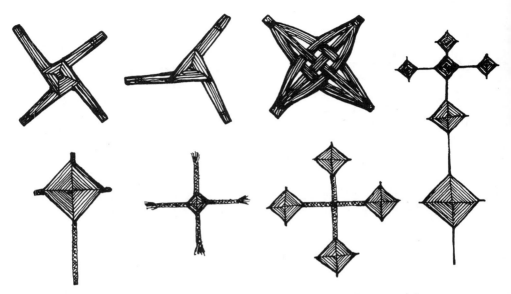

Fig. 16.5. St. Brigid's Cross, Ireland, and related straw plaits.

Brigid's cross was made on St. Brigid's day and hung up inside the house until replaced by another in the following year.

Many festive days were marked by bonfires, and in Geraardsbergen, Flanders (Belgium), the *Tonnekensbrand* is burned to mark the end of winter and the return of the light and the growing season. At sunset a tar barrel is set alight on the summit of the Oudenberg, and surrounding villages respond to the Tonnekensbrand with local fires. The *Tonnekensbrand* is a fire feast that has its own ritual food, the *krakeling*, bread in the form of a ring, thrown to the participants by the mayor. In Swabia (south Germany), on the first Sunday after Ash Wednesday (*Funkensonntag*), an effigy was burned in the *Funkenfeuer*.

At the end of winter, the ritual of spring cleaning the house takes place, usually in early March, and March 1 was the favored day in parts of England. The house had to be swept thoroughly before a threshold pattern was chalked on the front doorstep. In Cambridgeshire it was called Foe-ing Out Day. The belief was that if this day was not kept up, the household would suffer from an infestation of fleas for the following year.

Fig. 16.6. Foe-ing Out Day threshold pattern in chalk (Cambridge Box), South Cambridgeshire, England.

CARNIVAL AND EASTER

The beginning of the Christian fast called Lent (Shrovetide) was marked by the carnival (farewell to meat), culminating in Shrove Tuesday (Fastnacht, Fasnet, Fasching, or Mardi Gras). This was a time of festivity and license, characterized by parades of masked people guising as various local mythic characters and beasts. In Germany, Austria, and Switzerland, the tradition of wearing carved wooden masks continues. As with guising customs at other times of year, current performance has come through centuries of intermittent persecutions. In some places the ceremonial masks are kept hidden away for most of the year, to be brought out at the right time and ceremonially awakened. After the events they are carefully put back to sleep until the next year.

A man of straw can be just an empty straw effigy or may actually have a man inside, as the straw bears do. It is unnerving to see a seemingly lifeless straw man suddenly come to life. Straw men with wooden masks perform in central Europe in Slovenia, Slovakia, Serbia, and

Fig. 16.7. Masked performers on Shrove Tuesday at
Rottweil-am-Neckar, Germany.

Croatia. Straw Boys come out in Ireland and attend weddings, at one time whether or not they were invited. Unmanned straw men called Jack O'Lent were burned at mid-Lent in England. Jack O'Lent was beaten, kicked, shot at, or burned. In Cornwall he was identified with Judas Iscariot (Wright and Lones 1936, I 38). In Liverpool straw effigies of Judas were burned on Good Friday.

The German equivalent of Jack O'Lent appears on windowsills in south Germany now during the period of *Fastnacht* (Shrovetide). Breughel's painting *The Battle of Carnival and Lent* (1559) has a clothed stuffed straw figure sitting on just such a ledge. In Germany this straw man is alternatively called the *Todpuppe*: a symbol of death appearing in the ceremony of *Todaustragen,* "driving out death" (Flaherty 1992, 40–55). In his 1863 book *Das Festliche Jahr,* Freiherr von Rheinsberg-Düringsfeld described the effigy of Death being made of old straw with sticks as arms and legs, clad in old clothing with a face of white linen.

Young people danced hand in hand around it, singing and jeering, either dragging the effigy to a bridge and throwing it off into the water, or taking it to a cliff and throwing it over.

In 1880 William Bottrell wrote of the practice in Cornwall, western England, "In the spring, people visit a 'Pellar' (conjuror) as soon as there is 'twelve hours' sun,' to have 'their protection renewed,' that is, to be provided with charms; and the wise man's good offices to ward off, for the ensuing year, all evil influences of beings who work in darkness." The reason assigned for observing this particular time is that "when the sun is come back the Pellar has more power to good [do good]" (Bottrell 1880, 187). Easter is the festival of the vernal equinox full moon personified by Ostara (Eostre to the Anglo-Saxons), the Germanic goddess of springtime, which was absorbed by the church as its main festival but retained the traditional symbolic eggs and related customs from European

Fig. 16.8. Easter eggs bedecking a spring at St. Marien, Germany.

ancestral religion. Because hens begin to lay eggs only when days get longer than nights at the vernal equinox, eggs are symbols of springtime. It is traditional to paint them red or with complex patterns. The oldest extant spring "Easter" egg known was found at Wolin, in Poland. Covered with marbled patterns, it dates from the tenth century CE. In parts of Germany, springs and wells are decked with thousands of colored egg-shells. The Estonian runic calendars marked "ploughing day," April 14, with a tree with upward-pointing branches. October 14 was marked by a tree with drooping branches. In Britain and Scandinavia this day marked the commencement of the summer half of the year.

MAY DAY

In Britain the month is known as the Merry Month of May. Sir Thomas Malory's Arthurian epic *Le Morte D'Arthur* (1470s) tells of Queen Gwynevere informing her knights that on May Day she would go a-maying and ordering them all to be well horsed and dressed in green. Green is the ritual color of the Merry Month of May. In many

Fig. 16.9. Morris dancing at Oxford, England, on May Day morning.

parts of Britain and Ireland, a May bush (hawthorn, *Crataegus monog-yna*) was cut on the previous day and stuck in the ground in front of the house. An Irish tradition decorated the May bush with eggshells that had been saved up since Easter Sunday, along with ribbons, wildflowers, and candles. On May Night the candles were lit, and people danced around the May bush. The rite was said to be in honor of the Virgin Mary, to whom the month of May was dedicated. May Day marks the beginning of the summer Morris dancing season in England.

The iconic image of May Day is the maypole, a widespread custom across northern Europe. A German example is illustrated in figure 16.10.

Fig. 16.10. Maypole, Wenneden, Germany.

In Wales, May Day is *Calan Mai,* marking the beginning of the summer half of the year, as its former name, *Calan Haf,* the calends of summer, denotes. The earliest literary reference to a maypole in Wales is in a poem by Gruffydd ab Adda ap Dafydd, who died around 1344. The birch maypole was known as *y gangen haf* (The Summer Branch), and some were painted in various colors. In 1852 the Welsh bard Nefydd (William Roberts) noted that *dawns y fedwen* (the Dance of the Birch; i.e., Morris dancing) at maypoles was well known all over Wales. Nefydd described the ritual preparation of the pole. First, the leader of the dance would come and place his circle of ribbon about the pole, and each in his turn after, until the maypole was covered in ribbons. Then the pole was raised into position and the dance begun; each took his place in the dance according to the personal piece of ribbon placed upon the maypole (Owen 1987, 102). In the borderlands of England and Wales, it was traditional to cut a birch tree on May morning and set it up, bedecked with white and red rags or ribbons, next to the door of a stable. This maypole was left up for the whole year and taken down only on the next May Day, when a new one was set up. A birch set up in May prevented malicious sprites from riding horses at night and tangling up their tails and manes into "witches' knots." In the borderlands of England and Wales, crosses of *wittan* (rowan) and birch, tied with red thread, were set above the cottage door, on pigsties, and in garden seedbeds. On the Isle of Man they used rowan twigs alone, broken, not cut from the tree, tied with wool taken directly from a sheep's back, making the *Crosh Keirn.*

Là Beltain (May Day) in the highlands of Scotland was observed with bonfires. In the Scottish highlands in the eighteenth century, Beltane or Baaltein, the May Day festival, "was yet in strict observance." On May Day people cut a square trench in the turf, leaving a square of grass in the middle. A Beltane cake was baked upon it "with scrupulous attention to certain rites and forms." Then it was broken up, and the fragments, "formally dedicated to birds or beasts of prey that they, or rather the being whose agents they were, might spare the flocks and herds" (Scott 1885, 3). The ritual prayer, "This I give to Thee, preserve my [horses, cattle, etc.]" was recited as the fragments of oatcake were thrown over the shoulder. Fires were kindled upon high places in pairs and all the cattle of the district driven between them to protect them until the next *Là Beltain*. All house fires were put out and rekindled by fire brought from the sacred fire. Writing in the first half of the nineteenth century, Sir Walter Scott noted "remains of these superstitions might be traced till past the middle of the last century, though fast becoming obsolete, or passing into mere popular customs of the country, which the peasantry observe without thinking of their origin" (Scott 1885, 3).

In Wales, May Eve is one of the *teir nos ysbrydion,* the "three spirit nights" occurring each year. Divination traditionally took place on May Eve during the *Swper nos Glanmai,* the ceremonial May Eve supper, where future lovers could be called up, "though a hundred miles off." A *coelcerth* (ritual fire) was made for *Calan Mai.* It was prepared by nine men who first removed all metal from their persons. Then they collected sticks from nine kinds of trees, and took them to the place where the fire was to be. A circle was cut in the turf and the sticks arranged crosswise. It was kindled by friction with two pieces of oak. Two fires close to one another were made so that livestock could be driven between them to give them magical protection against diseases. A calf or sheep would be thrown in the fire whenever there was disease in the herds. This is the tradition of the needfire, which was often conducted in extreme conditions, such as famine and pestilence, as a magical attempt to bring the crisis to an end. Ashes from the *coelcerth* were kept for magical purposes (Owen 1987, 97–98). Until the nineteenth century, igniting gunpowder and firing guns in the air was part of May Day custom in some English cities with strong civic traditions, including London, Norwich, and Nottingham. Contemporary Pagans keep up the day whenever possible with a Beltane fire.

MIDSUMMER AND HARVEST

Throughout northern Europe there are customs of burning bonfires and fire wheels at midsummer. The summer solstice, June 21, was also celebrated with the erection of poles (inter alia in Wales, Sweden, and

Lithuania) and lighting fires. In Wales, birch poles were raised on two days in the year, May Day and St. John's Day. The latter was *y fedwen haf,* the Summer Birch. Magically, the Eve of St. John is one of the Welsh *teir nos ysbrydion,* when spirits can be more readily contacted. St. John's Day (June 24) is a former midsummer's day, calendar changes having made it out of kilter with the solstice. It is the day of the *Johannesfeuer* bonfire. Lammas, August 1, was the Celtic *Lá Lúnasa,* celebrating the god Lugus, called by contemporary Pagans by its Gaelic name: Lunassadh. It is the "loaf-mass," the festival of the grain harvest, when the first loaf of the new harvest was made and presented to the deity.

NOVEMBER, YEAR'S END

The old Celtic Samhain (Hallowe'en) in its traditional, precommercialized form signified the end of harvest, with slaughter of all livestock that could not be kept through the winter. The day marked the end of the summer half of the year and the beginning of winter. It was celebrated with bonfires and the blowing of horns (Owen 1987, 124). The ancestral dead were remembered at this time with festivals such as the Celtic *Lá Samhna* and *Nos Galan gaeaf* and the Lithuanian *Vėlinės. Nos Galan gaeaf,* "the eve of the calends of winter," October 31, is Allhallows' Eve or Hallowe'en. *Calan gaeaf,* November 1, was the old Celtic New Year. It was one of the *teir nos ysbrydion* ("three spirit nights") in Wales, a time when wandering ghosts and demonic entities walked abroad. They included the *ladi wen* (white lady) and *hwch ddu gwta,* the terrifying tailless black sow (Owen 1987, 123). The Welsh name for November, *mis Tachwedd,* denotes slaughtering, and in Anglo-Saxon England, November was *Blót-mónaþ,* "Sacrifice Month," when the farmers who were slaughtering farm animals that could not be overwintered dedicated them as sacrifices to the gods. Excavators of the Northumbrian Pagan temple site at Yeavering discovered a large pile of the bones and skulls of oxen inside the east door of the temple. Next to the temple was a smaller building, probably a cookhouse. The animals killed and dedicated to the gods were served up in the royal hall nearby.

In Ireland, well into the twentieth century, animals were sacrificed to St. Martin on Martinmas, November 11. In 1887 Lady Wilde noted, "There is an old superstition still observed by the people, that blood must be spilt on St. Martin's Day; so a goose is killed, or a black cock, and the blood is sprinkled over the floor and on the threshold. And some of the flesh is given to the first beggar that comes by, in the name and in honor of St. Martin" (Wilde 1887, II, 131). In the Aran Isles the sacrificial blood was poured or sprinkled on the ground, along the doorposts, and both inside and outside the threshold, and at the four corners of each room in the house. The blood was from a sacrificed goose or rooster, but if it was not possible to get one, "people have been known to cut their finger in order to draw blood, and let it fall upon the earth. In some places it was the custom for the master of the house to draw a cross on the arm of each member of the family and mark it out in blood. This was a very sacred sign, which no fairy or evil spirit, were they ever so strong, could overcome; and whoever was signed with the blood was safe" (Wilde 1887, II, 131–32).

Another Martinmas observance in Ireland was "a singular superstition forbidding work of a certain kind to be done on St. Martin's Day. . . . No woman should spin on that day; no miller should grind his corn, and no wheel should be turned. And this custom was long held sacred, and is still observed in the Western Islands" (Wilde 1887, II, 133).

Postscript

Tradition develops, it does not stand still. It is not an unchanging, rigid performance. It is a historical accident that certain customary rites, ceremonies, and performances have continued for a long time at certain places when similar or identical practices have ceased to be performed in others. In recent years, where the interest in vernacular performance has increased, new events have emerged. Apart from the long-standing assembly at Stonehenge at Midsummer, the Pagan community has established parades and other events, particularly in celebration of Beltane (May Day). These events draw upon traditional elements such as Jack-in-the-Green and May songs old and new. The older and newer events have one thing in common: they are keeping up the day. A particular day in the year is recognized and celebrated by a public performance, whether it be a sacred day such as Beltane or Fastnacht; a customary day such as Boxing Day and Plough Monday; or a day that has been designated by a modern interest group, for instance Apple Day. With everyday magic as well as customs, people who are alive now are performing their own interpretations of a tradition that is authentic, not because we are doing it by the book, but because we are doing it. Done properly, with respect, and on the right day, the magic is still implicit in the performance.

Glossary

ABBREVIATIONS

B	Breton
D	Danish
Du	Dutch
EAE	East Anglian English
G	German
Ga	Gaulish
Gr	Greek
I	Icelandic
Ir	Irish (Gaeilge)
L	Latin
LE	Lancashire English
ME	Midlands English
Nr	Norwegian
OE	Old English (Anglo-Saxon)
ON	Old Norse
R	Romani
Sa	Sámi
Sc	Scots
SG	Scots Gaelic
Sw	Swedish
W	Welsh
WE	West Country English

Abred: (W) This material world, the Middle World (Midgard; ON *miðgarðr*).

Acht Ort: (G) Ad quadratum (q.v.).

Ad quadratum: (L) Geometrical scheme based on the square and sub-divisions of the square, the octagram, and the sixteenfold.

Ad triangulum: (L) Geometrical scheme based on the equilateral triangle and its development, the hexagram.

Æsir: (ON) The gods and goddesses of the later Norse pantheon.

Ætt: (ON) Direction, place, family (see *Airt*).

Afhús: (ON) Sacred annex (Pagan chapel) on a farmhouse.

Agrimensores: (L) Roman surveyors.

Airt: (Sc) Direction, place, family (see *Ætt*).

Álag: (ON) On-lay, a spell or incantation laid upon a particular place.

Álfblót: (ON) Offering to the elves or genius loci (q.v.) of a place.

Álfreka: (ON) A place that has been spiritually defiled so the elves have been driven away.

Alraun: (G) (1) A natural humanoid root, usually mandrake. (2) A humanoid image fashioned from a root of bryony, bramble, or ash.

Amsterdam School: (D) An architectural school or movement in Amsterdam, the Netherlands, 1911–1940, characterized by ornamental, mythic, and symbolic forms, brickwork, stained glass, and sculpture.

Ankou: (B) Personification of death; the spirit of the last person buried in a graveyard in a particular year.

Annwn: (W). The Celtic underworld known as the Abyss, "the land invisible," or "the loveless place."

Ásatrú: (I) The contemporary religion of the Æsir (q.v.).

Asgard: (ON *Ásgarðr*) The heavenly realm of the gods.

Åsgårdsrei: (Nr) A spectral wild hunt thought to ride through the air on dark, wild horses, led by Thor, Gudrun, and Sigurd Fafnirsbane as evil spirits.

Ásmegin: (ON) *Megin* (q.v.) of the gods.

Aukinn: (ON) Augmented with power.

Awen: (W) The druidic threefold sigil of godhead, the heraldic Broad Arrow.

Axletree: The timber axle of a wagon.

Beltane: (Sc) May Day.

Besom: Traditional broom made with birch twigs.

Biddie: An old woman, but one who has the power of "bidding" animals and people (and possibly spirits) to do her will.

Black witch: (WE) A practitioner of malevolent witchcraft, bringing evil upon others.

Blast: Magical power projected from a staff.

Bor: (EA) East Anglian expression meaning friend, farmer, comrade, or neighbor.

Bought: (Scots and English dialectal) A circular magical enclosure, a magic circle.

Bregda Sér: (Ir) Shape-changing.

Buck: The body of a post mill.

Bull's noon: Midnight.

Cardinal directions: North, east, south, and west. Between each are the intercardinal directions.

Ceol-sidhe: (I) Fairy music (*òran sidh* SG, "fairy song"). Music and songs heard from the fairies and recalled. Examples include "Móraleana," "Bollan Bane," and "The Dunvegan Lullaby."

Ceugant: (W) The transcendent realm of the ineffable source.

Charivari: Riotous noisy assembly intended to express disapproval of an unpopular individual.

Charter: An unwritten code of conduct, such as eastern English *Fenman's Charter,* or the *Old Charter* concerning the license of Plough Monday.

Clim: Chimney spirit.

Closs: (Sc) Passage through a building constructed on a fairy path (q.v.), leaving the right of way unobstructed.

Compagnonnage: (Fr) The French journeymen's guilds.

Cosmic Egg: In the Pythagorean-Orphic tradition, the symbol of the coming-into-being of the cosmos, the emanation of the material world, renewal and regeneration, and rebirth.

Croomstick: A staff with a hooked end, used physically or magically.

Crowntree: Horizontal beam in a post mill upon which the buck (q.v.) is supported and turned.

Deal: Pine tree.

Deal apple: (EAE) Pine cone used ritually. The sacred emblem (*Stadtpyr*) of the Swabian goddess, Zisa.

Devil's Plantation: A piece of uncultivated ground at the corner of a field or road, like no-man's-land (q.v.), belonging to the otherworld. Also (Scotland) Gudeman's Croft, the Old Guidman's Ground, the Halyman's Rig, the Haliemann's Ley, the Black Faulie, Clootie's Croft, and (England) Gallitrap and the Devil's Holt.

Dewar: (Sc) A hereditary keeper of a spiritual heirloom or numinous place.

Dísarblót: (ON) Disting, the January festival of the *dísir* (female ancestral spirits).

Disciplina: (L) Customary and time-tested modes and traditions of doing things.

Dísir: (ON) The female ancestors.

Dobbie-Stane: (Sc) A cup stone used for offerings to the earth sprites and in wind magic.

Doctor: To doctor something is either to lay a spell on it or to add some substance to food or drink without the knowledge of the recipient. To fix up (q.v.).

Dod: (EAE) A peg or stick put in the ground on which a rig is lined up in ploughing.

Draugr: (ON) A revenant, ghost.

Drove: (1) A herd of cattle or sheep being moved from one place to another. (2) The road along which herds are driven.

Druid's cord: A string with twelve knots equally spaced, making thirteen equal units.

Ealh: (OE) A fully enclosed timber temple.

Electional astrology: Working out the optimal inceptional horoscope for a project in advance and founding the venture at that moment (punctual time).

Empyrean: The uttermost sphere in European traditional cosmology.

Enhardening: A spell that enables a person or animal to withstand an attack that otherwise would kill.

Enhazelled field: An area delineated by hazel poles for ritual combat to take place.

Épure: (F) Tracing ground used in traditional carpentry.

Etruscan Discipline: The divinatory arts of the Augurs of Etruria, Italy, from the early years of the first millennium BCE (from Latin *Disciplina Etrusca*).

Eurhythmy: The integrated interrelationship of all proportions within a structure or performance.

Evil eye: The supposed power to attack magically by looking at someone or something.

Ex-voto: (L) An artifact offered in thanks to a divine being who has granted a boon or an answer to prayer.

Fachwerk: (G) Timber framing.

Fainty grund: (Sc) The "hungry grass" or "hunger-stricken earth," ground where one felt faint; *fear gortha* (Ir).

Fairy path: A trackway across country, visible or invisible, along which the fairies were believed to process at certain times.

Fane: A Pagan sanctuary.

Far-sighted: Gifted with the ability to see into the future; *framsynn* (ON).

Farthest beacon: A distant landmark, used in lining up the first rig in ploughing and shepherds' (witches') dials.

Fastnacht (Fasnet, Fasching): (G) Carnival, Shrove Tuesday.

Faud Shaughran: (I) The fairy grass, or the stray sod, stepping on which causes disorientation.

Fear gortha: (I) The fainty grund (q.v.).

Fenland: The freshwater wetlands and former fens in the counties of Cambridgeshire, Huntingdonshire, Lincolnshire, and Norfolk, eastern England.

Fetch: See *Fylgja*.

Fix up: To alter an object magically, either to lay a spell on it or to add some substance to food or drink without the knowledge of the recipient.

Fjölkyngi: (ON) Skilled in the magical arts, literally "much knowledge."

Foundation: The act of marking the beginning of a building by laying a stone with rites and ceremonies. Traditionally the material foundations are called the Grounds.

Four Grounds: (of effective action) Judgment, distance, time, and place.

Four wentz ways: (EAE) A crossroads.

Fragmentation: See *Tileshards*.

Framsynn: (ON) Far-sighted.

Frau Percht: (G) Goddess of winter, also known as Perchta, Bertha.

Friðgeard: (OE) "Frith-yard," sanctuary enclosure.

Frith: (OE *frið*) Sanctuary

Frith: (Sc) Augury.

Fritheir: (SC) Diviner, seer.

Fur: A color in heraldry, a stylized pattern derived from the fur of squirrel or stoat.

Futhark: Runic "alphabet," so-called because the first characters are F, U, Þ (= th), A, R, K.

Fylgja: (ON) A spiritual entity connected with every person, a guardian angel.

Galdr: (ON) Magical call.

Gallitrap: (1) A "no-man's-land" triangle of ground. (2) A magic circle or triangle made by a conjuring parson to entrap spirits or a criminal.

Gandr: (ON) Staff or magic wand, also the power emanating from one (see *Blast*).

Gast: (EAE) A piece of ground bound magically to be unproductive; a piece of land from which all the spirits have been banished.

Gematria: The art of numerology, deriving numbers from names and words, mainly in Hebrew and Greek.

Genius loci: (L) The "spirit of the place," recognized in various ways as a literal spirit, as a discernable quality, or both.

Geomancy: (1) Divinatory technique using earth, stones, beans, nuts, and so forth to make figures that are read for their meaning. (2) The art of location of buildings, holistically in recognition of the site and the prevailing conditions, physical and spiritual, as in European Location (the Etruscan Discipline, q.v.), Indian *Vastuvidya,* Malagasy *Vintana,* Burmese *Yattara,* Chinese *feng shui.*

Goði: (ON) Priest of Norse religion.

Godsoog: (Du) The "eye of god," a protective pattern of diamond shapes.

Grey witch: A witch who uses her power for ill or good.

Grounds: Physical foundations of a building or the fundamental basis of a principle.

Guild: Cooperative organization of professional craftspeople.

Guiser (geezer): A person who wears disguise at a traditional ceremonial event.

Guising: Performing in disguise; in a mask, a costume that hides one's identity, or as an animal.

Gwynvyd: (W) The spiritual upperworld, the "white land."

Haever: (LE) Direction, airt (q.v.)

Haliarunos: Wise women of the Gothic tribes.

Hamfarir: (ON) To travel in a shape other than one's own; out-of-the-body soul-flight.

Hamhleypa: (ON) A shape-changer.

Hamingja: (ON) Mutable, transferable personal magic energy, luck.

Hammarrsettning: (ON) Sacred rite using a consecrated hammer for empowerment.

Hamramr: (ON) The power of shape-changing.

Harrowwarden: Guardian of a holy place; *heargweard* (OE).

Haugbonde: (Nr) Spirit that haunted burial mounds near farms of which it was the supernatural guardian; Orkney *hogboon* (cf. ON *haugbúi*, "mound dweller").

Hip knob: Post at the gable end of a house or other building, rising above the roofline.

Hlutr: (ON) A portable sacred image.

Hof: (ON) Hall used for sacred rites and ceremonies.

Höfuð-hof: (ON) Temple.

Hogback: Viking Age tombstone in the form of a small house of the dead.

Hokkiben: (R) Deception, confidence tricks.

Hoodoo: American folk magic.

Hörgr: (ON) Place of worship, an altar sheltered by a tent or canopy (OE *træf*).

Horkey: (EAE) Supper celebrating the successful conclusion of the harvest.

Hytersprite: (EAE) Benevolent earth spirit (eastern England).

Icon: (1) Original meaning: a sacred image that is a spiritual embodiment of the power or personification depicted; (2) a striking image in Modernism (q.v.) that is held to embody the character shown or the zeitgeist.

Inceptional horoscope: The horoscope of a project at its beginning (see *Electional astrology*).

Intercardinal directions: The directions lying at 45° to the cardinal ones: northeast, southeast, southwest, and northeast.

Invultation (invultuation): The practice of making and using images or effigies of people or animals for magical purposes.

Jarðar megin: (ON) *Megin* (q.v) of the earth.

Jordvättarne: (Sw) Earth spirits.

Kenning: An allegorical and poetic figure of speech, such as "carpenter of song" for a bard or "wave plough" for a ship.

Kirk-grim: (Nr) Ghostly guardian of a church, the spirit of the person or animal sacrificed at the foundation of the building.

Lammas: August 1.

Landvættir: (ON) Land wights, earth spirits.

Landwisdom: (Old Saxon *landwîsa*) Knowledge of the nature and custom of the country.

Legendarium: (L) The overall body of stories, legends, tales, poems, traditions, songs, and writings about any particular thing or place, without a judgment of veracity according to the precepts of historical research.

Lock: The interlocking pattern of swords in traditional sword dancers.

Locus: (L) A particular place.

Lykewake: The tradition of watching a dead body until it is taken away to be buried.

Main: Personal inner strength, ON *megin,* linked in the expression "might and main" with personal physical power.

Makelaar: (Du) A specially designed hip knob enabling millers to estimate the wind speed.

Materia Magica: (L) The materials, paraphernalia, and so forth used in the performance of magic.

Megin: (ON) Main (q.v.).

Meinvættir: (ON) Evil sprites who do one personal injury.

Mell: Hammer.

Meridional line: A line running north-south, literally to *meridies* (L), the middle of the day, due south.

Messedag stav: (Nr) Wooden runic almanac; also *primstav, rimstock,* clog almanac.

Metal: (1) The physical body of glass as well as what is commonly called metal, as in pot-metal glass; (2) a color in heraldry, white (silver, *argent*) and yellow (gold, *or*).

Mete-wand: Measuring stick.

Midgard: (ON *miðgarðr*) This material world, the Middle World (Welsh *Abred*).

Midwinterhoorn: (Du) Ceremonial horn blown during the period around midwinter in the Dutch provinces of Overijssel and Twente and the Achterhoek district of Gelderland.

Mjöllnir: (ON) The hammer of Thor. The "crusher" or "miller."

Modernism: A theory of art and life based wholly upon industrial production, with a deliberate rejection of tradition.

Monogram: A symbolic figure made from some or all of the letters of a name.

Ná-bjargir: (ON) Death rite conducted from behind the corpse so that the person performing it would not fall under the gaze of the deceased.

Nail down his (her) track: To hammer a nail into a footprint made by an ill-wisher to nullify his or her magic.

Nemeton: (Ga) Sanctuary, often a grove of trees.

Nimidas: (Ga) The "ceremonies of the woodland."

Noid: (Sa) Sámi shaman.

No-man's-land: A triangle of ground at a trifinium (q.v.), belonging to no individual, but to the spirit world, sometimes called a Cocked Hat. Closely related to the Devil's Plantation (q.v.).

Norn (pl. Nornir): (ON) One of the three female personifications of tripartite theory of the states of being: the past, the present, and the future.

Nowl: (EAE) The polar North Star, the Lode Star, Stella Polaris.

Ófreskr: (ON) Second-sighted, the ability to have visions of events in the spirit world.

Omphalos: (Gr) "Navel of the World," spiritual center point, frequently depicted as an egg-shaped stone.

Ogham: (I) An ancient Irish cypher-script with characters denoted by lines, and with correspondences with trees, birds, and other things.

Önd: (ON) Vital breath or universal soul, likened to Greek *pneuma* and Sanskrit *prana*.

Öndvegissulur: (ON). High-seat pillars in ancient Norse halls and temples.

On-lay: See *Álag*.

Orientation: The alignment of a building, originally toward *Oriens* (East), but with a more general meaning now.

Ørlög: (ON) The history of something, all the concatenation of events that have led up to the coming-into-being of the particular thing or person in question. Not to be confused with the Dutch word for "war" (*oorlog*).

Ostentum: (L) Something that appears or is noticed suddenly, with a meaning immediately apparent to the beholder.

Otherworld: The area of consciousness beyond everyday appearances; the spirit world or the Land of the Dead.

Outwright: (ME) A journeyman.

Overlooked: Bewitched, stricken with the evil eye.

Pargetting: Making symbolic patterns in plasterwork on the outside of timber-frame houses in eastern England.

Pentacle: A five-pointed, equal-sided star.

Pentagram: A five-pointed, equal-sided star.

Perisomata: (Gr) A person's individual temperament determined by the relative proportions of each of the four humors.

Primstav: (Nr) A wooden almanac with runes and sigils denoting day, month, solar, and lunar cycles; "Prime-stave."

Primum Mobile: (L, lit. "prime mover"). The Ninth Heaven, which is the realm of God.

Punctual time: The exact moment for a foundation according to electional astrology.

Put a pin in for someone: To stick a pin into an image, a pincushion, an onion, and so forth to magically harm someone.

Put the toad on: To put the toad on someone is to use toad magic to affect them.

Quarter Day: Significant days in British law: Candlemas, May Day, Lammas, and All Saints'.

Quincunx: (L) An arrangement of five items, four forming a cross with one at the center.

Rammaukinn: (ON) Possessed of superhuman strength.

Rath: (I) A fairy fort or hill.

Reginnaglar: (ON) Divine nails, driven into the posts of a building as a ritual act.

Rempham: An alternative name for a pentagram.

Rig: A straight line, as in ploughing.

Rimstock: (D) A Danish wooden almanac; (see *Primstav, Messedag stav*).

Rune: (1) a cryptic or magical sigil, carved, painted, written, or recited; (2) character of the ancient Germanic *futhark* (q.v.) legendarily gained by Odin through shamanic ritual.

Samain (Samhain): (Ir) (1) The month of November; (2) Modernly, Samhain is Allhallows' Eve (Hallowe'en), properly *lá Samhna* (Ir). Beginning of the Celtic year.

Sele: (EAE) Time of day, year, or season.

Shape-changing (shape-shifting): To alter one's appearance, or the ways others perceive one, by magic.

Sigil: A written figure signifying the existence and powers of a particular god, spirit, or energy.

Sill: Ground frame of a timber-frame building.

Skimmington: Riotous noisy assembly playing improvised percussion intended to express disapproval of an unpopular individual (also Charivari, Tin Can Band, Rantantanning. *Katzenmusik*).

Skinnleikr: (ON) "Skin-play," guising in an animal skin.

Smågubbar: (Sw) Elves, land wights, "little people."

Snor: (EAE) Ceremonial measuring cord, druid's cord (q.v.).

Snotches: (EAE) Knots on a *snor* (q.v.).

Sommarsblót: April 14, the beginning of the summer half of the year.

Sprite: A spirit, elf, fairy.

Stafgarðr: (ON) Sacred enclosure surrounded by a wooden fence of staves.

Stance: (Sc) A stopping place on a trackway or road, especially cattle-drovers' routes.

Sublunary realm: In traditional cosmology, the sphere of the Earth beneath the Lunar sphere, a realm subject to continuous change.

Sulcus primigenius: (L) The primal furrow made with a plough at the foundation of a city or a homestead.

Summer's Day: (*Sommarsblót*) April 14, the beginning of the summer half of the year.

Sway: East Anglian term for a magician's wand, made from blackthorn or hazel wood.

Tafl: (ON) An ancient northern European board game in which the one player defends the center from the opponent's attack from the four quarters. Also called Hnefatafl, Tablut, Brandub, Tawlbwrdd, and so on.

Taufr: (ON) A talisman, word related to the German *zauber,* "magic," and the red coloring material *tiver.*

Teir nos ysbrydion: (W) The three spirit nights: May Eve, St. John's Eve, Hallowe'en.

Temenos: (Gr) Sacred enclosure around a temple or shrine.

Tesselation: A geometric counter-change pattern in two colors with the interlocking shapes the same in either color.

Tetraktys: (Gr) Pythagorean concept of the fourfold.

Three holy names: Many traditional spells in northern European folk magic and American hoodoo use the three epithets of God from the Christian trinity as names of power: the Father, the Son, and the Holy Ghost.

Tileshards: Assemblage of new patterns in colored and stained glass from re-used older fragments.

Tincture: A color in heraldry.

Tiugunde Day: January 13, the midpoint of winter.

Toadman (Toadsman): A man or woman who has ceremonially obtained the toad bone.

Toadmanry: Magical skills and powers acquired by performing the toad-bone ritual, or *Water of the Moon* (q.v).

Town crier: Ceremonial civic official in Britain who makes public announcements after ringing a bell and calling "Oyez, oyez!"

Træf: (OE) Place of worship, an altar sheltered by a tent or canopy (ON *hörgr*).

Trifinium or trivium: (L) A junction of three roads, sometimes enclosing a triangular piece of ground, which is a no-man's-land (q.v.).

Troll-Knut: (Sw) Knotted string from Swedish magic, either interpreted as "troll knot," apotropaic against trolls, or more generally as a "magic knot."

Útiseta: (ON) "Sitting out," a meditative technique in which a person sat out on the skin of a sacrificed animal at night under the stars to hear inner voices or the voices of spirits.

Vé: (ON) Triangular sacred enclosure.

Vébond: (ON) The posts and connecting ropes surrounding a *vé*.

Waff: A human's spectral double, wraith, or doppelgänger.

Warlock: A man with the magic power of binding.

Warlock-brief: (Sc) A magic spell.

Wassail: (lit. "be whole," from OE *wes þú hál*) Ceremonial house-visiting and orchard-charming rites and ceremonies around midwinter.

Water of the Moon: The toad-bone ritual, performed at full moon or on St. Mark's Eve.

White witch: Witch who employs counter magic against black witchcraft, charging her clients money to do so.

Wíh: (OE) The place of a sacred image standing in the open.

Wild stud: The practice of letting a stallion and a number of mares loose in woodland to mate and produce foals, still practiced in parts of Scotland.

Wind shaft: Timber shaft that carries the sails on a vertical windmill.

Wintersblót: (ON). October 14, beginning of the winter half of the year.

Winter's Day: *Wintersblót* (q.v.).

Witch bottle: A magically prepared bottle intended to protect against magical attack and evil sprites.

Witch men: English guisers who went about on Plough Monday with their faces darkened.

Wittan: English-Welsh border word for rowan wood.

Wraith: A human's spectral double, doppelgänger, waff.

Xoanon: (Gr) Pagan sacred image made of wood.

Yarthkin: (EAE) Malevolent earth spirit, East Anglia, England.

Yule: The festival of midwinter, including Christmas.

Bibliography

Ackerman, John Yonge. 1855. *Remains of Pagan Saxondom*. London: John Russell Smith.

Adams, W. H. Davenport. 1895. *Witch, Warlock and Magician: Historical Sketches of Magic and Witchcraft in England and Scotland*. London: Chatto and Windus.

Addy, Sidney Oldall. 1907. "Guising and Mumming in Derbyshire." *The Journal of the Derbyshire Archaeological and Natural History Society* 29: 31–42.

Agrell, Sigurd. 1934. *Lapptrummor och Runmagi*. Lund, Swed.: Gleerup.

Agrippa, Heinrich Cornelius. 1993. (1531) *Three Books of Occult Philosophy*. Translated by James Freake. Edited by Donald Tyson. St. Paul, Minn.: Llewellyn.

Ahrens, Klaus. 1982. *Frühe Holzkirchen im nördlichen Europa*. Hamburg: Th. Dingwort and Son.

Ahrens, Walter. 1918. *Mathematische Unterhaltungen und Spiele,* 2 vols. Leipzig: Teubner.

Aksdal, Bjørn, and Jan Ragnar Hagland. 1987. "Strykelyren i norsk middelalder. En vurdering på bakgrunn av et funn ved de arkeologiske utgravningene i Trondheim." *Studia Musicologica Norvegica* 13: 97–112.

Albertus Magnus. 1569. *De mineralibus et rebus metallicis quinque libri*. Cologne: Birckmann & Baum.

Alford, Violet. 1968. "The Hobby Horse and Other Animal Masks." *Folklore* 79: 122–34.

———. 1978. *The Hobby Horse and Other Animal Masks*. London: Merlin Press.

Allcroft, Authur Hadrian. 1908. *Earthwork of England: Prehistoric, Roman, Saxon, Danish and Mediaeval.* London: Macmillan.

Allen, Richard C. 2001. "Wizards or Charlatans, Doctors or Herbalists? An Appraisal of the 'Cunning-Men' of Cwrt-y-Cadno, Carmarthenshire." *North American Journal of Welsh Studies* 1: 67–85.

Andersen, Sven Aage. 1945. *Guldehornen fra Gallehus.* Copenhagen: Populært Videnskabeligt Forlag.

Appulm, Horst, ed. 1994. *Johann Siebmeyers Wappenbuch* (1605). Dortmund, Ger.: Harenberg Edition.

Ash, Steven. 2001. *Sacred Drumming.* Old Alresford, U.K.: Godsfield Press.

Aswynn, Freya. 1988. *Leaves of Yggdrasil.* London: Aswynn.

Aveni, A., and G. Romano. 1994. "Orientation and Etruscan Ritual." *Antiquity* 68: 545–63.

Bächtold-Stäubli, Hanns, ed. 1927–1942. *Handwörterbuch des Deutschen Aberglaubens,* 9 vols. Berlin: Koehler und Amerlang.

Banks, M. M. 1935. "Tangled Thread Mazes." *Folk-Lore* 46: 78–80.

Barchusen, Johann Conrad. 1718. *Elementa chemiæ.* Leiden, Neth.: Theodorum Haak.

Baring-Gould, Sabine. 1909. *A Book of Devon.* London: Methuen.

Baring-Gould, Sabine, and John Fisher. 1907–1913. *The Lives of the British Saints: The Saints of Insular and Cornwall and such Irish Saints as have Dedications in Britain,* 4 vols. London: Honourable Society of Cymmrodorion.

Barner, Wilhelm. 1968. *Bauopfer und Hausschutzzauber im Land zwischen Hildesheimer Wald und Ith.* Hildesheim, Ger.: August Lax.

Barrett, Francis. 1801. *The Magus, or Celestial Intelligencer.* London: Lackington, Allen, and Co.

Bärtsch, Albert. 1998 [1933]. *Holz Masken. Fastnachts- und Maskenbrauchtum in der Schweiz, in Süddeutschland und Österrech.* Aarau, Switz.: AT Verlag.

Bede. 1943. *De Temporum Ratione.* Translated Charles W. Jones. Cambridge, Mass.: The Mediaeval Academy of America.

———. 1955. *Historia ecclesiastica gentis Anglorum: Ecclesiastical History of the English People.* Translated by Leo Sherley-Price, revised by R. E. Latham. New York: Penguin Classics.

Behrend, Michael, and Debbie Saward, translators. 1982. *Trojaburgen: The works of Aspelin, Hamkens, Sieber & Mössinger.* Thundersley & Bar Hill, U.K.: Caerdroia Project and The Institute of Geomantic Research.

Bewick, Thomas. 1790. *A General History of Quadrupeds: The Figures Engraved on Wood.* Newcastle-upon-Tyne, U.K.: S. Hodgson, R. Beilby & T. Bewick.

Black, William George. 1893. *Folk Medicine.* London: Elliott Stock.

Blécourt, Willem de. 1994. "Witchdoctors, Soothsayers and Priests." *Social History* 19: 285–303.

Blomefield, Francis. 1805–1810. *Topographical History of the County of Norfolk.* London: n.p.

Boeterenbrood, Helen, and Jürgen Prang. 1989. *Van der Mey en het Scheepvaarthuis.* The Hague: SDU Uitgeverij.

Bonser, Kenneth J. 1972. *The Drovers.* Newton Abbot, U.K.: Country Book Club.

Boone, Hubert. 1975. "De Hommel in de Lage Landen." *Brussels Museum of Musical Instruments Bulletin* 5: 9–153.

Bottrell, William. 1880. *Stories and Folk-Lore of West Cornwall.* Penzance, U.K.: F. Rodda.

Boudriot, Wilhelm. 1964. *Die altgermanische Religion in der amtlichen kirchlichen Literatur des Abendlandes vom 5. bis 11. Jahrhundert.* Bonn: Ludwig Röhrscheid.

Bradley, Richard. 2005. *Ritual and Domestic Life in Prehistoric Europe.* London: Routledge.

Branston, Brian. 1957. *The Lost Gods of England.* London: Thames & Hudson.

Bray, Olive, trans. and ed. 1908. *The Elder or Poetic Edda, Commonly Known as Sæmund's Edda. Part I—the Mythological Poems.* London: Viking Club.

Briggs, Katharine M. 1970–1971. *A Dictionary of British Folk-Tales in the English Language,* 4 vols. London: Routledge & Kegan Paul.

Brinton, Daniel G. 1890. "Folk-Lore of the Bones." *Journal of American Folk-Lore,* vol. 3, no. 8: 17–22.

Broadwood, Lucy, and J. A. Fuller Maitland. 1893. *English County Songs.* London: The Leadenhall Press; J. B. Cramer & Co.; Simpkin, Marshall, Hamilton, Kent & Co.; and Charles Scribner's Sons.

Brown, Terry. 1997. *English Martial Arts.* Hockwold-cum-Wilton, U.K.: Anglo-Saxon Books.

Brown, Theo. 1962. "The Dartmoor Entrance to the Underworld." *Devon and Cornwall Notes and Queries* XXIX: 6–7.

————. 1966. "The Triple Gateway." *Folklore* 77: 123–31.

Browne, Sir Thomas. 1862. *Religio Medici, A Letter to a Friend, Christian Morals, Urn-burial, and Other Papers.* Boston: Ticknor and Fields.

Bruce, John Collingwood. 1856. *The Bayeux Tapestry. The Battle of Hastings and the Norman Conquest.* London: John Russell Smith.

Bucklow, Spike. 2009. *The Alchemy of Paint: Arts, Science and Secrets from the Middle Ages.* London: Marion Boyars.

Bugge, Anders. 1931. "The Golden Vanes of Viking Ships: A Discussion on a Recent Find at Källunge Church, Gotland." *Acta Archaeologica* II: 159–84.

Bunn, Ivan. 1982. "'A Devil's Shield . . .' Notes on Suffolk Witch Bottles." *Lantern* 39: 3–7.

Burdick, Lewis Dayton. 1901. *Foundation Rites with Some Kindred Ceremonies: A Contribution to the Study of Beliefs, Customs, and Legends Connected with Buildings, Locations, Landmarks, etc.* New York: Abbey Press.

Burgess, Michael W. 1978. "Crossroad and Roadside Burials." *Lantern* 24: 6–8.

Burn, Ronald. 1914. "Folk-Lore from Newmarket, Cambridgeshire." *Folk-Lore* 25, 3: 363–66.

Burne, Charlotte. 1883. *Shropshire Folk-Lore: A Sheaf of Gleanings.* London: Trübner.

Burstein, Sonia Rosa. 1956. "Demonology and Medicine in the Sixteenth and Seventeenth Centuries." *Folklore* 67, 1: 16–33.

Burton, Robert. 1621. *The Anatomy of Melancholy.* London: G. Bell & Sons.

Buschan, Georg. 1926. *Illustrierte Völkerkunde.* Stuttgart: Strecker & Schröder.

Butcher, D. R. 1972. "The Last Ears of Harvest." *The East Anglian Magazine* 31: 463–65.

Cabrol, Fernand. 1910. "Canonical Hours." *The Catholic Encyclopedia.* New York: Robert Appleton Company.

Caciola, Nancy. 1996. "Wraiths, Revenants and Ritual in Medieval Culture." *Past & Present* 152: 3–45.

Campbell, Ewan, and Alan Lane. 1991. "Celtic and Germanic Interaction in Dalriada: The Seventh-Century Metalworking Site at Dunadd." In *The Age of Migrating Ideas: Early Medieval Art in Northern Britain and Ireland.* Edited by R. Michael Spearman and John Higgitt. Edinburgh: National Museums of Scotland and Alan Sutton Publishing, 52–63.

Canney, Maurice A. 1926. "The Use of Sand in Magic and Religion." *Man.* January: 13.

Carlie, Anne. 2004. *Forntida byggnadskult: Tradition och regionalitet i södra Skandinavien.* Arkeologiska undersökningar skrifter 57. Stockholm: Riksantikvarieämbetet.

Carmichael, Alexander. 1911. "Scotland: Introduction." In W. Y. Evans Wentz, *The Fairy Faith in Celtic Countries.* Oxford: Oxford University Press, 84–89.

———. 1997 [1900]. *Carmina Gadelica.* Edinburgh: Floris Books.

Carr-Gomm, Philip, and Richard Heygate. 2010. *The Book of English Magic.* London: John Murray.

Cassidy-Welch, Megan. 2013. "The Stedinger Crusade: War, Remembrance and Absence in Thirteenth-Century Germany." *Viator* 44, 2: 159–74.

Cater, Colin, and Karen Cater. 2013. *Wassailing: Reawakening an Ancient Folk Custom.* Castle Hedingham, U.K.: Hedingham Fair.

Cawte, Edwin Christopher. 1978. *Ritual Animal Disguise.* Cambridge: D. S. Brewer.

Chadwick, H. Munro. 1901. *The Cult of Othin: An Essay on the Ancient Religion of the North.* London: C. J. Clay.

Chambers, Edmund Kerchener. 1933. *The English Folk Play.* Oxford: Oxford University Press.

Chambers, Robert, ed. 1869. *The Book of Days: A Miscellany of Popular Antiquities in Connection With the Calendar, Including Anecdote, Biography & History, Curiosities of Literature and Oddities of Human Life and Character,* 2 vols. London: W. & R. Chambers.

Chambers, Vanessa. 2004. "A Shell with My Name on It: The Reliance on the Supernatural During the First World War." *Journal for the Academic Study of Magic* 2: 79–103.

Chaney, William A. 1970. *The Cult of Kingship in Anglo-Saxon England.* Manchester: Manchester University Press.

Chapman, Rod. 2007. *Seven: An Idiosyncratic Look at the Number Seven.* North Elmham, U.K.: Seven Star.

Cheape, Hugh. 1993. "The Red Book of Appin: Medicine as Magic and Magic as Medicine." *Folklore* 104: 111–23.

Chisholm, James Allen. 1993. *True Hearth: A Practical Guide to Traditional Householding.* Smithville, Tex.: Runa-Raven Press.

Chumbley, Andrew. 2000. *Grimoire of the Golden Toad.* London: Xoanon Publishing.

———. 2001. *The Leaper Between: An Historical Study of the Toad Bone Amulet.* Privately published and circulated.

Cielo, Astra. 1918. *Signs, Omens and Superstitions.* New York: George Sully.

Clark, H. F. 1962. "The Mandrake Fiend." *Folklore* 73: 257–69.

Clark, H. P. 1930. "Old Sussex Harvest Customs." *The Sussex County Magazine,* IV: 796–97.

Clucas, Philip. 1987. *Churches and Cathedrals of England.* London: Tiger.

Cohen, Sidney L. 1965. *Viking Fortresses of the Trelleborg Type.* Copenhagen: Rosenkilde & Bagger.

Collingwood, W. G. 1902. Translated by Jón Stéfansson. *The Life and Death of Cormac the Skald, Being the Icelandic Kormáks-saga.* Ulverston, U.K: William Holmes.

———. 1911. "Anglian and Anglo-Danish Sculpture in the East Riding, with Addenda to the North Riding." *Yorkshire Archaeological Journal* XXI: 254–302.

Constantine, Mary-Ann, and Gerald Porter. 2003. *Fragments and Meaning in Traditional Songs: From the Blues to the Baltic.* Oxford: Oxford University Press for the British Academy.

Conybeare, Frederick C. 1901. "The Paganism of the Ancient Prussians." *Folk-Lore* 12: 293–302.

Cooper, Emmanuel. 1994. *People's Art: Working-Class Art from 1750 to the Present Day.* Edinburgh: Mainstream Publishing.

Corrie, John. 1890–1891. "Folk-Lore of Glencairn." *Transactions of the Dumfries and Galloway Natural History and Antiquarian Society:* 37–45, 75–83.

Corrsin, Stephen D. 1997. *Sword Dancing in Europe: A History.* Enfield Lock, U.K.: Hisarlik Press.

Coverdale, Miles. 1846. Edited by G. Pearson. *Remains.* London: Parker Society.

Croker, Alec. 1971. *The Crafts of Straw Decoration.* Leicester, U.K.: Dryad.

Crooke, W. 1909. "Burial of Suicides at Crossroads." *Folk-Lore* 20: 88–89.

Cross, Pamela. 2011. "Horse Burial in First Millennium AD Britain: Issues of Interpretation." *European Journal of Archaeology* 14 (1–2): 190–209.

Curth, Louise Hill. 2000. "English Almanacs and Animal Health Care in the Seventeenth Century." *Society and Animal* 8, 1: 1–16.

Cyr, Donald, ed. 1990. *Full Measure.* Santa Barbara, Ca.: Stonehenge Viewpoint.

Dack, Charles. 1911. *Weather and Folklore of Peterborough and District.* Peterborough, U.K.: Peterborough Natural History, Scientific, and Archaeological Society.

Dacombe, Marianne R., ed. [ca. 1935]. *Dorset Up Along and Down Along.* Dorchester, U.K.: Longmans.

Dakers, Alan. 1991. *Ticklerton Tales: A History of Eaton-under-Heywood.* Church Stretton, U.K.: Privately published.

Dalton, Ormonde Maddock. 1915. *Letters of Sidonius Apollinaris,* 2 vols. Oxford: Oxford University Press.

Dalyell, John Graham. 1834. *The Darker Superstitions of Scotland.* Edinburgh: Waugh & Innes.

Dannheimer, Hermann, and Rupert Gebhard. 1993. *Das keltische Jahrtausend.* Mainz, Ger.: Prähistorische Staatssammlung München & Verlag Philipp von Zabern.

Davidson, Hilda Ellis. 1988. *Myths and Symbols in Pagan Europe.* Syracuse, N.Y.: Syracuse University Press.

———. 1993. *The Lost Beliefs of Northern Europe.* London & New York: Routledge.

Davidson, Thomas. 1956. "The Horseman's Word: A Rural Initiation Ceremony." *Gwerin* 1: 67–74.

Davíðsson, Ólafur. 1903. "Isländische Zauberzeichen und Zauberbücher." *Zeitschrift des Vereins für Volkskunde* 13: 150–67.

Davies, Owen. 1996. "Healing Charms in Use in England and Wales 1700–1950." *Folklife* 107, 1–2 (January), 19–32.

Davies, Owen, and William De Blécourt, eds. 2004. *Beyond the Witch Trials: Witchcraft and Magic in Enlightenment Europe.* Manchester: Manchester University Press.

Davis, J. Barnard. 1867. "Some Account of Runic Calendars and 'Staffordshire Clogg' Almanacs." *Archaeologia, or Miscellaneous Tracts Relating to Antiquity* 41: 453–78.

Day, George. 1894. "Notes on Essex Dialect and Folk-Lore, with Some Account of the Divining Rod." *The Essex Naturalist* 8: 71–85.

Day, James Wentworth. 1973. *Essex Ghosts: The Haunted Towns and Villages of Essex.* Bourne End, U.K.: Spurbooks.

De Hen, Ferd J. 1972. "Folk Instruments of Belgium: Part I." *Galpin Society Journal* XXV: 105–10.

Dennis, Andrew, Peter Foote, and Richard Perkins. 1980, 2000. *Grágás: Laws of Early Iceland*, 2 vols. Winnipeg: University of Manitoba Press.

Derolez, R. 1954. *Runica Manuscripta: The English Tradition*. Bruges, Belg.: De Tempel.

De Santillana, Giorgio, and Hertha von Dechend. 1969. *Hamlet's Mill*. London: Macmillan.

De Vries, Jan. 1956–1957. *Altgermanische Religionsgeschichte*, 2 vols. Berlin: De Gruyter.

Dickins, Bruce. 1915. *Runic and Heroic Poems*. Cambridge: Cambridge University Press.

Digby, Sir Kenelm. 1658. *A Discourse on Sympathy*. London.

Diószegi, Vilmos, ed. 1968. *Popular Beliefs in Siberia*. Bloomington: Indiana University Press.

Dixon, G. M. 1981. *A Heritage of Anglian Crafts*. Deeping St. James, U.K.: Minimax Books.

Dobson, R. B., and John Taylor. 1997. *Rymes of Robyn Hood: An Introduction to the English Outlaw*. Stroud, U.K.: Sutton.

Drechsler, Paul. 1903–1906. *Sitte, Brauch und Volksglaube in Schlesien*. Leipzig: Teubner.

Drinkwater, Peter I. 1996. *The Art of Sundial Construction*. Shipston-on-Stour, U.K.: Privately published.

Driver, Nicholas. 1994. *Nicholas Driver's Bodhran and Bones Tutor*. Horsham, U.K.: Gremlin Musical Instrument Company.

Durdin-Robinson, Lawrence. 1982. *Juno Covella: Perpetual Calendar of the Fellowship of Isis*. Enniscorthy, Ireland: Cesara.

Düwel, Klaus. 1988. "Buchstabenmagie und Aphabetenzauber: Zu den Inschriften der Goldbrakteaten und ihrer Funktion als Amulette." *Frühmittelalterliche Studien* 22: 70–110.

Dwelly, Edward. 1993. *Faclair Gàidhlig gu Beurla le Dealbhan / The Illustrated [Scottish] Gaelic-English Dictionary*. 10th edition. Edinburgh: Birlinn.

Dyer, T. F. Thistleton. 1878. *English Folk-Lore*. London: Bogue.

———. 1881. *Domestic Folk-Lore*. London: Cassell.

Dyggve, Ejnar. 1954. "Gorm's Temple and Harald's Stone Church at Jelling." *Acta Archaeologica* XXV: 221–41.

Easton, Timothy. 1999. "Spiritual Middens." In *Encyclopedia of Vernacular*

Architecture of the World. Edited by Paul Oliver. Cambridge: Cambridge University Press.

Eldjárn, Kristján. 2000. *Kuml og haugfé: Úr heiðnum sið á Íslandi*. Edited by A. Friðriksson. Reykjavík: Fornleifastofnun Íslands, Mál og menning, and Þjóðminjasafn Íslands.

Elliott, Ralph W. V. 1963. *Runes: An Introduction*. Manchester: Manchester University Press.

Ellis-Davidson, Hilda Roderick. 1964. *Gods and Myths of Northern Europe*. Harmondsworth, U.K: Penguin.

———. 1993. *The Lost Beliefs of Northern Europe*. London: Routledge.

Elworthy, Frederick Thomas. 1895. *The Evil Eye: An Account of this Ancient & Widespread Superstition*. London: John Murray.

Ericson, E. E. 1936. "Burial at the Cross-Roads." *Folklore* 47: 374–75.

Ettinger, Ellen. 1939. "British Amulets in London Museums." *Folklore* 50, 2: 148–75.

———. 1943. "Documents of British Superstition in Oxford." *Folklore* 54: 227–49.

Evans, E. Estyn. 1957. *Irish Folk Ways*. London: Routledge and Kegan Paul.

Evans, George Ewart. 1965. *Ask the Fellows Who Cut the Hay*. London: Faber & Faber.

———. 1971. *The Pattern under the Plough*. London: Faber & Faber.

Falk, Ann-Britt. 2006. "My Home is My Castle: Protection against Evil in Medieval Times." In *Old Norse Religion in Long-Term Perspectives: Origins, Changes, and Interactions*. Edited by Anders Andrén, Kristina Jennbert, and Catharina Raudvere. Lund, Swed.: Nordic Academic Press, 200–5.

Faucon, Régis, and Yves Lescroart. 1997. *Manor Houses in Normandy*. Cologne: Könemann.

Figura, Franz. 1896. "Das Schwirrholz in Galizien." *Globus* 70: 226.

Fingerlin, Ilse. 2005. "Gebäudefunde unter Dächern und zwischen Böden." In *Depotfunde aus Gebäuden in Zentraleuropa: Concealed Finds from Buildings in Central Europe*. Edited by Ingolf Ericsson and Ranier Atzbach. Archäologische Quellen zum Mittelalter 2. Berlin: Scrîpvaz, 14–20.

Fisher, Hal. 1936. *A History of Europe*. London: Arnold.

Fiske, Willard. 1905. *Chess in Iceland and in Icelandic Literature with Historical Notes on Other Table Games*. Florence: Florentine Typographical Society.

Flaherty, Robert Pearson. 1992. "Todaustragen: the Ritual Expulsion of Death at Mid-Lent— History and Scholarship." *Folklore* 103: 40–55.

Fletcher, Neville H., A. Z. Tarpolsky, and J. C. S. Lai. 2002. "Rotational Aerophones." *Journal of the Acoustical Society of America* 11: 1189–96.

Flowers, Stephen. 1986. *Runes and Magic: Magical Formulaic Elements in the Older Tradition*. New York: Peter Lang.

———. 1989. *The Galdrabók: An Icelandic Grimoire*. York Beach, Maine: Samuel Weiser.

———. *Northern Magic: Mysteries of the Norse, German and English*. Smithville, Tex.: Rûna-Raven Press, 1992.

Fox, Sir Cyril. 1955. *Offa's Dyke*. London: British Academy.

Fox-Davies, Arthur Charles. 1925. *A Complete Guide to Heraldry*. London: Thomas Nelson & Sons.

Frampton, George. 1996. *Vagrants, Rogues and Vagabonds: Plough Monday Tradition in Old Huntingdonshire and the Soke of Peterborough*. Tonbridge, U.K.: Privately published.

Franklin, Anna. 2002a. *The Illustrated Encyclopaedia of Fairies*. London: Vega.

———. 2002b. *Midsummer: Magical Celebrations of the Summer Solstice*. St. Paul, Minn.: Llewellyn.

———. 2010. *Yule. History, Lore & Celebration*. Earl Shilton, U.K.: Lear Books.

Franklin, Anna, and Paul Mason. 2001. *Lammas: Celebrating the Fruits of the First Harvest*. St. Paul, Minn.: Llewellyn.

Franklin, Anna, with Paul Mason. 2010. *Lughnasa: History, Lore and Celebration*. Earl Shilton, U.K.: Lear Books.

Franz, Leonhard. 1943. *Falsche Slawengöttger*. Brünn, Ger.: Rudolf M. Rohrer.

Frazer, Sir James. 1931. "Straw Bear at Jena." *Folk-Lore* 42: 87.

Frazer, Sir James, and G. C. Moore Smith. 1909. "Straw Bear Tuesday." *Folk-Lore* 20: 202–3.

Frazier, Paul. 1952. "Some Lore of Hexing and Powwowing." *Midwest Folklore* 2, 2: 101–7.

Garrad, Larch S. 1989. "Additional Examples of Possible House Charms in the Isle of Man." *Folklore* 100, 1: 110–12.

Gelling, Peter, and Hilda Ellis Davidson. 1971: *The Chariot of the Sun and Other Rites and Symbols in the Northern Bronze Age*. London: Dent.

Geoffrey of Monmouth. 1996. *The History of the Kings of Britain*. Translated by Lewis Thorpe. London: Penguin.

Gerish, W. B. 1895. "A Churchyard Charm." *Folk-Lore* 6: 200.

Gielzynski, Wojtech, Irena Kostrowicki, and Jerzy Kostrowicki. 1994. *Poland*. Warsaw: Arkady.

Gifford, George. 1587. *Discourse of the Subtle Practices of Devils*. London: N.p.

Giles, John Allen. 1849. *Roger of Wendover's Flowers of History Comprising the History of England from the Descent of the Saxons to A.D. 1235*, 2 vols. London: Henry G. Bohn.

Givry, Émille Grillot de. 1973 [1929]. *The Illustrated Anthology of Sorcery, Magic and Alchemy*. New York: Causeway Books.

Gjerset, Knut. 1915. *History of the Norwegian People*, 2 vols. New York: Macmillan.

Glanvil, Joseph. 1681. *Sadducismus Triumphatus*. London: N.p.

Glyde, John, Jr. 1872. *The Norfolk Garland*. Norwich, U.K.: Jarrold.

Godwin, William M. 1834. *Lives of the Necromancers*. London: Frederick L. Masson.

Goethe, Friedrich. 1971. "Der Schwan auf Kirchen Ostfrieslands und Oldenburgs." *Ostfriesland* 4: 7–19.

Gomme, Alice. 1894 & 1898. *Traditional Games of England, Scotland, and Ireland*, 2 vols. London: David Nutt.

Goodrich-Freer, A. 1899. "The Powers of Evil in the Outer Hebrides." *Folk-Lore* 10, 3: 259–82.

Gossett, A. L. J. 1911. *Shepherds of Britain, Past and Present: From the Best Authorities*. London: Constable.

Gouk, Penelope. 1988. *The Ivory Sundials of Nuremberg 1500–1700*. Cambridge: Whipple Museum of the History of Science.

Graf, Klaus. 1995. *Sagen rund um Stuttgart*. Stuttgart: G. Braun.

Green, Arthur Robert. 1978. *Sundials: Incised Dials or Mass-Clocks* (1926). London: The Society for Promoting Christian Knowledge.

Green, Dennis Howard. 1998. *Language and History in the Early Germanic World*. Cambridge: Cambridge University Press.

Green, Thomas. 1832. *The Universal Herbal; or, Botanical, Medical, and Agricultural Dictionary*, 2 vols. 2nd revised edition. London: Caxton.

Gregor, Walter. 1881. *Notes on the Folk-Lore of the North-East of Scotland*. London: Folk-Lore Society.

Grieve, Maud. 1931. *A Modern Herbal*. London: Jonathan Cape.

Griffiths, Bill. 2003. *Aspects of Anglo-Saxon Magic*. Hockwold-cum-Wilton, U.K.: Anglo-Saxon Books.

Griffiths, Bruce, and Dafydd Glyn Jones. 1995. *The Welsh Academy English-Welsh Dictionary*. Cardiff: University of Wales Press.

Grimm, Jacob. 1888. *Teutonic Mythology*, 4 vols. Translated by James Steven Stallybrass. London: George Bell and Sons.

———. 1965. *Deutsche Mythologie*, 3 vols. Darmstadt, Ger.: Wissenschaftliche Buchgesellschaft.

Groves, Derham. 1991. *Feng-Shui and Western Building Ceremonies*. Singapore: Graham Brash & Tynron Press.

Guidon. 2011 [1670]. *Magic Secrets and Counter-Charms*. Hinckley, U.K.: The Society for Esoteric Endeavour.

Gundarsson, Kveldúlf Hagan, ed. 1993. *Our Troth*. Seattle: Ring of Troth.

Gurdon, Camilla. 1892. "Folk-Lore from South-East Suffolk." *Folk-Lore* 3, 4: 558–60.

Gurdon, Lady Evelyne C. 1893. *County Folk-Lore: Suffolk*. London: David Nutt.

Gurina, N. N. 1948: "Kammenye labirinty Belomor'ya" ("Stone Labyrinths on the White Sea"). *Sovetskaya archaologiya* 10: 125–42.

Gustafson, Mark. 2000. "The Tattoo in the Later Roman Empire and Beyond." In Caplan, Jane, ed. *Written on the Body: The Tattoo in European and American History*. London: Reaktion Books.

Gutch, Mrs., and Mabel Peacock. 1908. *Examples of Printed Folk-Lore Concerning Lincolnshire*. London: David Nutt.

Haddon, Alfred C. 1908. *The Study of Man*. London: John Murray.

Hadow, Grace E., and Ruth Anderson. 1924. "Scraps of English Folk-Lore IX (Suffolk)." *Folk-Lore* 35: 346–60.

Hall, Alaric. 2007. *Elves in Anglo-Saxon England: Matters of Belief, Health, Gender and Identity*. Woodbridge, U.K.: Boydell.

Hall, Samuel Carter, ed. 1867. *The Book of British Ballads*. London: Jeremiah How.

Halliday, Robert. 2010. "The Roadside Burial of Suicides: An East Anglian Study." *Folklore* 121: 81–93.

Hambling, David. 2013. "Weatherwatch: How to Catch the Wind in a Trap of Stone." *The Guardian* (London), Friday, June 28.

Hamkens, Freerk Haye. 1938. "Heidnische Bilder im Dom zu Schleswig." *Germanien* 6: 177–81.

Hammarstedt, Nils E. 1920. *Svensk Forntro och Folksed.* Stockholm: Nordiska Museet.

Harland, John. 1865. "On Clog Almanacks, or Rune Stocks." *The Reliquary* (January): 120–30.

Harland, John, and Thomas Turner Wilkinson. 1867. *Lancashire Folk-Lore Illustrative of the Superstitious Beliefs and Practices, Local Customs and Usages of the People of the County Palatine.* London: Frederick Warne.

Harrison, Frank, and Joan Rimmer. 1964. *European Musical Instruments.* London: Studio Vista.

Hartner, Willy. 1969. *Die Goldhörner von Gallehus.* Stuttgart: F. Steiner.

Haseloff, Günther. 1979. *Kunststile des frühen Mittelalters.* Stuttgart: Württembergisches Landesmuseum.

Hasenfratz, Hans-Peter. 2011. *Barbarian Rites: The Spiritual World of the Vikings and the Germanic Tribes.* Translated by Michael Moynihan. Rochester, Vt.: Inner Traditions.

Haust, Jean. 1946. "Les Gnomes dans les parlers de Wallonie." *Enquêtes du musée de la vie wallonne* 41–42: 141–46.

Hayes, R. H., and J. G. Rutter. 1972. *Cruck-Framed Buildings in Ryedale and Eskdale.* Scarborough, U.K.: Scarborough Archaeological and Historical Society.

Hayhurst, Yvonne. 1989. "A Recent Find of a Horse Skull in a House at Ballaugh, Isle of Man." *Folklore* 100, 1: 105–9.

Haynes, Edmund Sidney Polluck. 1906. *Religious Persecution: A Study in Political Psychology.* London: Watts.

Heanley, Rev. R. M. 1902. "The Vikings: Traces of their Folklore in Marshland." *Saga-Book* 3: 35–62.

Helm, Alex. 1981. *The Mummers' Play.* Ipswich, U.K.: D. S. Brewer.

Henderson, William. 1866. *Notes on the Folk-Lore of the Northern Counties of England and the Border.* London: Longmans Green.

Hennels, C. E. 1972. "The Wild Herb Men." *The East Anglian Magazine* 32: 79–80.

Henschen-Nyman, Olle. 1980. "Kring ett frågetecken angående bildstenen Lärbro Källstäde." *Riksinventeringens rapport* 25: 8–9.

Herbord. 1894. *Herbords leben des Bischofs Otto von Bamberg.* Leipzig: Dyk.

Herity, Michael. 1993. "The Tomb-shrine of the Founder Saint." In *The Age of Migrating Ideas*. Edited by Michael R. Spearman and John Higgitt. Edinburgh: Alan Sutton, 191–94.

Herrick, Robert. 1902 [1648]. *The Poems of Robert Herrick*. London: Grant Richards.

Herrmann, H. A. 1939. "Ein unbekannter Runenstabkalender." *Germanien* 6: 266–77.

Herrmann, Paul. 1929. *Das altgermanische Priesterwesen*. Jena: Eugen Diederichs.

Hewett, Sarah. 1900. *Nummits and Crummits: Devonshire Customs*. London: Thomas Burleigh.

Hickes, G. 1970. *Linguarum Vett. Septentrionalium Thesaurus: 1703–1705*. Facsimile reprint. London: Scolar Press.

Hissey, James John. 1898. *Over Fen and Wold*. London: Macmillan.

Hodson, Geoffrey. 1925. *Fairies at Work and Play*. London: Theosophical Publishing House.

Hoggard, Brian. 2004. "The Archaeology of Counter-Witchcraft and Popular Magic." In *Beyond the Witch Trials: Witchcraft and Magic in Enlightenment Europe*. Edited by Owen Davies and William De Blécourt. Manchester: Manchester University Press.

Hole, Christina. 1977. "Protective Symbols in the Home." In *Symbols of Power*. Edited by Hilda Roderick Ellis-Davidson. London: Folklore Society, 121–30.

Hone, William. 1827. *The Every-Day Book; or, Everlasting Calendar of Popular Amusements, Sports, Pastimes, Ceremonies, Manners, Customs and Events,* 2 vols. London: Hunt and Clarke.

Honko, Lauri. 1962. *Geisterglaube in Ingermanland*. Helsinki: Academia Scientiarum Fennica.

Howard, Michael. 2009. *West Country Witches: Witchcraft of the British Isles*. Richmond Vista, Ca.: Three Hands Press.

Howlett, England. 1899. "Sacrificial Foundations." In *Ecclesiastical Curiosities*. Edited by William Andrews. London: William Andrews.

Hukantaival, Sonja. 2009. "Horse Skulls and 'Alder Horse': The Horse as a Depositional Sacrifice in Building." *Archaeologica Baltica* 11: 350–56.

Hull, Eleanor. 1913. *The Northmen in Britain*. New York: Thomas Y. Crowell.

Hultkrantz, Åke. 1961. *The Supernatural Owners of Nature*. Stockholm: Almkvist & Wiksell.

Hutton, Ronald. 1996. *The Stations of the Sun: A History of the Ritual Year in Britain*. Oxford: Oxford University Press.

———. 2001. *The Triumph of the Moon. A History of Modern Pagan Witchcraft*. Oxford: Oxford University Press.

Inman, Thomas. 1875. *Ancient Pagan and Modern Christian Symbolism, with an Essay on Baal Worship, on the Assyrian Sacred "Grove" and Other Allied Symbols*. New York: J. W. Bouton.

Ivanits, Linda J. 1989. *Russian Folk Belief*. Armonk, N.Y.: M. E. Sharpe.

James, David. 1997. *Celtic Crafts: The Living Tradition*. London: Blandford.

Jans, Everhard. 1977. *Het Midwinterhoornblazen*. Enschede, Netherlands: Witkam.

Jekyll, Gertrude. 1904. *Old West Surrey*. London: Longmans Green.

Jobson, Allan. 1966. *A Suffolk Calendar*. London: Robert Hale.

Johansons, Andrejs. 1964. *Der Schirmherr des Hofes im Volksglauben der Letten: Studen über Ort- Hof- und Hausgeister*. Stockholm: Almqvist & Wiksell.

Johnson, Hildegard Binder. 1976. *Order Upon the Land: The U. S. Rectangular Land Survey and the Upper Mississippi Country*. New York: Oxford University Press.

Johnson, Walter. 1912. *Byways in Archaeology*. Cambridge: Cambridge University Press.

Jones, Prudence. 1982. *Eight and Nine: Sacred Numbers of Sun and Moon in the Pagan North. Fenris-Wolf Pagan Paper #2*. Bar Hill, U.K.: Fenris-Wolf.

———. 1990. "Celestial and Terrestrial Orientation." In *Astrology and History*. Edited by Annabella Kitson. London: Unwin Hyman.

———. 1991a. *A "House" System from Viking Europe*. Bar Hill, U.K.: Fenris-Wolf.

———. 1991b. *Northern Myths of the Constellations*. Bar Hill, U.K.: Fenris-Wolf.

Jones, Prudence, and Nigel Pennick. 1995. *A History of Pagan Europe*. London: Routledge.

Jones, Sydney R. 1912. *The Village Homes of England*. London: The Studio.

Jonson, Ben, and W. Gifford (notes and memoir). 1816. *The Works of Ben Jonson*, 9 vols. London: W. Bulmer.

Kallenberg, Dorothea. 1989. *Was dr Schwob feiert: Feste und Brauche in Stadt und Land*. Stuttgart: DRW-Verlag.

Kamp, Jens. 1877. *Dansk Folkeminder, Æventyr, Folkesagn, Gaader, Rim och Folketro.* Odense: N. Nielsen.

Kandinsky, Wassily. 1997. *Concerning the Spiritual in Art.* Translated by M. T. H. Sadler. New York: Dover.

Kern, Hermann. 1983. *Labyrinthe.* Munich: Prestel.

Kodolányi, J., Jr. 1968. "Khanty (Ostyak) Sheds for Sacrificial Objects." In *Popular Beliefs in Siberia.* Edited by Vilmos Diószegi. Bloomington: Indiana University Press, 103–6.

Kolltveit, Gjermund. 2000. "The Early Lyre in Scandinavia: A Survey." *Tiltai/Bridges* 3 (12): 19–25.

Kottenkamp, Franz. 1988. *The History of Chivalry and Armour.* Translated by Rev. A. Löwy. London: Bracken Books.

Kõuts, Eric, and Heinz Valk. 1998. *Rist ja raud: Cross and Iron.* Tallinn, Estonia: SE & JS.

Kraft, John. 1983. "Götlands Trojeborgar." *Götlandsk Archiv:* 59–90.

———. 1986. "The Magic Labyrinth." *Caerdroia* 19: 14–19.

Krause, Rhett. 1996. "Traditional and Invented Sword Locks." *Rattle Up My Boys* 6, 1: 1–7.

Kristensen, Evald Tang. 1885. *Skattegraveren,* 3 vols. Copenhagen: Glydendal.

Kristensen, Tenna. 1994. *Middelalderlige musikinstrumenter.* Höjbjerg, Denmark: Moesgård Museum.

Laing, Gordon J. 1931. *Survivals of Roman Religion.* London, Calcutta, Sydney: George G. Harrap.

Lake, Jeremy. 1989. *Historic Farm Buildings.* London: Blandford.

Lambert, Margaret, and Enid Marx. 1989. *English Popular Art.* London: Merlin Press.

Lambeth, Minnie. 1969. *A Golden Dolly: The Art, Mystery and History of Corn Dollies.* London: John Baker.

Lämmle, August. 1935. *Brauch und Sitte im Bauerntum.* Berlin: de Gruyter.

Langford, J. A. 1875. "Warwickshire Folk-Lore and Superstitions." *Transactions of the Birmingham and Midlands Institute* 6: 9–24.

Larrington, Carolyne. 2006. "Diet, Defecation and the Devil: Disgust and the Pagan Past." In *Medieval Obscenities.* Edited by Nicola Macdonald. Woodbridge, U.K.: D. S. Brewer, 138–55.

Larson, Laurence Marcellus. 1912. *Canute the Great (995–1035) and the Rise of Danish Imperialism During the Viking Age.* New York: G. P. Putnam's Sons.

Larwood, Jacob, and John Camden Hotten. 1908. *The History of Signboards from the Earliest Times to the Present Day*. London: Chatto & Windus.

Latham, Charlotte. 1878. "Some West Sussex Superstitions Lingering in 1868." *The Folk-Lore Record* 1: 1–67.

Lawrence, Robert Means. 1898. *The Magic of the Horse Shoe*. Boston: Houghton Mifflin.

Lawson, G., and S. Rankin. 2000. "Music," "Chant," & "Musical Instruments." *The Blackwell Encyclopaedia of Anglo-Saxon England*. Edited by Michael Lapidge. Oxford: Blackwell.

Leather, Ella Mary. 1912. *The Folk-Lore of Herefordshire*. Hereford, U.K.: Jakeman and Carver; Sidgwick and Jackson.

———. 1914. "Foundation Sacrifice." *Folk-Lore* 24: 110.

Lebech, Mogens. 1969. *Fra runestav til almanak*. Copenhagen: Theijls.

Le Braz, Anatole. 1982. *La Légende de la mort chez les Bretons armoricains*. Marseille: Lafitte.

Lecouteux, Claude. 1995. *Au-délà du merveilleux: des croyances au Moyen Âge*. Paris: P.U.P.S.

———. 2013. *The Tradition of Household Spirits: Ancestral Lore and Practices*. Translated by Jon E. Graham. Rochester, Vt.: Inner Traditions.

Lethaby, William Richard. 1974 [1891]. *Architecture, Mysticism and Myth*. London: Architectural Press.

Lethbridge, Thomas Charles. 1957. *Gogmagog: The Buried Gods*. London: Routledge & Kegan Paul.

Lidén, H. 1969. "From Pagan Sanctuary to Christian Church: The Excavation of Maere Church, Trondelag." *Norwegian Archaeological Review* 2: 23–32.

Linden, Stanton J. 2003. *The Alchemy Reader: From Hermes Trismegistus to Isaac Newton*. Cambridge: Cambridge University Press.

Lindig, Erika. 1987. *Hausgeister: Die Vorstellung übernaturlicher Schützer und Helfer in der deutschen Sagenüberlieferung*. Frankfurt: Peter Lang.

Lip, Evelyn. 1979. *Chinese Geomancy*. Singapore: Times Books International.

Lundqvist, Sune. 1923. "Hednatemplet i Uppsala." *Förnvannen* 18: 85–118.

MacCulloch, John Arnott. 1911. *The Religion of the Ancient Celts*. Edinburgh: T. and T. Clark.

Mackenzie, William. 1895. *Gaelic Incantations, Charms and Blessings of the Hebrides*. Inverness: Northern Counties Newspaper.

Magnus, Olaus. 1655. *Historia Septentrionalium Gentibus.* Rome: N.p.

Mair, Craig. 1988. *Mercat Cross and Tolbooth.* Edinburgh: John Donald Publishers.

Malchus, Marius. 1960. *The Secret Grimoire of Turiel.* London: Aquarian.

Malory, Sir Thomas. 1472. *Le Morte d'Arthur.*

Manilius, Marcus. 1977. *Astronomica.* Translated by G. P. Gould. London: Heinemann.

Manker, Ernst. 1938. "Die lappische Zaubertrommel 1." Acta Lapponica 1. Stockholm: Almqvist & Wiksell.

———. 1950. "Die lappische Zaubertrommel 2." Acta Lapponica 6. Stockholm: Almqvist & Wiksell.

Mann, Ethel. 1934. *Old Bungay.* London: Methuen.

Maple, Eric. 1960. "The Witches of Canewdon." *Folklore* 71, 4: 241–50.

March, H. Colley. 1899. "Dorset Folk-Lore Collected in 1897." *Folk-Lore* 10: 478–89.

Marshall, Sybil. 1967. *Fenland Chronicle.* Cambridge: Cambridge University Press.

Martin, Eugène. 1903–1904. "Le coq du clocher." *Memoires de l'Academie de Stanislas* 6: 1–16.

Mason, Hugo. 2001. *All Saints' Church Brockhampton Herefordshire.* Brockhampton, U.K.: Brockhampton Parochial Church Council.

Massey, Alan. 1999. "The Reigate Witch Bottle." *Current Archaeology* 169: 34–36.

Mathers, Samuel, Liddel MacGregor, and Aleister Crowley, eds. 1997. *The Goetia: The Lesser Key of Solomon the King.* York Beach, Maine: Samuel Weiser.

Matthews, William Henry. 1922. *Mazes and Labyrinths: A General Account of Their History and Developments.* London: Longmans, Green & Co.

Maylam, Richard, Mick Lynn, and Geoff Doel. 2009. *Percy Maylam's The Kent Hooden Horse.* Stroud, U.K.: History Press.

McAldowie, Alex. 1896. "Personal Experiences in Witchcraft." *Folk-Lore* 7: 309–14.

McCrickard, Janet E. 1994. "Brief History and Development." In Nicholas Driver, *Nicholas Driver's Bodhran and Bones Tutor.* Horsham, U.K.: Gremlin Musical Instrument Company, 20–22.

McFadzean, Patrick. 1984. "Heraldry and the Planetary Colours." *The Symbol* 4: 19–20.

McNeill, F. Marian. 1957–1968. *The Silver Bough,* 4 vols. Glasgow: William McClellan.

Meaney, Audrey. 1981. *Anglo-Saxon Amulets and Curing-Stones.* Oxford: British Archaeological Reports.

———. 1989. "Women, Witchcraft and Magic in Anglo-Saxon England." *Superstition and Popular Medicine in Anglo-Saxon England.* Edited by D. G. Scragg. Manchester: Manchester Centre for Anglo-Saxon Studies.

Merrifield, Ralph. 1987. *The Archaeology of Ritual and Magic.* London: Guild.

Meyer, Wilhelm. 1882. "Ein Labyrinth mit Versen." *Sitzungsberichte der philosophisch-philologischen und historischen Klasse der k.b. Akademie der Wissenschaften zu München* 2, 3: 267–300.

Michell, John. 1975. *The Earth Spirit: Its Ways, Shrines and Mysteries.* London: Thames & Hudson.

———. 1981. *Ancient Metrology: The Dimensions of Stonehenge and of the Whole World as Therein Symbolised.* Bristol, U.K.: Pentacle.

Miles, Clement A. 1912. *Christmas in Ritual and Tradition.* London: Fisher Unwin.

Mockridge, Patricia and Philip Mockridge. 1990. *Weathervanes of Great Britain.* London: Robert Hale.

Monger, George. 1997. "Modern Wayside Shrines." *Folklore* 108: 113–15.

Monikander, A. 2006. "Borderland-Stalkers and Stalking-Horses: Horse Sacrifice as Liminal Activity in the Early Iron Age." *Current Swedish Archaeology* 14: 143–58.

Monson-Fitzjohn, Gilbert John. 1926. *Quaint Signs of Olde Inns.* London: Herbert Jenkins.

Montagu, Jeremy. 1975. "The Construction of the Midwinterhoorn." *The Galpin Society Journal* 28: 71–80.

Moora, Harris, and Ants Viires. 1964. *Abriss der estnischen Volkskunde.* Tallinn: Estonian State Publishers.

Moore, Arthur William. 1891. *The Folk-Lore of the Isle of Man.* London: David Nutt.

Morgan, James R. 1990. "The Druid's Cord." In *Full Measure.* Edited by Donald L. Cyr. Santa Barbara, Calif.: Stonehenge Viewpoint, 109–13.

Morris, Carole A. 2000. *Wood and Woodworking in Anglo-Scandinavian and Medieval York.* York, U.K.: York Archaeological Trust.

Morrison, Sophia. 1911. "The Isle of Man: Introduction." In W. Y. Evans

Wentz, *The Fairy Faith in Celtic Countries*. Oxford: Oxford University Press, 117–20.

Mortensen, Karl. 1913. *A Handbook of Norse Mythology*. Translated by Clinton A. Crowell. New York: Thomas Y. Cowell Publishers.

Mortimer, Bishop Robert. 1972. *Exorcism: The Report of a Commission Convened by The Bishop of Exeter*. Edited by Dom Robert Petitpierre. London: Society for Promoting Christian Knowledge.

Mössinger, Friedrich. 1938. "Die Dorflinde als Weltbaum." *Germanien* 10: 388–96.

——. 1938. "Maibaum, Dorflinde, Weihnachtsbaum." *Germanien* 10: 145–55.

——. 1940. "Baumtanz und Trojaburg." *Germanien*: 282–89.

Mössinger, Friedrich, and Siegfried Sieber. 1978. *Troytowns in Germany*. Translated by Michael Behrend. I.G.R. Occasional Paper 10. Bar Hill, U.K.: The Institute of Geomantic Research.

Muecke, Mikesch W., and Miriam S. Zach. 2007. *Resonance: Essays on the Intersection of Music and Architecture*. Ames, Iowa.: Culicidae Architectural Press.

Munch, P. A. 1846. "Sagnet om Aasgaardsreien." *Annaler for nordisk Oldkyndighed og Historie*.

Munrow, David. 1976. *Instruments of the Middle Ages and Renaissance*. London: Oxford University Press.

Neat, Timothy. 2002. *The Horseman's Word*. Edinburgh: Birlinn.

Newall, Venetia. 1978. "Some Examples of the Practice of Obeah by West Indian Immigrants in London." *Folklore* 89: 29–51.

Newman, Leslie F. 1940. "Notes on Some Rural and Trade Initiations in the Eastern Counties." *Folklore* 51: 33–42.

——. 1946. "Some Notes on the Practise of Witchcraft in the Eastern Counties." *Folklore* 57: 12–32.

——. 1948a. "Some Notes on the Pharmacology and Therapeutic Value of Folk-Medicines I." *Folklore* 59: 118–35.

——. 1948b. "Some Notes on the Pharmacology and Therapeutic Value of Folk-Medicines II." *Folklore* 59: 145–56.

Newman, L. F., and E. M. Wilson. 1952. "Folklore Survivals in the Southern 'Lake Counties' and in Essex: A Comparison and Contrast." *Folklore* 63: 91–104.

Nicholson, John. 1890. *Folk-Lore of East Yorkshire.* London: Simpkin Marshall.

Nichomachus of Gerasa. 1994. *The Manual of Harmonics.* Translated by Flora R. Levin. Grand Rapids, Mich.: Phanes Press.

Nicolaysen, Nicolay. 1882. *Langskibet fra Gokstad.* Christiania, Norway: Alb. Cammermeyer.

Nodermann, Maj. 1973. "Hem in Redning." *Arbete och Redskap.* Edited by Nils-Arvid Bringéus, et. al. Lund, Swed.: Gleerup.

Nørlund, Poul. 1948. *Trelleborg.* Edited by John R. B. Gosney. Copenhagen: Gyldendal.

North, C. N. McIntyre. 1881. *Leabhar Comunn nam Fion Ghael: The Book of the Club of True Highlanders,* vol. 1. London: Club of True Highlanders.

Notebaart, Jannis C. 1972. *Windmühlen.* The Hague: Mouton.

Novati, Francesco. 1904–1905. "'Li Dis du Koc' di Jean de Condé." *Studi Medievali* I: 497.

Nylén, Erik, and Jan Peter Lamm. 1981. *Bildsteine auf Gotland.* Neumünster: Karl Wachholz.

Olsen, Olaf. 1966. *Hørg, Hof og Kirke.* Copenhagen: University of Copenhagen.

Omurethi [Lord Walter Fitzgerald]. 1906–1908. "Customs Peculiar to Certain Days, Formerly Observed in the County Kildare." *Journal of the Co. Kildare Archæological Society and Surrounding Districts* 5: 439–55.

Ord, John. 1920. "The Most Secret of Secret Societies: Ancient Scottish Horsemen." *The Glasgow Weekly Herald,* November 13.

———. 1995 [1930]. *Ord's Bothy Songs and Ballads of Aberdeen Banff and Moray Angus and The Mearns.* Edinburgh: John Donald Publishers.

Osborn, Marijane. 1981. "*Hleotan* and the purpose of the Old English *Rune Poem.*" *Folklore* 92: 168–93.

Owen, Trefor M. 1987. *Welsh Folk Customs.* Llandyssul, U.K.: Gomer.

Paine, Sheila. 2004. *Amulets: A World of Secret Powers, Charms and Magic.* London: Thames & Hudson.

Pakenham, Thomas. 2001. *Meetings with Remarkable Trees.* London: Cassell.

Pálsson, Hermann, and Paul Edwards, translators. 1972. *Landnámabók: The Book of Settlements.* Winnipeg: University of Manitoba Press.

Pareli, Leif. 1984. "Sørsamenes Byggeskikk." *Foreningen til norske Fortidsminnesmerkers Bevaring Årbok:* 116.

Parsons, Catherine E. 1915. "Notes on Cambridgeshire Witchcraft."

Proceedings of the Cambridge Antiquarian Society, XIX, LXVII: 31–52.

Pattinson, G. W. 1953. "Adult Education and Folklore." *Folklore* 64, 3: 424–26.

Paulsen, Peter, and Helga Schach-Dörges. 1972. *Holzhandwerk der Alamannen.* Stuttgart: W. Kolhammer.

Peacock, Edward. 1877. *A Glossary of Words Used in the Wapentakes of Manley and Corringham, Lincolnshire.* London: Dialect Society.

Peacock, Mabel Geraldine W. 1896. "Executed Criminals and Folk Medicine." *Folk-Lore* 7: 268–83.

———. 1897. "Omens Of Death." *Folk-Lore* 8: 377–78.

———. 1901. "The Folk-Lore of Lincolnshire." *Folk-Lore* 12: 161–80.

Peacock, Mabel Geraldine W., Katherine Carson, and Charlotte Burne. 1901. "Customs Relating to Iron." *Folk-Lore* 12: 472–75.

Pennick, Nigel. 1979. *The Ancient Science of Geomancy.* London: Thames & Hudson.

———. 1985a. *Natural Measure.* Bar Hill, U.K.: Runestaff.

———. 1985b. *The Cosmic Axis.* Bar Hill, U.K.: Runestaff.

———. 1986. *Skulls, Cats and Witch Bottles.* Bar Hill, U.K.: Nigel Pennick Editions.

———. 1987. *Einst war uns die Erde Heilig.* Waldeck-Dehringhausen, Ger.: Felicitas-Hübner.

———. 1989. *Practical Magic in the Northern Tradition.* Wellingborough, U.K.: Thorsons.

———. 1990. *Das Runenorakel* (with rune cards by Hermann Haindl). Frankfurt: Droemer Knaur.

———. 1992. *Rune Magic. The History and Practice of Ancient Runic Traditions.* London: Aquarian/Thorsons.

———. 1993. *Wayland's House.* Bar Hill, U.K.: Nideck/The Way of The Eight Winds.

———. 1995. *Secrets of East Anglian Magic.* London: Robert Hale.

———. 1996. *Celtic Sacred Landscapes.* London: Thames and Hudson.

———. 1998. *Crossing the Borderlines: Guising, Masking & Ritual Animal Disguises in the European Tradition.* Chieveley, U.K.: Capall Bann.

———. 1999a. *Beginnings: Geomancy, Builders' Rites and Electional Astrology in the European Tradition.* Chieveley, U.K.: Capall Bann.

———. 1999b. *The Complete Illustrated Guide to Runes.* London: Element.

———. 2001. *The Pagan Book of Days.* Rochester, Vt.: Destiny.

———. 2002a. *Masterworks: Arts and Crafts of Traditional Buildings in Northern Europe.* Wymeswold, U.K.: Heart of Albion.

———. 2002b."The Goddess Zisa." *TYR: Myth—Culture—Tradition* 1: 107–10.

———. 2003–2004. "Heathen Holy Places in Northern Europe: A Cultural Overview." *TYR: Myth—Culture—Tradition* 2: 139–49.

———. 2006a. *Folk-Lore of East Anglia and Adjoining Counties.* Bar Hill, U.K.: Spiritual Arts & Crafts.

———. 2006b. *The Eldritch World.* Earl Shilton, U.K.: Lear.

———. 2011a. *In Field and Fen.* Earl Shilton, U.K.: Lear.

———. 2011b. *The Toadman.* Hinckley, U.K.: Society of Esoteric Endeavour.

Pennick, Nigel, and Paul Devereux. 1989. *Lines on the Landscape: Leys and Other Linear Enigmas.* London: Robert Hale.

Pennick, Nigel, and Helen Field. 2004. *Muses and Fates.* Milverton, U.K.: Capall Bann.

Pennick, Nigel, and Marinus Gout. 2004. *Sacrale Geometrie: Verborgen Lijnen in de Bouwkunst.* The Hague: Synthese.

Pennick, Nigel, and Nigel Jackson. 1992. *The Celtic Oracle.* London: Aquarian.

Pennick, Rupert. 1984. "The Secret Vehm." *The Symbol* 3: 20–23.

Petrie, Sir Flinders. 1934. *Measures and Weights.* London: Methuen.

Pfister, Freidrich. 1924. *Schwäbische Volksbräuche.* Augsburg, Ger.: Benno Fisher.

Pliny. 1989. *Natural History,* 10 vols. Translated by W. H. S. Jones. Cambridge, Mass.: Harvard University Press.

Pokropek, M. 1988. "Interior." In *Folk Art in Poland.* Edited by Aleksandra Czeszunist-Cicha. Warsaw: Arkady. Pp. 46–75.

Pollington, Stephen. 2000. *Leechcraft: Early English Charms, Plantlore and Healing.* Hockwold-cum-Wilton, U.K.: Anglo-Saxon Books.

Porter, Enid. 1969. (Fenland material provided by W. H. Barrett.) *Cambridgeshire Customs and Folklore.* London: Routledge and Kegan Paul.

Pritchard, V. 1967. *English Medieval Graffiti.* Cambridge: Cambridge University Press.

Propping, Walter. 1935. "Das 'Dag' Zeichen am niedersächsischen Bauernhaus." *Germanien:* 143–46.

Puckle, Bertram S. 1926. *Funeral Customs: Their Origin and Development.* London: T. Werner Laurie.

Pughe, John, trans., and John Williams ab Ithel, ed. 1861. *The Physicians of Myddfai.* Llandovery, U.K.: Welsh Manuscripts Society.

Puhvel, Martin. 1976. "The Mystery of the Cross-Roads." *Folklore* 87: 167–77.

Raglan, Lady. 1939. "The 'Green Man' in Church Architecture." *Folk-Lore* 50: 45–57.

Randall, Arthur. 1966. *Sixty Years a Fenman.* Edited by Enid Porter. London: Routledge and Kegan Paul.

Ranke, K. 1969. "Orale und literale Kontinuität." In *Kontinuität? Geschichtlichkeit und Dauer als volkskundliches Problem. Festschrift Hans Moser.* Edited by H. Bausinger and W. Brückner. Berlin: E. Schmidt.

Rayson, George. 1865a. "East Anglian Folk-Lore, No. 1. 'Weather Proverbs.'" *The East Anglian, or, Notes and Queries on Subjects Connected with the Counties of Suffolk, Cambridgeshire, Essex and Norfolk,* vol. I: 155–62.

———. 1865b. "East Anglian Folk-Lore, No. 2. 'Omens.'" *The East Anglian, or, Notes and Queries on Subjects Connected with the Counties of Suffolk, Cambridgeshire, Essex and Norfolk,* vol. I: 185–86.

———. 1865c. "East Anglian Folk-Lore, No. 3. 'Charms.'" *The East Anglian, or, Notes and Queries on Subjects Connected with the Counties of Suffolk, Cambridgeshire, Essex and Norfolk,* vol. I: 214–17.

Read, D. H. Moutray. 1911. "Hampshire Folk-Lore." *Folk-Lore* 22: 292–329.

Redknap, Mark. 1991. *The Christian Celts: Treasures of Late Celtic Wales.* Cardiff: National Museum of Wales.

Redman, Nicholas. 2004. *Whales' Bones of the British Isles.* Teddington, U.K.: Redman Publishing.

Rees, Alwyn, and Brinley Rees. 1961. *Celtic Heritage: Ancient Tradition in Ireland and Wales.* London: Thames and Hudson.

Rees, Rev. R. Wilkins. 1898. "Ghost Laying." In *The Church Treasury of History, Custom, Folk-Lore, etc.,* ed. William Andrews. London: William Andrews, 240–70.

Regardie, Israel. 1977. *How to Make and Use Talismans.* Wellingborough, U.K.: Aquarian.

Rennie, William. 2009. *The Society of the Horseman's Word.* Hinckley, U.K.: Society of Esoteric Endeavour.

Reuter, Otto Sigfrid. 1934. *Germanische Himmelskunde.* Munich: Lehmann.

———. 1985. *Sky Lore of the North*. Translated by Michael Behrend. Bar Hill, U.K.: Runestaff.

Riley, Henry Thomas. 1868. *Memorials of London and London Life*. London: City of London.

Robbins, Russell Hope. 1963. "The Imposture of Witchcraft." *Folklore* 74, 4: 545–62.

Roberts, Robert. 1816. *Arweiniad i Wybodaeth o Seryddiaeth (A Guide to a Knowledge of Astronomy)*. *Daearyddiaeth (Geography)*. Chester, U.K.: Carlleon Lloegr.

Robson, Vivian E. 1969. *The Fixed Stars and Constellations in Astrology*. Wellingborough, U.K.: Aquarian.

Rohrberg, Erwin. 1981. *Schöne Fachwerkhäuser in Baden Württemberg*. Stuttgart: DRW-Verlag.

Roper, Charles. 1883. "On Witchcraft Superstition in Norfolk." *Harper's New Monthly Magazine*, 87, 521: 792–97.

Rosecrans, Jennipher Allen. 2000. "Wearing the Universe: Symbolic Markings in Early Modern England." In *Written on the Body: The Tattoo in European and American History*. Edited by Jane Caplan. London: Reaktion, 46–60.

Roud, Steve. 2003. *The Penguin Guide to the Superstitions of Britain and Ireland*. London: Penguin.

Rudbeck, Olof, Sr. 1702. *Atland eller Manhem* [= *Atlantica* in the Latin translation by Andreas Norcopensis]. Uppsala, Swed.: Henricus Curio.

Rudkin, Ethel. 1933. "Lincolnshire Folk-Lore." *Folk-Lore* 44: 279–95.

———. 1934. "Lincolnshire Folk-Lore, Witches and Devils." *Folk-Lore* 45: 249–67.

Rushen, Joyce. 1984. "Folklore and Witchcraft in Tudor and Stuart England." *Popular Archeology* (April): 35.

Ryan, M. 1991. "Links between Anglo-Saxon and Irish Early Medieval Art: Some Evidence in Metalwork." In *Studies in Insular Art and Archaeology*. Edited by C. Karkov and R. Farrell. Oxford, Ohio: American Early Medieval Studies, 117–26.

Sandford, Lettice. 1983. *Straw Work and Corn Dollies*. London: Batsford.

Sandklef, A. 1949. *Singing Flails: A Study in Threshing-Floor Constructions, Flail-Threshing Traditions and the Magic Guarding of the House*. FF Communications 136. Helsinki: Suomalainen Tiedeakatemia.

Sanger, Keith, and Alison Kinnaird. 1992. *Tree of Strings (Crann nan Teud): A History of the Harp in Scotland.* Shillinghill Temple, U.K.: Kinmor Music.

Saward, Deb, and Jeff Saward. 1984. "Let Sleeping Dogs Lie." *The Symbol* 4: 10–11.

Saxo Grammaticus. 1905. *The Nine Books of the Danish History of Saxo Grammaticus.* Translated by Oliver Elton. New York: Norroena Society.

Schefferus, Joannes. 1673. *Lapponia, id est Regionis Lapponum et Gentis Nova et Verissima Descriptio.* Frankfurt: Christian Wolff.

Schmidt, Friedrich Heinz. 1926. *Osterbräuche.* Leipzig: Bibliographisches Institut, 1936.

Schmidt, Johann Georg. 1988 [1788–1722]. *Die Geistregelte Rocken-philosophie oder aufrichtige Untersuchung derer von vielen super-klugen Weibern hochgehaltenen Aberglauben,* 2 vols. Leipzig: VCH Verlagsgesellschaft.

Schnippel, Emil. 1926. "Die Englischen Kalendarstäbe." *Leipziger Beiträge zur Englischen Philologie:* 24–105.

Schuldt, Ewald. 1976. *Der altslawische Tempel von Gross-Radern.* Schwerin, Germany: Museum für Ur- und Frühgeschichte.

Schumacher, Hermann Albert. 1865. *Die Stedinger: Ein Beitrag zur Geschichte der Weser-Marschen.* Bremen: C. E. Müller.

Schwedt, Herbert, and Elke Schwedt. 1984. *Schwäbische Bräuche.* Stuttgart: W. Kohlhammer.

Schwedt, Herbert, Elke Schwedt, and Martin Blümke. 1984. *Masken und Maskenschnitzer der Schwäbisch-Allemannischen Fasnacht.* Stuttgart: Konrad Thiess.

Scot, Reginald. 1584. *The Discoverie of Witchcraft.* London: William Brome.

Scott, Mackay Hugh Baillie. 1906. *Houses and Gardens.* London: George Newnes.

Scott, Sir Walter. 1885. *Letters on Demonology and Witchcraft.* London & New York: George Routledge and Sons.

———. N.d. [1885]. *Waverly Novels: Chronicles of the Canongate.* Philadelphia: Porter & Coates.

Seymour, St. John Drelincourt. 1913. *Irish Witchcraft and Demonology.* Dublin: Hodges Figgis.

Seznec, Jean. 1940. *La survivance des dieux antiques: Essai sur le rôle de la tradition mythologique dans l'humanisme et dans l'art de la Renaissance.* Studies of the Warburg Institute 11. London: Warburg Institute.

Shaftesbury, Edmund. 1943. *Universal Magnetism: A Private Training Course in the Magnetic Control of Others by the Most Powerful of All Known Methods.* Marple, U.K.: Psychology Publishing Company.

Shakespeare, William. 1970. *The Complete Works of William Shakespeare,* 2 vols. Garden City, N.J.: Nelson Doubleday.

Shetelig, H. 1912. *Vestlandske graver fra jernalderen.* Oslo: J. Grieg.

Shippey, Thomas A. 1976. *Poems of Wisdom and Learning in Old English.* Cambridge: D. S. Brewer.

Seidel, H. 1896. "Das Schwirrholz in Westpreussen." *Globus* 70: 67–68.

Sieber, Siegfried. 1936. "Ein Trojaburg in Pommern." *Germanien:* 83–86.

Simmonds, L. 1975. *Welsh Witchcraft. Ofergoeliaeth Cymru.* St. Ives, U.K.: James Pike.

Simpkins, John E. 1912. *Country Folk-Lore: Fife.* London: Folk-Lore Society.

Simpson, H. F. Morland. 1895. "Notes on a Swedish Staff-Calendar, Presented to the Museum by the Hon. John Abercrombie, F.S.A. Scot., Dated 1710." *Proceedings of the Society of Antiquaries of Scotland* XXIX: 234–40.

Simpson, Jacqueline. 1972. *Icelandic Folktales and Legends.* Berkeley: University of California Press.

———. 1975. *Legends of the Icelandic Magicians.* Cambridge: D. S. Brewer.

———. 1987. *European Mythology.* London: Hamlyn.

Singer, William. 1881. *An Exposition of the Miller and Horseman's Word, or the True System of Raising the Devil.* Aberdeen: James Daniel.

Sirelius, U. T. 1921. *Suomen kansanomaista kulttuuria. Esineellisen kansatieteen tuloksia,* II. Helsinki: Otava.

Sjömar, Peter. 1995. "Romansk och gotisk—takkonstruktioner i svenska medeltidskyrkor." *Hikuin* 22: 219–22.

Skinner, F. G. 1967. *Weights and Measures.* London: Her Majesty's Stationery Office.

Smedley, Norman. 1955. "Two Bellarmine Bottles from Coddenham." *Proceedings of the Suffolk Institute of Archæology* XXVI: 229.

Solheim, Sval. 1958. "Draug." *Kulturhistorisk Leksikon for Nordisk Middelalder* 3: 297–99.

Spamer, Adolf. 1935. *Die Deutsche Volkskunde.* Leipzig: Bibliographisches Institut.

Speth, G. W. 1894. "Builders' Rites and Ceremonies." Margate, U.K.: Keeble's Gazette.

Stephen, H. J. 1868. *Commentaries on the Laws of England.* London: Butterworth.

Sternberg, Thomas. 1851. *The Dialect and Folk-Lore of Northamptonshire.* London: John Russell Smith.

Stevenson, Joseph, trans. 1861. *The Church Historians of England,* 4 vols. London: Seeley.

Stone, Alby. 1998. *Straight Track—Crooked Road.* Wymeswold, U.K.: Heart of Albion Press.

Storms, G. 1948. *Anglo-Saxon Magic.* The Hague: Nijhoff.

Stracherjan, Ludwig. 1867. *Aberglaube und Sagen aus dem Herzogthum Oldenburg.* Oldenburg, Ger.: G. Stalling.

Strohecker, Hans Otto. 1978. *Canstatter Volksfest.* Stuttgart: Konrad Thiess.

Strömback, Dag. 1935. *Sejd.* Stockholm: Geber.

Strygell, Anna-Lisa. 1974. "Kyrkans Teken och Årets Gång." *Finnska fornminnesföreningens tidskrift* 77: 46.

Sturluson, Snorri. 1907. *Heimskringla, or the Chronicle of the Kings of Norway.* Translated by S. Laing. London: Norroena Society.

———. 1964. *Heimskringla: History of the Kings of Norway.* Translated by Lee M. Hollander. Austin: University of Texas Press.

———. 1966. *The Prose Edda.* Translated by Jean I. Young. Cambridge: Cambridge University Press.

Tacitus, Publius Cornelius. 1959. *Germania.* Edited and translated by Eugen Fehrle and Richard Hünnerkopf. Heidelberg: Winter.

Tebbutt, C. F. 1984. *Huntingdonshire Folklore.* St. Ives, U.K.: Norris Museum.

Theophilus. 1979. *On Divers Arts.* Translated by John G. Hawthorne and Cyril Stanley Smith. New York: Dover.

Thijsse, Wim. 1980. "De Midwinterhoorn en zijn functie." *Mens en Melodie* XXXV: 24–32.

Thompson, Charles John Samuel. 1934. *The Mystic Mandrake.* London: Rider.

Thorsson, Edred. 1984. *Futhark: A Handbook of Rune Magic.* York Beach, Maine: Samuel Weiser.

———. 1992. *Northern Magic.* St. Paul, Minn.: Llewellyn.

Tongue, Ruth L. 1958. "Odds and Ends of Somerset Folklore." *Folklore* 69, 1: 43–45.

Topsell, Edward. 1658. *The Book of Living Creatures, or The History of Serpents.* London: E. Cotes.

Torrance, D. Richard. 1996. *Weights and Measures*. Edinburgh: SAFHS.

Toulson, Shirley. 1980. *The Drovers, Shire Album 45*. Princes Risborough, U.K.: Shire Publications.

Trevelyan, Marie. 1909. *Folk-Lore and Folk Stories of Wales*. London: Elliot Stock.

Trinkūnas, Jonas, ed. 1999. *Of Gods & Holidays: The Baltic Heritage*. Vilnius, Lithuania: Tvermė.

Trollope, E. 1858. "Notices of Ancient and Mediaeval Labyrinths." *Archaeological Journal* 15: 216–35.

Trubshaw, Bob. 1995. "The Metaphors and Rituals of Place and Time. An Introduction to Liminality." *Mercian Mysteries* 22: 1–8.

———. 2005. *Sacred Places, Prehistory and Popular Imagination*. Wymeswold, U.K.: Heart of Albion Press.

Tupper, Frederick, Jr. 1895. "Anglo-Saxon Dæg-Mæl." *Publications of the Modern Language Association of America* N.S. III, 2, vol X, 2: 112–241.

Tuzin, D. 1984. "Miraculous Voices: The Auditory Experience of Numinous Objects." *Current Anthropology* 25, 5: 579–96.

Tyack, George S. 1899. *Lore and Legend of the English Church*. London: William Andrews.

Valebrokk, Eva, and Thomas Thiis-Evensen. 1994. *Norway's Stave Churches: Archaeology, History and Legends*. Translated by Ann Clay Zwick. Oslo: Dreyer.

Valiente, Doreen. 1984. *An ABC of Witchcraft Past and Present*. London: Robert Hale.

Váňa, Zdeněk. 1992. *Mythologie und Götterwelt der slawischen Völker*. Stuttgart: Urachhaus.

Van der Klift-Tellegen, Henriette. 1987. *Knitting from the Netherlands: Traditional Dutch Fishermen's Sweaters*. London: Dryad.

Van Gennep, Arnold. 1903. "De l'Emploi du Mot 'Chamanisme.'" *Revue de l'Histoire des Religions* XLVII, 1: 51–57.

Van Hammel, A. G. 1935. "De ijslandse gang tegen de zon." *Neophilologus* XX: 212–23.

Vésteinsson, O., T. H. McGovern, and C. Keller. 2002. "Enduring Impacts: Social and Environmental Aspects of Viking Age Settlement in Iceland and Greenland." *Archaeologia Islandica* 2: 98–136.

Villiers, Elizabeth. 1923. *The Mascot Book*. London: T. Werner Laurie.

Von Alpenburg, J. N. Ritter. 1857. *Mythen und Sagen Tirols.* Zürich: Meyer & Zeller.

Von Negelein, Julius. 1906. *Germanische Mythologie.* Leipzig: Teubner.

Von Zaborsky, Oskar. 1936. *Urväter-Erbe in deutscher Volkskunst.* Leipzig: Koehler & Amerlang.

Voss, J. A. 1987. "Antiquity Imagined: Cultural Values in Archaeological Folklore." *Folklore* 98: 80–90.

Wagner, Anthony R. 1956. *Heralds and Heraldry in the Middle Ages: An Inquiry into the Growth of the Armorial Function of Heralds.* Oxford: Oxford University Press.

Waite, Arthur Edward. 1911. *The Book of Ceremonial Magic: Including the Rites and Mysteries of Goëtic Theurgy, Sorcery and Infernal Necromancy.* London: Rider.

Warrack, Alexander. 1988 [1911]. *The Scots Dialect Dictionary.* Poole, U.K.: New Orchard Editions.

Weber, Martha. 1940. "Kaiser- und Königsmonogramme des Mittelalters." *Germanien:* 334–42.

Webster, David, ed. 1820. *A Collection of Rare and Curious Tracts on Witchcraft.* Edinburgh: T. Webster.

Weinstock, Stefan. 1946. "Martianus Capella and the cosmic system of the Etruscans." *Journal of Roman Studies* 36: 101–29.

Weiser-Aal, Lily. 1947. "Magiske Tegn på Norske Trekar?" *By og Byd Årbok:* 117–44.

Wellcome, Henry S. N.d. [1903]. *Hen Feddegyaeth Kymric (Ancient Cymric Medicine).* London: Burroughs Wellcome & Co.

Wentz, W. Y. Evans. 1911. *The Fairy Faith in Celtic Countries.* Oxford: Oxford University Press.

West, Trudy, and Paul Dong. N.d. *The Timber-frame House in England.* Newton Abbot, U.K.: David & Charles.

Weston, Jessie L. 1903. *Sir Gawain at the Grail Castle.* London: David Nutt.

———. 1907. *Sir Gawain and the Lady of Lys.* London: David Nutt, 1907.

Wiesinger, Alfons. 1980. *Narrenschmaus und Fastenspiese in Schwäbisch-allemannischen Brauch.* Konstanz, Ger.: Südkurier.

Wilde, Lady Jane Francesca Agnes. 1887. *Ancient Legends, Mystic Charms, and Superstitions of Ireland,* 2 vols. Boston: Ticknor & Co.

William of Newburgh. 1861. *Historia rerum Anglicarum.* In *The Church His-*

torians of England, 4 vols. Translated by Joseph Stevenson. London: Seeley.

Wilson, David. 1992. *Anglo-Saxon Paganism.* London and New York: Routledge.

Wirth, Herman. 1934. *Die Heilige Urschrift der Menschheit,* 9 vols. Leipzig: Koehler & Amelang.

Wood-Martin, W. G. 1902. *Traces of the Elder Faith of Ireland,* 2 vols. London: Longmans.

Wordsworth, Rev. Christopher. 1903. "Two Yorks Charms or Amulets: Exorcisms and Adjurations." *The Yorkshire Archaeological and Topographical Journal* XVII: 376–412.

Wortley, Russell. "Notes Made By Russell Wortley 1938–1975." Unpublished manuscript, Cambridgeshire Collection, Cambridge.

———. 1972. *Traditional Music in and around Cambridge.* Unpublished manuscript.

Wright, Arthur Robinson, and T. E. Lones. 1936. *British Calendar Customs I: Movable Festivals.* London: William Glaisher.

———. 1938. *British Calendar Customs II: Fixed Festivals, January–May, Inclusive.* London: William Glaisher Ltd.

———. 1940. *British Calendar Customs III: Fixed Festivals, June–December, Inclusive.* London: William Glaisher.

Young, A., and T. J. Glover. 1996. *Measure for Measure.* Littleton, U.K.: Blue Willow.

Youngs, Susan, ed. 1989. *The Work of Angels. Masterpieces of Celtic Metalwork, 6th–9th Centuries AD.* London: British Museum.

Zeiten, Miriam Koktvedgaard. 1997. "Amulets and Amulet Using in Viking Age Denmark." *Acta Archaeologica* 68: 1–74.

Zerries, Otto. 1942. *Das Schwirrholz: Untersuchung über die Verbreitung und Bedeutung der Schwirrholz im Kult.* Stuttgart: Strecker and Schroder.

Ziolkowski, T. 1961. "Der Karfunkelstein." *Euphorion* 55: 313–16.

Zupko, Ronald Edward. 1968. *A Dictionary of English Weights and Measures: From Anglo-Saxon Times to the Nineteenth Century.* Madison: University of Wisconsin Press.

———. 1977. "The Weights and Measures of Scotland before the Union." *Scottish Historical Review* 56: 119–45

———. 1978. *French Weights and Measures before the Revolution: A Dictionary of Provincial and Local Units.* Bloomington: Indiana University Press.

Index

Page numbers in *italics* refer to illustrations.